SERVED HIM RIGHT

Also by Lisa Unger

Angel Fire
The Darkness Gathers
Twice
Smoke
Beautiful Lies
Sliver of Truth
Black Out
Die for You
Fragile
Darkness, My Old Friend
Heartbroken
In the Blood
Crazy Love You
Ink and Bone
The Red Hunter
Under My Skin
The Stranger Inside
Confessions on the 7:45
Last Girl Ghosted
Secluded Cabin Sleeps Six
The New Couple in 5B
Close Your Eyes and Count to 10

SERVED HIM RIGHT

LISA UNGER

PARK ROW BOOKS

Recycling programs
for this product may
not exist in your area

ISBN-13: 978-0-7783-6005-6
ISBN-13: 978-0-7783-0599-6 (International Trade Paperback Edition)

Served Him Right

Copyright © 2026 by Lisa Unger

All rights reserved. No part of this book may be used or reproduced in any manner whatsoever without written permission.

Without limiting the exclusive rights of any author, contributor or the publisher of this publication, any unauthorized use of this publication to train generative artificial intelligence (AI) technologies is expressly prohibited. Harlequin also exercises their rights under Article 4(3) of the Digital Single Market Directive 2019/790 and expressly reserves this publication from the text and data mining exception.

This is a work of fiction. Names, characters, places, and incidents are either the product of the author's imagination or are used fictitiously. Any resemblance to actual persons, living or dead, businesses, companies, events or locales is entirely coincidental.

TM is a trademark of Harlequin Enterprises ULC.

Park Row Books
22 Adelaide St. West, 41st Floor
Toronto, Ontario M5H 4E3, Canada
ParkRowBooks.com

HarperCollins Publishers
Macken House, 39/40 Mayor Street Upper,
Dublin 1, D01 C9W8, Ireland
www.HarperCollins.com

Printed in U.S.A.

For my nephew Grant
You're a bright light and a sweet soul.
This one's for you, kiddo.
Love,
Aunt Lisa

PROLOGUE

She really needed this job. That's why she was always there a half an hour before her boss got in, why she was often the one to turn the lights off after everyone else had left, sometimes even there when the cleaning crew arrived at night. She came in on weekends when she knew Paul's work week ahead was heavy to make sure he had everything he needed for his various meetings, that his calendar was in order.

"You're meticulous," he told her. "What would I do without you?"

Meticulous. She carried the word around like a gold star. Meticulous. On top of things. Never missing a step. And her boss, Paul, he was good to her. When he stopped at Starbucks on the way into the office, he picked her up an oat milk latte, left it on her desk. He praised her in meetings, and to his own boss. He put in for her raise, and she got it. She hadn't even asked.

Of course, she knew all the rumors about him. How he was a different man when he'd had too much drink. How he took credit for his colleagues' work. How he got aggressive, handsy. But Jessica had never seen a hint of any of that. He did his job. She did hers.

Sure, there were a couple of office affairs—Beth in Marketing, Marie in Social Media. There had been some drama there;

she wasn't sure what. She tried to stay out of it, didn't hang out in the break room where people gathered to whisper about this and that. She wasn't like them; they all seemed so carefree, meeting for brunch and happy hour, driving new cars, taking expensive trips.

But Jessica wasn't carefree. She had debts—massive student loans. There was no safety net. Her parents both passed and had left her with nothing except more debt. It wasn't their fault. They'd worked hard, too. That was the way of it for some people, wasn't it? Work hard and still can't get ahead. But Jessica was steadily chipping away at her debt, even managing to save and invest a little.

Though this job paid well, if she was doing what she went to college for, she'd make more. But when she'd been applying, this position was offered first. She figured she'd take it just to pay the bills and keep looking. She'd make a change soon. But for now, she needed to be here. She *wanted* to be here.

So, today when Paul asked her to stay late to help with his client presentation, she didn't hesitate.

"Of course," she said. She had plans; she'd cancel them.

"Don't worry about dinner," he told her. "I'll order in Thai."

Truthfully, she liked Paul, even though many of the women in the office did not. He was funny, kind to her, hardworking. No, no. It wasn't like that. Jessica had someone special in her life, someone she loved. Paul wasn't her type. Like, not at all.

The project he needed help with was a big pitch for a brand-new client, a bespoke gym founded by an influencer who needed a full suite of services from traditional advertising buys to a publicity campaign, to website design and social media management. If Paul landed this account, it would mean a lot to the firm, which had lost a few clients last year for various reasons—some said because of the rumors swirling around Paul. But she didn't believe that.

Anyway, Jessica had been researching the client all day, and she had some ideas that she was excited to share with Paul. She'd dressed for it, too. She wore her new black suit, with a white silk blouse and pumps. Dress for the job you want. Isn't that what they said? She wasn't going to be like some of the people her age, showing up in hoodies and pants that could be pajamas.

Now the office was emptying out, people heading out for happy hour. They always invited her. Her colleagues at the firm were warm and inclusive. But Jessica kept herself apart, mainly because she was shy, not a bar person. And her partner worked here, too, in another department. They kept their relationship out of the office. Even the contact in her phone was just the letter *M*, because they didn't want to be the subject of the office gossip mill.

Her phone pinged.

Hey, there. Ready to go? Still feel like a movie?

Sorry, babe. I have to stay late to help Paul with his presentation.

. . .

Alone?

It's fine. He's not like that with me.

Okay. Well, stay in touch. If things get weird, get out.

Jessica smiled. Because M worried about her, and also because Jessica thought all the rumors about Paul were simply not true. She'd never seen that side of him, not even a glimmer. And wouldn't she have? Working so closely?

She hustled to the conference room down the hall, got set up. She was a little bit nervous. But when Paul joined her, she presented her research, all her ideas; they used the whiteboard to brainstorm. After a while, he ordered the food. And they continued working.

It was after ten by the time they'd finished, the office dark and empty, even the cleaning crew gone. She'd received a couple of worried texts from M, but Jessica offered assurances that all was well and that she'd come by after and spend the night.

As she tidied up the room, keeping her notes so that she could do the PowerPoint for the presentation, Paul left and returned with a bottle of vodka and two glasses.

Jessica really didn't drink.

"You know," he said, pouring generous portions into the glasses, "I wouldn't have been able to do this without you. Especially the social media stuff. You have a real gift for that."

She had always been good with tech. In fact, her degree was in computer science, which she didn't talk about much because it was a little embarrassing that she'd worked so hard for it only to find she wasn't using it at all in this job. She had a gift for coding, too. She'd applied for work in the IT department, but there wasn't an opening. And she needed the work. So, when they offered the assistant job, she took it, hoping to move when she proved herself.

Her life after college had been fraught. She'd struggled to find her footing after her parents passed. She knew she should be trying harder to get a job in her field; M was always encouraging her. But truthfully, she liked it here. This is where she met M. She'd made real friends here, even though she rarely attended the group outings. She felt safe, secure. There was time for the big job she hoped to have. She was young.

"Social media is such a big part of marketing these days. Maybe the biggest piece," she said. "People are living online, getting all their news and advice there. And the owner already has such a big following. We can really leverage that."

"And the idea about pitching the owner for big podcasts and

podcast advertising," he went on, handing her a glass. "I love that."

She took the glass, even though she didn't want to. She was driving and she didn't do well with alcohol. It was a big part of the reason she didn't go to happy hour. Liquor hit her too hard, and she didn't like who she was, or how it made her feel. But she didn't want to disappoint her boss. So she raised the glass to her lips and took a swallow. It burned going down and she must have grimaced, because Paul laughed a little.

"Oh, that's right," he said. "You're a lightweight."

It was easy, good-natured. Jessica laughed, too. "I guess so."

"To you, Jessica. Thanks for always having my back and going the extra mile. You're the best assistant I've ever had. You have a bright future here at the firm."

He raised his glass again, and she took another deep swallow. She'd call an Uber if she had to, or text M to come get her.

"Thank you," she said. "For being such a great boss, for encouraging me."

Another big swallow.

Her phone pinged again.

Hey, it's getting late. All good?

Truthfully, that's the last thing she remembered clearly, that text, those words swimming on the screen.

She reached for her phone—she remembered that—and the world seemed to tilt.

Paul's voice, heavy with concern. "Oh, hey, there, steady."

His hands on her arms, holding her up. She tried to apologize but the words wouldn't come, and then his mouth was on hers, and his arms tight around her. And she didn't have any strength to push him away, or any voice to say no. *This isn't happening*, she remembered thinking. *It's a dream.* And then everything was just fuzzy, then black.

The next moment Jessica was aware of herself, she was sitting in the driver's seat of her car. Her seatbelt was fastened. The lights in the lot glowed, casting everything in grayish sodium flicker. The office building was completely dark and there wasn't a single other car. The moon was high and full.

Her mind grappled for context. *How* had she gotten here?

She'd been working late. With Paul. Then—

She ached. The skin on her face felt raw. In the visor mirror, she saw that her lipstick was smeared across her face, her hair wild. She felt him on her—her arms where he gripped her. Her back where she knocked against the table. Her skirt was hiked high up on her thighs. Her panties. They were gone. She could feel him *down there*, a terrible sore rawness.

The truth broke over her like a wave, swamping her, knocking her under.

She leaned over the steering wheel and wept, body heaving, wailing.

What had he put in her drink? How could she be so stupid? She should have known. Women don't start rumors like that about men unless they're true. They don't warn you to watch your back and stay away and don't get caught alone with him anywhere, unless there's a good reason. She felt a rush of shame. How could she not have seen it?

She reached for her phone. The screen was filled with missed calls and texts from M, who was frantic.

Where are you?

What's happening?

Please, please, pick up, honey. I'm so worried.

She looked at the time and was shocked to find that hours had passed since she took the first drink. She was shaking, couldn't even bring herself to call M. How could she say what had happened to her? She didn't even remember. She'd been alone with him, drinking with him. She'd taken off her suit jacket, hung it on the chair. She knew her silk blouse was flattering. She'd clocked his gaze. She should have put her jacket back on then. But she hadn't.

She started the engine, shivering from fear and pain and the cold. Her windows were frosted. She could still smell his cologne.

She pushed open the door and vomited onto the blacktop.

Take a deep breath, her mother would say when Jessica was upset. *Just breathe.*

She did that, slow and deep, pulled herself together. She texted M.

I'm on my way to you.

She didn't read the replies that came one after another in quick succession. Ping. Ping. Ping.

Jessica started to drive, moving slowly through the lot. She wondered if she should be driving. She'd go slow; she'd be okay.

That's when she saw him, waiting. He sat in his Porsche over by the exit, just idling. As her car approached his, he rolled down the window.

"Great job tonight," he said. "Glad you're feeling better."

He gave her a wide smile and she saw what others before her had seen. A predator. A monster. He lifted a single manicured finger to his lips.

"Hush now," he said. "Not to worry. I won't tell anyone how you behaved tonight. It's between us."

Then he closed his window and roared away.

The shaking—it was almost comical. Her hands could barely hold the wheel, her teeth were chattering. The fear. The shame. The rage.

The tangle of feelings manifested themselves not in a scream, but in a deluge of tears.

That rage. It would find a home in her belly, a pot of pure molten lava.

She would drink from it, and it would make her stronger.

Everything that came next would come from that place.

PART ONE

AMUSE-BOUCHE

əˌmo͞ozˈbo͞oSH/

NOUN
A small savory appetizer offered before a meal.

"Girls, remember this, the only difference between poison and medicine is the dose."

Aunt Agnes's *Book of Cures*

ANA

This is a mistake. One of many, if you want to know the truth.

Still, I pull my car into the nearly empty parking lot and come to a stop, tires crunching on gravel. A blue neon sign that has seen better days flickers and buzzes over the roadside bar. *Gina's*, the sign reads in aspirational cursive when all the letters light at the same time. A tilted martini glass glows green, until it goes dark and stays that way a while before stuttering to life again. The sun is sinking hot pink beyond the stand of pines that reach to the horizon line.

Sunset is always beautiful, isn't it? Even in the parking lot of a dump like this, the kind of place that's always empty until it isn't. Where truckers stop for the night, or maybe biker gangs gather for a rowdy afternoon. This evening, there's only a smattering of other cars parked. And I wonder why he chose this place. Forty minutes from anywhere, anything.

I should probably go, right? This is a bad idea.

Instead, I kill the engine and look at his picture on my phone, then freshen up my makeup in the visor mirror and climb out of the car into the chilly twilight. I'm aware, as I often am, of a kind of hunger, a low hum of need. When I act from this place, that's when I am my worst self, do the things I later regret. But knowing this doesn't stop me tonight. Sometimes there's no stopping me.

In the lot beside the bar, there's an impressive collection of junk. Rusted-out cars, discarded appliances, shattered televisions, a waist-deep pile of computer keyboards, white and brittle as bones. As the electric-pink sun disappears below the horizon line, the broken and unwanted things are slowly, subtly painted rose. There's a strange, sweet reek of rot.

That's when I see them. The stray cats. Too mangy, too rangy, prowling in their bony elegance, leaping weightless from dangerously precarious mounds of sharp edges, peering yellow-eyed from shadows. I stop to watch them a moment. I'm comfortable in feline company. Cats are survivors like me. They always seem to think a lot of themselves despite their circumstances, like the black tom missing an eye who perches imperious as a king, watching as I continue moving toward the bar.

I swear I still feel that yellow eye on me as I step through the door.

What's a nice girl like you doing in a place like this? I imagine the tomcat would ask, licking his lips.

Well, Tom, I would answer, *the truth is, I'm not a nice girl. Not at all.*

Inside, it's a surprisingly decent space, with wood floors and cozy booths, a glowing jukebox, several pool tables and a long bar, lit and mirrored, rows and rows of colorful liquor bottles, lined up like soldiers in the war against good sense and right behavior. A predictably muscled and tattooed bartender in a black tank top and too-tight jeans wipes surfaces clean, gives me a nod.

"Welcome in," he says, eyes lingering.

In one of the booths toward the back, I see the man I've come to meet. He offers a wave and then gets to his feet to greet me. Unbelievably, he's better looking than his picture on the app. How often does that happen? We're all such liars, aren't we? He's tall and clean-cut, stylish if a bit rumpled in black jeans and suede bomber jacket. I imagine telling my sister, Vera, that

I've driven out of town to meet a man I connected with on an app that exists only for no-strings-attached sexual encounters called HookUp. *What are you thinking?* she'd surely ask, her tone striking all the notes of disappointment and disapproval I expect from her.

I catch my reflection in the mirror, slim, high-heeled, dressed all in black, my go-to color. My posture is erect, gait easy, expression flat, uninterested. But that's just the outer shell, the projection that I allow you to see. I'm a matryoshka doll. You could spend all day looking for the real woman, the hard, tiny kernel of truth inside all my painted-on selves. But you won't find her; I'll never allow that.

He reaches out a hand as I approach, and I find that appealingly nerdy considering the reason we've both come. His hand is warm in mine, handshake firm but not one of those that seems to need to prove how strong he is. This man is not buff and styled like my pretty ex with his moisturized skin and yoga-toned ass, the bespoke wardrobe he could ill afford. But there's something in this stranger's smoky dark hazel eyes that gets my heart to pumping as we slide across from each other into the leather booth. There's something familiar, though I know I've never seen him before.

He asks me what I want to drink, then walks over to the bar to order. I look at the items he's left on the table. A set of keys, a phone. I tap the screen, wondering what picture will pop up—a girlfriend, his wife and kids, his dog—but there's nothing, just a black screen with the time and, strangely, the lunar phase. Waxing gibbous.

Which reminds me, we're approaching the Wolf Moon, the first full moon of January, of the new year. It's meant to be a time of reflection on what has been, and what is ahead. It is a moment when we celebrate that in the dull gray cold of winter, the rebirth of spring approaches. The old will fade, the new will blossom green and bright. It's an important night in my circle, and for reasons I can't fully explain I'm always on edge as it approaches.

The stranger returns with my vodka soda, places it on the table as I thank him.

"I've never done this before," he says. "The app. I'm new to it."

"So am I," I lie. "I'm just getting out of a bad relationship. I'm not looking for anything serious."

That much is true. Sometimes a girl just needs to have a little fun, right? Long-term relationships with men are all handholding and ego-stroking, then it's cooking and picking up socks off the floor. And that's the best-case scenario. Things got ugly with my ex. I rub at my arm, which still aches a little, more like a ghost pain than a real injury.

"Got it," he says. No ego, no rush to say how *he's* not looking for anything serious either, no defensive posture. Just a slow, knowing smile. Those eyes—there's intelligence, a kind of seeing that makes me a little nervous. Like maybe he could see through all my layers, to the person inside, the one I have to protect.

A little more flirty chitchat. And then I kick off my shoe under the table and put my foot on the inside of his calf feeling the roughness of his jeans against my toes. The muscles of his leg are toned and strong. He startles a little, color coming up on his cheeks. He *is* new to this. I find that charming.

I take a deep swallow of my drink, then slip back into my shoe and rise, walk toward the rear of the bar, through the door that leads to the restrooms. He follows.

In the women's bathroom, he shuts and locks the door. It heats up fast, his arms around me, his lips on my neck, breath in my ear, then his mouth on mine, hot and sweet. I unbutton his shirt, feel the smooth heat of his skin. He's not ripped, but solid. He backs me up against the wall. He's strong, taking what he wants, but somehow gentle.

"Is this okay?" he asks. "Are you alright?"

Normally I find this a turnoff. But I don't mind it from him.

I nod, press my mouth to his so that he doesn't talk anymore. He hikes my skirt and lifts me onto the sink. And then I'm lost in the heat of him, of us, the rhythm of our bodies in this seedy place, the cracked mirror where I can only see fractured pieces of myself, the graffiti-covered walls filled with names and numbers and lines of bad poetry.

And it's good, deep, pleasure. There's no note of violence or undercurrent of malice, as there was with my ex, and so many of the other men in my life.

I know. I need to look at that.

When I open my eyes, he's staring at me.

"You're so beautiful," he whispers, pupils dilated slightly in the dim light.

I'm not one of those who feels the need to match a compliment with another one, so I just smile and kiss him again. And then we're both lost, not even bothering to stay quiet.

Afterward, he gives me another slow, deep kiss before he leaves, tender and respectful in spite of our tawdry ladies' room romp. "I'll wait for you outside."

"Okay," I say, fully expecting him to be gone when I return to the table. I am *not* new to this. I know how it goes. How it *should* go.

I pull myself together, wipe the smear of lipstick from around my mouth, feeling him all over me. My legs are shaking as I tug down my skirt. Well, then.

When I step outside, he's sitting in the booth, waiting like he said he would. There's a moment when I see him, and he doesn't see me. There's something about him, both virile and almost boyish. He's not staring at his phone like most people would, on to the next thing, the next hookup, the next whatever, but off into the distance at nothing. It's weird. I think I actually like him. Which was not the plan.

I turn around and find the back door, slip outside into the

night, pick my way through the alley, make my way past the junk in the lot next door.

There, on top of one of the rusted-out cars, is that one-eyed cat again. Black with a white star on his chest. He meows mournfully as I pass him by, headed for my car.

I told you I wasn't a nice girl, Tom. Didn't you believe me?

VERA

"What I need," says my sister, her voice filling my car over the Bluetooth speakers. "Is an exorcism. An *ex*-orcism."

She leans heavily on the syllable, the *x* catching in her throat like she's trying to hack up a hairball.

"Just forget him," I say, trying and probably failing to keep the impatience from my voice. "He was a loser. You can do better."

She blows out a laugh. "Easy for you to say, Mrs. Perfect Life."

Far from it and she knows it, so I don't even bother to respond. I keep my eyes on the road. Little Valley Academy, where my daughter, Coraline, is a senior and my son, Grant, is a freshman, looms ahead like a stone battlement—all iron gates and turrets, mullioned windows, sweeping green lawns. The aroma of entitled privilege wafts like the scent of cut grass.

"Seriously," she goes on, reception breaking up a little. "It's a thing now. After a breakup, you get together with your best girlfriends and basically eradicate your ex from your online life. You take down posts, eliminate tags. Your friends do the same. Block. Delete. Fuck off. And—poof—he disappears. He basically doesn't exist anymore."

It's interesting how people like my sister think that the world online is more real than the actual world in which people live and breathe. I'm glad I don't have to keep myself from rolling my eyes.

The security guard nods me through the open gate; he never smiles though he sees me every day. They take security seriously at Little Valley Academy, because the rich always think they're in terrible danger even though they rarely are. No one without the ID sticker in the window gets through the gate unescorted. After drop-off and dismissal, the gate is closed and locked.

"Would it make you feel better? An *ex*-orcism?" I ask, pulling onto the circular drive, getting in line to pick up the kids. Bentley, Porsche, Jag, Beemer. Chauffeur-driven Lincoln Town Car. Even though I'm behind the wheel of a Mercedes GLS, I still remember my dad's rattling, ancient Bronco. Every time he turned the ignition, he offered words of encouragement, *come on baby, one more time*. I linger on the memory, one of the few of him that make me smile. There was something I preferred about that life, I think. It was hardscrabble and ultimately tragic. But it was *real*, not buffed and shined, cropped and filtered like this one. Above me the sky is crisp, cold blue.

"I think it would," Ana says, thoughtful. "It would be like *cathartic* or whatever."

She *has* been taking it hard, this breakup with Paul. Who, by the way, I despised. And she has been behaving extraordinarily well. I'm actually quite proud of her restraint, her maturity. Her other breakups have been—messy. I'm eager to keep her stable. I don't have the bandwidth for a cleanup.

Coraline's senior year and the battle over where she wants to go to school, among other things, is taking up all my resources.

"How about a brunch this Sunday?" I offer. "At the house. Invite whoever you want. My treat."

There's a pause, a sigh. Then, "You'd do that?"

Her voice is soft, almost as if she's experiencing true emotion.

"Of course," I say. "Brad's away this weekend, that company golf thing. He leaves on Friday, doesn't get back until late Sunday. The kids are busy all weekend, sleepovers on Saturday. So, we'll have the house to ourselves Sunday morning."

Over the years, Ana's group of close friends have become my friends, as well. So, the idea of having them for a girls' Sunday brunch is pleasant enough, and if it helps Ana feel better, keeps her stable, why not?

"What can I bring?" she asks, sounding excited now, eager.

"Nothing," I say. "Just yourself."

"You're sure?"

"Consider it done. Let's say 11:00?"

I am already ticking through what I'll need. A large charcuterie board from Sal's, flowers from The White Orchid. Place cards from Papier. Quiche Lorraine and Waldorf salad, maybe a fruit platter from Mise en Place. Champagne for mimosas. A vegan option, too. Maybe April will come to help me set up, serve, clean up after. She's a magician in the kitchen. I'll ask her to make some scones.

As the car line snakes, I catch sight of my daughter, Coraline, with her wild shock of spiky black and pink hair, and Doc Martens chunky beneath the plaid pleats of her uniform skirt. It's a look. I let my kids be who they are, or who they think they are right now anyway, at least when it comes to what they're wearing. Anything else is to make everyone miserable. A truth most parents I know in this environment don't seem to grasp, as they try to bend and mold their children into versions of themselves, or the selves they wish they'd been.

Though I know Coraline would get a charge out of this idea of me as a parent who just *lets my kids be*, our most recent argument ringing back to me, one which ended in tears and slammed doors.

You don't even know me, she'd shrieked. Oh, my little girl, I know you better than you know yourself. This is an example of the kind of thing our family shrink would ask me not to say. *It's infantilizing, Vera*, the doctor chastised me last session.

Yeah, but! *But!* She *was* an infant—like five minutes ago!

Now Coraline stands with her two closest friends. Ethan, with his wild tangle of curls, towers lean and smiling over Coraline. He's messy, gangly, but handsome in his way, the way of youth. He whispers something in my daughter's ear and whatever he says causes Coraline to look into the crowd of kids exiting the school and laugh.

Autumn, a ginger blonde, freckled and bespectacled, looks worriedly at her phone, head bent, thumbs tapping. Her hair is pulled tightly into braided pigtails. Coraline tugs on one. Autumn leans into her, and Coraline drops an arm around the girl who's been her best friend since preschool. They both seem unformed to me, not awakened really. So different from Ana and me as teenagers. We had to grow up fast, learn to take care of ourselves, survive. Especially me, the elder.

And there are so many open questions about gender and sexuality now, plus the arrested development from the years of the pandemic. The devices stealing attention and awareness, taking kids out of their bodies and the real world, telling them stories about themselves and others that are less than true. All of them, it seems to me, are yet to *become*.

Not like when I was young, losing my virginity in the back seat of my dad's Bronco to my next-door neighbor Billy. An arrangement of proximity really, rather than of any real desire. There was no question of consent, just a magnetic pull from his body to mine, a wild curiosity guiltily satisfied. But it was real, alive, not an image on a screen. The world vibrated when I was young, felt electric with possibility.

"Vera, did I lose you? Let me guess. Car line."

Ana, just two years my junior (though it seems and feels like much more), resents my children, even though I know she loves them in her way. They draw most of my attention now. And Ana, who used to be my main focus, has had to take a distant back seat to Coraline and Grant. She doesn't always bear it graciously.

"No kids at the brunch, right? Sleepovers you said?"

No, we wouldn't want anything to take focus from *Ana* and her *ex*-orcism.

"They won't be home," I repeat. "But what about Iggy? Isn't she breastfeeding?"

An annoyed sigh. "I think she can leave the thing with its father for a couple hours, right? Don't they have like that pump or whatever?"

Nice.

Who was it that said that the world is sharply divided between people who have children and those who don't? Parents remember what it was like before. But single people can't imagine what it's like after. The choices you have to make, the sacrifices, the negotiations for even a few hours out. What you would do to protect and provide for your kids. It changes you. I don't even like to think about who I would be if I hadn't met Brad and had Coraline and Grant.

The back door opens and Grant climbs in. He doesn't even bother jockeying for the front seat. Coraline is the dominant personality, the elder, the more confident, outspoken. Though he towers over her now, she still bosses him around like she always has. The car bucks and pitches as he heavily lands in the back.

"Hey, pal," I say. "How was your day?"

"Good."

For Grant, that's a rave. It might be: "Sucked." Or: "I don't know." Or maybe no answer at all, AirPods in, barely a nod to acknowledge my existence. He looks at me with his deep, dark eyes as I turn, pushes his floppy brown bangs away though they slide right back. The girls like a floppy-haired boy these days, skinny, asexual; the clean-cut, masculine look that Brad would prefer is *out*. Grant tugs off his blue blazer, loosens his tie. He has purple shiners of fatigue under his eyes. I don't need to ask if he was up late gaming. *Red World*, the bane of every parent's existence.

"Expound," I press.

He digs through his bag and hands me a clipped stack of

paper. Mr. Wilson is the only teacher at school who insists that work be turned in on real paper instead of submitted via one of the digital platforms available at the school. I love the man for this—a real English teacher who has forced his students to learn how to write well and clearly, to analyze and annotate texts, take notes in paper notebooks, keep a planner. They spent a month on *Hamlet*. Mr. Wilson is funny and wise, with a deep love of language and literature. For Grant, at least, it's been contagious.

There's a big *A* emblazoned across the title page of Grant's short story, which is twenty-five percent of his grade this unit focused on creative writing. Coraline is a much better student, though she's operating far below her abilities, just coasting because she can. Grant struggles in every area—academically, socially. So, this is a big deal.

"Holy wow, kiddo," I say, flashing him a grin. "That's fantastic."

"He said it was up there with the best he's seen in his years as a teacher."

That's the longest sentence Grant has uttered in a week. My heart swells.

"That's awesome." I lift a palm and he high-fives me. "I'm proud of you. Can I read it?"

He hesitates a moment, then nods, and I slide it in my bag. I don't ask twice. I'm eager for any window into my fourteen-year-old son who used to be attached to my body, and who is now so totally self-possessed that he's nearly a stranger. That's the way of it, I suppose. But I miss the nights where he slept between Brad and me, and we had no idea how we were going to get him to sleep in his own bed. "I'll read it tonight."

The front passenger door opens, bringing with it the sound of youthful exuberance—laughter and shouts, screeches and hoots.

"God," Coraline says, blustering in like a little thunderhead. "I hate this place *so much*."

"I'm still here, you know." Ana, on the Bluetooth. The kids both roll their eyes.

"Rough day?" I ask Coraline.

"Ugh. I'm *exhausted*."

"Oh, right. Because life's so hard for the child of extreme privilege," says Ana, breaking up a bit over the speaker. "Let me tell you about how your mom and I grew up."

"You don't know about *my life*," snaps Coraline, flashing me an angry look like *why is she even here?*

"See you Sunday, Ana," I cut in. She's saying something else when I hang up. Did I hear cassoulet? I'll put an end to that. Ana has no business in the kitchen. She's a terrible cook. Really, dangerous is more like it. And cassoulet is a whole thing.

"Tell me," I say, as I pull though the rest of the driveway.

Coraline is talking about her day, how she barely got a 90 on her chem lab because her partner didn't do his part of the work, and she had to hustle during study hall to complete what he'd forgotten. How Emma, the meanest girl in school, told her that *no one* wore Doc Martens anymore. Like, that they weren't even cool in a *retro* way. There was something about how weird Ethan is acting. And some rumor about Mr. Wilson and Ms. Crabtree, that they'd been caught by a student making out in the break room.

Huh, good for them.

Little Valley Academy, never a dull moment. Well, truthfully, *nothing but* dull moments. Still always abustle with rumors and mini-dramas, banal events, ridiculous conflicts. I find it all fairly amusing. As much as I am a fixture here, donating preposterous sums for the new gym, or the scholarship program, running fundraisers, and volunteering for committees on diversity and inclusion, or student mental health initiatives, I am not really a part of it all. I float above, move through, smile and nod.

Ana's right, of course. This life in no way compares to how we grew up.

"She's so—*needy*," says Coraline, conversation veering back to Ana again.

This is actually dead-on. Because Ana has a shiny veneer

of icy beauty, a sharp tongue, and exudes a nearly pathological apathy for the feelings and needs of others, it's hard to spot. I've been taking care of her since before we lost our parents, and I know that beneath it all is a scared little girl, one who still relies on me in ways that she shouldn't. And I'm a bit of an enabler, because for so long it was just the two of us.

"She's right," I say. "We didn't have it easy."

"Yeah," says Coraline. "But she's like almost forty. Time to grow up, right? She needs her own life."

My daughter, wise beyond her years, is not wrong about this either. But Ana and I are too entangled; there's too much history. I reach for Coraline and put a hand on her thigh, give her a look. She softens, smiles. Even with all the rough-and-tumble between us, there's a closeness, a mother-daughter love that is foundational to our relationship, also hard to spot most days.

"I know," she says. "We're all she has."

"Family," I say. "Imperfect, but indelible."

She mouths the words along with me because I've said it a million times.

A glance in the rearview mirror reveals that Grant's got his AirPods in now. Then Coraline is tapping on her phone. My thoughts turn to the brunch, creating a mental checklist of everything that will have to be done between now and then for it to be perfect. Because perfection and order are a comfort to me, a need, really. It's a kind of wall that keeps the chaos at bay. One little crack and the whole thing can crumble.

And Ana and I know too well what the world looks like when that wall comes crashing down.

As I pull on the road and head toward home, I hear the distant wail of a fire engine siren, and after a few moments the truck rounds the bend and is barreling in our direction, lights flashing, horns blaring.

I find myself cringing against the assault of sound as it passes, a red wall of angry urgency—though the kids barely seem to notice, only Coraline side-eyeing the passing vehicle because the noise is an annoyance to her. Then the truck disappears around the next bend—leaving a ghostly echo in the air and a cold finger of worry pressing into my belly in its wake.

I flip on the radio to the local news channel and listen for any information about what has burned. But no news comes.

I am aware of a white noise of unease, the slight sense that something is wrong. It lingers as we drive, even though Coraline has turned off the news and has her music blaring, and the kids are safe in my care. Usually, if this feeling came up, I'd reflexively check the LifeWatch app where I can track the kids, my husband, my sister. But I just talked to Ana, and Brad is in a big meeting at the office. Everyone's safe. For now.

Stop it, I chastise myself. Free-floating anxiety. The child of trauma, I am no stranger to this feeling. I used to think I had some powers of prediction, largely because my mother always claimed I was borderline psychic. I know better now. The world dishes up more beauty and horror than you can ever conjure in your own imagination, and it usually comes out of nowhere.

When we arrive home, pulling up the circular drive in our neighborhood, each house grander than the next, I come to a stop and the kids thunder out of the car, leaving me in silence.

After a moment of gathering my things, I follow them. They've left the door ajar behind them.

I almost miss it, am over the threshold before it catches my eye.

On the ground behind the enormous potted plant, a small, tied collection of sticks in the shape of a person. I put down my things inside the door and reach for it, hold it in my hand. The tiny arms and legs are tied with red ribbon; inside the collection of sticks there are small feathers, crystal shards.

My heart thuds a little.

I know what it is.

The question is—who put it there? And why?

IGGY

Doesn't it just seem like little girls get handed this bill of goods about what life is going to be like if they only do this, or do that? There's the whole fairy tale, right? You spend your entire life in a state of expectation. And then what *comes*—the *truth* of it all—bears very little resemblance to the fantasy.

Like, it's not even close.

I'm thinking this as I stare at the downy crown of Noah's head. He's four months today. And he's just drifted off after nursing, his head heavy in the crook of my arm, a little drop of milk trailing from the corner of his pouty pink mouth. The nursery is dim, and quiet, the only sound the wind pushing at the windows. Brock and I chose, after careful deliberation and hours cruising around online, a jungle theme—a kind of gentle, cheerful baby jungle with smiling monkeys, and big-eyed giraffes, tumbling tigers, and pleasingly roundish elephants. In the peaceful stillness, the happy animals watch us.

Noah is what the nurses called an angel baby—one who latched on right away, who was easily comforted, who seemed awake and alert, observant, while others were squalling, protesting their entrance in this cold, cruel world.

"This one's special," the night nurse in the hospital told me. She'd lifted him from his bassinet and placed him in my arms. He immediately started to suckle ferociously, looking at me with these super-intense blue eyes. "He's a star."

Probably, she said that to all the drug-addled, stunned mothers in her care. But it seemed true to me, still does.

Twinkle, twinkle little star, I whisper to him each night when I put him to bed.

"And you're a natural mother," the nurse said when she observed our easy connection. "That's not true of everyone."

I'm not. I studied, determined to do better than my own mother.

I wipe the milk from Noah's mouth. And he's out, even snoring a soft little baby snore. I should get up from this chair and put him down in his crib; I'm late. But one of the things they don't tell you about your baby is that you'll be hypnotized by your love for him. Really, it's a spell they cast. Sure, you're exhausted, overwhelmed, stressed and out of your league in every way. And sometimes I just lie in Brock's arms and cry, so swept away by emotion I can barely express myself. But mostly I'm just awed by this tsunami of love that matches no other I've ever experienced.

It makes me wonder about my own mother, who was not what the night nurse would have called a "natural mother." Everything about my mother—who she was with me, her choices, the things she did and said—makes even less sense to me now that I have my own child.

Finally, I rise carefully, and place Noah on his back in his empty crib. His onesie is covered in little stars and his chubby legs fall open. I spend another untold amount of time watching his curling fingers, the way the light dances in the scant hair on his head, the fullness of those big baby cheeks. I think he looks like Brock. But Brock insists he looks like me, around the eyes especially.

In our bedroom, I pull on the flowered dress that I ordered online with a prayer that it would fit. At the moment, I am not small enough for my pre-baby clothes, and all my maternity things look like muumuus. Soft and crepey, the new dress is perfect, skimming my fleshier areas and highlighting my boobs, which, if I must say so myself, look spectacular. The soft pink brings out the high color in my cheeks. I even managed to go to the salon yesterday, with Noah in the BabyBjörn. All the ladies at the salon gathered and cooed; the little ham, he lapped it up, smiling and gurgling. And he loved the blow dryer; it put him right to sleep.

I'm not one of those Instagrammable post-pregnancy people, killing myself to "get my body back." To be honest, my body was never that great to begin with and it's always been good enough for Brock. So, I'm just walking with the baby in the mornings and eating healthy and hoping for the best at the moment.

I pull a brush through my honey hair and put a light pink gloss on my lips. I think of Ana, impossibly svelte and always chic. Her skin is a flawless peaches and cream; her long glossy black hair gleams almost purple when it reflects light. Vera is older than us, but in an aspirational way, like she's *ahead*. Her life is seemingly perfect with ultrarich Brad and that insanely big house that looks like it belongs on someone's vision board. Those thick auburn tresses are always blown out to perfection, nails a simple gel French. I saw a dress she wore to a girls' night out last year on Nordstrom's website. It cost *a thousand* dollars. Though those kids do seem like a handful. And Brad? Well, he's Brad. We like to call him "the ghost." He's rarely there, and when he is, he's on his way somewhere else.

Payton will also be at brunch. Payton, who, before her thirty-third birthday, is the first Black partner at her law firm. Tiny but mighty, a stick of TNT in a perfectly tailored designer suit. And Esme, CEO of a gaming company, dresses like a very wealthy teenage boy in hoodies and baggy jeans, expensive sneakers. She wears her hair in a platinum buzz cut, has a line of gold hoops along her right ear. A tattoo on the inside of her left forearm reads: Carpe Diem. Her wife, Claudia, won't be joining today. Apparently, she's *off to Asia* for her work in a finance firm.

These are all women of a certain type. High achieving and exacting, powerful in their different ways. I fell into this friend group because Ana and I have been friends since college, where we were roommates and inseparable until I left in junior year. Which I don't like to think about, how I never finished my degree. So, I guess I'm Ana's friend and I'm connected to the rest through her. It doesn't matter, I tell myself, that they all have accomplishments and successes. I have something they don't, except for Vera maybe. True love. A child. I am—after years of therapy—happy.

Before I make it to the top of the staircase, my phone pings. There's a message from a number but no name.

I can't sleep. I can't stop thinking about it.

I thumb out my answer quickly. **Don't text me again.**

I don't like to be harsh. But I can't handle this right now. What happened, happened. It's done. I'm good at putting things in a box and locking them up. I'm like my mother that way. I don't dwell on the past. I have a brunch to attend.

Another text: I'm all alone out here.

I don't answer, delete the chain. Brock is on my phone all the time, and I'm on his. We don't have secrets. Or we didn't.

Downstairs, my husband is lying on our plush sectional couch, the game volume low on the enormous television we bought for ourselves when I got pregnant. We spent the latter half of my pregnancy when things were dicey, and the first months of Noah's life, watching movies, bingeing shows, cheering for our various sports teams. Honestly, it was paradise. I'm not ready to rejoin the world yet, not really.

"Whoa," Brock says, getting up. "You look—amazing."

He put on weight during my pregnancy, too. Of course, it looks good on him.

He takes me into his arms, kisses me deep. He's beefier, broader through the shoulders. His arms feel bigger, stronger. I run my hand through his dark hair in its usually wild tousle, touch the three-day stubble on his jaw. He pulls away, looks down at his baggy jeans and worn flannel shirt. He's hot, my hubby, even on a Sunday morning in.

Brock pats his stomach, looking at his reflection in the big bay window. "I better get myself back in shape if I'm going to be in your league."

"You're in a league of your own," I tell him, giving him a peck on the cheek.

Suddenly, I'm thinking of canceling plans I really didn't want to accept in the first place.

I take another quick glance at my phone. Nothing. That text. It rattled me. I just want to stay here where it's safe.

I was a little surprised to get Vera's invitation. Hey, Iggy, hope you're well. Join us for brunch on Sunday? Ana's been taking her breakup with Paul pretty hard, and we're planning an "ex-orcism."

I had to look it up. Apparently, it's a thing you do now. After you break up with someone, get together with friends and digitally remove the ex from your lives. Block. Delete. Unfollow. Fuck off—according to Ana.

I *tried* to tell Ana about Paul, the things I knew about him. But she didn't believe me. In fact, Ana and I didn't talk for a while after that little chat. Which was hurtful. But maybe not surprising. Ana does what she wants, doesn't like to be told otherwise.

I know it's hard with the baby so small, Vera's message went on. But Ana would love to see you. And so sorry, but no kids. Do you think you can sneak away for a couple of hours?

No kids? Wouldn't most gatherings of women allow for a friend's newborn? But of course, no kids. So that all the attention can be on Ana and her drama du jour.

My husband leans in for another kiss, and then his hands

are roaming my body. Heat comes up fast. Our sex life, after a couple months' hiatus, has ramped up again, hotter than ever. It's different—more reverent, deeper. Like we're awed by what our bodies—especially mine—can do.

"Stop," I say, pulling away reluctantly. "I'm late already. Are you sure you're okay?"

He lifts his palms. "What is this, the 1950s? I am a woke husband and dad. I got this. We'll watch the game. Play with some soft blocks. Boys' day in."

I could just put my sweats back on and stay. There are a thousand excuses I could give. The baby was fussy. Or Brock got called into work. No one would judge me.

Not true.

Ana would. Those icy eyes, the way they bore in and see everything.

Brock helps me with my coat in the foyer, where I almost lose my resolve again. He must see it. He puts a hand to my cheek, brow wrinkling with concern.

"What is it? Are you okay?"

I nod and smile. It's not about Noah being safe; Brock is the best dad in the world.

It's about me. It's not safe out there.

"Maybe I'm not ready."

He runs a hand down the back of my head, hand gentle and warm, kisses my forehead.

"It'll be good for you. To see your friends. To have a couple of hours of girl time. We're fine here. I promise. I'll call if things get hairy."

"I know," I say weakly.

"Talk to me," he says, frowning now.

There are so many things I wish I could tell him; it's all right there, ready to spill. Then in my bag, the phone pings again. I ignore it and try for a smile. "No, you're right. Some girl time is just what I need."

We start walking toward the door. "Oh, the cookies," I say. "I'll get them."

He jogs back to the kitchen, then follows me out the door with the tray of gluten-free, dairy-free, carob-chip cookies I stayed up late to make. Vera said not to bring anything, but I can't go empty-handed.

Outside, the air is cool and clean, the day overcast and windy. I feel a rush of energy, of confidence. It *does* feel good to be out, to be dressed. Brunch will be a nice distraction.

I wave to my sexy husband, then back out of the drive. The electric car is so quiet, like it's not even running. The house and our pretty neighborhood grow smaller in the rearview mirror.

At the stop sign just a few doors down on my street, I glance at the phone again.

The text there reads: I'm sorry.

I delete it, push my feelings down deep. I can forget things, people.

Brock's right. The brunch *will* be good for me. Won't it? Isn't this what they tell you you're supposed to want? To get your body back, your life back, yourself back? Time away just for you? Except the reality is, I don't want to *go back* anywhere.

The Iggy I was before Noah, before Brock? It's like those memories are in black-and-white, something distant and less. Motherhood has made me stronger, more able. And that person—who I was in college, and after I left. That person doesn't even exist anymore. It's like I've *exorcised her*. She's gone.

The only person in my life who still remembers her is Ana.

I'm still at the stop sign, no one else behind me to honk and bring me back to myself.

Out of the corner of my eye, I see a parked car. An older black BMW with a dent in the side. Inside a figure sits in the driver's seat, stock-still. The windows are tinted, so I can't tell, but I feel like he's staring at me. Watching. My heart starts to thud.

I drive away, keeping watch in the rearview mirror.

After a moment, the car pulls out and follows me.

The man at the wheel is older, with a full graying beard. He's wearing sunglasses and a baseball cap. I don't recognize him. Who is he? Why is he following me? I speed up a little, heart racing.

But after a while the car makes another turn and is gone. I let go of a laugh that sounds more like a cough. I'm paranoid.

Still shaking, adrenaline pulsing, I keep checking my mirrors all the way to Vera's.

I can't shake the feeling, an anxious unease.

Is somebody watching me?

My phone pings again. I'm scared.

So am I.

I keep driving.

VERA

What is it about *don't bring anything* that people fail to understand? Entertaining is an art; it takes time and planning. Last-minute additions to the buffet I've set up on the sideboard in the dining room will require rearranging and replating because—no. I'm not putting Iggy's *aluminum foil* tray of gluten-free, dairy-free cookies out. April quickly arranges them on a Lennox serving platter. Or Esme's special meal ordered from a website that, after extensive DNA testing, delivers weekly organic entrées specially calibrated for Esme's specific dietary needs. It's in a biodegradable paper container that apparently must go in the microwave for two minutes. April dutifully heats and plates it. I don't have to say a word about any of it. April just *knows* how I like things. Which is such a relief since I feel like I'm constantly explaining myself to my kids and my husband, who stare at me like I'm speaking a language they don't understand and don't care to learn.

Then she transfers Ana's cassoulet from the dirty Dutch oven she brought it in to my Fitz and Floyd Toulouse soup tureen with a bluebird on a branch as its handle. Ana is proud of herself, chattering on about Aunt Agnes's old recipe and how it's perfect for this cold and blustery day. It does smell good; maybe her skills have improved.

"Remember how Mom loved this?" Ana reminisced as she put the big pot on my stove.

I don't, but okay.

Payton is the only one with any sense. Plus, she doesn't cook, or entertain. She works seventy hours a week. And like all women, she must work twice as hard at her law firm to achieve half as much. And as a woman of color, double that. She brings a hostess gift, which is appropriate, if unnecessary, and very much appreciated—a bottle of Veuve and a box of Belgian chocolates in an elegant gold box, noting that she has to be on her way by 2:00 at the latest. She always has an exit strategy for these gatherings. I respect that.

Anyway, we're seated now, the meal underway. Late morning light streams in from the big windows. And the table is—if I do say so myself—set to perfection with woven placements and a simple runner of fresh greenery and fairy lights. And everyone is oohing and aahing over the brunch offerings. I notice that no one touches the cassoulet. Ana's reputation in the kitchen is well-known. No one except Iggy, who I can only imagine is just trying to be nice. She dutifully praises Ana's efforts. I'll stick with the quiche and Waldorf salad.

"Anyway, we have Payton to blame for this," says Ana, her voice rising over the other conversations.

Payton raises her eyebrows, glass halfway to her glossed lips. Her hair is a lush cloud of silky curls, eyes shadowed in glittering copper. That watch on her wrist costs more than the used car I'm planning to buy for Coraline—if she ever passes her driving test.

"How is it *my* fault?" Payton asks coolly.

"You introduced us," says Ana.

Payton offers an elaborate eye roll. "*Ana*, you met Paul at the firm Christmas party last year. I don't recall personally introducing you. And—if I remember correctly you invited *yourself* to that party. My friend, you were trawling."

Ana gives an assenting nod, a devilish smile. "Fair enough."

"Where is Paul, anyway?" Payton asks, sipping from her wineglass. I notice that she wrinkles her nose in distaste when she says his name. "I didn't see him at the food bank board meeting on Friday."

"Apparently, he's off to Aruba," says Ana tightly. A flash of something across her face. Sadness? Maybe she did really like him. "With the new girlfriend."

"He was cheating," puts in Esme.

She's found her way to the sideboard, is eyeing the creamy quiche Lorraine, her mail-order meal untouched. It sits gray and unappetizing on her plate. "Ana found an errant thong in his gym bag. Lacy, red, wasn't it?"

Ana launches a glare like a Chinese star. "You were always good at remembering details." But Esme only grins. She has a way of gently teasing Ana that appeals to me.

Iggy, who arrived late with a flurry of apologies and is seated to the right of my place at the head of the table, has been mostly silent. She watches Ana like a sparrow watches a hawk. I don't understand their relationship. I like Iggy. She's a sweet girl, but she's a bit of an outlier in this group. A college dropout, she has flitted between jobs since then. Last I heard she was the office manager at a startup company, a job Esme got her and one to which Ana doubts Iggy will return now that she has a baby. *The girl is apparently on the mommy track*, complained Ana.

I stopped myself from asking Ana what type of track she considers herself to be on. Her work as a freelance public relations and social media consultant can be lucrative when she has the right client. But the work is sporadic. And even though she's always rushing off to this meeting or that, Brad and I are still paying most of her bills.

Iggy is eating the cassoulet with gusto. Ana, true to form, has only a few pieces of lettuce on her plate and has barely eaten a bite. She hands her untouched serving of cassoulet to Iggy, who keeps eating.

"So," says Ana. "My sister was kind enough to host this little gathering. Welcome to my exorcism."

"Here we go," says Payton. She's seated on the other side of Ana. In spite of another eye roll, she reaches for my sister's hand. They, too, have been friends since college.

Ana goes on. "This is where we eliminate Paul Hayes from our digital life. We unfollow him on any social media platform and block him from interacting on ours. I've already gone back through my feed and deleted images of him, and untagged any images he's shared of me."

"So," says Payton, raising a hand as if she's a student in class. "I can't really exorcise Paul, you know. His agency works for our firm."

"You don't have to socialize with him, though, right? It's not like you're *friends*."

Something rushes across Payton's face, a worried wrinkle of the eyes. What's going on there? "No," she says stiffly. "We're not friends."

"I'm *happy* to exorcise Paul," says Esme. "I only interacted with him because of you." She's already got her phone in hand. Tap. Tap. Tap. "Done. Paul Hayes just stopped existing for me. Good riddance."

There's an uncharacteristic edge to her voice.

"I never followed him," says Iggy. "I'm not following any more of the men in your life until you get married."

"Which will be *never*," says Ana, sharply. "I don't want that life."

Iggy flushes, fingers the diamond *N* at her neck. She's pretty in a lush, feminine way, a kind of country-girl-next-door look in the flowery dress she probably got online. I flash her a smile, which she weakly returns. You can't take Ana's declarations too seriously. If it suits whatever agenda she happens to be running, she'll change her mind about marriage and anything else in a heartbeat. Iggy, if she knows Ana as well as she should by now, knows that.

"Fine," says Payton. "I'll unfollow in socials. But I have to stay connected to him in ConnectIn for professional reasons."

Ana concedes with a pouty nod. "What about you, Vera?"

"You know I'm not on socials much."

That is a lie. What's true is that I don't participate. I don't comment and like, share or argue. I don't post recipes or pictures of the kids. I'm not interested in broadcasting my life for approval. And I definitely don't want my image out there any more than necessary. It's bad enough that our life as community business owners and local philanthropists is so high-profile, hard enough to dodge the camera at functions. I hate seeing my own image in newspapers or online. I like to control how I am seen.

But I do watch. I'm what Coraline would call a social media stalker. You don't see me. But I see you. I watch Ana, the kids, the kids' friends. You learn a lot about people that way.

So, for example, though I couldn't care less about Paul, I followed him because of his connection to Ana. So, I did see the post that sent Ana over the edge. The sunset shot from Aruba, his feet beside the pedicured feet of a woman, two martini glasses held to the sky. *Paradise found.* That's one of the things I disliked about Paul the most, his utter lack of imagination. He was so—dull.

The post did seem taunting, though. Which is a bit off-brand. I wouldn't have imagined him cheating, breaking up with Ana, dashing off to Aruba, and then posting an image that he clearly knew she would see. That showed a lot of imagination, a creative mean-spiritedness worthy of a woman. Men are usually so basic in their hurtfulness, in their violence.

But my sister does have a way of pushing people to their limit, making them do things they wouldn't do without her subtle influence.

Ana's watching me. We know each other too well. We almost don't need to talk anymore. Sisters. Just a look, what is left unsaid, can speak volumes.

"But yeah," I say. "Of course. Consider him social media dead to me."

"He was never good enough for you," says Iggy.

Ana puts a hand to her heart, beams. "Thank you, lovey. Maybe someday I'll find someone as wonderful as your Brock."

There's another layer to it though, and Iggy's sweet smile falters.

Ana raises her glass. I've shared around the champagne that Payton brought as a gift. April filled some flutes and brought them out on a tray as we sat. Hardly anyone noticed her, except for Iggy, who thanked her quietly. April's like that, a person who prefers to go unseen. She does whatever job I hire her to do efficiently and quietly. She disappears until I need her again. April and I share the rare perfect relationship—unemotional, discreet, transactional. I pay her in cash.

"To Brock," says Ana. "Who reminds us that there *are* good men in the world."

We clink. I notice that Ana only pretends to sip, while Iggy nearly drains her glass.

"And good riddance to cheating slobs like Paul," says Esme, lifting her glass again. "May he never darken our social media feeds again."

Another round of clinking flutes.

Then the doorbell rings. Everybody freezes, glasses still raised. Looking around the table, I clock fleeting expressions, those little twitches on the face that tell the truth. Ana looks guilty. Trust me, I've seen that look a thousand times, underpinned by a kind of dark glee. What's she up to? Iggy looks briefly scared. Esme, angry. Payton glances at her watch, like she's counting the minutes until she can leave.

I nod to April, who scurries off to answer the door.

AGNES

Vera and Ana, just two years apart, are very different. I watch them in the rearview mirror, my eyes darting away from the road to the two slender girls in my back seat. One dark, one fairer as they sit still, each looking out her respective window.

Vera, the elder, has big eyes, weirdly black, and thick lashes, eyebrows angry slashes, mouth wide and full, high cheekbones. Her auburn hair, glossy and thick, is tightly braided to a single rope that slides over her shoulder like a snake. To someone else, those still features might communicate calm. But her aura is wild—grief, anger, fear. She holds her sister's hand.

Ana is silently crying, tears streaming from icy blue eyes. Her hair is so black it's almost purple. Heart-shaped and pale, her face is a mask of sadness. Downturned pink lips, inky eyebrows knitted. Her energy however is as cold as a blade. She's the one to watch. That's what my sister, the girls' mother, Sadie, said. Vera has a golden center. Ana's is steel through and through. Sadie loves them both, fiercely.

"Not much longer," *I say, catching Vera's eyes in the mirror as she offers a tight nod. There's something there that gives me a little jolt, like a mini electric shock to the solar plexus.*

I wonder if Sadie was right about the girls. She often made mistakes about people. Take, for example, the girls' father. She was clueless about him, though I saw right through him from the first. I knew he'd be her undoing. But what woman ever listened to reason when she was in love?

The road winds on, the sun sets. I flip on my headlights. And finally, I turn onto the drive that leads to the house, come to a stop. Then I climb out to unlock and swing open the gate, return to the car to drive us through.

"Why is there a gate?" asks Ana, her voice soft.

"To keep people who don't belong here out," I say.

She seems to consider this but doesn't respond.

"We don't want this," says Vera, those fierce dark eyes on me. "We don't want to live with you. We don't even know you."

"I understand," I tell her, gripping the wheel. "You're a child, but you do have a choice. Come live with me here, or you and your sister will go into state care, the foster system. I think I can promise you that won't be better."

Ana throws Vera a frightened look, tugs at her arm urgently, shaking her head. Vera will make the decisions for them, and Ana will do what she says. This much is clear.

"I want to go home," says Ana, voice wobbly.

"This is home for now," I say as gently as I can. Ana reminds me so much of Sadie. I hope she's stronger, wiser. I am not the mothering type, lacking patience and that essential tenderness. But maybe I have something to teach both of them, if they'll learn.

I wait, the engine rumbling. In the trees, the mournful call of a barred owl. Above, a dusky sky starting to glitter with stars.

"What's it going to be, girls?"

I turn to look at them. Vera wraps her arms around her middle. Her red coat is too small, exposing delicate wrists. Another nod.

I drive.

"Where are we?" asks Vera as the big house rises into view. "What is this place?"

"This is your birthright, the place where your mom and I grew up."

Something in Ana's eyes glitters. And strangely I'm reminded of a baby rattlesnake. How its bite is rumored to be more deadly than that of a mature rattler because it can't control the amount of venom it releases. Adult rattlesnakes supposedly know to leave some venom in reserve. Young snakes unload it all.

"Whoa," Ana says.

The house is actually kind of a wreck. The porch needs shoring up, the roof repair. The whole thing could badly use a coat of paint. But it's huge, and its decrepitude is masked by the crepuscular gloom. I admit there's a grandness to it in the shadows.

I help them get their tiny suitcases from the trunk. They have so little, and I try not to feel sorry for them because pity is disempowering, and I want better than that for them. They're right that we don't know each other well, but they're my blood.

Inside, I ask them to follow me upstairs. "I'll show you girls around properly tomorrow," I say as we climb the creaking steps. "But for tonight let's just try to get some rest."

I hear them whispering as they climb the stairs, past the row of portraits and photographs. Their family—aunts, their grandmother, Sadie and me as children. In time, I'll teach them all about the family Sadie was so eager to leave behind.

At the end of the hallway, I swing open the door to the bedroom that I shared with their mother when we were girls. The room is cozy with two twin beds made with fluffy pink comforters and soft pillows, matching dressers, thick overstuffed chairs by the window. There's a working fireplace, and a tall bookshelf packed with the novels that Sadie and I devoured as young people. Vera enters and offers an imperious nod, as if she finds the space just barely acceptable. I know for a fact it's about a hundred times nicer than their room in the hovel they called home.

She moves inside and claims the far bed, putting her suitcase down by the dresser. She stares at a picture of Sadie and me; we stand hand in hand in the garden, which I'll show them one day.

"Is it haunted?" asks Ana, still lingering at the door. "It looks haunted."

"Don't be stupid," snaps Vera. But she doesn't fool me; fear pulls *the features of her face taut as she gazes out the door, down the long dark hallway.*

"It's not haunted by anything but memories," I answer truthfully.

What I don't say is that memory can be the most relentless haunting of all.

ANA

The sound of the doorbell moves through me like an electric shock, sitting me bolt upright, leaving my skin tingling.

I don't know why the doorbell should have this effect; this is not even my house. No one else seems bothered, or to have even registered the interruption.

Iggy glances at her phone, looking at photos of the baby sent—every few minutes it seems—by Brock. Payton and Esme are whispering about something obviously *very* important, because they're so smart, *such* power brokers. Only Vera acknowledges the ringing doorbell. She doesn't rise but looks to April, who gives a nod and heads to the door.

What is it with those two?

How much is Vera paying the mousy little thing that she's always at my sister's beck and call, lingering in the shadows of all our functions? She's barely there, wisp thin with prematurely graying blond hair, big glasses, and weird eyes—one brown, one green. The only detail that hints at all at any kind of inner life are the tattoos snaking out the cuff of her (always) long-sleeve tee, or at the crew neck. Plain white Keds, faded loose-fitting jeans. Basic. If I passed her on the street, she wouldn't even register.

She comes back and whispers to my sister. Vera's eyes catch mine. Then she rises, straight-backed and regal as a queen, and glides from the room.

"What's going on?" asks Iggy, still gazing at her phone. Gawd, all she does is look at pictures of that baby.

I shake my head, get up and follow my sister. Stopping in the entrance to the octagonal foyer with its black-and-white tile floor, I peer around the towering vase of flowers on the round table in the center. Through the open door I see that there are two police cruisers in the drive. A pair of uniformed officers stand behind a tall man in a suit, who holds out a gleaming gold shield in a leather case.

Him.

I didn't think we'd be seeing each other again. My mind starts to grapple for why he would be here at my sister's door. Under my confusion, there's a little thrill.

I don't like his expression, like he's in on a joke the rest of us aren't getting. Eyes heavily lidded, face stubbled, a thick head of dark hair, mouth kind of pouty. He obviously thinks a lot of himself. One of those men who's always sure of his position. A very different bearing than when I first met him.

Also: He's a *cop*?

I can tell by Vera's rigid posture, the way her hand covers her heart, that my sister is distressed. Did something happen to Brad? One of the kids? I should go to her, but I stay rooted, blood rushing, a loud swish-swishing in my ears, so loud I can't hear. Sometimes I just freeze like this, rebuffering.

I force myself to move forward.

"What is it?" I hear myself say. "What's happened?"

My sister turns to me. She doesn't utter a word, but I hear it all the same. *What did you do?*

I'm through a wormhole, back to Agnes's house, the first time the police came to the door. I was young, still reeling from our crash course in the world and all its varied cruelties.

"Honey," Vera says softly. The loving older sibling, offering kindness and support. Her stare is like a cattle prod. "I'm so sorry."

She moves and puts her arm tight around my shoulders.

"What?" I ask, heart in my throat. "What's happened?"

"Ms. Ana Blacksmith?" I don't like his voice. It's cold, official, hard like a concrete wall. I guess we're acting like this is the first time we've met. I'll go along with that.

"That's right." My throat constricts.

"I'm Detective Timothy Bandeau from the Little Valley Police Department. I am afraid we have some difficult news. The body of Paul Hayes was discovered by hikers this morning. We understand you were in a relationship."

The space tilts a little. A veil comes down, separating me from reality.

"We broke up," I manage to say. "A few weeks ago. How? How did he die?"

"It's unclear at the moment, but we suspect foul play. Can you think of anyone who might want to hurt him?"

Wow. He doesn't waste any time, does he? I guess that shouldn't come as any surprise.

This is where I'm supposed to break down, right? Let my legs buckle and allow Vera to ease me to the ground. But I stand rigid, eyes locked with the detective's. Can I think of anyone who would want to hurt Paul?

Ha.

They are legion. Some of them are even in this house.

"No," I whisper, leaning into my sister, whose grip on my shoulders is too tight, almost painful like she's trying to keep me from getting away. It's weirdly comforting.

"Paul Hayes's sister, who we notified as next of kin, thought you might be someone who wished him harm. We went to your apartment. Your neighbor said you'd be at your sister's today."

Paul's *sister*? That little witch; she always hated me. And my unbelievably invasive, cloying neighbor Tina. God, she's never *not* watching me. I think she steals my mail.

Instead of saying this, I stay silent. The detective and I lock eyes.

"When was the last time you spoke with Mr. Hayes?"

Agnes's words bounce around my head. *Never answer the precise question they ask. Never offer anything of your own volition.*

"I'm not sure. A while."

"Can you be more specific?"

"I don't understand." My voice doesn't even sound right. "I thought he was in Aruba with his new girlfriend."

"Apparently not."

He pulls his mouth into a sympathetic grimace. But it's all an act. "Can I ask you to come with us to the station, Ms. Blacksmith?"

What did he say his name was? Timothy? I'd have expected something more manly—like Frank, or Jake. The broadness of his shoulders, the hard line of his jaw. Those hands are like bear claws. When I met him before, let's just say names weren't exchanged.

"As if." A voice from behind me. "That's a hard no. Unless you have a warrant for my client's arrest."

Payton presses up beside me—all Jimmy Choo and Chanel Number 5. I practically cry out with relief.

The detective smiles wanly, gives Payton an up and down, then takes a step back. She's intimidating as fuck.

"This is a first," he says. That smile. It's infuriating. "Your lawyer got here before I did."

"It's brunch," I say weakly. "Sunday brunch."

It was supposed to be girl talk and flowers, mimosas and croissants. I leave out the part about how this gathering was called to erase Paul Hayes from our online lives, the *ex*-orcism. It seems inappropriate now. Potentially incriminating, actually.

Iggy and Esme join us. "What's going on?" says Esme.

"Paul," says Vera, voice taut. The color has drained from her cheeks. She's very slightly quaking. "He's dead."

Iggy draws in a sharp gasp. *"Oh my god."*

I never do get to play the fainting card. Iggy beats me to it. She goes down like a stone.

VERA

I remember the first time I saw Agnes go out to the garden. I didn't sleep much those first few weeks, still trying to understand the things that had happened to Ana and me, lying awake at night listening to the sounds of the old house. It seemed to have a heartbeat, to shift in sleep like an old crone, moaning and creaking. Ana had burrowed herself into the crook of my arm and curled into a fetal position, the way she did most nights, sneaking into my bed after she thought I'd drifted off. It was like sleeping with a warm, soft stone, she was so still. I never told her that I needed that comfort as much as she did. The smell of her hair, the baby-soft soles of her feet pressed against my legs.

I heard Agnes on the stairs, then banging around the kitchen. The back door opened and closed. I shifted away from Ana and went to our window. It looked out on the path that led into the woods. Agnes was wearing a set of protective coveralls that would become familiar over the years, carried a burlap sack. There was something about the way she moved, cautious, watchful. Where was she going?

"Your mother and I slept here," she'd said when she'd showed us to our room. Two twin beds with clean pink comforters, a wicker bedside table between. The walls were papered, pink roses on a white background, wood floors worn, the windows cloudy. My mother's equestrian trophies on a shelf. There was a picture of her straight-backed on a gleaming black horse; she looked so powerful, so confident. It was hard to reconcile her with the woman I'd so fiercely defended from my father's rages, the one who was always afraid.

Ana and I would spend hours in that room over our years there, piecing together our mother's childhood, our ancestry, by poring over the books and pictures we'd find, the journals and letters stuffed in drawers and keepsake boxes. But that wasn't until later, when we had our bearings. When we understood ourselves better.

That night, I watched Agnes disappear into the woods, wondering how we were going to survive the fact that my mother was in jail for poisoning my father, that he now lay in a coma clinging to life. And if he died, she'd likely be in prison for the rest of her life, or worse. The injustice of it was acid in my gullet. Because everyone who knew my dad, a gambler and a con man with a violent streak who'd brutalized my mother for years, knew he had it coming. I didn't know whether to pray for him to live or die. If he died, my mother would be gone forever, too. If he lived, she'd probably go back to him, and we'd have to go with her. Which was worse? I don't remember feeling grief or pain or sadness. I don't recall missing them, or our life as a family. All I felt was a cold calculation as to how Ana and I would survive, and under that was the heat of a simmering anger.

Over the next couple of weeks, I watched Agnes leave the house almost nightly after she thought we were sleeping and head into the woods. The curiosity of the situation distracted me from my nighttime litany of worries and fears.

Finally, one night I followed her.

"Help me get her up," I say to Ana now, who is looking at Iggy on the floor like she's something she wants to scrape off her shoe. I've always puzzled over their friendship. I can't imagine two women more different.

"I'm sorry," says Iggy as she gets to her feet, leans heavily on me. I help her to the couch where she sits, head in her hands. Her skin has a grayish tinge, eyes glassy.

"Get her some orange juice," I say to April, who hustles off.

The detective, weirdly stiff about the shoulders, and just—*tall*—in my foyer, seems mildly amused, also curious. Esme joins Iggy on the couch; she's managed to make a cold compress out of a hand towel she must have found in the guest bathroom. Which annoys me. We have ice packs if she'd only asked, items designed specifically for this function. That Italian linen hand towel will never be the same.

Iggy leans her head against Esme. "Just take some deep breaths, Ig. You're okay," Esme soothes.

Ana hovers over Iggy, her back to us.

"Does she know Paul Hayes?" the detective asks me, nodding toward the obviously shaken Iggy.

"Only as someone Ana was dating," I say. "I think."

But maybe that's not true. Did they work together once? Another entry-level job, one that Ana helped her get. I can't remember the details of everyone's life.

He asks for her name, and after a moment's hesitation I give it to him. Iggy Rose. Ignatia, actually. It means "fiery one." Which doesn't suit her, really. She's as meek as a lamb. Or so she seems.

He offers a kind of squint and tight smile; I don't like it. It's somehow condescending, like he knows more than other people. It strikes me as very typically male.

"Iggy just had a baby," says Payton, mercifully placing her body between the detective and the living room so that he doesn't feel like he can follow us. "She's not back to form. The shock must be too much. Why are you still here, Detective?"

"I have questions for Ms. Blacksmith," he says.

"My client is happy to cooperate with the police." Payton hands him a card; her manicured nails look like claws. "Please call my office to make an appointment."

"It would be easier if I could just talk to her now."

"Easier for you, you mean," says Payton crisply.

He turns up his palms. "Well, yeah."

"Detective, may I see your ID and have your shield number? Did you know that the police commissioner and my boss are old Harvard Law School friends?"

"Seriously?" The corner of his mouth ticks up, an almost smile.

"Quite serious, yes."

He reaches into his pocket and opens a cheap pleather identification wallet. That gold shield shines, though. Payton snaps a picture with her phone.

"We don't need to play games," he says, putting it away.

"I assure you that I am not playing."

Payton has a bearing. It's not her height, or the boost her three-inch heels gives it. It's not the width of her shoulders, or even that searing gaze. It's confidence, a finely tooled knowledge of the law and how to navigate it. She wields it like a honed blade.

The detective releases a sigh. He's a full head taller than Payton, but she backs him to the door like they're doing some kind of dance.

"Thank you for coming and sharing the news, Detective."

He's only just stepped outside as she shuts the door quietly behind him and turns the lock for good measure. When he's gone, everyone seems to exhale.

I move into the living room and take my sister into my arms. "I'm so sorry, honey. What a shock," I say loud enough for everyone to hear.

"I didn't do anything," she whispers fiercely into my ear, sounding slightly panicked. "I swear."

That's the thing about Ana. You never know when to believe her.

AGNES

I am about halfway up the path when I realize that I'm being followed. I saw her watching from the window the other night and I wondered how long it would be before curiosity got the better of her.

Vera. She's a little soldier. Once she resigned herself to living with me, she took over the care and feeding of herself and her sister, got them both enrolled in school, signed up for the school bus route, which will pick them up at the end of the drive starting next week. Of course. She's Sadie's daughter; she'd be in charge of everything because Sadie could barely manage herself. I have to admit, I'm surprised Sadie found the intrinsic motivation to "take care of" Mac. But then again a wild animal backed into a corner is capable of pretty much anything.

"Don't let them come back here to visit him or me," Sadie said over the phone last night, a collect call from jail. "Mac's going to die and I'm going to prison for the rest of my life. They need to move on."

"They want to come," I told her. I wanted to see her, too. If only to say goodbye. "They miss you."

She was silent on the phone; I could hear the chaos of clanging and shouting voices on the line. I experienced a flutter of panic. I was losing my sister. I could feel her fading. Though in many ways she'd been lost to me for years. What I was losing was hope, the hope that she'd return to the fold.

"Sadie."

"Agnes. You know what to do."

Then she just hung up.

It's part of the code, the one handed down through our female ancestors. If you get caught, you pay the price in silence. You don't defend yourself. You reveal nothing about yourself or your practices, your garden, or your recipes.

The path now is narrow but well-worn, the night humid and starry. Little Vera probably thinks she's being quiet, but she's clumsy behind me, not accustomed to the dark. A twig snap here, a trip, a brush against the branches. I keep moving, then come to a stop at the locked gate in the high stone wall and turn around.

"I hear you," I say. "Come on out."

She slips from the shadows, moves closer then comes to a stop. She's the perfect blend of Sadie and Mac, wide mouth and high cheekbones, Sadie's deep-set dark eyes and auburn mane of hair, Mac's freckles and pale skin. She wears Mac's skeptical frown.

"What are you doing?" she asks.

"I could ask you the same thing."

"You come out here every night. What are you wearing?"

I'm wearing a white vented beekeeper suit with a hat and round veil. The bee, another venomous creature. But like most, they only defend what's theirs. They're not predators. They're creators—they make hives and honey, are friends to trees and flowers.

"Are you a beekeeper?" asks Vera.

"Not exactly."

"What is this place?" She stares at me, at the wall. I wonder if she knows. I'm not sure what Sadie has told her, or what is coded into her DNA. I remember when our mother brought me here for the first time, I felt like I had been here a thousand times before. It was known to me. I heard the centuries whispering, full of secrets.

"Answer me," she says. There's fire in this one; that comes from Mac. He is the one with rage in his spirit. The other one is ice. That comes from Sadie; a practiced smile that masks a cold heart. Both properties have their dangers—and their strengths.

"If I take you inside with me tonight, you won't be able to unlearn what I teach you."

She's very still in her tattered jeans and baggy sweatshirt, Converse high-tops. I think she might turn and run. I reach into my sack where there's another suit, hold it out to her and wait. There's a scurry in the underbrush. An owl hoots, questioning.

Some of us decline the life, The Knowledge. Sadie declined to practice, to the very bitter disappointment of our mother. But The Knowledge stayed strong within her. I'm not sure which way Vera will go.

Finally, she offers a quick nod, reaches for the suit.

I unlock the gate.

VERA

Ana lies on my couch now, her Louboutins kicked to the carpet, a heated eye pillow on her face, her breath shallow. April is in the kitchen; I hear her dutifully cleaning up the brunch mess. Likely she'll leave by the back door without saying goodbye. I've handed her the envelope of cash already, told her to take all the leftovers. If only all relationships were so easy.

The air in the room is thick with tension—all my questions, the shock of the news. A man we know has died. He's been in my home, eaten with my family, had a relationship with my sister. Foul play. According to the police, they suspect murder.

My sister takes a shuddering breath. I'm about to speak, then don't. As long as I don't ask the questions, I won't have to face the truth.

We're alone.

Esme has taken the visibly shaken Iggy home, leaving Iggy's car in my driveway. Which I don't love, only because it's something out of place.

Payton has left as well, said that she'd make the arrangements for Ana to go to the station to talk to Detective Bandeau tomorrow.

"I wish I could take her myself. But it's best that she has someone with teeth," she said at the door, looking concerned.

Payton is a business attorney, but her on-again, off-again boyfriend, Victor, is in criminal defense, has a big city firm.

"They'll send someone suitably intimidating, if Victor can't come himself," she assured us. "Just to let that detective know that Ana is not an easy mark. The 'ex-girlfriend did it' is way too easy a narrative."

Of course, it goes without saying that I'll be footing the bill. Ana, with her walk-in closet full of designer clothes, bags, and shoes, is as broke as ever. According to her tax returns, which are done by our accountant, she makes a decent living. But my sister has never met a dollar she didn't spend.

We sit in silence until we hear the back door close. April's vehicle pulls down the driveway, the sound of the engine disappearing up the street.

The kids could be back anytime. They both have a raft of homework, and Sunday night is sacred in this house. Family dinner, without fail. Early to bed.

"Talk to me," I say.

She draws in a breath, holds it a moment before releasing a heavy sigh. Then she removes the pillow, looks at me.

"You think I did this?"

"Did you?"

"No," she says flatly. "I had *nothing* to do with this."

Ana's face is her best asset. She's as pretty as a porcelain doll with big blue-gray eyes and false lashes, apple cheeks, and a Cupid's bow mouth. And she has absolute control over her expressions. You'll only ever see what she plans for you to see when you look at her. Even me, who knows her better than anyone.

"Then who?" I ask.

"How should I know?" she snaps. "Paul. He's a dick. *Lots* of people didn't like him."

I grab my laptop from the desk over by the window, start a search for "dead body found Little Valley."

There are already a couple of short news items.

Hikers find dead body in shallow grave off the Big Bear Trail at Black River Park.
Local man found dead at Black River Park. Foul play suspected.

This is early coverage from stringers alerted by police scanners. The real news won't hit until tonight. He's been identified and next of kin notified; the bigger news channels are likely waiting for Detective Bandeau or someone to make a statement. I flip on the television to the local news station, turn the sound down.

"I think maybe I loved him," says Ana, putting the eye pillow back in its place.

"Oh, please."

"No," she says, her voice just an exhale. "Really. And I thought he loved *me*. He just dumped me. A text. Then he just disappeared. Who does that?"

"You've ghosted a thousand people."

A pout. "That's not true."

I'm about to say something like, *Stop being an idiot*. But I hold my tongue.

I'm trying to be softer with people. Something Coraline said in family therapy about being afraid to show emotion around me, that I viewed *feeling* as *weakness*. She's right of course. I do view giving in to emotion as weakness. Because it is.

"I'm so sorry he hurt you," I say instead. It practically pains my mouth, it's so saccharine.

Ana peeks out from under the mask. "Shut up."

Maybe you can fool your kids into thinking that you're working toward real inner change; but you can't fool your sister.

Her eyes fall on the screen, and she sits up. "Turn up the volume."

There he is on the television. The too-tall, bad-attitude Detective Timothy Bandeau. He's uncomfortable in front of the camera, like he's more accustomed to being behind the scenes.

He glances shyly down at the notes on the podium in front of him. I reach for the remote and bump up the volume in time to hear him nervously clear his throat.

"This morning at 6:00 a.m., two hikers who'd ventured off Big Bear Trail at Black River Park found the body of entrepreneur and philanthropist Paul Hayes buried in a shallow grave disturbed by local wildlife."

I glance over at Ana. She's come to sitting, chin in her hands, eyes on the screen. A single tear trails down her cheek. I should move over to comfort her as any good sister would. But I don't.

"Our forensics team is currently at the scene, and we will share information as it comes to light."

I wouldn't say the detective is good-looking exactly. *Virile*, that's the word I'd use. Big through the shoulders, maybe too thick through the middle. There's something wolfish about his dark eyes, his thick head of hair, like when the moon is full maybe he's a different kind of man. He impresses me as someone my sister might find attractive. A glance at her reveals that she's transfixed, tears dried.

"Are there any suspects?" The question drifts up from the audience.

"At the time we have no suspects. But an investigation is underway, and we'll be questioning people close to Mr. Hayes in the coming days. In the meantime, if anyone has any information, please call the tip line."

He gives the number, and it comes up on a banner at the bottom of the screen.

Detective Bandeau looks at the camera. Why do I feel like he's looking directly at us? "No further questions at this time. Thank you."

I flip off the television. The silence around us expands. Down the hall, the ticking of the grandfather clock from Brad's side of the family is measured and quietly relentless.

"If there's something you need to tell me, tell me now."

I walk over to the table beside the couch and open the drawer there. I remove the item I found on my porch, hold it up.

"Where did that come from?" she asks, frowning.

I tell her.

Ana looks at me, and I see it. We come from a long line of secret keepers, of women who do bad things, sometimes for the right reasons, sometimes not. There's something moving behind her eyes.

She opens her mouth to speak, and just at that moment, the front door opens. The kids burst in, apparently dropped off at the same time, already arguing about something. I stash the item again, rise to greet them, stand in the door and wave at the parents in their big SUVs as they pull away on to normal Sunday activities that surely don't include murder investigations.

"You're an idiot, Grant," says Coraline, slamming the door. She looks exhausted, pale with dark circles under her eyes like she hasn't slept a wink and probably she hasn't.

"I'm just saying." He drops his bag by the stairs even though there are hooks by the door just for this purpose. They each give me a kiss, then head straight for the kitchen, their conversation teetering between talking, teasing, arguing. A pleasant, familiar rise and fall, usually punctuated by laughter.

Ana's already up, pulling on her slim sky-blue coat.

"I need to think," she says, tugging it tightly around her. She stows her phone in a bone-colored Louis Vuitton tote that by the way costs more than her rent. And I know this because we pay her rent. *Ana*, I told Brad when he proposed, *is part of the package. I take care of her. She's more like my child than my sister.* He's never once complained except to suggest that maybe our taking care of Ana prevents her from learning to take care of herself. Maybe he's right. Of course he's right.

"Where are you going?" I ask her now.

"I told Iggy I'd take back her car. Brock will drive me home from there."

She took an Uber here in the expectation of drinking too much champagne. But we never got more than a sip. So much for the exorcism. Even in death, Paul is going to be a problem.

"Ana."

But she's already out the door.

There's a very strong urge to call her back and interrogate her. But the kids are here, and there's something about their presence that makes it impossible for me to focus on Ana and whatever mess she's in. My brain has shifted to the checklist of what must be done for the week ahead.

"Be ready in the morning," I say on the stoop. I glance at the bare flower bed; soon it will be time to plant for spring. "I'll pick you up and go to the station with you."

She nods, gives me a quick squeeze, then leaves. I watch her pull away in Iggy's shiny blue electric car, cheap but decent. I feel a twinge of regret; maybe I should have been more comforting. But then I notice that she turns right, instead of left. Away from, rather than toward Iggy and Brock's.

My phone dings. Oh, great. It's Lisander. I don't answer to her, but I often feel like I do. My Aunt Agnes's mentee, she occupies a position of quasi-authority in our circle. And I owe her. Or Ana does. I'm used to shouldering Ana's debts.

> I'm assuming that you've heard the news about Paul Hayes.

Well, I think but don't type, *I have heard because the police came to my door.*

How did the news make its way to her? I don't answer.

> I doubt I have to tell you that if this is Ana's mess, we won't be able to clean it up.

I feel a pulse of fear, of defensiveness for Ana, and it impels me to thumb out a response.

She didn't do this.

Are you sure, Vera?

Am I sure? When it comes to Ana, the only thing I'm sure about is her unpredictability.

I open the app that tracks all my family members, LifeWatch, and stare at Ana's pulsing blue dot. Nowhere near Brock and Iggy's, she winds down a rural road, then gets on the highway. She's speeding, a little flame next to her dot.

Lisander again: **We need to talk.**

Again, I decline to answer.

I stare at the screen on my phone. Where are you going, Ana?

IGGY

Brock hovers, fussing with the blanket, pulling the shade. Noah is napping; I can hear his soft breathing over the monitor, deep and even. It's maybe the most soothing sound on the planet. Your baby, content and cozy, safe.

My nerve endings are frayed; I'm buzzing with anxiety. Have been since I thought I was being followed on my way to brunch. False alarm but still, it rattled me. The events of the brunch have further unsettled me, and truthfully it wasn't much fun to begin with. Ana was being Ana. And I felt out of place as soon as I arrived, was counting the minutes until I could go home to Brock and Noah. Then the police. The shock of it all just took my breath away. A murder.

Now nausea and an unpleasant reflux have me wondering if I'll be racing for the bathroom. Ana is the *worst* cook. Why did I eat so much of that cassoulet? Just to please her, I think. Because she noticed that no one else had touched it, felt hurt. The brunch was supposed to make her feel better, after all.

"I'm okay," I assure Brock now. But he doesn't seem convinced.

"You're really pale, Ig. Like, gray." He sits behind me, puts his hand on my forehead. "You feel warm."

"It was the shock," says Esme, bringing me a glass of water. She's been attending to me since I fainted. Drove me home.

Her presence is soothing. She's one of those people, confident, knowledgeable, in control. Always kind, even when she's not at her best. "Maybe the champagne. And the food. I'm a little queasy myself. I should have stayed with my planned meal. There's something. A weird aftertaste."

"I can't believe Paul is—dead," she says, sinking into the chair across from our bed. She shakes her head, looks out the window. A large diver's watch glints on her wrist, catching the light from the window; her earrings are huge diamond studs. She likes the bling, which I always find a funny contrast to her down-to-earth sweetness.

"How?" asks Brock, brow furrowed. "How did he die?"

He looks tired, faint circles under his eyes. He hasn't shaved today. Brock's been taking the 3:00 a.m. feeding with the pumped milk, even though he has to go work in the morning. He likes it, that time alone with the baby. But we're both a little out of it, and I know he hasn't been sleeping well. The other night Noah woke me, and Brock wasn't there. He came in from outside while I was nursing.

"Where were you?" I asked in the dim of the nursery.

He knelt beside us. "I took a walk. I couldn't sleep."

The night, its solitude and quiet, soothed him, he told me. I'm the opposite. I seek light and warmth, company.

Now Brock sinks onto the foot of the bed, puts a comforting hand on my leg. He rubs a hand up and down my shin. His touch always relaxes me.

Esme glances at her phone. "There's nothing about cause of death in the news. Just that he was found at Black River Park."

"I hike there all the time," says Brock, running a hand over the crown of his head. There's something odd to his tone, but when I look at him I don't see anything but fatigue. He rubs his eyes, something Noah does too when he's tired. What night was that? That he was out walking? I can't remember, these new-parent days and nights just run together.

"So do we," says Esme, shuddering a little.

We. I notice things like that. How Brock said "I," even though I often join him on those hikes or did before the baby came and we had to decide to take turns exercising unless his mom can sit. How Esme said "we." They're very *coupled*, Esme and her wife—both of them always say "we." There's just an energy to their relationship, a bond that seems very solid, unbreachable.

Unlike, say, Vera and Brad. Their relationship has the vibe of a very successful business partnership. You might catch Esme and Claudia whispering to each other, sharing a private touch or eye roll. At a party Vera and Brad orbit each other, never connecting it seems, not even looking at each other, working the room. That's the only time I've seen them together though, at parties to which Ana has invited me. So maybe I'm only seeing the public-facing version of Vera and Brad. Maybe there's something deeper between them that they only show in private. Probably there is. There's always something we only show in private.

Ana and Paul. Once I caught them coming out of the men's bathroom together at a restaurant where we were all having dinner to celebrate Payton making partner. Ana gave me that bad-girl smirk I know too well, and Paul flushed when our eyes met, his hair tousled.

"You might want to pull up your fly," Ana whispered to him as they passed me, loud enough for me to hear.

"Oh, shit," he said, then laughed. I hated the sound of his voice.

But no, I wouldn't call them coupled. Nothing with Ana ever seems permanent. Paul was her longest relationship, though. Which shocked me. Because how could she not see what he was? Or maybe that's why she liked him. She's always had dark appetites. Usually, she grew bored quickly, or got angry about something, turned off. She's the dumper usually, not the *dumpee*.

I *have* wondered if Ana hadn't gotten tired of Brock and dumped him if he and I would have ever found our way to each other. I try not to think about that too much; certainly, Brock and I don't talk about it. I think maybe he loved her, or thought he did for a while. I'm sure he doesn't know the kinds of things she used to say about him. *He's like one of those modern "un-men." All feelings and no backbone. For fuck's sake if he asks for consent one more time I'm going to punch him in the face.*

There's tension between Brock and Ana. They don't like each other much anymore. Not one of those former couples who can still be friends. It's another reason things have been difficult between Ana and me.

Truthfully, after the places I've been and the men I've known, the things that annoyed Ana are the traits I love most about my husband. He's gentle and good. Anyway, Brock and I both have complicated histories with the opposite sex; we don't judge each other. And *so what* if we fell in love when I was comforting him after his breakup with Ana? Relationships have started under worse circumstances, right? Meanwhile, *kind* doesn't equal *weak*. Something people like Ana never understand until it's too late.

My vision is a little blurry, my stomach roiling like a vat of acid. God, what did I eat?

"Who do you think killed him?" asks Brock.

"My money's on Ana," says Esme flatly. There's a beat of silence, then they both start laughing. I, however, don't find it funny. They don't know her like I do.

"There's no shortage of people who hated Paul," I say. Though I'm not sure why I'm always rushing to her defense.

"He really *was* a dick." Esme steeples her heavily ringed fingers. "Not to speak ill of the dead."

"What was so bad about him?" asks Brock, who maybe met him once.

"We can start with misogynist," says Esme. "A woman in

his office filed a harassment complaint, after which a number of others came out to say they had been mistreated. Psychological stuff—social media stalking, spreading rumors, sabotaging work. Some women claimed he drugged and raped them. Though there was no physical evidence to support that."

"Oh my god," says Brock, frowning deeply. "Wait. Didn't you work there, Iggy?"

"I did but not in the same department," I say. "I heard all the rumors, but it was kept very quiet."

God. My stomach.

"So, what happened to him?"

"No charges were filed. The women took a payout in exchange for signing NDAs. Paul was fired from that advertising agency, then started his own firm, taking a good deal of his high-profile clients with him. His new firm, Hayes & Associates, became very successful. Last year he was featured in *Business Journal*'s '50 under 50' issue."

"Ok, wow," says Brock. "How did that happen?"

"He maintained his innocence. Said he was the victim of a conspiracy of hateful women trying to bring him down. He and the *Business Journal* editor-in-chief went to the University of Florida together. Frat brothers."

"Huh."

Brock glances back at me. I give him a wan smile. Men find these things surprising. Women do not. A certain kind of man can get away with almost anything. And likely the women who came out against him suddenly found that their lives are harder. Promotions didn't come. Perhaps they got laid off in a department downsizing, had a hard time finding another job in their field. It's all very subtle.

"He was investigated for tax fraud," Esme goes on. "Charges dropped somehow. A client accused him of billing for ads he never bought on the client's behalf. That went away, too. And yet, somehow, he and I are—were—up for the same award this year. It's kind of a big deal, but I know who I'm putting my money on. He'll probably still get it even though he's dead."

The baby fusses. We all pause, listening.

"And that's just the stuff people know about," says Esme. "But he was a big donor to a lot of high-profile causes—the children's hospital, the local youth center, the church, the library. Give big money and people ignore the rest. *If* you're a handsome, cis, rich white man."

She wears an uncharacteristic scowl. It's not like her to sound bitter. Esme was not included in that *Business Journal* article, though she's made millions, employs almost a thousand people, and donates generously. Her company is known for its humane work environment, diverse staff, great benefits, and flex hours for parents.

And she's probably right that Paul will win Businessperson of the Year. Dead or alive.

"What are you trying to tell us, Esme?" I say with a smile, just to lighten things up.

She seems to snap back to her normal upbeat self, tosses me a grin. "I'm too busy to go around killing people. That's *a lot* of work. Besides, I would have done a better job hiding the body."

Brock laughs too loudly, and the baby fully wakes.

"I'll bring the baby to you," he says, getting up and leaving the room before I can protest that I'll go. The truth is I'm feeling worse and worse, weak and foggy.

"Brock's a good guy," says Esme, looking after him. "A keeper. You guys are lucky to have each other."

"You and Claudia, too."

Something flashes across her face, but it's gone before I can read it.

"Everything okay?" I ask. She gives me a wave, is about to answer, but then Brock is walking in with Noah in his arms.

Esme gets up to coo and fawn, and Noah rewards her with a giggle and wide, toothless smile. He's friendly, easily goes to people. *Most* people; he squalls when Ana approaches. I know she resents him and doesn't approve of the life I've chosen—one she might have had for herself but discarded.

Then Noah's in my arms.

The room disappears even as Esme and Brock keep chatting. Esme's talking about a young woman who came to work for her, someone who had an ugly encounter with Paul. But I'm not listening. I lose myself in the bright blue sea of Noah's gaze, that flood of oxytocin through my veins—the love hormone.

And I forget about Ana, the strange, stricken look on her face at Vera's after the cops came. I forget all about Paul in his too-shallow grave.

After a while, Esme comes to kiss Noah and me both on the head, and she heads home.

When Noah's done, Brock lies on the bed next to me and we talk about the brunch, his week ahead, the baby's checkup this week. It's nearly dark outside, the wind howling. And I'm washed over with a sense of peace, of gratitude for our little family and how much I love them both.

"You okay? You still look a little off," Brock says.

I'm aware of a growing pain in my stomach.

I hand the baby to Brock and try to rise to go to the bathroom. But then I'm doubling over, the pain in my abdomen like a hundred knives. I struggle to the bathroom and vomit in the toilet. Brock puts the baby, who is crying now, into the bassinet and comes to help. He hovers over me, but the world is strange and distant; I vomit again and again.

Oh, god, is that blood?

"Iggy? Ig, what is it, sweetie? Are you okay?"

I try to answer, but only vomit again. Then I can't hold myself up, fall to the cold tile floor.

Noah's wailing now. And I try to struggle up, to get to him. *Please*, I beg whoever happens to be in charge, *let me get to my baby*.

Then everything goes black.

TIMOTHY

The heat in the car blows overwarm, the world outside gray. Dead of winter. Bare tree branches reach into the dove sky, patches of white from the last snowfall on the brown ground.

I pull into the shoulder, then sit looking at the map on my phone. The radio buzzes and hums. Judy from dispatch requests a response to a vagrant on Main Street. A patrol officer answers. But I'm not really listening, processing the discovery of Paul Hayes's body, the things I've learned so far.

There are other, more defined, access points to Black River Park than where I have stopped.

There's the main entrance with its big parking lot, bathrooms, and gift shop in summer. There are various trailheads with smaller parking areas, as well as lesser-known unmarked accesses mostly used by locals.

But at any place along this particular road, Old Mill Road (RR63), you might walk in through the trees, hike the incline through the forest, and wind up on one of the park trails eventually.

Where I have stopped here, according to my map, is the point at which Old Mill Road is closest to where Paul Hayes's body was found. A straight shot, if a difficult one, from here to there through the thickly wooded area.

I glance away from my screen and look outside.

Breathe. Think.

"He wasn't killed here," Beck had said when we first arrived at the site early this morning. He'd stood beside the grave, looking down impassively at the grisly scene. He's young to be a chief medical examiner, also the first trans person to hold the post.

He'd pulled an e-cigarette from his pocket and gave it a surreptitious drag cupped in his hand. A sweet-smelling cloud disappeared over his head. Vapers always seem like they're keeping some kind of dirty secret.

"You should give that up," I'd said, though it's none of my business.

He ignored me, as I expected he would.

"I keep telling him," said his assistant, Miranda, as she took a soil sample. She's also the Medical Examiner's Office receptionist. Like every municipal department in the underfunded town of Little Valley, they operate on an impossibly tight budget, the two of them doing nearly every job of the morgue and ME's office. When my partner, Hitch, retired last year, his salary went to cover shortfalls in the budget, and he wasn't replaced. Since then, I've worked alone.

"Someone moved him," Beck had continued, his eyes drifting past the corpse into the trees. "It couldn't have been easy. He's a big guy."

I remember noting his size the first time I met Paul Hayes. Broad through the shoulders, thick, heavy arms, a handshake like a challenge. Men do that; we size each other up. Decide who would win if it came to a fight. I also noted: the soft skin of his hands, his manicured nails, the light waft of aftershave.

Paul Hayes died ugly, mouth open, eyes wide, hands clawing at his throat. Later animals got to him in the shallow grave; his innards were exposed, ropy and red, frozen solid in the cold. It shouldn't bother me; I've seen enough gore in my life and career that I could be one of those who resorts to gallows humor to cope. It still gets me every time. I know too much about the human body and how it comes apart, breaks down, comes undone.

Mainly these days what I see is overdose. Fentanyl is a scourge, especially in semirural communities like this. A thousand people last year died in this county alone. All kinds of people. Last month a wealthy doctor; the month before that, a waitress after a night out with friends. Two college students found in the library; they thought, according to friends, that what they were taking was Adderall. Died over their textbooks.

There have been car accidents, suicides, assaults, domestic violence, but in my five years on the Little Valley PD, this is only my fourth murder. The three others were open and shut, domestic violence turned deadly. That's the truth of it. Overdoses and men killing women who they supposedly love. Like the flower he hadn't meant to pick, or the bug he hadn't meant to stomp.

"Why?" I heard one man wail. "Why did you make me do this?"

This is strange work, to be the person they call when the worst thing happens. To observe it, try to understand it. Solve it if you can. Though there's no solution to the violence we do to ourselves, to each other. Sometimes it feels like there's no justice either.

It keeps me up at night sometimes, how unfair it all is. Who gets away with what and why.

Now I step out of the car into the cold. The sun already seems low in the sky even though it's only mid-afternoon; the temperature is dropping. It's that mean winter light, bright with no warmth. I dream of beaches; white sands and jewel-green water, swaying palms.

I step in through the tree line, start hiking up the incline. It's pretty hard going—the wet forest floor, icy patches. Just a few feet and I am already breathing heavily. Imagine dragging a body, a big dead body. As I huff and puff, I think: You'd have to be strong, fitter than I am.

Also: You would have had to transport the body from the kill site to the point of entry on Old Mill Road in a vehicle. Can't do that without leaving DNA evidence in the trunk, or wherever you hauled it. You think you cleaned it up. You didn't. Blood and bodily fluids leak, work their way into cracks and crevices. Somewhere there's probably a vehicle hiding evidence, or a tarp, or a rug, whatever was used to wrap and transport.

Meanwhile, there's a camera at every traffic light, each gas station, every shop; most residential homes have doorbell cams that detect motion. People don't realize that there's a network of electronic eyes; facial recognition software improves every year. It's very hard to hide these days, harder to hide what you've done.

I'm fully panting now, air cold in my lungs, the smell of wet leaves pungent. Oh my god, I seriously have to get back to the gym. No more late-night pizza with the guys after the game.

If they came up this way and not from the trail above, there had to be more than one person.

I stop, a stitch in my side, look around for evidence of something being dragged, and think I need to bring in the tracker, a guy I know called Old Bob. He sees things that most of us don't; he can tell you if a deer or a rabbit nibbled on a branch, identify a game trail. I've seen him follow crows to a dead body deep in a corn field—a lone hunter who had a heart attack. We went looking for him when his wife called to say he hadn't come home. Old Bob found him in the early morning hours the next day.

People have stopped seeing what's right in front of them, he told me once. *I'm only paying attention.* I stop to send him a text, ask if he can meet me here. He answers right away. **See you in an hour.**

I keep walking. Picking my way up, cracking branches beneath my feet, grabbing trunks for support. I stub my toe on a root, leaving a scuff on my boot. That's what we do, how we leave traces of ourselves everywhere.

Ahead, through the barren trees, I spot the red and blue

flashing lights of the vehicles at the scene. As I get closer, I hear voices. Someone guffaws. Not even a half mile from Old Mill Road to the grave site, all up hill, heavily forested. A hard passage hauling a heavy load.

But there would have been no way to get a vehicle from any of the park entrances onto the hiking trail; the narrow gates prevent it. Park rangers use Gators, small all-terrain vehicles; all of those are accounted for. It's nearly three miles from the main trailhead to where Paul Hayes was found.

It was Beck who said that they *probably came up through the trees from the road*, between puffs on his e-cigarettes. After my hike up, I'm thinking he was right.

I stop again, try to catch my breath, look around me. Cold air in my nostrils, crows overhead. The sky threatens snow, a grim watercolor. I breathe into the stillness, eyes falling on the ground littered with leaves, the trunks of the trees.

If there's something to see, I'm not seeing it.

I crouch down. Think.

I'm still puzzling over my encounters today:

Delivering the news to Paul Hayes's sister, listed as his emergency contact at the DMV.

The interrupted brunch hosted by the wealthy and connected Vera Blacksmith, her husband a big donor to the police department, as well as one of its biggest contractors.

Ana Blacksmith, who—well, I don't want to think about where we've met before, and why I didn't know her name. It's a personal problem.

I found Hayes's sister in a barn that doubled as an art studio, down a path from her house seated on a large swath of property just outside of town. When there was no answer at her front door, I followed the sound of blaring music to the other structure and found her in front of a giant canvas that was painted in angry swaths of red and black. Regina Hayes has a gallery in town, where she sells her own art and the art of other regional artists. I knew this from the quick web search I did before heading her way.

I knocked on the door that stood open, once, twice, then loud enough to startle her over the music. She spun, the expression of blank concentration morphing to concern. Wearing just a tank top and leggings on her too-thin frame, she reached for a robe.

"Who are you? What are you doing here?" Annoyed. Scared underneath.

"Detective Timothy Bandeau." I offered my shield. She moved in to take a closer look, tightening the robe about her. "Regina Hayes?"

She ran a hand through close-cropped orange hair. Her fingernails were painted black. "What's happened? Is it Paul?"

It seemed odd. Why would she ask that? I made a note of it.

"I'm afraid I have difficult news," I said when she turned off the music.

There's no good way to deliver this type of information. I've learned to just let it drop, as gently as possible, keep my voice low and matter of fact. People take it all kinds of ways. I try not to read too much into that initial response.

"I'm sorry to inform you that your brother, Paul Hayes, was found dead this morning at Black River Park."

Some people wail, collapse. Some freeze. Some are stunned, go glassy. The first word they usually utter is "no." Confusion. Refusal. Denial.

Regina stumbled forward a step, steadied herself on a stool before I reached her, but stayed silent, eyes darting, hand to her throat. We stood like that a moment, awkwardly close as I waited to see if she would fall to the ground, trying to catch her, before she backed away, wrapped her arms tight around her middle.

"I'm so sorry," I said. "Is there anyone else at home? Can I call someone for support?"

She shook her head. "Was it a—what? A hiking accident?"

I flash on the look of horror frozen on Hayes's face, his fingers stiffened, clawing at his throat.

"Doesn't look like that, no. Hikers found his body when they ventured off the trail just after 6:00 a.m. His body had been buried."

A frown, a flare of the nostrils, then tears trailing helplessly down her gaunt cheeks.

"Murder?"

"It's too soon to offer anything definitive. But initial evidence points to foul play, yes."

She reached for a pack of cigarettes, lit one with a Zippo she produced from her robe, took a deep drag. How have people not gotten the memo on this? The scent of tobacco met my nostrils immediately.

She stared off, thinking hard. "If someone killed him, I can tell you who it was right now."

"Oh?"

"Ana Blacksmith, his bitch ex."

She blew out an angry puff. I'd go back to smoking in a heartbeat if I hadn't seen the way COPD wasted my father, hadn't had to watch him die. After his funeral I went cold turkey. Still, the smell makes me twitchy.

"What makes you say that?" I asked.

"He broke up with her. She's been stalking him. She was enraged, following him, harassing him at work, in social media. She was threatening his new girlfriend, too. That woman Ana Blacksmith. She's batshit crazy."

Regina started to cry harder then, stubbed out her cigarette. I walked her back to her house. We talked a while about Paul, where he worked, his last few days, this alleged trip to Aruba with the new girlfriend.

"I haven't met her," Regina said, pulling a blanket from the couch. The living room was cozy, eclectic—crowded with art pieces, books piled high on every surface, a stone Buddha sat impervious on the hearth of a big stone fireplace. "He didn't even tell me about her. I just saw some pictures on Instagram. I thought he went away with her. I was a little pissed about it. He owes me money, like quite a bit."

"Oh?"

"I gave him a loan to start his new business."

She was still crying, not sobbing but tears falling steadily.

"The girlfriend. Do you have a name?"

She shook her head. "Maybe Amy or Mandy or something like that? I can't remember. He never introduced me to the women in his life, rarely talked about them."

As we talked, there was a key in the front door. A big, bearded man walked in, taking up lots of space, baggy flannel shirt, chunky work boots.

"What's up?" he asked, looking back and forth between us, reading the room. "Everything okay?"

That's when she really lost it, dumped her head in her hands and started to wail. The man moved over to her quickly, took her in his arms.

"Paul's dead," she managed, voice muffled in his chest. "My *brother.*"

He looked over at me with a deep frown; I held up my shield and he nodded. I may have seen him before at the local pub. It's a fairly small town; you maybe don't know everyone by name, but there's a familiarity of visiting the same restaurants, grocery stores, gas stations. There's something girlish about his eyes. They're big and heavily lashed, a contrast to his robust maleness.

"Oh, shit," he said, eyebrows knitting. "What happened?"

"She killed him." It's just a wail, the very sound of helpless misery.

He shot me a questioning glance.

"Initial evidence points to foul play," I answered. "But it's too early to make definitive judgments and we don't have any suspects at this time."

"Okay," he said, voice a comforting baritone. "Okay. I got you. I'm here."

Something about its gravely timbre had me thinking about my dad and I felt a familiar stab of loss. Once you've lost someone, any grief connects you to your own.

Ross Avidon, sculptor, welder, I'd learned before I left them to the unhappy days and nights stretching before them. They both agreed to come in for further questioning the next morning. Ross saw me out, gentle, softspoken, said he would do whatever he could to help. Seemed like a nice enough guy.

Still, of all the people I talked to today, he was the only one big and strong enough to haul a dead body up this hill.

Now, up from my crouch and approaching the scene, I'm slightly nauseated, that side stitch amping up. Am I really this out of shape? I try to remember the last time I went for a run. I can't. The sun is an unblinking white eye in the sky, staring down on the winter day, more crows overhead. The body has been bagged, is being lifted onto the stretcher.

I scan the crowd that's gathered behind the crime scene tape. There's a hum, whispers between people who stopped to see what's happening. I hear the notes of awe, disbelief, fear. In the back I note the slim figure of a woman dressed all in black, a black wool cap on her head, coat zipped up to her chin, a pair of large sunglasses obscuring her face. She's alone, watching. Earbuds in. She must sense me watching, turns her head my way. Then she pivots and starts to run, just a jog up the path, maybe just continuing with her workout. But I follow, move around the crowd and head in her direction.

She rounds a bend, and I pick up my pace.

But by the time I turn on the path, she's gone. I stand, breathless again, watching as the trees rustle in the breeze, listen for her footfalls but hear nothing.

I don't have my radio, so I call dispatch on my cell, ask Judy to tell the detail at the trailheads to stop a slim woman all in black and big glasses if she tries to exit. To call me if they see her.

When I return to the scene, Beck stands by, hands in his pockets, head bowed. A moment of silence for the dead.

There's a beauty to it. Even in its horror, in its ugliness. There's something elegant to the end of suffering, to the silence that falls. A single black crow on the branch above me caws his agreement.

After the crew leaves and the crowd of lookers disperses, I remain, scanning the trees around me, the ground. Is there something to see that I'm not seeing?

My phone rings. Dispatch.

"Bandeau."

"No one matching your description has been seen leaving from any exit since you called. They'll pass the information to the next detail."

I'm not holding out much hope. If she's local, if she has something to hide and doesn't want to get caught, she'll exit through the woods. I imagine her slight and fast, weaving through the trees. Who was she?

I wait another moment, approach the grave again, make a slow circle. An odd tingle, the sense of being watched. I glance around at the trees.

But I'm alone.

AGNES

Even though Sadie doesn't want me to, I take the girls to their father's funeral. It's only right. Neither one of them cry as the three of us stand by his grave alone. There was a smattering of his drinking buddies at the service. But no one cared enough to follow us to the burial.

"Can we bury him in the family plot?" Vera had asked when the news came. I regretted showing her the small graveyard at the edge of our property, a place where my parents and grandparents, my aunts and great aunts, were laid to rest. It's a private place, peaceful with a big weeping willow and an oak bench for contemplation. Willow. Salix. The ancient Greeks believed it helped people pass safely to the underworld.

"No," I said, too sharply. "He's not family."

She blinked at me, hurt disappearing behind anger. "He's our father."

"I'm sorry." He was an abuser and adulterer who essentially ruined Sadie's life. If it comes down to a question of who poisoned who, I'd say he gave as good as he got in the end. He was a toxin that slowly destroyed her. Good riddance. We're not spending eternity with that piece of shit. Naturally, I didn't say any of this out loud to the girls.

Vera hasn't spoken to me much since, as if she read my mind.

"I'm glad he's dead," says Ana now graveside, her small voice wobbling. Of course she doesn't mean it. She's just being brave the way the women in our family have had to be.

"Don't say that," Vera answers harshly. "Don't."

Ana looks ashamed for a minute, but then, no, she sticks to her guns. "He was a bad man. He hurt us, hurt Mom. That's not love. And if he didn't love us, why do I have to love him?"

Vera looks about to argue but then she presses her mouth closed a moment, a thin pink line of sadness and anger. Finally, "He wasn't just that. He didn't only hurt us."

My heart clenches a little at that, what's left of it. It's true that none of us are just one thing, that few people are all bad. And that Mac could be loving and charming, generous. He played the guitar and had a good singing voice, which is what I think did Sadie in, the music in him. How she loved him. Like a sickness, an addiction she couldn't shake.

And truthfully it was his addictions that turned him rotten. Maybe he would have been a better man if he hadn't given himself over to drink and drugs.

There are so many types of toxins you might choose from in this life.

But what difference does that make? We are what we do. I'm not sure it matters who we might have been if we'd done better.

"When people love you, they don't hurt you. Not ever," Vera says. A child's view of the world. We hurt the people we love all the time, don't we? "That's what Mom said. No one is sometimes-mean. Mean is always there, beneath the surface, even when they're being nice."

Ana looks at her sister, big eyes searching, but Vera is looking up where birds circle high above and the sky is an indifferent blue, flowers blooming all around the pretty church graveyard—daisies and lavender, daffodils and wormwood, larkspur. I paid for all of this, by the way—the funeral, the burial. I did it for the girls, for Sadie.

Not for you, Mac. Just to be clear in case you're listening. I'm glad you're dead, too. At least the girls are free now, though it certainly doesn't seem like it to them.

Vera clutches a bouquet we picked from among the wildflowers. Daisies. Now, there's an interesting flower. So pretty and sweet, the very symbol of innocence and purity, and the perfect example of selective toxicity. Pyrethrins are derived from the flower and used as a power-

ful insecticide. Harmful to bugs, but not to people. Matricin, another daisy derivative, is used in pain relief. We're none of us just one thing.

I can think of a few other flowers I'd like to throw in Mac's grave—rue for regret, petunia for anger, tansy for hostility. I could go on.

Vera walks to the edge of the grave and lets the flowers fall. Now it's her sister's turn to look away, batting at tears she doesn't want to shed. Vera is stone-faced.

I watch the flowers in the dirt atop the coffin for a moment as the sun dips behind a cloud, the air cooling. After a few more moments of silence, we walk back to the car.

I'm about to get in and drive us away from this place when the little soldier finally breaks down. Vera drops to her knees, wailing. It's young and helpless sounding, striking all the notes of misery, rage, and despair. Ana drops beside her, wraps her sister up in skinny arms.

"Don't cry. Please don't cry," Ana pleads.

I join them on the ground, hold on to them both.

"No, that's good," I tell her. "Let it all out."

When she's spent, weak with the exhaustion of grief, Ana and I help her to her feet. In the car I hand her a little cotton pouch of dried lavender, give one to Ana, too. Lavender, or Lavandula, it calms and soothes. "Here," I say. "Put these under your noses and breathe deep."

In floriography, its meaning is distrust, maybe because asps frequently make their homes in the same hot climates where this particular flower thrives. Lavender is a thing of beauty providing shelter for a venomous snake. But its effect on the body is powerful, with antioxidant components that lower stress hormones and settle the nervous system.

Both girls do as they're told. Vera still drawing in shuddering breaths until eventually she eases. Ana wrinkles her nose, as cool and still as a glacial lake.

"I want to see my mother," Vera says as I put the car in gear and start up the road that winds through the graveyard. The tires crunch on the gravel; the trees outside the open window are alive with birdsong.

I glance in the back at Ana, who has receded to that place she goes when things are too much. It's a glassy stare into nowhere that reminds me of Sadie. My sister used to do that, too. It's a dark place, I think. Vera, like me, stays grounded in the real world. Someone has to.

"She doesn't want you to see her in that place," I say carefully. "She loves you both, so much. But she wants you to move on and not look back."

"Did she kill him?" asks Ana.

Vera's eyes meet mine when I glance at them, then look back to the road.

I don't answer because the truth is that I don't know for sure. Sadie of course hasn't told me what happened. I know she served him beef Wellington, and there's a variation to that recipe that could make it deliciously deadly.

"How did she do it? Poison?" presses Ana. "Did you help her?"

Vera is glaring at me, eyes burning but her expression slack.

"Sadie never needed my help with anything."

That was always true until now. Last night she called. "It's time," she told me. "I need you."

"I can take you to your mother," I say to my elder niece. "But she won't see you. She's already told me as much."

A quick intake of breath. She turns to look out the window where I see her wan face reflected.

"Doesn't she even want to say goodbye?" asks Vera.

"We don't always get that in this life. Write her a letter if you have things to say."

She casts me a bitter side-eye but stays quiet.

I don't mean to sound cold. But the truth is not always kind, and it's not always pretty. It's better swallowed whole, to avoid that bitter taste in your mouth and throat, even if it sticks in your gullet for a time.

Finally, Vera's shoulders sag. Defeat. We all take the rest of the ride in silence.

Back at the house, Vera leaves the car and runs up the stairs, slams the door to the bedroom with such force that the fine china in the dining room sideboard clatters.

"She made him beef Wellington that night," says Ana as I serve *her some warmed-up macaroni and cheese.* "She wouldn't let us have any, even though we both love it. She said it was special just for him."

I nod.

The death cap mushroom, or amanita phalloides, is delicious. Similar in shape, size, and color to the common mushroom, it is often mistaken for its benign cousin. An invasive species, the death cap frequently grows in the roots of live oak, elm, or birch, blooms in the darkness of their shade. People who have ingested it—and survive—describe its rich, earthy flavor. You feel fine for a while, until the toxins go to work on your kidney and liver. Then come the abdominal pains, the nausea, vomiting, and diarrhea. The symptoms may subside for a while, delaying necessary medical treatment. But the amatoxins, phallotoxins, and virotoxins have most likely done irreparable damage to your organs. You will probably fall into a coma as one by one those organs fail, death coming soon after.

What scientists don't understand about this mushroom that crept into North America, actually every continent except Antarctica, from Europe on the roots of an imported decorative shrub, is why it has evolved to be so terribly deadly. Why has it developed this weapon in the war of nature where predator and prey struggle in a terrible dance of survival? From whom exactly is it trying to protect itself? The answer is known only to Mother Earth. We, her most difficult children, are often in the dark about her many mysteries.

Mac was a big eater. He scarfed his food, had an insatiable appetite. Just a tiny piece of the death cap is enough to kill. He likely ate more than his share.

"I've seen it," Ana says, her face smooth, eyes big. "The garden. My mom told me about it. And I saw you go inside."

"Don't go in there without me," I say maybe too harshly. I keep the door locked of course. But was there ever a kid that didn't find a way into trouble when she was truly motivated? "It's dangerous until you know what you're doing."

"You're teaching Vera," she says, polishing off her food. "I want to learn, too."

I'm not sure about Ana. There's a coldness to her, a blankness that I don't like. The Knowledge, as we call it, is a dangerous thing; its keepers must be trustworthy. There's a code. An order.

"Maybe," I say finally. "When you're older."

When our eyes meet again, she's just a kid who has lost her parents, with a little bit of cheese on her lip. I see her sadness, her vulnerability, and something else. The desire to take her in my arms and assure that everything is going to be fine, someday, is strong. Instead, I find myself thinking of fields of lavender that hide the deadly asp. I tell her to clear her plate and go to her room.

Later, alone in the garden, I pick a bouquet for my sister. The delicate white flower of hemlock, or conium maculatum. The cheerful violet monkshood, or aconitum. The pretty pink foxglove, or digitalis. The bouquet is delicate, feminine, a gift of love for my sister. I'll go to see her on my own tomorrow. She's right. It's time.

Our relationship to the natural world, to plants and trees, to the whole big spinning orb, is complicated. It's a twist, a dance, a struggle. Nature nourishes us, an endlessly giving mother. But unsheltered exposure to her whims and moods can end your life. The plants we use to heal ourselves, in different doses become toxic. The substances we use for recreation can stop our hearts, irreparably addle our minds, invade our cells, and change our behavior. Consider tobacco, one of the most dangerous plants on earth, killing nearly five hundred thousand people a year. And yet some of us pick it up willingly and daily suck that poison into our lungs because of the way it makes us feel. And the poppy, the beauteous red flower of misery and death. Untold millions have died from the drugs concocted from her compounds, drawn over and over again to the promise of that state of euphoria, the blessed relief from the pain of living.

There's no such thing as an unnatural death. Nature has devised a million ways for us to die, even if it's by way of human nature.

There are some that believe humans have dominion over the earth. But it's not so. As we trample and destroy her, so does she wreak her havoc upon us. Eventually, she will eradicate us like the virus we have proven ourselves to be. And then she'll heal herself, take back everything that she has given. The scars we've left will heal. And there will be silence again.

There's a kind of comfort in that, isn't there? That there's only so much damage that we can do?

I'm thinking about this as I finish collecting what I need and tie it all together with a swatch of muslin. Like so much of nature the bouquet is beautiful, to the untrained eye a pretty bit of innocent prettiness, but lethal in the right hands.

Sadie will know what to do.

VERA

I tidy up, wiping surfaces that don't need wiping, sweeping floors that April has left spotless. It helps me to think, to be moving, eradicating any dirt or grime, ridding a space of negative energy. I turn over the visit from the detective as I fluff pillows; consider things my sister said and didn't say as I wipe down baseboards. I think about that detective standing in my foyer, then holding his news conference as I spray and polish already gleaming surfaces.

The house where Ana and I grew up was always filthy, walls in need of painting, carpet frayed and stained, dishes in the sink, grime in the bathrooms, refrigerator empty most of the time. Sadie and Mac were only into themselves, either having a good time or hurting each other. They loved us, each in their own measly way. There were good times, too, believe it or not. But they didn't take care of us the way I take care of Coraline and Grant. They didn't make a home, the way I've made one for my family. Because that takes work and a capacity for self-sacrifice, constant vigilance. And neither one of them were equipped for that. That's why I always had to take care of Ana. Still do.

On the couch where Ana was lying, there are strands of her long raven hair. I pick them up and guiltily put them in my pocket. Then I also take the stick figure from the drawer and stow it in the other. Just as I do so, I see that Coraline has come to stand at the archway that leads to the living room.

"What's wrong?" she asks.

"Nothing," I say, forcing a smile. "Why?"

Coraline, unlike Grant, is a watcher. She reads expression and tone, listens for nuance. Grant is like a Labrador retriever, happily crashing through life, not worried especially about what's going on around him. Though I have to admit there was a depth and a sensitivity to his short story that surprised me. A thriller of sorts about a detective trying to solve a case that winds up forcing him to confront a truth about someone he loves. It was smart and edgy, thoughtful. I told him as much and watched him blush.

Coraline bites at her thumbnail now, a nervous tic. "Lizzie from up the street texted me. She said the police were here?"

Fucking nosy neighbors.

"Is this about work?" she asks.

"Oh. No."

Truthfully, there have been problems with the company. We try to keep our professional and home lives separate. But Brad has been a wreck, tense at home, snapping at the kids, which is unusual because I'm the one with all the moods, according to Coraline. And Brad is usually the moderator, the level one.

"What then?" she asks, sitting on the arm of the couch.

I'm the first to admit that I'm a bit of a helicopter parent. Although I'm not sure that's an apt analogy. I'm more like a Bubble Wrap parent, protecting the kids if I can from the worst the world has to offer. We never turned the news on when they were little. I always offered to drive to every event, chaperone every field trip, hosted sleepovers because I didn't like to let them out of my control. They've never been out of my sight, technologically speaking. Not because I don't trust them. I actually do. Despite Coraline's fiery defiance and Grant's occasional cluelessness, they are both smart, good humans. It's because I don't trust the world, other people, that I keep an electronic leash on them.

Our family shrink brings this up a lot, my "desire for control." *When our children are little we have all the power. It's our job and our biological imperative to protect. As they grow, we have to believe that we've taught them well, hand them some autonomy over their lives and decisions, let them make mistakes. That's how they learn to become adults.*

Let's just say I'm having trouble with this part. My instinct here, right now, is to lie to my daughter. Make something up.

But she's almost eighteen, will be going to college this fall. Where and if she'll get in to any of the schools I imagined with her just decent grades and middling test scores is a big source of angst in the house, lots of battles, tears, raised voices.

"Do you remember Ana's ex?" I ask.

"Which one?"

True, there has been a parade of them over the course of the kids' lives. The only one I've ever liked was Brock. I knew he was too nice for Ana. That she'd tire of him and eventually dump him.

"Paul?" I say.

She moves from her uncomfortable perch to sit in the big wingback chair by the window. I sit across from her. "I guess, yeah," she says. "The thirsty one?"

"He's—um," I say, stumbling over the words. "He passed away."

I can't bring myself to say he's been murdered, that Ana might be the prime suspect.

She stares at me, two big blinks, mouth dropping open. "He's *dead*?"

"That's right."

"Like—*how*?"

I steel myself and like a grownup tell her at least as much as the detective told the reporters at the news conference. *When we hide things from our children, we're telling them that we don't think they can handle the truth.* Just for the record, our family shrink is ridiculously young, has no children yet of her own. So how is she qualified to school me? Even though she's often right.

"Holy shit," says Grant, who's come to join us. "He was *murdered*?"

"Language," I say weakly, still fighting a battle I lost long ago.

Grant flops on the couch, stares at his phone, is well trained enough to keep his shoes off the fabric by hanging them over the side.

Coraline is still staring. I struggle for words.

"You spent some time with him at that July 4th barbecue. So, this must come as a shock," I say finally. "Would you like to talk about your feelings?"

See? I'm doing a lot better with this.

But neither of them answers. They're both on their phones now, searching for more information. You can't protect them anymore, not once you put that phone in their hands. It helps you keep track of them, sure. But it's a portal to every awful thing the world can offer up.

Grant starts listing off facts from whatever news article he's found. Coraline is scrolling, too, frowning deeply.

"So why did the police come here?" she asks.

"To question Ana. Because they were dating."

Coraline stays quiet, but I can see the wheels turning. We both know Ana very well. There is another knowledge we share as well, much as I've tried to keep her from it. Grant on the other hand is oblivious.

"What's for dinner?" asks Grant, stowing his phone. He's already lost interest in the murder of his aunt's ex-boyfriend. Should I be concerned about that?

I smile, grateful for now for the self-centeredness of youth, the desensitization to violence that comes from overexposure to video games, film and television, true crime podcasts, or whatever it is that's making us so cold.

"Roast chicken and sweet potatoes, maple-roasted Brussels sprouts. Dinner in an hour. Your father's on the way home."

If Coraline has more thoughts, she's distracted by a text she says is from Ethan, and soon they've both headed upstairs, leaving me alone with my thoughts.

I am filled with anxiety as I take the big roasting pan from the fridge and pop the already-prepped chicken to cook in one oven, vegetables on baking sheets into the convection oven above it. Even as I busy myself in the kitchen, I can't stop thinking about Ana, Paul, the kids. I take some cleansing breaths, try to center myself.

Finally, I head downstairs to the basement. I pass the boxes of old toys and outgrown baby clothes, the old furniture from other style iterations in the house. There's my father's guitar. Grant's crib. Clutter, I'm sure some would say. But everything feels like a piece of the past, the physical manifestation of memories. So, they remain.

Behind Brad's untouched workbench filled with the most expensive possible tools that have rarely been used, I unlock a door by pressing a code into the keypad.

This is my space, and only Brad and I know that it's here. I already feel better just stepping over the threshold.

From my stores, I pull some dried lavender, basil, chamomile, some white sage, and a stick of palo santo wood. I take Ana's hair from my pocket and use it to bind the items together with a big piece of tigereye. If I had time, I'd make a doll, a little effigy like the one I found on my porch, but I don't. Or I'd put the whole concoction outside to absorb the light of the sun.

Instead, I place it all in a metal bowl, sprinkle it with salt for protection and purity, then light a black candle to drip wax to absorb negativity. Then with a match, I light the palo santo and let it burn, the scent of all the herbs wafting up in a single twist of smoke.

I whisper, "Protect my sister, and my family. Surround us in love and positive energy. We do no unnecessary harm, and no harm is done to us. Light is my weapon and my shield."

A warmth fills my body, and the wood burns. I repeat the mantra several times, as the words and the scent soothe me. Finally, when my nervous system has calmed, and the wood has turned to ember, I turn on the exhaust fan, then cover the bowl with a lid. The scent lingers; I draw it in deeply.

From my pocket, I lift the doll I found on the porch. I might recognize the handiwork. It could have come from a number of places. I inspect it more closely—the dove feathers, tiny rose quartz crystals, rose petals, lavender embedded in the dried sticks tell me that it's for protection, not for harm. But who put it on the porch? I prop it up on my workbench.

"Who left you?" I ask. No answer comes.

I am startled by a sound outside the door, realizing that I've left it ajar. But when I look out into the basement, there's no one there. After a moment, I hear the door at the top of the stairs close quietly.

My cheeks burn. It could only have been Coraline. Grant doesn't have it in him to be quiet. If he was looking for me, he would have thundered down the stairs, calling for me. I've tried to keep Coraline from The Knowledge, but I know she's learning from Ana and Lisander. I've discouraged her and am embarrassed that she caught me doing something that I have told her not to do. That's extremely poor parenting.

"You should be the one to teach her these things," Lisander admonished when last we discussed it over tea at Aunt Agnes's place where we often meet.

"I never wanted this for her."

"Or for yourself. But you have it all the same."

I heard the notes of sadness and resentment in her tone. My Aunt Agnes was Lisander's mentor, but I was Agnes's star pupil. *You have the gift*, she used to tell me. *You can have The Knowledge without it. But you have both. There's great power in that. You'll be a leader to others.*

Aunt Agnes bestowed something upon me that Lisander wanted for herself, but I tossed it away. We've never discussed it, but it's a wall between us.

I make sure that the palo santo has gone cold, leave it in the metal bowl just in case some embers remain smoldering. Then I exit the space, pull closed the door.

Often it feels like there are two selves within me. The person I am in that room, and the one I am in the world.

Which one of them is real? I have no idea.

TIMOTHY

Old Bob meets me at the main entrance of Black River Park as the afternoon is growing dim, and I give him the details I have. He doesn't say much, just offers a nod and a grunt. Then starts walking toward the trailhead, up into the park. I follow.

Our footfalls crunch on the path and all around me the trees whisper. I am aware of the scent of wood smoke probably coming from the chimney of a nearby house, the light odor of wet and rot.

I still can't shake that feeling of being watched. The woman in black, disappearing on the trail. Who was she? Maybe no one. Just a jogger. A curious onlooker.

And then there's Ana Blacksmith. On the app, she called herself Jinx, an obviously fake name. Not that it matters; that particular app is not for people looking for long-term relationships. What matters is that I was disappointed when she snuck out the back, and that she's been on my mind since. And now, she's the ex-girlfriend of a murder victim. Bad luck? Bad karma? Something else? Bad in any case.

"Are you with me, Detective?" Old Bob has stopped in his tracks and is giving me a look, like the sound of my thoughts is annoying him.

"I'm here. One hundred percent." Not really.

He's a strange one. Gulf War vet, covered in ink. On his back is the tattoo of a crossbow, expanding across his shoulders and down his spine. I happen to know this because he works out occasionally at the youth center gym where I volunteer with some at-risk kids, teaching them about the value of exercising yourself into exhaustion, teaching them to box and weight train. There's a Buddha inked on Old Bob's enviably hard middle. A study in contradictions, there's also an AK-47 rifle up his right arm with text in cursive: *Go ahead. Try to take it.* He's wiry, smallish, but he works the heavy bag like it insulted his mother.

We continue the trek. And I try to be more *present*. When Old Bob walks, his breathing gets slow and deep, his eyes moving from the path to the sky, into the trees that surround the trail. There's no chitchat, no discussing the case. He seems to listen to the air around him, every so often stopping to bend to the ground, examine this branch or that one, touch something with the toe of his boot.

I let him walk ahead of me, keeping my distance so as not to distract him. He cuts an odd figure on the trail with his long gray hair, dark, deeply wrinkled skin, a fleece-lined denim jacket, red cap, work boots, torn cargo pants. He lives in a shack off the grid. Sometimes you don't see him all winter; then maybe he'll come riding into town on his snowcat to get supplies, disappear again until the spring thaw. He does have a cell phone, though. And when I call he never fails to respond.

We hike the three miles in total silence to where Paul's body was found by the hikers. And I'm hating on myself a little less than I did on the walk up from the road, because this trail is fairly level, and I don't feel like I'm going to puke by the time we see the yellow and black of the crime scene tape. I'm not in the *worst* shape, right? I work the kids pretty hard, but during that time I'm mostly standing around. I need to get in the ring more. It goes on like this, the mental chatter.

Finally, we stand at the edge of the scene, the crime scene

tape flapping. With the light fading, it's not the best time to track. But the more hours pass, the less evidence, if any, there will be. When the snow falls, even less.

Bob circles the grave site, bends down and takes a deep breath. I don't smell anything, maybe just that faintest aroma of wood smoke lingering. For some reason I can't name, the scent always makes me think of my mother. When I think of her most often, she's in her garden where she grew herbs and flowers, kept a beehive on our modest expanse of property. She sold teas and honey for extra cash; my dad was always sick with the lung disease that eventually took his life. They struggled to make ends meet. But there was always laughter in our house.

"When we lose ourselves in memory, we fail to see what's right before us," Old Bob says, reprimanding me again, maybe intuiting that I'd once again left the present moment behind to time travel.

"Point taken," I say, even though I'm not the tracker. I'm a thinker, a puzzle solver, a student of human nature. Thoughts are my thing.

A stiff wind bends the branches. Old Bob ducks under the crime scene tape and starts to walk straight along the path I took up. He bends down when we come to the place where I scuffed my boot against the root.

"That was me," I say, embarrassed. I should have let him walk it first, shouldn't have been tramping around like an idiot.

He gives me a look. "I know."

We walk a while longer; he moves slowly, touches trees. Is he whispering? Hitch, my old partner, absolutely hated Old Bob, said he was like an old witch casting spells. *Gives me the creeps.*

My mother used to say that nature holds all of our secrets, all the cures to what ails us. The plants and trees, they'd talk to us if we would only listen. Maybe that's why I like Old Bob. He's listening in the same way my mother did.

"Here," Bob says. "They dropped him."

I see the scratch on the tree, the way the debris has been swept away. There's a tiny tear of fabric on a low broken branch.

He points to the ground. It's hard and frozen, so the impressions there are light. But now that he shows me, I see them. One looks like the edge of a treaded boot, the other smooth and pointy. I snap pictures with my phone; they're not the best. I pull gloves and an evidence bag from my pocket, retrieve the fabric. It looks like black denim, consistent with what Paul was wearing.

I tie crime scene tape around the tree.

"Two people?" I ask.

He points to the ground, and I see another tread. A sneaker maybe. "Three."

I nod. Carrying a body is hard work. Three people could do it better than two.

We keep walking, Bob pointing to this broken branch, this disturbed area of path, so obvious now that he's here to point it out. At each point I tie off a bit of tape, marking the trail. We come out at the road about a tenth of a mile north from where I had parked earlier. Not bad, but just wrong enough to miss everything.

We look around the shoulder for tire treads and nothing is apparent.

Then Old Bob stops suddenly, eyes on the ground, and kneels at the edge of the trees.

"Gloves," he says, and I hand him a fresh pair from my other pocket. All my pockets are filled with gloves and evidence bags. Which one ex-girlfriend found odd enough to list as one of the (many) reasons she wanted to break up with me. *It's gross, Tim. It's just—weird.*

When he stands again, he's holding what looks like a bunch of sticks tied together.

But as I get closer, I can discern arms and legs, a torso, a head with dried leaves for hair. Around the neck, a twist of barbed wire. Old Bob hands it to me and I shine the light from my phone on it. I can see that entwined with the twigs and branches there's hair, fabric, dried flowers, a small black feather along the spine, tiny black beads sewn in for eyes.

Loathe as I am to admit I feel a tingle of fear.

"Is it—a doll?" I ask.

Old Bob nods.

"A voodoo doll."

ANA

This car has no spine. I press my foot to the pedal, and it hums along. It's like driving a cell phone. No fuel. No combustion engine. No *guts*.

In fact, it's a lot like Brock. It *looks* like a car on the outside. But nothing under the hood where the muscle should be.

I zip along the highway, veering for the exit when it comes up. I press my foot to the "gas" and see how fast it will go when I'm on the rural road. Pretty fast, surprisingly. The satellite radio is tuned predictably to an '80s alternative station, volume down low. The Cure—somehow mournful and upbeat all at once. Iggy's into all that retro shit, like she was born in the wrong decade. In the back, there's Noah's empty car seat, all padded and puffy for maximum comfort and safety for its screaming little passenger.

Babies. The ultimate friendship killer. Once those little narcissists come along, it's all about them.

My phone pings, and I glance at the screen face up on the seat beside me. My heart flutters a little. Fear. Something else.

We need to talk.

I don't answer and the road stretches ahead of me, an unfurling black ribbon, lined by tall pines, bows dusted with snow.

I *feel* something. An unfamiliar ache in the center of my chest. Paul.

The last time I saw him—it was ugly. I was my worst self. There's a part of me that stays caged most of the time. But every once in a while, I unlock the door and let it out. Things rarely go well when that happens, and I know it. But you can't keep the beast in a cage forever, hard as you try, especially when it's always screaming and rattling to get out. It goes mad, becomes even more dangerous.

Things got out of hand.

But to be honest, with Paul, there had always been a kind of dark current beneath all the flowers and jewelry, the surprise trips. Yeah, he took *me* to Aruba. And I wasn't the first. It was apparently in his go-to seduction playbook. (Do I feel a tiny bit gratified that he didn't make it there a final time? I do.) It took about six months for that other layer to breach the surface. But I think I knew it was there all along.

Sudden sharp words. Then fingerprint bruises on my upper arm. A cut under his eye.

The sex, which had always been shall we say edgy, got really rough. We started actually hurting each other. Both of us enjoying the pain a little, giving and receiving.

He reminded me of my father.

The way Mac used to grab my mother hard by both her upper arms like she was a beer can he was trying to crush, how she jutted her chin out at him, flashed a wicked grin.

"Do you feel like a man now?" she'd taunt.

And he'd either deflate, start to weep, or slap her or worse depending on his mood and how much he'd had to drink. And I swear there was something about those encounters that they both enjoyed. Something about that razor's edge between passion and rage. Even as a kid, I saw it. I didn't understand it until much later. But I saw the way their eyes gleamed, how utterly alive and engaged they were.

And I liked it when Paul bit me so hard that it left a throbbing black and blue mark that I could feel under my clothes days later. That little pulse of pain hidden from everyone else beneath the silk of my blouse excited me somehow.

"That's sick," Vera said when I confessed this to her. "You need help, Ana. Like for real."

Ha. Don't we all? Little Mrs. Perfect Life. Vera has a beast, too. The difference is that she *does* keep it muzzled and caged and locked away. It never gets any light or air, nourishment. I shudder to think what happens the next time it finally breaks free.

The familiar red mailbox tilts by the side of the road ahead of me. I stop and retrieve what's inside through the window, toss the pile in my tote to look through later. Then I pull up the long drive, Agnes's house rising ahead as I make the final turn.

The first time I saw this place, it filled me with dread. Now it's home in a way. I don't live here anymore, but sometimes I retreat to the room I shared with Vera after our parents were gone. Vera thinks I should move back here, has been making noise about how she's paying my rent and paying all the upkeep on this place. Which is bullshit because I do pay my own rent. Most of it. Most months. But so far I've refused to come back to Agnes's house. You know, because I shouldn't even *be here* in this one-horse town. That's why my business is always floundering. There's a real dearth of celebrity clients, which I need if I want any real money. I should be in Paris or London, New York City. That was the plan. There's more for me than this. I'm sure of it. I just can't seem to get where I'm going.

Paul said he was going to help me bag some bigger clients. He made promises. But they were all lies. That's what unstitched me most. All the lies he told me. That's why the beast emerged.

I pull to a stop, and the old house seems to acknowledge my arrival. I remember asking Agnes if the place was haunted and she said no.

But I feel her presence here now. And my mother's, and all the women in my family who lived here since it was built in the early 1900s. Not the men. They're all dead and gone, barely made a mark on this earth. All of them varying degrees of abusive or useless, weak or criminal. It's a family curse. The women in my family choose badly when it comes to men.

There are a million secrets and stories inside the walls of this house.

The car hums to a stop. There's no difference in sound between on and off with this thing. My father loved muscle cars, big machines in bold colors that roared and ate the road. Like women, he'd say, wild, untamable, thrilling.

What would he think of these electric cars?

My phone pings again.

Ana. Answer me.

Oh. We're on a first-name basis now? I stuff the phone in my pocket and enter the house. There's a scent when I enter the front door, must and sage. The wood floor creaks, welcoming me.

In the kitchen, I drop my bag. I take a smudge stick from the jar by the sink, light it from one of the gas burners on the old stove. Sage, its botanical name *salvia* meaning "to cure," cleanses. Its antiseptic and astringent properties rid a space of negative energy, bring in clarity and healing wisdom.

I walk through rooms, blowing gently on the embers, catching ash in an abalone shell. I fluff throw pillows, straighten blankets. All the while I'm thinking about Paul, the words the detective used.

Dead. Buried. Foul play.

I breathe in the sage. Hoping to cleanse myself.

I can distance myself, push the bad things away and away, until it doesn't seem real.

Finally, I find myself at the door to the library. Here I pause, because it's usually locked, but this afternoon it stands ajar. I feel a little pulse of concern, push inside.

In the distance, windchimes tinkle softly on the back porch below. I notice right away that something is out of place.

Aunt Agnes's *Book of Cures* sits on the desk, thick and leather bound. It's open, not as I left it the last time I was here. I put my hand to the parchment page.

The only other person who has keys to this place is Vera. I know she comes here, too. Sometimes we meet to talk, to tend the garden, to go through the hundreds of old volumes, and boxes of books, letters. Sometimes we sit under the weeping willow by the graveyard where both my mother and Agnes rest. Last autumn Vera and I came to winterize the garden, to harvest what we could, mulch the beds.

This place is ours, hers and mine.

And Brad's I guess. Since he pays all the bills. Or at least is aware that Vera pays all the bills involved in the upkeep, taxes, insurance, etcetera. I don't pretend to understand their relationship or how it works or what negotiations take place. He seems more like a boy than a man. But he makes all the money and lets her do whatever she wants, doesn't fight her, isn't violent. So, I guess that's what she likes about him. Because if there's one thing Vera needs it's total control. And maybe Brad needs to feel controlled. *Marriage is a negotiation*, Vera likes to say.

She's all romance, that one.

I sit down in the leather chair and look at the page that's open. There's a colored pencil drawing and Agnes's scrawling hand filling the parchment.

Agnes was a gifted artist. The delicate green leaves seem to move; the white flowers like tiny clouds gathered at the top of the plant bloom and billow. The telltale purple spots dot the stem. Like all flowering plants, it's pretty, looks harmless.

Hemlock.

It's meaning in floriography, the language of flowers, is death.

Its innocent appearance conceals the fact that it is viciously poisonous. Common and hearty, it can find a home anywhere—by roadsides, in waste areas, by fences. If ingested, depending on the amount, and the toxicity level of the plant, it can cause paralysis, renal or respiratory failure, and ultimately death. It is particularly threatening to livestock, though its unpleasant odor tends to ward most creatures away unless there's nothing else to eat.

Its leaves can be mistaken for parsley, which is a common mode of accidental ingestion.

There is currently no antidote for hemlock poisoning. You can only hope to stave off seizures, respiratory failure, and the other grievous effects with modern medical intervention until the body repairs itself. *If* it does.

I touch my hand to the page. Outside the window, even through the glass, even though it's the dead of winter there's the faint sound of birdsong. The room, overwarm and dusty, feels close; I lean against the leather back of Agnes's chair, then swivel to look at her wall of books, most of them older, leather bound, spines printed in gold.

Floriography: The Language of Flowers. Medicinal Herbs: A Beginner's Guide. Encyclopedia of Herbal Medicine. Salves and Tinctures. Poison. Healing Teas. Broths and Teas for Common Ailments. Botanical Curses and Poisons. Curative Plants. Natural Pain Relief.

Agnes had no formal education after high school, but her knowledge of plants for medicinal and nefarious purposes would put most PhDs on the subject to shame.

I swivel again in her chair.

Someone has been in this room. I feel it, see it in things left just slightly out of place. The crystal paperweight on her desk, a book on herbs pulled out from its spot and replaced. And I'm pretty sure it wasn't Vera. She's meticulous. She would never leave Agnes's book open, the door unlocked. The leather-bound volume, fully three inches thick, is crammed with generations of study, recipes, anecdotes, antidotes, and advice. Agnes called it "The Knowledge."

"It's only for those who know their place on this planet, who understand the truth about nature, and our relationship to her," she told me before my first lesson. "The Great Mother with all her whims and moods, her fury, her grace, her power, protects us, destroys us at her pleasure. Do you understand, Ana?"

I did and I didn't then. Like all human children, and most adults, I was a bit ignorant of my place in the ecosystem.

I close the book, a vein throbbing in my throat.

The dust motes dance and the couch over by the fireplace still has an Aunt Agnes–sized dent in one of the cushions. How many hours did she spend here reading and writing, drawing? I can almost see her sitting there, looking up to peer at me over her wire-rimmed specs, frizzy hair wild, when I interrupted her for this or that.

"Who was here?" I ask her.

She doesn't answer. But the ideas come just the same.

The other members of The Cove know about this place, but each of them has her own books, her own recipes and ways, special skills. Lisander, Agnes's mentee, often joins us here to work on the garden. Who else? Another name comes to mind.

I rise and shut the heavy volume. The smudge stick has burned out in the shell, a final thin line of smoke snaking up in a twist, then dissipating.

I grab the shell, exit the room, and lock the door behind me.

Down in the mudroom, I don one of the beekeeper suits we keep there, kick off my heels, pull on a pair of rubber-soled boots. Outside, I walk the path to the garden.

It's winter so when I unlock the heavy wooden door and push inside, there's little to see.

A dormant garden in winter, though it appears dead, is a promise of what's to come in spring. Beneath the surface, there is life gestating, just waiting for its moment to burst forth. One of my favorite Agnes-isms.

Vera and I came in the fall together and cleaned and mulched the beds. Some of the other members of The Cove were here, as well—Lisander, Camille and Bree, of course Vera's little helper, April. We harvested leaves, flowers, and berries to be dried and stored, composting what wasn't needed out behind the greenhouse, pruned branches, and covered the beds to protect the roots from winter chill.

Lisander and Vera had words after the work was done. There's always been tension there, a kind of love triangle between Lisander, Vera, and Agnes. Lisander worshipped Agnes. Vera was Agnes's star pupil, the one she wanted to pass The Knowledge to as her heir apparent. Vera rejected the life completely, refusing Agnes's seat in The Cove.

The Cove doesn't even exist, Vera likes to say. *It's a fantasy.*

Lisander and many others disagree.

I linger on the path.

This is not a garden like other gardens, though it has its share of roses and snapdragons, hydrangeas, other spectacularly colored blooming plants, leafy green ferns, and climbing ivy. And if you come here in the late spring, early summer, when nature's color show is at its most audacious, you will marvel at its beauty. Surrounded by a tall stone wall, it's a peaceful place with a gurgling fountain and tidy white graveled paths. We keep this place as pristine as Agnes did, fully operational. We provide herbs, seeds, flowers, petals, and stems to many of the area practitioners. It helps with the cost of keeping this place.

In spring or summer, you might not even notice the hemlock growing white and pretty in the shade of the oak. Or the oleander, slender and elegant as a debutant at the ball. The flowering rosary pea is long and thin, a climber, her berries as pretty as ladybugs. Lovely purple belladonna with her ball gown blossoms seduces. Deadly nightshade sprouts fat blue berries so similar to the harmless fruit in your fridge. At the far end of the garden, a tall tree with plump leaves offers small green apples that are sweet to the taste, its sap milky white—the manchineel tree. Not native to this region, it takes some work to keep it alive.

All of these plants can harm, burn, blind, or kill you. Some can heal you. Often both—depending on the dose, or on which part of it you ingest or come in contact with.

Girls, Aunt Agnes used to tell us, *often the only difference between poison and medicine is the dose.*

But today, the garden is fallow, waiting for spring. Winter is a time of paucity, of fearful shortfalls, where once upon a time, animals and humans alike might have despaired as their winter stores dwindled and hunger was the constant companion.

Hence the name for the upcoming January full moon, the Wolf Moon, so named it's said for the wolves howling in the bitter cold of winter, lamenting the lack of nourishment. But it's also a time of reflection and looking forward to the rebirth of spring just weeks away. It's a time of gathering, of coming together to help each other through.

I think about this as I move through the garden. There will be a great deal of work to do here soon. Vera and I will take turns preparing for the season. Making a loop along the gravel paths, I'm satisfied that everything is undisturbed.

As I look at the hard, cold earth, I think of Paul in his shallow grave.

His body was so warm; he gave off so much heat. He was a copious sweater. Turned red if he ate too much spice. At night, he was like sleeping next to a space heater.

Not anymore. I allow a tear to fall, wipe it away.

Vera doesn't believe me.

But I *did* love him.

In my way.

At the west wall of the garden, I stop. Another door that should be locked stands ajar. I study the handle. It does not appear to have been pried or forced. Whoever opened it, did so with a key. Maybe someone picked it? There are only two keys to this place, as well, again mine and Vera's. I know myself to be sloppy, distracted, and often careless. But my sister is a machine. There is no way she left the door to this place unlocked. It would be like leaving a gun cabinet open wide.

I stare a moment longer and then exit, thinking as I turn the key that we need better security.

Who has been here?

I keep walking west up the path, tromping clumsily in my boots and this ridiculous beekeeper suit that Agnes loved. She was always wearing it.

The dead branches around me whisper, desiccated. I'm not alone.

A sound behind me causes me to turn quickly. I grip the tiny silver switchblade I only occasionally remember to carry with me in my pocket. *A woman must always be ready to defend herself, psychologically and physically.* Another Agnes-ism.

She stands in the trees staring, frozen.

A doe. She is still, watching, so close I can see the gleam of her tawny fur, hear her breath. We lock eyes. On another day, I might be the hunter and she the prey. But not today. Today, we are just two creatures in the forest, each up to the business of existing, surviving. And truthfully, I've never hurt anything or anyone who didn't deserve it.

After another moment she bolts, startled by something I didn't hear, and I continue down the path to the greenhouse. Past that is a small stone house with a chimney and mullioned windows. It has stood on the property for a hundred years at least, the original house before my grandfather built the house where Agnes and my mother grew up. Inside it's been gutted and thoroughly modernized. Agnes called it "The Kitchen."

An accomplished herbalist, Agnes used ingredients from her garden and some she had to import from other countries. She was a sought-after purveyor of teas, tinctures, salves, and cures. She spent hours out here—chopping, cutting, drying, mixing, storing, experimenting, developing recipes. Below the house is a cellar, where there are even more stores.

On the door to The Kitchen there's a thick modern lock with

a keypad. I'm relieved to find it firmly closed. I key in my code and push inside, greeted by warmth and the heavy scent of sage.

Something about this place always soothes me.

Maybe it's the shelves of books, journals, and bound handwritten recipes left by my aunt, mother, grandmother, her sisters, and their mother, reaching back generations. The enormous maple apothecary chest built by my great-grandfather, topped with a marble work surface. There's a brand-new industrial-size stove and oven, thanks to moneybags Brad. There's a bright green herb garden on the windowsill, a long wooden table in the open space. Stacks of well-used pots and cauldrons hang from a ceiling rack. I used to think this place was magic and that Agnes and my mother were witches.

But what happens here isn't magic. It's science. Nearly fifty percent of modern medicines were derived from the work of indigenous healers.

Plants and their powers to heal and harm have a long, largely ignored and unknown history. It was the sap from the manchineel tree, dipped on the tip of an arrow, that killed Ponce de León when he returned to settle Florida; the Calusa tribe had other ideas about his returning to pillage their sacred land. Socrates was executed for his ideas by being forced to drink hemlock tea. Penicillin is derived from mold, a fungus that grows on plants. Its discovery has saved untold millions of lives.

I don a mask and gloves, then kneel in front of a drawer labeled "Hemlock" and open it, careful to lean away. The drawer is empty, the sprigs we dried and stored last season are gone.

My heart is thumping a little, as I close the drawer, discard the mask and gloves, wash my hands thoroughly with charcoal soap. Outside a crow alights on the windowsill, looks inside then flits away.

Someone came here, looked up a recipe in Agnes's book, then came to The Kitchen to gather ingredients. My brain clicks through options, none of them good.

Using Agnes's big copper kettle, I brew myself a cup of peppermint tea, the way she used to when we were upset. Peppermint calms the nerves, an agitated stomach; its oil can ease a headache. It's an antibacterial, an insect repellent, a performance enhancer.

But as I sit at my aunt's big table drinking, it's just a way to comfort myself, thinking about Paul, and wondering who was in the house and the garden.

I think I might have an idea. I sip my tea, then thumb out a text. Someone has been in the study, the garden, and The Kitchen. **Have you been at Agnes's place?**

I wait, but as usual there's no answer. She's difficult, reticent, unpredictable. At least she comes by it honestly.

When my phone finally pings, it's not in answer to my most recent text.

Ana, don't ignore me.

I stare at the bubble, which seems to throb with menace. I almost delete and block. My go-to move. The ultimate modern day fuck off. Instead, I bite.

What do you want?

Let's meet.

Am I really going to do this? What would Vera say? She'd tell me I was crazy, reckless, not considering consequences. But there's something tugging at me, something thrilling and familiar, an almost magnetic draw to danger.

Where and when?

The sender drops me a pinned location.

Now.

CORALINE

I stare at my phone and think about how to answer the text there.

Have you been at Agnes's place?

And then I just *don't* answer, stuff my phone into the front pocket of my hoodie.

Grant is slouched on my bed when I get back to my room, leaning against the stuffed animals and throw pillows that are piled high.

"Get out," I say, almost out of habit. I don't really care if he's in my room. He flops back on the mattress instead, puts his sock feet up on the spread.

"Ew," I say. "Get your disgusting feet off my sheets."

"Want to play *Red World*?" he asks, ignoring me.

"Don't you have to study for chem?"

"Just one game," he says, holding up his iPad, offering me his goofy smile.

I push him off my bed, and he rolls dramatically onto the floor, landing with a thud on the beanbags there. I put on my headset, grab my iPad, and enter the game. He's already in the locker room, choosing his skin. Tonight, he's a werewolf, clad in a torn-up denim jacket, holding a chainsaw. The Wolf is ripped, and snarling. The complete opposite of my geeky, wimpy brother, who in spite of his size is tenderhearted. Literally will not even kill bugs, carefully removes flies, spiders, even mosquitos outdoors instead of screaming and smashing them like I do. *They're alive, Coraline! They have meaning!*

I keep a lower profile on *Red World*. My avatar wears a simple black dress with tall lace-up boots, rocks a pink crew cut. My weapons of choice are carried in a messenger bag, not immediately visible. Aunt Ana likes to talk about the pit viper. How it's small and slow, doesn't dart off on your approach. It doesn't have to. It's the deadliest snake in the world. One bite and you're done. Hence my name: Viper.

In my bag I have a silver blade, Chinese stars and magic beans, deadly potions, harming herbs, also a first aid kit to tend to wounds, which is often more powerful than the ability to hurt.

Grant and I make a good team in *Red World*. Brawn and brains. Sometimes you need both. We barely talk at school. Honestly, I actively avoid him because he's so fucking needy, always asking me for money, wanting to sit with my friends at lunch. But in the game, we slay.

"What's up, *mofos*?"

It's Autumn. *Red World* must have notified her that we were dropping in. Grant and I exchange a look. Because as much as I love my lifelong friend and she's a literal genius vying for the valedictorian spot at school, she is a liability in *Red World*. She is always getting killed or getting me killed. I'm constantly having to rescue her. And she has no assets—no Red Coin, very few weapons, just the minimum of skins. And her avatar? Honestly, it's embarrassing. "Fairy" has wings and an iridescent shift dress, striped tights and pink shoes. She *can* fly; so that's something.

I give her a high five on the game because I love her, and because in the real world *I'm* the liability a lot of the time. I wouldn't be getting higher than a C in pre calc or chem if not for her. We've had each other's backs since kindergarten. And her parents only let her play *Red World* on the weekends, so it's not like I have to deal with it all the time.

"Let's do this," she says, as the timer counts down.

"Slay," says Grant, making his voice deeper.

Gawd, they are such hopeless nerds.

And then we're in. Looks like we've landed in Haunted Amusement Park, and as soon as we hit the ground we're fighting off the zombies. The Wolf uses his chainsaw to behead a few of them. I fling a Chinese star, getting one right between the eyes. Fairy is running away, screaming.

"Let's try to find the Purple Diamond," says The Wolf when Fairy calms down and returns.

"I've never seen it," I answer, feeling a jolt of adrenaline: it's a huge find that doubles your Red Coin balance.

"So hey," says Autumn over my headset. "Wasn't your aunt dating that guy who they found dead today?"

I blow a pouch of paralyzer dust into the faces of a couple of zombies coming up from behind us and they all fall to the ground stiff as branches, then turn to red dust.

"Yeah," I say, feeling a little flutter of unease.

"Are you freaked out?"

"They broke up."

When Mom told us about Paul, I could tell that she was doing that new thing she's doing since we all started therapy—speaking more softly, asking about our feelings.

You spent some time with him at that July 4th barbecue, she said. Which was like a hundred years ago. *So this must come as a shock. Would you like to talk about your feelings?*

She sounded like our family shrink. At least she's *trying* to be less of a controlling hard-ass.

Honestly, I never pay attention to Aunt Ana's boyfriends. They're like NPCs in the game. They're just there. They don't interact, have a point, talk. They're just set dressing essentially.

But that guy? He was creepy and weird. When he shook my

hand, I got a weird feeling in my stomach. I caught him watching me when I took off my cover-up by the pool. I didn't like the way Ana acted around him—meaner, edgier, somehow not herself.

The 4th of July barbecue wasn't the last time I saw him.

"I don't even really remember him," says Grant, staring at his iPad.

"The tall one," I said. "The one with the hair."

Thick and shiny brown, it was all coiffed and stiff like LEGO hair.

I feel like my mom wanted to say more when we were talking about it but then didn't. Also, she was looking at me like she does when she thinks (or knows) I've done something bad and she's just waiting for me to admit it. She's been off and rattled since we got home.

Ana, who was lying on the couch when we got in, left without saying goodbye. Usually she doesn't leave, stays through dinner, is annoying.

Then my mom went into the basement, to the room she thinks no one knows about. She only does that when she's really upset.

"Do we have to go to the funeral?" asks Grant.

"Doubtful. I mean, we didn't really know him."

"You guys must be freaking out," says Autumn. Her avatar Fairy is doing a little dance, and I have to zap a vampire that comes up behind her.

"Yeah, I guess. Maybe a little."

That seems like the right thing to say even though I couldn't care less. And anyway, it doesn't even seem real, like something you would hear about on a true crime podcast.

"My mom knew him," says Autumn. "They were on some charity committee together. She's been crying all day."

That makes me a little uncomfortable, like maybe I should be feeling more than I do. But something I've learned—you can pretend to have the right feelings, but you can't fool yourself into feeling something you don't. I've tried.

"Yeah," I say, trying to make my voice heavy. "It's so sad."

Another look from Grant, who knows me better than anyone. He's wearing a ridiculously oversized T-shirt with some Lord of the Rings map on it. *Mordor Fun Run*, it reads in old-timey lettering. *We don't simply walk.*

Autumn is about to say something else when her avatar disappears into a burst of rainbow glitter. Behind her stands a towering leather-clad, muscle-bound beast with a purple mohawk who we know in the game as Black Dahlia.

"There was no need for that," I say into my headset.

"I just can't deal with her tonight."

"No one invited you."

"Grant did."

I look over at my brother, who avoids my eyes now but is turning a bright red. He has a mad forever crush on Dahlia; that's her name in the real world. Which I honestly don't get. She's not even that pretty; she's got issues, is always in trouble.

"Hear about that guy who got killed?" says Dahlia. "They buried him in the park."

"We knew him," Grant jumps in. "He dated my aunt."

"No shit?"

"*Used to date* him. They broke up a while ago," I correct him, feeling a sudden rush of defensiveness for Ana. *Family protects family. No matter what.* A mom-ism, of which there are so many.

"My sister works at the ME's office. They're saying poison."

My throat goes a little dry. A text bubble pops up on my phone.

My phone pings and there's a text from Autumn: **Wtf? She killed me for no reason.**

"That's messed up," says Grant vaguely, though he shoots me another look.

I think about one of the other times I saw Paul. He was with a woman, not my aunt. That's when I knew for sure he was a bad guy. I put him on "The List." The list I keep of people I don't like, who have hurt me, or someone I love, or who are just objectively bad. The list is getting pretty long. The only people who know about it are Autumn and Ethan.

So, what's your plan for these bad people? Ethan wanted to know.
I don't know.
And is there any way to get off the list if you're on it? And what if someone is just having a bad day when they wind up on your list?

That's Ethan for you. He's a deep thinker. Me, not so much.

Grant's avatar runs off to fight a group of zombies. Black Dahlia gives chase. Together they make short work of the undead. I follow. I have to use some of the energy in my first aid kit to reattach The Wolf's arm when it gets macheted off, spewing digital blood everywhere.

The sky is turning pink. There's not much time to find the doorway to the next level.

"Hey," says Dahlia. "It's over there."

I see it now, too. She just saved us.

"Check it out," I say. "Behind the tree. What's that? Is it the Purple Diamond?"

Grant looks at me. "There's no time."

The Wolf starts moving toward the exit. But Dahlia heads over to the tree and I corner her there. No one, and I mean *no one*, fucks with the people I love.

I take a Chinese star from my bag, spend extra Red Coin for a death shot, and hit her right between her eyes.

"What the actual fuck?" she says, before her avatar disappears into a cloud of black glitter.

"What did you do that for?" asks Grant, scowling at me.

"I don't like her."

"You don't just kill people you don't like, Coraline."

We both run then, heading for the doorway, and make it through the portal *just before* the red sky closes in and we both die.

VERA

After the flurry of dinner, the house has gone quiet again. Brad missed the meal, his flight delayed, and is on his way from the airport now.

Sitting at the kitchen bar, I watch Ana's dot pulse on Life-Watch. She's been at Agnes's house for a while.

What is she doing? Destroying evidence? My impulse is to call her, or to get in my car and go to Agnes's. Instead, I decide to use the time before Brad comes home to scour the web for more information about Paul's death. There still isn't much. His body found this morning by hikers in a too-shallow grave. Cause of death unknown.

All the detective said was that foul play was suspected. He didn't say *shot* or *beaten*. He didn't say *robbed*.

No suspects. No leads.

I watch a replay of his earlier press conference. That detective; I really don't like the look of him. Too watchful, seeing. An arrogance. Somehow he seemed to hone right in on Ana. It fits a narrative, like Payton said, the jilted girlfriend. It certainly makes things a lot easier when the story has already been written and you just have to plug in the characters. He won't have to dig very deep into my sister before she starts to look more and more the likely culprit.

I type the detective's name into the search bar.

"Who are you?" I say to no one.

I thought about brewing some chamomile tea but needed something stronger. I poured myself two fingers of Brad's favorite bourbon, Blanton's. Taking a deep swig of it now, it's smooth and hot in my throat, taking the edge off almost right away even as it burns.

Timothy Bandeau. We're all out there for anyone to see these days, the internet like a catalog of our deeds. I click link after link. Homicide detective at Little Valley Police Department. John Jay College graduate, a dual degree in psychology and criminal investigation. In his uniform he looks stiff, clean-shaven, with that weirdly erect posture of his like there's a rod up his back. His brow line is heavy, high cheekbones, a wide mouth.

I stare at the image of him as a younger man, clean-shaven, thinner. That look again, a person who thinks a lot of himself. Also, something else, something subterranean. There's something in the eyes when you've witnessed the truth of the human condition. You see it in soldiers, cops, firefighters, EMTs. They know things about life, about death, about the human body that they can't unknow.

I take another sip of bourbon, scroll through the smattering of articles in which the detective is quoted about various cases over his years on the job in this little town. Why here? I wonder. In this little place where nothing happens. Until it does.

Down a little further there's another story, a feature. *Local Detective Volunteers at the YMCA; Teaches Boxing to Area Underprivileged Youth.* There's a picture of him smiling, surrounded by a group of teenage boys. He has his arm draped over one, is fist-bumping another.

There he is—the real man.

Out of uniform, off duty, he is easy, affable, boyish. *Boxing saved me when I was a kid. It taught me control, discipline. The daily physical activity helped me to stay calm, deal with my anger issues. Without it, I'd probably be in jail instead of a cop*, he's quoted as saying.

Some interesting layers to Detective Bandeau. Know your enemy; that's what Agnes always said. Not that he's our enemy. Yet.

There's another article, more recent, about how the Little Valley Youth Center is in trouble, that some federal funding and money promised from a donor fell through. There's a GoFundMe link, a fundraiser coming up.

My phone pings, alerting me that my sister is on the move again. Looks like she is heading to Iggy and Brock's now. She's been at Agnes's all this time and I have no idea why. We both tend to retreat there when things get hot. There's always work to do, especially now that spring is approaching. You can lose yourself in the care and upkeep of that old money pit. Brad thinks we should sell it. But that's not an option, and he never makes me do things I don't want to do. Which is part of the reason I married him.

I drain the glass just as I hear him come in through the front door. As if an alarm has sounded, both kids come bounding from their rooms just as they've always done since they were old enough to walk. Brad is the FP, as we call it. The favorite parent, the good guy, the easy one. I am the workhorse, the disciplinarian. I don't mind it. Someone has to keep watch.

I rise and walk out to the foyer to greet him. We've been married a long time, but I still feel a little rush at the sight of him—the silk of his sandy-blond hair, that strong jaw and easy smile, his impeccable wardrobe. The kids are already on him.

He's got a stuffed bear for Coraline, a graphic novel for Grant. I know he'll have a gift for me, too. This is his love language, the giving of thoughtful presents.

They push by me through the swinging door into the kitchen as a group, attached, exuberant, laughing.

"Way to drink alone, Mom," quips Coraline, clocking the bourbon bottle on the counter.

"I'm not alone," I say, following. "I haven't been alone in years."

"Rough day?" asks Brad, giving me a worried frown.

"You could say that."

He leans into me, snakes a strong arm around my waist and kisses me on the mouth. The kids wail in disgust. We try to model a good relationship for them, even though as a couple we are far from perfect. We think about these things. What Grant and Coraline see between us is what they'll expect from their own spouses. I could fill a book with what I had to unlearn about Sadie and Mac's sick marriage. Brad, too, comes from trauma and pain.

We try to do better.

He fills my glass again and pours himself one, too. He looks tired, shiners of fatigue under his eyes. Though the lines around his eyes seem more defined, he's still boyish, like he should be all dusty on a Little League mound somewhere ready to throw a pitch.

"I saved you a plate," I say. "Can I heat it up for you?"

"That would be great. I'm starved." Doubtful, but he knows I take pleasure in feeding him. That's *my* love language, caretaking. Making beds and doing laundry, handing out water on the soccer field. Old-fashioned, silly maybe. But I take a comfort in it. Homemaking, *life* making, is a lost art. Coraline told our therapist that she feels controlled by my constant presence at home, at school. Maybe that's part of it, too. Control all the little details, and it keeps the chaos at bay.

Grant comes in for a quick hug, then he's bounding up the stairs again. Coraline lingers a while, chatting with her dad about this and that, then she's gone, too, and it's just us.

"What is it?" he says to my back as I put his plate in the microwave. "You seem tense."

When we met, I was a wreck. But then again, so was he. Both in our twenties, I had just lost my job because of a boss who couldn't keep his hands to himself and how I handled it. Brad was trying to save his failing business, outrun all his demons.

"You look how I feel," he'd said all those years ago. It was a bar in town, a place I'd just happened into after wandering the streets for a while, trying to figure out what I was going to do with my life. He sat next to me as The Rolling Stones played on the jukebox, and a happy hour group was getting loud around the pool table.

"That good?" I said, tipping back my glass, checking him out in the mirror behind the rows of bottles.

"Don't get me wrong," he said, flashing that boyish grin. "You look *good*. Just maybe . . ."

I turned to look at him. There was a jolt of attraction, a notch in my heart chakra.

He searched my face. And there was something about his eyes—dark brown and heavily lidded—his easy slouch, the bad boy smile. "Just maybe a little sad."

"Just tired, I think," I admitted though on another night I might have just gotten up and left. I wasn't looking for Brad or anyone. I'm not like Ana. I'm perfectly happy without a man in my life. "But like on an existential level."

"I hear that."

He ordered a Blanton's neat—one for him, and one for me. When we clinked glasses, he said, "I have a feeling we're going to be good for each other."

He was right about that, in many ways. We were like two parts of a whole, each of us capable of less alone than we were together.

"Paul's dead," I say now.

The microwave beeps. I retrieve the plate, the savory aroma wafting.

"*Who?*" he says, squinting at me over his glass.

"Paul? Ana's ex."

It takes a moment for it to register. "Oh," he says finally, the implications dawning. He puts down his glass, gets still. "Oh, shit. Did she—?"

"She claims not. But I don't know. Foul play is suspected."

I run down the details, the brunch, the visit from the detective, the scant information I found online.

"Where is she now?" he asks.

He eats like a teenager, shoving food in his mouth as though he thinks someone is going to try to take it away from him. He grew up in foster care, had to fight for everything he has in life. Watch his back. These things don't die—even when you're driving a Porsche and gave a million dollars to the free clinic last year. In public, he's cool and measured, the very picture of style, grooming, and manners. Charming. At home, he's different. Sometimes I think of him less as my husband, and more like one of the kids; someone I occasionally have to soothe or reprimand.

"She was at Agnes's. Now it looks like she's on her way to Iggy's. She has their car. I'm taking her to the station in the morning with a colleague of Payton's to answer questions."

He nods. Then, "I thought you had her under control." Like he's my boss. He's not. I'm no trophy wife.

I give him a look, and he raises his palms in surrender. "I'm just saying. You said she was in therapy. That she was handling her anger issues better."

"She was. She *is*."

He comes around the kitchen island to take me in his arms. I sink into him. He's strong, body warm and solid. He holds me tight and some of the tension releases from my shoulders. He kisses me on the head, says into my hair, "She's a liability. We can't keep bailing her out of trouble. At some point she's going to pull you under with her. You have the kids to worry about."

"I'll handle it."

"I know you will."

"What about the fire?" I ask.

He blows out a long breath. "There's going to be an investigation," he says. "The police suspect arson."

I pull back from him, look up into his tired eyes. "What does that mean?"

"Someone sabotaged the system. Or it failed. Either way, it's not good for us. The system is supposed to be fail proof, tamper proof. Files that were meant to be turned over as evidence in a case against the company were destroyed. A man died."

We stand like that awhile. I can hear the beating of his heart, matching the thrumming of my own. This is what I mean. If you don't control everyone, everything, the world can just spin out. But no matter how hard you try, something always seems to get away from you.

"Anyway, we'll put out a press release. Say that we're standing behind the integrity of the system and are launching an investigation of our own into what might have happened."

"Okay," I agree.

"Anyway," he says, looking down at me. "I'll handle the business. You handle Ana."

Coraline is talking loudly on the phone upstairs. Music comes from Grant's room, something I don't recognize. The house smells like Sunday dinner. I can almost believe that the world we have made inside these walls is enough to keep us safe from everything out there. But I'm old enough to know that it's not.

Yes. I'll handle Ana.

In Brad's arms, I'm thinking about Detective Timothy Bandeau and that too-watchful, too-seeing gaze, that smarter-than-you smile. He's a wolf at our door, huffing and puffing.

It's okay. I've got this, as Coraline likes to say even when she's not sure she means it. Protecting the badly behaved women in my family is my birthright.

Brad heads down to the basement to knock out a couple miles

on the treadmill, and I walk out to the back deck. The pool is covered for winter, and leaves blow across the surface in the wind. It's cold. Above me, the moon is almost full.

"Have you forgotten about the Wolf Moon?" Lisander wanted to know when we last spoke.

"Of course not."

"I didn't think such things were important to you anymore." There's always that note of sadness, of resentment.

Truthfully, I've moved far from the kind of life Agnes and Lisander wanted for themselves, for me. I've turned my back on The Cove. But it's still with me. Still in my blood. I still practice, though just for myself.

The waxing gibbous moon is white-blue and rising bloated over the trees.

"Can we count on you to be there?" Lisander asked. "There's unfinished business."

Unfinished business. Maybe for her. My business was finished long ago. I have a life, a family. I've joined the real world.

"I'll see what I can do."

I have no intention of attending the Wolf Moon ceremony. The last time I did, Agnes was still alive. And I promised myself that I'd never attend again. And so far, I've kept that promise to myself. Though I'd be lying if I said I didn't feel the tug, a tinge of sadness when I'm at Agnes's place, like I've given up something out of spite that part of me still craves.

"I strongly urge you to attend," Lisander pressed.

I didn't answer and ended the call. I don't take my orders from her, or anyone.

The fact is I have bigger problems than whatever "unfinished business" needs to be resolved on the night of the Wolf Moon.

I need to find out who killed Paul before the police do, and there's no time to waste.

ANA

I arrive at the roadside diner just beyond the town limits, pull into the nearly empty parking lot, and wait. Through the windows I can see the few customers inside, a waitress in a silly pink uniform shuttling between booth tables and the counter. I park toward the far edge, near the exit in case I change my mind. Every nerve ending is buzzing—fear, excitement. Vera likes to refer to these as my dark appetites. Says I'm happy where other people are unhappy. Maybe she's right.

The last of the light is disappearing from the sky. I roll down the window a bit and the air smells like snow. I imagine it falling and covering Paul's grave. Probably if the predicted snow had fallen last night, the hikers would never have found him. At least not until spring. He'd have been discovered missing of course. But his body would have stayed in the cold earth, decomposing, his whereabouts a mystery.

The last time we were together, we made love on his living room floor. Afterward we fought—I don't even remember about what. That was how things were going—fuck, fight. A terrible, familiar dance that often ended in violence. He grabbed my arm, called me a spoiled, vapid bitch. I threw a glass of wine at him, it hit him, spraying red everywhere, shattering against the fireplace hearth.

Later I got a text. **We're done.**

Relief and rage mingled. I'm the dumper, not the dumpee. But truthfully, I was already done with it, with him, with the person I was with him. Vera's not the only one in therapy.

Anyway, I already suspected he was seeing someone else. That lacy thong in his gym bag. Red flag, right?

As time passes, five minutes, ten, I start to get annoyed. The person I'm waiting for is not in the diner, vehicle nowhere in sight. Have I been stood up?

I don't even bother texting. I know when I'm being played with. I wait another few minutes, then leave, anger and annoyance on simmer in my center.

My mood hasn't improved as I turn into Iggy's neighborhood.

Gawd, I'd rather *die* than live in a neighborhood like this with all its predictably pretty normie houses with their tidy lawns, bicycles twisting on the driveway, basketball hoop over the garage. A husband and baby and this idiotic woke-mobile. If boredom could kill this would be the zombie apocalypse.

I hum up the street thinking how different Iggy was when she and I first met. A wild child with her mop of white-blond hair and ready smile. Her easy, devil-may-care approach to everything from boys to homework thrilled me after sharing a room all my life with my drill sergeant of a sister. Honestly, it was love at first sight when I entered our college dorm room and found Iggy smoking a joint out the window. There was a stack of her things in the middle of the room.

"Hey," she said. "I waited to see what bed you wanted. I'm cool with whatever. Want a puff?"

I looked around for Vera, who had dropped me off and sped away, angry at me for something I'd said or done—as usual. I was alone for the very first time. Vera had been this controlling, organizing presence in my life, even before we went to Agnes's, the one who held us together while the adults around us made a mess of their lives and then the whole world fell apart. I relied on her, but I couldn't wait to break free from her. I know she was just trying to keep us safe, but she was always—still is—such a bossy little bitch.

Iggy was bongs and belly laughs, stay up all night and miss class, eat pizza in bed, sleep with whoever, then ghost him. She reminded me of my mom *before*, the person Sadie was when I was home sick from school and it was just the two of us, or when Dad was in a good mood. There *were* happy times, which is weird to say given how it ended. Even Vera was happier once, less afraid and uptight. Iggy reminded me what it was like to feel free, the way I felt before I understood that violence and murder were the flip side of love, a coin that was forever being tossed by some unseen hand.

Now all Iggy thinks about is Brock and that stupid baby, who honestly I have only ever seen squalling and squirming. *That's your life now? Just tending to that thing?*

As I turn onto Iggy's tree-lined street I slow, trying to process what I'm seeing.

Flashing red and blue lights, a jam of vehicles, one of them a police cruiser, another an ambulance. Blood rushes in my ears, my heart a tiny drumbeat in my chest.

As I get close, I realize that they're gathered in front of Iggy and Brock's place, the front door swung wide open. On the lawn is the detective standing six feet tall, rangy and watchful as a wolf.

For the love of gawd. What now?

I pull the car to the side of the road and step out into the night chill, jog up the lawn. The detective puts himself between me and the house.

"Ah, Ms. Blacksmith," he says. "Twice in one day. What are the odds?"

"What are you doing here? What's happened?"

I try to move around him, but he keeps blocking my path.

"911 call for medical assistance," he says. "Small department. Dispatch alerted me."

My mind is reeling, searching for data. Why are the police here? The ambulance?

"What's happened?" I say again.

"Maybe you know better than I do?"

I shake my head at him, feel the heat coming up my throat, which happens when I'm angry. I have and suppress the very strong urge to shove him hard out of my path. "What are you *talking about*? Get out of my way."

With a slight smile, he lets me pass and I run to the house just as paramedics are coming out the red front door onto the pretty brick stoop with a stretcher, easing it down the shallow steps.

"Iggy!"

Those blond tresses fan around her. She's Sleeping Beauty, fragile, gorgeous, and deathly pale. Brock follows holding that baby, who is, as usual, screaming his head off.

"What's going on?" I demand.

Why won't anyone answer me?

"I—I—I don't know," Brock stammers over the baby's wails.

Ugh, it's like a *siren*.

"She wasn't feeling well after the brunch. Then she started to have really bad stomach cramps, like she was doubled over. She passed out and I called 911."

I take her hand; it's ice-cold. I keep walking as the paramedics move toward the waiting ambulance. She's so white she's almost blue, so slight she's barely a bump on the stretcher. She's not faking it, though I wouldn't put it past her under the right circumstances. She turns her head toward me. I think she's opening her eyes, about to say something, her powder-blue gaze filled with fear, locking with mine.

"Tell me," I say, squeezing her hand.

But then she's seizing, mouth puckering, back arcing, limbs flailing.

"Iggy!"

The EMTs rush her to the ambulance, Brock close behind, still holding the wailing baby.

"Let me take him," I hear myself saying, almost as if I were a normal person. "So you can focus on Iggy. I'll meet you with him at the hospital."

"Are you sure?" He looks deeply worried—about Iggy, about handing me the baby.

"Of course." I reach for it, and then squirmy little Noah is warm in my arms.

"All his stuff is in the baby bag by the door," says Brock. "There's pumped breast milk in the fridge."

Great. Shit. Maybe this was a bad idea. Noah and I lock eyes. What do I even do with it?

But it's too late because Brock's disappearing into the ambulance, the doors closing hard behind him and the vehicle wailing away.

The world is spinning. None of this makes any sense. I have that same helpless feeling I've been running from since I was a kid, when Sadie and Mac seemed hell-bent on ruining everyone's life until they finally succeeded.

When we're used to chaos in our lives, sometimes we seek to create it. Because it's what we know. That's what the shrink who Vera thinks is too young to know anything said to me last session. We see her as a family to work on what Vera calls our *generational issues*. But some of us have individual sessions—Coraline and me, because we're the ones who do the most *acting out* supposedly—with her. I suspect Vera sees the doctor alone, too, even though she pretends not to like her.

But I'm not creating this, am I?

Mercifully, inexplicably, the little monster goes quiet as the sirens fade away down the street. I look down at baby Noah, and he up to me. Weirdly, suddenly, there's a connection. Those watery blue eyes are just like Iggy's. I snug him in close up on my hip. It feels—dare I say it—natural.

Detective Bandeau has joined me to watch the ambulance speed away.

I think of our first encounter, not at the house today. How long ago was it? A week? More?

"I wouldn't have figured you for the babysitting type." I don't like his tone, like he's laughing at me even though his face is stone still.

"You stood me up," I say.

"Like I said, I got a call. Anyway, I guess that makes us even, since you snuck out the back door after our—encounter. I'm trying not to take it personally."

"It *was* personal."

"You didn't enjoy yourself."

I flash on the heat of his body, the taste of his lips on mine. His strength, his presence, the gaze of those dark eyes. The truth is I haven't been able to stop thinking about him. How even though he was physically powerful, he was somehow gentle. How even though our "encounter" was debauched and tawdry, he was respectful. My body betrays me, tingling.

"What was it about the concept of 'no strings' that eluded you?" I manage.

We lock eyes a moment, and I'm gratified to see color come up in his cheeks, his gaze drop. I win.

Noah chooses this moment to spit up on my blouse. I look down at the baby.

"Seriously, dude?"

He coos happily now, kicks his legs. I press back a smile. It's almost as if maybe he likes me. But maybe he just feels better after puking. He *is* soft and warm.

I push past the detective and move toward the house.

"I find myself wondering," says the detective, following close behind. "Your ex was found dead this morning. It's too early for the toxicology report. But it *does* look, according to the medical examiner, as if someone poisoned him. Blue around the mouth, clawing at his throat. No other visible cause of death."

The image jars, but I say nothing, just as Agnes would have advised.

"Now your friend from the brunch is being rushed to the hospital. Her husband said severe stomach pains, loss of consciousness. A seizure."

I move through the threshold, but he's right at my heels. I stop in the door frame, make it clear that he's not welcome inside. He's too close. I can smell his clean scent, feel his heat. I think about running my fingers through that inky black hair. I know it to be soft and silky.

Stop. *Stop.*

"Baa," says Noah. Bad man, that's right. Smart kid.

"In my business, you're always looking for connections," says the detective, rubbing at his stubbled jaw. "The ways in which seemingly separate events are linked."

"Is that what you were looking for the night we first met?"

He moves another step close, and I move back. A dance.

That brief uptick of a smile. "What were *you* looking for?"

"I got what I was looking for."

"I'm flattered."

"Don't be."

It was a particularly seedy bar, the wee hours when it's not yesterday and it's not tomorrow. There was some classic rock ballad on the jukebox. The bathroom mirror had a big crack in it, and when I caught my reflection there, I looked like a cubist version of myself, fractured and strange. Holding on to him, I let him take me hard and desperate against the cold porcelain sink. I had a painful bruise on my back afterward.

I've really got to get off that app.

I start to close the door, but he places his foot there to stop me.

We might have had a drink together after, even maybe laughed a little about how crazy it was to meet people like this—if I hadn't snuck out the back.

"I waited," he says. "You took off. Something I said?"

He never said anything about being a cop. Of course he wouldn't. And I never said anything about being dumped by my boyfriend, or how sometimes I meet people on the app just to feel something, anything, even if it's the tingling fear of risk, or the thrill of risky behavior of which Vera would vehemently disapprove. Vera would *never* hook up with some random man on an app strictly for no-strings sexual encounters. Not Little Mrs. Perfect Life.

Noah starts squirming in my arms, making unhappy noises.

"It's time for you to go," I say.

A beat. A breath.

"So, as I was saying," he says, slipping back into detective mode. "Today, I have a dead body buried in a shallow grave in the park. Now a young woman rushed to the hospital. At the moment, there's only one obvious connection."

"What's that?"

"You."

Well, I walked right into that one. I offer him a wan smile.

"I'm asking you to leave. Unless you have a warrant, you need to go. I know my rights."

"Of course you do. Everyone does these days thanks to all the crime fiction, podcasts, docu-dramas, what have you."

He pauses a second, our eyes locked, and I find myself thinking about the feel of his lips on my throat. Then he removes his foot. I quickly close the door between us, hard.

"See you at nine tomorrow, Ms. Blacksmith." He raises his voice so that I can hear him through the door.

"With my attorney," I say loudly enough for him to hear.

Noah thinks that's funny, offers me a drooly smile. He's a decent audience. I touch my finger to his nose.

"As is *your right*," says the detective.

I decide to let him have the last word because I'm reeling from this day, exhausted, and, yes, as loathe as I am to admit it—afraid.

I don't have an attorney *per se*. I have a text from Payton saying that her ex—big-shot city defense lawyer Victor Freeman—will take us to the station tomorrow morning. I wonder if my good pal Payton would be as willing to help me if she knew that I slept with Victor very shortly after they broke up. It was just a one-night thing after we'd bumped into each other at that notorious law firm Christmas party, the same night that I met Paul actually, though Paul and I wouldn't hook up for a while. I just hoped they didn't get back together because then I'd have to carry this dirty little secret to their wedding, their kid's baptism, birthday parties, whatever. This is an example (okay, another example) of the behavior that Vera says needs improvement. *Consequences, Ana! It's like you have the frontal lobe development of a twelve-year-old boy.*

Now at the station tomorrow I'll have slept with both of the men in the interrogation room. Relationship status: complicated.

"Good night, Detective," I say because I know he's still standing there.

There's a moment, with him on one side of the door and me on the other, when I could see my way to opening it and letting him inside. Not to search the premises. But to let his hands roam my body. To tell him everything. He seems so familiar. I feel like he's known to me, and I am known to him. But that's just fantasy, right? We're strangers. Maybe even enemies.

Question your impulses. More advice from the shrink.

Noah makes another unhappy noise, reaches out and grabs a big fistful of my hair, yanking painfully.

"Easy, tiger," I say, unfurling his little fingers.

Babies and therapists. Major cock-blocks.

"Good night, Ms. Blacksmith."

I watch out the side window as Bandeau walks down the path and gets in his car.

Finally, he drives away, the other vehicles clearing, the police cruiser included. It was just an ambulance call, someone sick needing medical attention. There's no reason for the police to be here except maybe protocol, or because they had nothing better to do on a slow Sunday night.

Still, I'm jumpy, edgy. Are they coming back? Will they bring a warrant? Will they want to search *my* apartment? I had better get back there at some point and clean up.

That detective is going to be a problem.

Now Noah is bobbing his head toward my breast with an open mouth. It takes me a second to get it.

Oh.

I find the bottle in the fridge, then pop it in the warmer the way Iggy showed me. Feeding him, it turns out, is easy and a decent distraction. He rests in my arms, and sucks away like a little gremlin, feet kicking. The kitchen is bright and big box store chic, everything white and flat, stainless steel appliances. But it is all cheap, shiny on the outside, particle board on the inside. Not like at Vera's where everything might as well be carved from marble—bespoke cabinetry, lavish walk-in closets, an espresso machine that cost more than a trailer home.

Iggy is prone to those little signs with inspirational sayings. *You have to look through the rain to see the rainbow*, in bold type on a dish towel hanging from the oven handle. *Sing like no one is listening* on a little wooden key rack by the door leading to the garage.

Poor Iggy. She's always been so desperate to make lemonade out of the lemons life has served her, over and over. It was only after we knew each other for a while that I would learn that her young life was almost as unstable and chaotic as mine and Vera's.

I'm thinking, wheels turning.

Stomach cramps, loss of consciousness, seizure. Solanine,

the active ingredient in deadly nightshade, is a possibility. Foxglove, a digitoxin, might also present first as an upset stomach—vomiting, cramps, dizziness. I flash on the open drawer in The Kitchen, the missing hemlock.

I am mentally running through the brunch menu, when a horrible smell wafts up from the little monster.

I *am not* changing him. No way.

"That's where I draw the fucking line, kid."

I swear he winks at me.

I rise quickly, leave the bottle in the sink, grab the diaper bag by the door. Something catches my eye on the counter. Iggy's phone. I grab it and stuff it in my pocket. Then I'm buckling the little stinko into the car seat in the back of Brock and Iggy's car. I roll down the windows, all of them, and head to the hospital.

Poison, Agnes always said, is a woman's weapon. Because female power must be subtle, a secret. It must hide itself in whispers and spells, incantations and prayers. And harmful substances are all around us, often masquerading as something beautiful, a pretty flower you might put in a vase, one that might grow peacefully in your garden.

The herbalist embraces her female side, in that she nurtures a garden, uses her skills and the earth to produce, to bring life. The herbalist heals, using nature's gifts to soothe and even cure. But some plants are more deadly than any venomous creature, any gun or knife you might wield. It's stealthy. Like a snake in the grass, you'll never see it coming. And by the time you're bitten, it might already be too late.

When I get to the hospital, I find Brock slumped in the ER waiting room, eyes rimmed red. He's been crying, which I suppose is appropriate but fills me with disgust.

"How is she?" I say, coming to stand in front of him. Noah is squirmy and smelly in my arms. Brock rises and I shove the baby at him.

"I don't know," he says, taking Noah, who pumps his legs in delight. "No one has come out."

"He needs to be changed."

He nods, takes the diaper bag, and walks off looking shell-shocked. If there's anything I can't tolerate it's male weakness.

"Kindness isn't weakness," Iggy said about Brock just after I dumped him. I was listing his many flaws and all the things about him that had grown to annoy me. I should have known she had her sights on him. In fact, maybe I did know that, and that's why I initially wanted him.

"Strength isn't just about power," she said. "It takes strength to love someone well."

But that sounded like one of her insipid inspirational plaques.

The emergency room stinks of blood, illness, and fear. I gaze around at the mess of humanity. Everyone here is in a state of disrepair. A thin frightened-looking young girl holds an ice pack to her bruised head. An old woman coughs wetly in the corner. We're so fragile, aren't we? Our bodies so susceptible to breaking down. I feel a rush of fear and sadness, which I tamp down with anger.

Brock returns with the baby, who has gone quiet, head lolling against his father's shoulder. Noah rubs at his eyes with a tiny fist. He's tired; it's way past his bedtime.

"I fed him," I say. I touch his fat little hand and he grabs for my finger and holds on tight.

Ew. I'm not going to start liking this little brat. It's bad enough that I have "feelings" for Coraline and Grant, the little terrorists who literally take up every bit of Vera's emotional bandwidth.

Noah reaches for me, and I grudgingly take him. He nestles in, rests his head against my chest.

"How about that?" says Brock with an unpleasant smirk. "You *are* human."

There's bitterness between us, an edge. He wishes Iggy and I weren't friends. Maybe he wonders if we compare notes on his sexual prowess, or lack thereof. We don't. Iggy refuses to dish on Brock, even when she's drunk.

"My mom's on her way," he says when I don't bother to respond. "She'll take Noah."

"Good," I say. The baby suddenly feels five pounds heavier in my arms and he's a little chunker to begin with. I look down and he's fast asleep.

"What happened at that brunch, Ana?" Brock is looking at me, suspicion etching lines between his thick brows. "She was fine before she went."

But then the doctor is approaching, a hot, young Indian guy with dark skin and a lustrous mane of black hair. I notice a simple gold wedding ring. Not a deal breaker.

"I'm Dr. Pavesh," he says to Brock. "I'm afraid we've had to intubate your wife. She's in a coma."

"Oh, god," moans Brock.

The doctor keeps talking, the room spinning.

Low blood pressure.

Loss of kidney and liver function.

"Can you tell me what she's had to eat in the last twenty-four hours?"

All eyes are on me. "I don't know," I say, voice rasping. "I wasn't paying attention at brunch."

"Maybe we can get a list of items that were served?"

"Of course," I manage. "My sister was hosting. I'll call her."

They let us back to see her. In the intensive care unit, she looks like a puppet, pretty and still, with tubes from her arms, her mouth. A machine is breathing for her, its mechanical sigh filling the room. A rhythmic beeping assures us she's still alive.

I take her cool, delicate hand. Brock has taken the baby and stands in the corner, crying again.

It's just the two of us, like it used to be. Just Iggy and Ana, no secrets between us, inseparable, devoted. I guess that was a long time ago. We've both changed.

For some poisons, there's no antidote. You just have to treat the symptoms and hope the body survives the toxins' ravages.

"I'm sorry," I whisper so no one can hear me.

Brock is sniffling behind me. A pretty blonde charge nurse comes in and takes the baby from his arms. "He can't be in here," she tells him. He reluctantly lets her take the baby, and then we're alone, the sound of Noah squalling growing fainter. Nurses crowd around him outside the door; soon the baby is smiling, and his adoring audience coos.

Brock stands behind me now. "What happened at the fucking brunch, Ana?"

I shrug, looking at Iggy's blue-veined eyelids, her jutting cheekbones. "I don't know. Nothing. It was just mimosas and girl talk until that detective came."

"What did she eat?" he hisses.

But my head is spinning, words jammed in my throat. Paul is dead. Iggy's gravely ill. Shallow grave. Coma. This is bad. Really bad.

"I wasn't paying attention."

"Well, that tracks, doesn't it? Because you're only ever thinking of yourself."

I've never seen him like this—angry, afraid. Even when we broke up, there was no heat, no yelling or harsh words. Just: *If that's what you want, Ana, I'll respect it.*

"That's not true," I protest, even though of course it is. But he's already turned back to Iggy.

I edge toward the door. Brock sits down beside the bed, takes her hand, presses it to his lips. He doesn't even seem to notice me slipping out the door, his focus on his wife so total now, his questions of me forgotten.

Down the hallway, his mother—who always disliked me—is marching toward the room. A domineering, thick-bodied hausfrau, she'll take over here. I give a quick glance at the gaggle of nurses cooing over the baby, move quickly in the other direction.

Then I'm outside in the dark, cold night. Another ambulance is approaching, sirens bleating.

I take their car again and hum out of the lot, heading where I always do when the shit hits the fan.

To Vera.

VERA

The first time the police came to Agnes's door, we'd been living with her a year. We'd been dropped off by the bus and wandered up the long driveway toward the house.

Surprisingly, we'd both adjusted to the new school fairly well. Ana was guaranteed to be popular everywhere she went: beauty, charm, a titanium backbone. And I was happy to linger in her shadow, a good student, teacher's pet. We were survivors. Our parents were gone; the pain of it had formed us. Ana had nightmares. I slept too little, the night haunted by memories and fear. But we moved ahead, as we knew Sadie would have wanted. *Be strong, girls. This world has no patience for weakness.*

When we turned the corner, there was a black-and-white cruiser parked in front of the house. I felt Ana freeze as I stopped in my tracks. By that point, we were accustomed to visitors. They came at all hours, often in the middle of the night, would talk with Agnes in hushed tones at the kitchen table. Most often women, occasionally men. Once a boy.

But we hadn't seen a police cruiser since Sadie and Mac were alive. In our other life, the police would come to our house often, called by worried neighbors when things got loud. And their arrival always brought some mingling of dread and relief. It meant an end to the evening's violence. Sadie would turn on the charm. Mac, if she'd convinced them that all was well, would be contrite. *I'm sorry. I'm sorry, baby.*

But I also knew, long before it actually happened, that one day things could get so bad that they'd come and take Mac away for good. Or us.

Until that late spring afternoon, I never thought about what would happen to us if something happened to Aunt Agnes. Our situation was far from perfect, but it was safe, manageable. Agnes loved us in her way, and she let us be.

"What's happening?" asked Ana. She grabbed my hand.

"Nothing," I said. "Probably nothing."

I peered inside the cruiser. There was a computer mounted on the dash, a radio, a notebook on the passenger seat. There was a picture of a woman and two small boys, wrinkled and creased, held to the driver's side visor with a rubber band. A shotgun was mounted on the grate that separated the front of the car from the back. It was like another world in there, a place of black-and-white, right and wrong.

I looked across to see Ana peering in the other window with wonder.

Inside the house, maybe I expected to see Agnes in cuffs, like one of the nights they took my father away, when Sadie's bleeding nose or blackened eye belied her claims that everything was fine. Instead, Agnes was sitting at the kitchen table with a beefy older man with a white head of hair and tired eyes. They spoke quietly, both going silent and then turning in our direction as we entered the room.

"Girls," said Agnes. "This is Little Valley Police Chief Royer. He's an old friend."

He stood, seemed huge, with his Kevlar vest beneath his flannel shirt and denim jacket, big gun holstered at his waist. He shook each of our hands with his big bear paw.

"Vera, Ana, you go to school with my boy, Chuck."

Chuck was one of those golden boys, star athlete, heartthrob, a senior graduating with honors, dating the homecoming queen. We both nodded.

"Well," he said, looking back and forth between us. There was something about him—a quiet seeing that made me squirm. "I'd best be getting on. Agnes, you let me know if you think of anything else."

"Of course."

And then he was gone. We were all quiet as we listened to the engine start, then the car pulling away.

"He just had some questions," said Agnes after he'd gone, answering a query neither of us had dared issue.

"About?"

"A girl from your school. She got ill from food poisoning. Seems she missed cheerleading tryouts and another girl got the spot. Her mother suspected foul play, went to the police."

Agnes's visitors came often late at night, but every so often we'd get home from school, and someone would be sitting where Chief Royer had been. Maybe pale with anger. Maybe crying. We knew enough to scuttle by, not ask questions. In the night, we might sit at the top of the stairs and listen. Most often Agnes's visitors weren't local, came from far away. Sometimes Agnes spoke to them on the phone. The next day maybe a package would go out in the mail. These visitors were the people who came to Agnes for her help.

Not everyone needs a permanent solution, she taught us. *Some just need a leg up, a head start, a way out of the situation they're in.*

"Daphne?" asked Ana.

It was all the buzz at school, how Daphne projectile vomited at the lunch table, was moaning in the nurse's office with stomach cramps. Her period came. A gusher, she bled through her clothes.

Agnes frowned, put her finger to her lips. "Shh. No names. Not in any diary you may keep, not on your tongue."

"What did you do?" asked Ana without heat, just curious.

"What she did, she did to herself," said Agnes, taking a sip from the cup in front of her. I could smell licorice root, her favorite tea.

Agnes had a code, but it was less a set of metrics than it was a feeling. Does this person truly need my help? How can I do the least harm? Does the help I offer this person outweigh the harm I am going to cause someone else? She made her decisions quickly and never changed her mind. She never regretted the consequences or collateral damages. *My remedies are organic, and like nature they are powerful and sometimes unpredictable. When you agree to avail yourself of these recipes you assume all the risk.*

"The girl was pregnant," said Agnes, setting her cup down. "She is no longer."

"And she's no longer the captain of the cheerleading team," I said.

Agnes nodded slowly, holding my eyes. "Our actions often have unintended consequences, girls. You make a choice, and it alters the course of your life, or the life of someone else. You change one thing, and you can't predict what else will change because of it."

Agnes was a good teacher, and I was her willing student. I miss her, even now, though I wouldn't say I ever really loved her. Or forgave her.

In my "mom tank" as Coraline calls it, I roll down the drive, glancing back at the warm, glowing windows of our house, the lit landscaping. I have worked hard for the relative safety and peace of this life. I would be lying if I didn't say I resented Ana sometimes for her various dramas. Or whoever mucked with the fire protection system, the damage such an event can do to our livelihood. I should be focused on helping Brad with damage control, keeping our company in the black, not on my sister's latest mess.

But here we are.

I turn onto the road to town. I am a careful driver, slow and always following the rules. I don't push the speed limit. I make a full stop at stop signs even when there's no one else on the road. Where am I going?

I'd like to start at Paul's place, but I have no explainable reason to go there. If the police are watching his place, I'll have some talking to do about why I've turned up hours after he was discovered murdered. Not the actions of someone unconnected to the crime.

The park where the hapless hikers discovered the body would be my next choice. But all the same concerns apply.

Then, where? It's been a while since I had to clean up after Ana. I'm out of practice. I guess I'll start at her place. I have the keys, know that she's not home. No one would question my right or reason to be at my sister's place.

As I turn in that direction, my phone chimes three times. The messages from Ana pop up on the dashboard screen, one after another.

Iggy's sick. She's in a coma.

The doctors want to know what she ate at brunch.

Something's going on. Something bad.

My stomach bottoms out. Shit. Who brought what? Who *ate* what? *What* is happening?

"Hey, Siri, text Ana," I say. "Meet me."

Her reply is quick, desperate in its single syllable. **Where?**

"Lisander's," I say and watch the message bubble populate.

When she doesn't answer, I take it as an affirmative. I make the next right, and head toward the house of Agnes's mentee. No need to call ahead. Like Agnes, Lisander is always ready to answer the door at any hour.

As I make my way there my phone rings with Coraline's signature tone, the theme from *Stranger Things*. I didn't announce my departure, figuring I wouldn't be missed—since no one usually comes looking for me unless they need something.

I answer the call and see Coraline's pretty face fill the screen.

"Where are you?" she asks.

"I had an errand. Do you need something?"

"I forgot I'm supposed to make something for Spanish class tomorrow."

"Make something?"

"Like food."

This is one of those moments when I usually get annoyed, say something I shouldn't. I try the child shrink's technique. *Stop. Breathe. Be.*

"Okay," I say. "How are you going to solve that problem?"

See. That's how good I am at this now.

She's opening and closing cabinets in the kitchen. I glance at the phone to see she's put it down on the counter.

"There's rice. And black beans. I'll just make that."

Basic, lazy, but okay.

"Mom?"

"Yeah, kiddo."

"Is something wrong? Is Ana in trouble?" I forget how young Coraline is because she's so smart, so wily. But it wasn't that long ago that I had to lie on the floor next to her bed while she fell asleep because she was afraid to close her eyes.

"I heard you say that you had to take her to the police station tomorrow."

"We have a good lawyer. It will be okay."

"Did she?" She leaves the rest of the question unspoken. And I feel a fresh wash of anger for Ana, who has taught Coraline things I didn't want her to learn. Not yet. Maybe not ever.

"No," I say firmly. "No."

I almost believe it.

"Can I help?" she asks. "Is there anything I can do? To help Ana?"

The question makes me go a little cold. What is she asking? "Like what?"

She's quiet for a moment. "I don't know."

"Better get cooking," I say. "It's late."

"When are you coming home?"

"Soon. I love you. I'll come tuck you in when I get back."

"Love you."

She ends the call, and I consider turning around, leaving Ana to handle her own mess and face Lisander alone. But I keep driving, thinking about my daughter and what she meant by "can I help?"

Lisander's sprawling Victorian is dark. But as I approach a light goes on upstairs. I know that there is a motion sensor camera at the gate through which I just passed. Her phone would have chimed, alerting her to my arrival. I envision her climbing from bed, putting on her robe, and heading downstairs.

As I bring the car to a stop, Lisander's generous form fills a downstairs window. By the time I've stepped onto the porch, she opens the door. Clad in a long nightgown and flannel robe, she reminds me startlingly of Agnes. Maybe it's the long unapologetically gray hair, the fragrant softness of her embrace, the cool discernment of her dark-eyed gaze.

She idolized my Aunt Agnes. So maybe it's no surprise that she emulates her.

"What is it?" she asks with concern, ushering me through the door. "What's happened?"

She's always been good to us, even though our arrival into Agnes's life disrupted hers. Before we came, Agnes was her mentor, giving Lisander all her knowledge. Lisander doted on Agnes, more like a daughter than a student. But after we came, so broken and in need, Agnes's attention was necessarily diverted to us. As we grew, Lisander graciously became our teacher, as well. Even later, when Agnes made a choice that clearly showed her favoritism, Lisander never faltered in her care of us.

If she missed what she had with Agnes before we arrived, she didn't show it, was Agnes's devoted friend and student until the end.

In her warm kitchen, I sit at the long wooden table where we've gathered for meals and meetings over the years, and tell Lisander about Paul and Iggy while she brews a pot of tea, listening.

We stay silent with it as the kettle comes to a boil, both of us thinking. The copper pots hanging over the oven gleam, picking up the dim light. Over by the big bay window, there's a small indoor greenhouse where Lisander grows herbs in winter, the glass fogged with humidity. Along the counter there are large glass jars of dried flowers, leaves, sprigs, berries—lavender, elderberry, white sage, licorice root.

In a stack, by the big cauldron that always sits on the stovetop, are her leather-bound volumes of recipes, drawings, notes, so like Agnes's. Lisander's specialty is healing teas for all ailments from anxiety to indigestion, from women's troubles to the common cold. If you have a problem, Lisander has a brew. I've come here often for the blend she makes for flu, which she calls Flame, because it heats away illness. It's her proprietary recipe of elderberry, echinacea, licorice root, lemon balm, yerba santa, slippery elm, and other herbs that even I can't discern just by taste. With its immune-boosting and antiseptic properties, it cures what ails you—from sore throat to lingering cough.

Tonight, it's a simple blend of fresh spearmint and peppermint, reviving, refreshing. The aroma fills the cozy kitchen.

"So, Paul, Ana's ex," says Lisander finally as she pours the brewed fresh mint tea into dainty porcelain cups. "Iggy, Ana's best friend."

"That's right," I say as she comes to the table with a tray, sets it on the old wood.

"Who was at the brunch?"

"I was there, of course. Ana, Esme, Payton, Iggy. April was there to serve."

"And the menu?"

I run it down. The quiche, the Waldorf salad, the elaborate charcuterie board, all catered from local places in town. Ana's cassoulet. Esme's special meal. Iggy's cookies.

Lisander drops a single sugar cube into my cup, just the way I like it. The scent of mint wafts pleasantly. She sits across the table from me, chair creaking. She has the bearing of an earth mother, welcoming bosom, high color in her cheeks, powerful arms. She was Agnes's most beloved student, her best friend. What is she to us now? We've called on her help more than once since Agnes has passed.

"Any issues between Ana and Iggy?"

"Not that I'm aware," I say. "I mean other than Iggy married Ana's *other* ex, Brock. And Iggy just had a baby that's annoyingly taking attention from Ana."

I think of Iggy's baby, Noah, still breastfeeding, his mother in a coma, and feel a crush on my heart.

Lisander raises her eyebrows at me.

"She wouldn't," I say quickly. "She loves Iggy."

Loves. Whatever that means to Ana, who can love you and still manage to dislike you sometimes, become magnificently annoyed with you. Betray you. Then save you.

"They've been best friends since college. Even if anything, that's against the code." I'm talking too much. Anxiety.

"Our Ana," says Lisander with a grim smile. "Not exactly a rule follower."

This is true. Lisander and I have had to clean up her messes before. Last time, Ana was nearly expelled from The Cove.

"It wasn't her," I say, that powerful instinct to protect and defend rising. "She was *over* Paul. And she dumped Brock long before he and Iggy got together. They asked her blessing. She was happy for them, in her way. As happy as Ana can be for anyone but herself."

The chime sounds and Lisander glances at her phone. "She's here."

I feel a tension I didn't know I was carrying release from my shoulders. Ana's here, where I can protect her from herself.

Lisander leans across the table and grabs my hand. "You won't be able to defend her to The Cove again. You know that. And you'll have to answer for it, too, if you've involved yourself with her mess."

I nod, a dump of dread in my gut, a cold finger of fear down my spine. Anger at Ana is an eternal flame. I love my sister, but she's put us all in danger too many times.

We sit in silence a moment before Ana blusters in. She brings in with her a burst of anxious energy, the scent of a homemade floral perfume made from essential oils. She looks frazzled, hair a wild raven cloud, still wearing what she had on at brunch today.

"I know what you two are thinking," she says, dropping her bag on the counter. She gets a cup from the cupboard. "I did not do this. I swear."

Again, I find myself believing her. The truth is since the last time, she's been on the straight and narrow. She has been building her business, *is* slowly getting her finances in order with our help. Until he turned up dead, she seemed to be taking the breakup with Paul pretty well.

"There are plenty of people who hated Paul," says Ana, sitting heavily beside me.

"Like whom?" I ask.

"Like *everyone*. In fact, I can't think of a single person who liked him except for his new girlfriend. And it was only a matter of time before she realized he was a malignant narcissist."

"But who specifically might want him dead?" I press. "To what end?"

She makes a point of counting off on her manicured fingers,

blue eyes flashing. "Esme hated him. Payton had *multiple* run-ins with him. Didn't Brad have some kind of professional dispute with him?"

"Don't even," I say, putting up a palm. I need to keep Brad and the business as far away from this as possible. We have our own problems.

But. Yes, that's right. Paul did use his relationship with Ana to try to pitch his advertising firm to Brad. There was a meeting, but Brad declined his services. Mainly because I said no; never a good idea to get into bed with Ana's boyfriends. There's no telling what the blowback will be. Obviously.

Paul didn't take it graciously. Started badmouthing Brad and the company to clients. So, no, Paul wasn't Brad's favorite. Or mine. But when I told him about Paul's death, he didn't even know who I was talking about at first. My husband doesn't hold a grudge.

I, on the other hand, do.

"I'm just saying," she says, looking at me sheepishly. She's tapping her finger annoyingly on the table. I put my hand on hers to stop it. A little too hard. She gives me a pout, pulls her hand back.

"His sister," she says, eye widening. "She immediately put the police onto me. But Paul and Regina were in some kind of a legal tangle over their parents' will."

"Oh?" Lisander and I say in unison, both leaning forward.

That could be something. People get more murderous over money than over almost any other issue. And speaking strictly from experience, there's not a person alive who can press your buttons like your sibling.

"What was the dispute exactly?" I ask.

"I don't know. I wasn't paying attention. But they were fighting about it." I note the circles of fatigue under her eyes, the worried set of her mouth. This is not like her. Usually, she's ice. "He owed her a lot of money, too."

Lisander is watching Ana carefully. I'm not sure I love the expression on her face. Distrust, concern. She wrings her hands, seems to catch herself, then folds them on the table in front of her.

Ana is tapping again. "Also! One of the women Paul was accused of harassing at his old firm couldn't drop it. She was social media stalking him, leaving angry messages on his voicemail. She took a payout from the firm and signed an NDA, but apparently that didn't do it for her."

"Yes, *so* inconvenient when victims won't be easily bought off," says Lisander darkly.

"But she *did* take the money," says Ana.

Lisander scowls. "Maybe she *needed* the money because she couldn't get a job in her industry after the harassment case. Because that's what happens when women come forward. The men skate away, and the women are psychologically damaged, find their earning potential decreased, other companies suddenly reluctant to hire them."

"Okay, she was still pissed. Rightly so. So maybe *she* killed him."

"What was her name?" I ask.

"I don't remember."

"Find out."

She nods.

"And what about Iggy?"

A flash of sadness ripples across Ana's doll-like features. She wraps her arms around her middle. "I don't know what happened. An accident? A virus? Everyone loves Iggy."

That's true; even I like Iggy. It's hard to think of anyone more harmless and normie than Iggy with her aluminum tray of dairy-free, gluten-free cookies, so sweet and thoughtful. Ana's opposite in so many ways. An odd friendship, but they seem to complement each other. Iggy can calm Ana like no one else. Ana connects Iggy to her inner fire, her birthright. Ignatia means *fiery one*.

Truthfully, though, their friendship has been strained since

Iggy married Brock, especially since they had Noah. There was some other argument, too. So maybe Ana is angry at her on some level, jealous and looking to create damage.

I look at my sister and for some reason remember how she used to climb into bed with me at night. For all her wildness, just a scared little girl, looking for safety.

"So, lots of possible suspects," I say. "We just have to move the detective in one of those directions and away from you."

Something flashes across Ana's face—fear, guilt? It's gone before I can read it.

"Let's hope the other members of The Cove don't draw any unfortunate conclusions," says Lisander, leaning back. There's something about the way she says it that gives me a chill.

Ana has the good sense to look a little scared. "I didn't do this. Any of it."

"But after everything, what are the chances anyone believes that?" says Lisander.

I reach for my sister's hand again. It's cold. She squeezes tight.

The Cove is a self-governing body of herbalists and healers. At one point, Agnes was at the helm. Lisander was next in line to take her place. But before Agnes's death, she named someone else to succeed her. Someone who didn't want the seat. So, there's been a kind of council running The Cove, with Lisander as the default leader since she has the most experience.

Under new leadership, the rules are strict. Their punishments unforgiving. If Ana has broken code again, we'll both be in trouble.

The three of us sit in silence for a moment. The hanging pots knock softly against each other in a draft, making a low clatter that sounds vaguely like voices.

"Payton called," says Ana into the heavy silence. "Our appointment with the detective is at 9:00 a.m. Victor will pick you up, then me."

"Ana," says Lisander. There's antipathy between them, always has been. They were in competition with each other for Agnes's favor. Ana's natural talent drawing Agnes's admiration in a way that Lisander's devotion to The Knowledge didn't seem to.

Ana's too impulsive, Agnes told me. *Lisander maybe lacks her gifts, but she makes up for it with diligence, with care. Vera, you are the natural person to lead The Cove when I am gone.*

Never, I told her. *I don't want this life.*

Some of us don't get to choose. We are chosen.

You can't make me into something I'm not.

And you can't turn away from the truth of your heritage. The Cove needs you, Vera.

This was a very typical row between Agnes and me; it's not lost on me that Coraline and I have a similarly heated argument now, just with the sides reversed. And my daughter is every bit as stubborn and immoveable as I am.

"Ana," says Lisander again.

Ana is staring at her phone now, purposely ignoring her. Who is she texting with? If I know my sister, she probably already has another boyfriend. She's never gone more than a few weeks in her adult life without a man.

"If there's something you need to tell us," Lisander goes on, even though Ana doesn't acknowledge her, "do it now while we can still fix this."

Ana looks up, wraps her arms around her middle again. "*Somebody* was at Agnes's. In her office and in the garden. There are materials missing. The hemlock stores were depleted."

I feel a little jolt of alarm. "What? Who was there?"

"How should I know?" Her voice has gone a little shrill. "Who has access? You do and I do. That's it, right?"

She looks at Lisander, who is frowning deeply, hands wringing again. Ana dangles her key ring. "My key is right here. I always have it with me."

Mine is on a hook in the laundry room by the door to the garage. I tell her as much.

"So," she says. "Anyone at the brunch might have taken it. Or anyone who has access to your house. The maid. The handyman. The kids, their friends. Brad, anyone who comes to his poker games."

For some reason my conversation with Coraline rings back. *Can I help?* What did she mean? Could she have made the doll I found on my porch? And if so, what else is she up to?

I shake my head. "No."

But yes, that's true. I should have safeguarded that key. But I have let thoughts of Agnes and The Cove drift away. My life is busy, grounded in the now, rooted in the immediate care of my family and our life—the meals, the house, the kids' various mini-dramas. I don't have time for The Cove. I don't think much about cures and salves, tinctures and potions. Today is the first time I've been in the basement in ages. Though I keep my hand in with various healing teas, which I make with herbs from Agnes's garden. I certainly don't think about what Agnes called "cures." I don't think about poison.

"Is the key there now?" asks Ana.

"Of course." I'd have noticed if it was gone. Wouldn't I?

She looks back and forth between Lisander and me. "Why are you two always willing to think the worst of me?"

Lisander lets out a little laugh. "Are you really asking that, Ana?"

Ana stands. Her icy veneer is back. "I didn't do this and I'm going to find out who did."

She grabs her bag and moves toward the door.

"Be careful," I say. Because what else can I say? She's a grown woman; she'll do what she wants, what she needs to do. I can't save Ana from her worst excesses. Lord knows I have tried. "And be ready when Victor and I pick you up tomorrow."

She pauses, doesn't turn around, then keeps walking, closing the door behind her with a quiet click.

"She's been trying," I say. "She's matured. A lot."

"I hope you're right. For all of our sakes."

Lisander's expression is stern, her bearing steely. There's a coldness to her that Agnes never had. Ana's headlights sweep the room, then disappear.

I feel the first lick of real fear.

Our appointment with Detective Bandeau tomorrow is quite frankly the least of our worries.

AGNES

The girls are quick studies, with more natural aptitude and discipline than either Sadie or I had at their ages. Sadie was always boy crazy; she liked to party. I was, as my mother never failed to point out, essentially lazy as a young person, more prone to daydreaming and getting lost in romance novels than I was to learning about horticulture, herbology, floriography, chemistry, biology.

"Agnes," my mother would chide. "Join us in the real world."

But Vera is a straight-A student, and Ana is fiercely competitive with her sister, never to be outdone. So, they sit still, attentive, scribbling. In the garden, they follow directions with care, are gentle with the plants. Ana has the gift; I can see it. Vera does as well, but she also has the discipline, the aptitude. Talent is not enough for what I need from the girls. There must also be strength, self-control, wisdom.

We're in the greenhouse. The day outside is cold, snow in patches on the ground, but it's warm and humid in here.

This is my favorite place; somehow it always seems magical, apart from the rest of the world. Green and moist, it is like an eternal spring, safe from the white and gray of winter desiccation. Most of the plants in here are harmless, bred only for their beauty. With the flowers from here and in my garden, I create bespoke boutonnieres, corsages, and bridal bouquets to supplement my income and to provide a legitimate business cover for my other activities. The irony of this cover profession, town florist, bringer of beauty and joy, is not lost on me. Then again, life and nature are nothing but dichotomy. The most beautiful flower, or lushest ripe fruit, can kill. The rot of compost is black gold for the hungry roots of plants. What looks to the untrained eye like a pile of twigs can be powerful medicine.

Vera and Ana have been quiet, careful since Chief Royer paid his visit. The Knowledge and its dangerous power is only just starting to dawn.

The girl Daphne had come to me during the school day. She'd stayed home sick and walked the long distance between her house and mine. A friend had told her about the tea that can end a very early pregnancy, a potent blend of pennyroyal, mugwort, blue cohosh, and bitter parsley, among other things. I generally don't deal with children, and at seventeen she was exactly that.

"They'll kill me," she said, shivering at my table. "My parents. They'll never forgive me for this."

Something about the way she said it, about how pale and afraid she was. Normally, I'd counsel her to talk to her mother, even offer to help her have the conversation. Once upon a time, a woman had no choice but to harm herself to end a pregnancy; now there are safe and legal ways to do so, a right we've fought for and won. But I sensed there was something else, something Daphne didn't want to share. She was poised, in possession of herself, and had the bearing of a much older person. It was clear to me that she'd made her choice.

"The levels of toxin required to end your pregnancy could also be harmful to you. You will, at the very least, be extremely ill," I warned.

She nodded, her strawberry-blond hair framing her freckled face, her pouty pink mouth. She twisted at a silver locket she wore around her slender neck.

In this culture, we don't have dominion over our bodies, not really. We are not allowed to say when we will die. As women, we have often been prohibited from preventing or terminating pregnancy, as if our bodies were just vessels to be filled by men.

My work is to give people, women especially, back their power.

I went to the kitchen and retrieved a bundle of the tea from my stores. It is by far my bestselling cure. I ship it all over the country for "menstrual discomfort." In history, women have died from drinking this blend, but never from mine. It is ancient, this brew, with stories of its use in texts from China, India, and the African and Latin American continents. Over my years of study, I have refined my recipe. But I would never claim that it's safe or even always effective.

Nature and the human body, the mind and the spirit, how they all mingle, is an unpredictable tangle. Modern medicine will claim that they have it all worked out with their processes of chemical synthesis. They don't.

I told all this to Daphne, and she seemed to understand. She looked at the bundle in her hand, then up at me.

"Am I a bad person?" she asked.

She was so young. And already she'd internalized the message that as women we are not allowed to choose the course of our lives, that we belong to our parents, then to men, then to our children. That we're not allowed to say yes, or no, that we will or won't.

"It's your body, your life," I told her. "You choose the course."

She nodded uncertainly, staring down at the muslin pouch in her palm. "How will I know if it worked?"

"You'll know," I told her. I gave her instructions. Told her how to dispose of the tea bag when she was done. She lingered a moment as if uncertain. Then she nodded, offered a payment that I refused, and then she left. I watched her disappear down the path. I don't usually doubt myself, but then again, I don't usually deal with children. Twice I almost called her back. Finally, I just let her go. I believe strongly that a woman should have dominion over her body, even a young woman who is not necessarily of legal age, another thing determined by men.

Now I feel the heat of Vera's gaze.

"You nearly killed Daphne," she says. It's like she's been carrying it. Waiting for the right moment to set it down.

She's tying a bundle of pink, white, and red tea roses with a skein of blush ribbon. Ana's working on a boutonniere, clipping thorns from *white roses, wrapping the stems in floral tape. A young bride and groom are to be married in the park this afternoon.*

"There are risks associated with the cures," I say, touching a gentle finger to a rose petal. The rose is a bit hackneyed, but I appreciate its perfect beauty, its delicacy. Its oils are healing if brewed fresh in tea, soothing for skin, antiseptic, with antibacterial properties.

"And if she'd died?"

"She knew the risks."

"Are you always so sure of yourself?" asks Ana.

What a question. "I'm sure of The Knowledge, the science. I'm aware that things don't always go as planned in this work. That unintended consequences are the norm."

There. A large bouquet for the bride, smaller ones for her bridesmaids. I've carefully removed all the thorns, wrapped the stems. For a wedding day, there should be only beauty, no chance of pain.

Together we place the arrangements in a box designed to hold them. The larger for the bride in the center, surrounded by smaller white and red bouquets for the bridesmaids. The grooms and groomsmen each get a white rose boutonniere, tied with ivory ribbon. The boutonnieres are pinned in a narrow box on greenery. Sometimes I offer the end of something. Today, it's a joyful beginning. The balance of it all gives me some satisfaction.

Vera has gone silent. A lot goes on behind those dark eyes. I can tell she's processing all the layers of this thing we do. Ana is singing quietly to the orchids now. She's not a deep thinker in the same way. Her mind is quick, her conscience easy. The plants seem to turn toward her. She's one with them.

"How much does Chief Royer know?" Vera asks. "Why did he come here?"

My relationship with the chief is complicated. We have a history. He has come to me for various reasons over the years. We have an understanding, a shared past. I've known him since we were children. None of those things explains what I have with him. What he knows about me and what I do. I guess in many ways he's a protector, someone who understands that often the wrong thing might be the right thing. Or so we tell ourselves.

"He wanted to know if anyone had come to me looking to harm Daphne. The truthful answer was no."

"And if someone had, would you have told him that?"

"First, I wouldn't have helped someone looking to harm a child. And second, no, I would not have. The foundation of my practice is—"

She finished my sentence, narrowing her eyes. "Secrecy. Lies."

I correct her gently. "Confidentiality."

Vera remains angry at me for killing her mother. Or rather for providing her the means to end her life rather than live out her days in prison. The bouquet I brought her, brewed in a tea, was her end. The cause of death was found to be heart failure; my bouquet was never suspected. For some of us, sometimes, life is harder, more unpleasant than death—a thing the young rarely understand.

"It's what she wanted," I say, answering the accusation she hasn't voiced.

"You didn't have to give her what she wanted."

She's right.

Almost nightly I dream about my sister. In my dreams, she sips from a cup our mother used for her morning coffee. The bright red mug was hand painted with flowers, a gift from one of my mother's clients. In the dream, Sadie drinks deeply, nearly chugging it.

"Thank you, Agnes," she says. Then she starts to gag. The cup drops, shatters on the ground. As I reach for her, I wake up feeling desperate, hopeless.

I miss my sister terribly, and wish she was still here with me. We weren't always close; we had our battles. But we understood each other. In the end, we followed the code as it was taught to us. But the girls and I have paid a high price. Maybe Vera's right to be angry.

"What's done is done," I say tightly.

My niece stares daggers at me, then storms from the greenhouse, *slamming the door, the panes rattling. I watch as she disappears down the path. The sky has gone gray, threatening rain, as if her temper has brought on a storm.*

"What's wrong with her?" Ana asks. "You only did what she asked. No one forced her to drink that tea."

I'm not sure if she's talking about Sadie or Daphne, maybe both. I stay quiet, tightening the ribbon on the final boutonniere. It's something I think about a lot. Who is to blame? The one who delivers the poison or the one who deliberately takes it?

"If Sadie wanted to live for us, she would have. She left us."

Ana's angry, too, but mostly at Mac and Sadie for making such a mess of it all. She only calls them by their first names when she talks of them. Not Mom and Dad, Sadie and Mac.

"It might be easier for your sister to be mad at me than at your mom," I offer. I feel the sting of tears, blink them back. Though there is much pain in this life, I rarely cry. It's pointless, isn't it? Sadness hobbles. Anger energizes.

Ana nods sagely. "I'll talk to her."

She helps me load up for delivery. The car fills with the scent of roses. As I'm placing them, arranging them just so, I snag my finger on a single thorn I failed to clip from the stem. A drop of blood blossoms dark and fat on my thumb. Ana giggles, girlish.

"You can never get them all, can you?"

No. You can't. For every beautiful thing in this life, there's pain.

TIMOTHY

I spent too much time in a hospital as my father lay dying and, for me, it will always be a place of fear and sorrow. Regret. Things left unsaid.

I stand outside the doorway to Iggy Rose Caine's room, knock on the frame.

Brock Caine's drawn, pale face reminds me too much of the way I felt as my father slowly faded away, nothing anyone could do, monitors beeping, at the end the machine breathing for him. He waves me in; I flash my shield.

Brock's mother, Marge Caine, paces the room, holding the baby who has fallen asleep in her arms. Her lined face is a mask of concern, even as she softly hums to her grandchild.

Usually, we look to the husband when harm comes to the wife. But I don't view Brock Caine as a suspect; his love, his grief and fear are too evident. He's as straight as they come, not even a parking citation or an overdue library book that I can find. And besides, just because it's often the husband, doesn't mean it always is.

The young intern holds Iggy's chart, listing off the various ways in which Iggy's organs are failing, that's she's febrile, that her blood oxygen levels are dropping. That they don't quite understand why. Poisoning or virus could be the cause, but so far nothing conclusive has turned up in her blood. Has she traveled? Walked in the woods? Tick-borne illness is possible. Neurotoxins. Salmonella. Listeria.

Brock and his mother, Marge, seem at a loss.

When the intern leaves us, I stay by the door. It seems wrong to move farther into the room, invasive, but I have questions. And maybe the answers will lead to help for Iggy.

"Sorry to trouble you at a difficult time," I say. "Detective Timothy Bandeau. I'm investigating the murder of Paul Hayes."

Brock looks at me with a furrowed brow. "You think that has something to do with what happened to Iggy?"

I shake my head. "Too soon to say. Just asking questions at this point."

"Was Iggy having any trouble with anyone? Maybe at work?"

Brock looks to Iggy, as if she might answer. "She's been on maternity leave. She wasn't even sure she was going back."

"Did you want her to go back?"

"I mean—" He looks at me earnestly. "I wanted her to do what she thought was best for her and the baby. I want her to be happy with her choices down the road, and for Noah to have everything he needs. She hasn't decided."

"Money issues? Debt?"

"No," he answers. "We're careful with money. She's always been frugal."

A single tear trails. He wipes at it angrily.

"I'm sorry for all the questions." Sometimes I apologize even when I don't have reason to. It seems to make people feel better, more comfortable. And sometimes that helps them to be more open.

He lifts a palm. "No, I get it. You're just being thorough. That's your job."

"Problems in the marriage? Infidelity?"

"No, no." He shakes his head vigorously. "She's the best thing that ever happened to me."

I glance at his mother, but she's focused on the baby. If she has an opinion about her son's marriage, she's keeping it to herself.

"What about Iggy? Angry exes? Anything like that?"

"No, I don't think so. We've both been with other people. But like I said she just had a baby. We've both been home, like all the time. The brunch was one of her first outings without Noah, except a few date nights when we left him with my mom."

"Anybody unstable in *your* past?"

He shrugs, seems reluctant. Then, "I—uh—dated Ana. We broke up long before Iggy and I got together."

I almost let out a laugh. Another connection to Ana Blacksmith; Brock and Ana used to date. Now Brock is married to her best friend, Iggy. Who is currently languishing in a coma. Ana's ex is in the morgue. Are these loose connections enough to get a warrant to search her place? Probably not.

"You found her unstable."

"Maybe not unstable? Just, I don't know, she has a bad temper. I suppose our breakup—well, *she* broke up with *me*—was amicable enough. I got the sense after a while that she just didn't like me all that much, you know? In a lot of ways, if I'm being honest, it was a relief that I didn't have to break up with her. She's a lot."

In my experience, when a man says that a woman is "a lot," it generally means that *he's* not enough, can't handle intensity or passion, intelligence or independence.

I can see that fire in her, how she'd be a lot to handle in a relationship. How she was a lot to handle in a bathroom romp, fiery and passionate, present, lots of biting and nails in my back. I don't mind a little heat. Actually, I enjoy it. I'm still feeling that bite of disappointment when I realized she slipped out the back. I think about the way she looked at me tonight. Fire. But something else. What was it?

"No bad blood there?" I say now.

"No," he says emphatically. "We're all adults, right? Ana was with Paul until—you know—recently. She seemed happy with him. He was maybe more her type."

"What type would that be?" Not strictly a professional interest.

"I think she likes bad boys."

Marge gives a huff but keeps quiet.

"Something to add?" I ask.

"I've known Ana and her sister since they came to live with their Aunt Agnes. And those girls have always been trouble. Especially Ana."

My thoughts turn—again—to our encounter a few weeks ago. Stupid. Careless. I really need to delete that app from my phone. Sex in a bar bathroom with a stranger is behavior that would certainly be frowned upon by my superiors. Probably I should report it, maybe even recuse myself from this investigation.

But embarrassment keeps me from doing so. Plus, I'm the only homicide detective in a sadly underfunded department. We don't even have money in the budget for coffee in the break room. Anyway, it's not relevant to this case, that I randomly slept with someone who later might be a murder suspect. Right? That's what I'm telling myself.

From the pocket of my jacket, I remove my phone and show Brock pictures of the extremely creepy doll we found at the scene. Not really a doll. More of a bound pile of sticks that looks like a human figure. I've dropped the actual item at the lab for analysis.

"Any idea what this is?"

Brock looks at the strange stick figure. The image is grainy, eerie. Does he go even paler? "What *is* that?"

"We found it at the scene where Paul's body was discovered."

He doesn't say anything, just stares at it. It *is* strange and mesmerizing. His mother leans in for a look. She owns an organic herb and vegetable market in town, is vocal at town meetings, formed a committee to clean up some abandoned lots and turn them into community gardens. At the youth center, she teaches the kids about healthy eating. She's one of the people working to save the center, as I am. We've lost funding—an expected donation never came in. And if we don't find money soon, we might have to close the doors. I push those thoughts away for now, though it's a big deal to me. The kids who I work with there really rely on that place as a safe haven. They rely on me.

"The tracker who found it said that it was a voodoo doll," I offer.

Marge snorts. "A voodoo doll," she repeats. "That's ridiculous. It's just a bunch of sticks and leaves."

"Have you ever seen anything like it?" I press.

Marge shakes her head.

"Never?"

"No," she says. "Never."

Brock averts his gaze, watching Iggy. Okay. Change tack.

"Did Iggy have any kind of a history with Paul Hayes?"

Brock releases a deep breath. "They worked together a long time ago. She wasn't a fan. Said he was the kind of guy who was handsy and overly solicitous one day, mean and insulting the next. She warned Ana to stay away from him. But Ana wouldn't listen."

More connections. Ana used to date Brock. Iggy used to work with Paul. Feels *entangled*.

"When was the last time she had contact with him?"

"That I know of? Not for years."

Secrets and lies have a vibration, a kind of hum that sounds beneath all the other sounds.

There's something. What am I missing?

I am about to press about the doll when Iggy's monitor starts beeping wildly, her eyelids fluttering.

"Iggy?" says Brock. He presses the button for the nurse, and footsteps start moving hurriedly up the hall. "Iggy!"

I step outside and leave as the nurses rush in. It seems right to leave. Maybe Iggy can hear us, something we said upsetting her. The young intern comes running, starts barking orders. Soon Iggy is surrounded, Brock pushed away. The baby starts crying, Marge trying to comfort them both.

As I start to leave, I turn and catch Marge's gaze. But she turns away, back to her distressed family.

As I step into the frigid night, my phone pings.

I don't suppose you would believe me if told you I didn't do this.

Ana.
The truth is I don't know what to think about this woman. I only know that I've thought of little else since our first meeting.
Faith is not part of my job, I answer, moving quickly into the warmth of the car. Inside, I start the engine and crank the heat. A few moments pass and I think she's not going to say any more. Then,

What does that mean?

I follow the evidence.

A couple of pings come in quick succession. A link to a blog article. A screen shot of Paul's ConnectIn page. Another screen shot of what looks like an angry text exchange between Paul and someone in his contacts listed as The Witch.

Paul Hayes had a lot of enemies.

The first link is to a website called *Jezebel*, a post entitled *What Happened to #MeToo?* An anonymous writer provides details on how she was harassed at work, took a payout, signed an NDA, and finally had to leave the company anyway because she was "frozen out" and passed over for promotions. Paul Hayes is not mentioned by name. *How are these men still getting away with it?* The article concludes, *When does it end?*

There's a screen shot of an angry post on Paul's professional page. *One day, you're going to pay for things you've done*, someone calling herself Jezebel, same as the site, no picture, threatens. I make a note.

Finally, there's the screen shot of a text chain.

The Witch: I'm tired of asking. You owe me 100K.

Paul: I don't have it.

The Witch: That's bullshit. I don't want this to get ugly.

Paul: What is that supposed to mean?

The Witch: Pay me by the end of the month or you'll find out.

Another threat. The Witch. Jezebel. Is it the same person? Did Paul owe money? Or was he being blackmailed?

I send the links to my Gen Z tech nerd, the only nod our small department has made to the changing times. Birch is young, savvy, too often reduced to IT and keeping our aging computers alive, recovering lost documents. *Can you do your magic with any of this? Real names? Addresses?*

He's also wildly overeager for anything the resembles detective work.

On it! he replies almost instantaneously.

I take a moment to consider how much of my work and communications are digital, how the trails that often lead to the truth are online and not in the real world. Strange how things have changed, how fast. I still think about my childhood, sandy, salty, catching lizards, and getting sunburned. Skim boarding. Always out in nature. Here, I walk the miles of trails, try to immerse myself in the same way, but the phone is always with me now. Has something changed in me that doesn't allow for disconnection anymore?

I think of the voodoo doll, of the woman in the park, the one who disappeared into the woods. Real-world clues that leave no trail I can follow.

A knock on the passenger side window moves through me like an electric shock. I drop my phone.

There she is. A darkly beautiful mirage shimmering in the glass. I hesitate a second, unlock the door, and Ana climbs inside, fills the car with her scent, her energy.

The pull to her is magnetic. I want my lips on hers, her hands in my hair. This is so wrong.

"Did you get my texts?" She tugs at a strand of her hair, then holds her hands up to heat coming from the vents.

"I did."

"Well?" She turns to lock me in her gaze.

I take a breath. "I'm following every lead. I promise you that."

She wraps her arms around her middle, looks suddenly young, vulnerable. I guess she is both of those things. "You haven't just decided it was me?"

"I haven't decided anything."

"He had enemies."

"I'm getting that."

Lithe as a cat, she moves over the center console, straddles me. In spite of every better instinct, I wrap her up in my arms, feel her warmth, her softness.

"We can't do this," I moan, as she presses herself against me.

"I know," she says, breath hot in my ear. "This is bad. Will you come visit me in jail?"

I put my mouth on her delicate throat, feel her life force pulsing there. There's something wild between us, something untamable. And I'm going to lose my job for sure if I don't get it under control. She smells of flowers and sex. *Goddamn.*

"Stop," I say.

She leans back and smiles at me, runs a finger along my cheek. I take her hand, on impulse press it to my lips. "Okay," she says. "No means no, Detective."

And then she's getting out of the car, taking her heat, the frigid night air like a cold shower.

"I'm innocent," she says. "Of this anyway."

Sauntering into the dark, she disappears.

CORALINE

My dad's in the shower, my mom off on whatever errand. Grant is supposedly studying but who knows what he's actually doing, his door closed.

Downstairs, I grab the keys I'm not supposed to use on my own and slip out the door to the garage.

I walk my bike out the side door, don my helmet, and head quickly, quietly into the night. It's freezing and even my puffer jacket doesn't feel warm enough. Agnes's place is just a few miles. There's a hooting owl, and the lights of houses glow orange and warm, as I zip through quiet streets. All in black, I imagine that I'm invisible, a ghost.

My mom tracks me, so if she looks at the app, she'll expect to see me at home. But what she doesn't know is that I have *another* app, which allows me to trick LifeWatch. If my mom looks at LifeWatch, she'll see my last location, home in this case. But the trick only lasts for an hour, so I don't have much time.

At Agnes's, I get off my bike and unlock the gate, push through, then close and relock it behind me.

The driveway up to the house is long and dark. I turn on my little headlight. I am not afraid, though. This place, the nighttime, they don't scare me. I'm not afraid of anything. Or anyone.

The house is quiet, unlit. I pull my bike around the side and walk the rest of the way to The Kitchen, past the garden and the greenhouse.

The night is alive with sound—my crunching footfalls, some skittering in the underbrush, wind in the branches. Winter. It feels like a magical time to me, when everything you see *appears* desiccated and dead, but underneath, a whole other season is preparing to burst forth.

Above me the moon is almost full. The Wolf Moon is nearly here.

In the kitchen, I get to work quickly. I have to make my recipes, get home, and replace the keys before my mother realizes I'm gone.

If she knew how I spent my time, or the things I'm doing, she'd be angry.

So, I take it back. I'm not scared of anything, or anyone.

Except my mom.

TIMOTHY

It's getting late when I pull up to Amanda Alessi's little house in a modest neighborhood in the part of Little Valley that they call The Pink Streets because of the brick roads that characterize it. It's kind of a young, hip enclave nestled between the richer neighborhoods where Vera Blacksmith and her family live, and the more working-class areas—where I happen to live.

The neighboring houses are dark. Somewhere there's the faint sound of windchimes. The smell of pine is heavy in the air.

I push through that wired, vaguely nauseated feeling that comes from too little sleep and too much caffeine. A headache teases behind my eyes. I can still feel her on me. Ana. She's a dangerous distraction. I try to forget her, focus on Amanda.

A few calls around to co-workers we found on social media, and to family and friends, confirmed that no one had heard from Amanda Alessi in a few days, that she hadn't showed for work, but hadn't put in for vacation time. Most thought, because of the social media post, that she'd taken off with Paul. Everyone agreed that this was out of character.

Amanda Alessi, by all accounts, was always on time, reliable, and thoughtful. She called her parents every other day—except for the last few days. Her parents are on their way from

California. They gave me permission to enter the house, which they own and Amanda rents from them.

I sent a unit here earlier to knock on the door, but there was no answer. A quick perimeter check and some peering in windows revealed nothing suspicious. Neighbors hadn't seen anything. I should have gotten here earlier.

Still in the car, I look at the picture I took from Amanda's best friend, Jessie, who also gave me the keys to her place. Her parents told me Jessie would have a set, and they were right.

Amanda is young, just turned thirty, with a blond pixie cut and dark, thickly lashed eyes. Smiley with a full, curvy body. In the photo, she's fashionable in a shirt dress and expensive tote, surrounded by her friends. Girls' shopping day, according to Jessie. In the photo, she looks happy, smile broad, cheeks pleasantly dimpled, the crinkles of laughter around her eyes.

"I didn't believe it," Jessie said, when I dropped by her place to get the keys. "That she'd take off with him. It just wasn't her—they'd just met. But that social media post."

The photo on Amanda's Instagram feed. Toes, cocktails, sunset. Turns out it was a stock image. Posted on her page and Paul Hayes's page. Birch, the young tech guy at the precinct, tracked it down. It was featured on a half dozen ads for beach vacations. Paradise found.

I have a bad feeling that whatever Amanda Alessi has found, it isn't paradise.

"Do you think she's—?" Jessie couldn't finish the sentence.

"Let's not jump to any conclusions," I said.

She shook her head, dark bob cut shimmering. "She just wouldn't do this. Take off without telling anyone. I should have called earlier—her Insta post, though."

"It's too soon to know anything," I told her.

Which was true—because we never really know each other. People snap, disappear, leave their lives, suddenly steal and take off. Even people like Amanda. You never know when people have had enough with whatever they're managing, or what pushes them over the edge.

"She could be a little crazy when it came to men," Jessie called out to me as I was walking away.

I looked back at her; she was a contrast to Amanda—dark where Amanda was fair, bony where Amanda was curvy.

"Threw herself into new relationships, you know?" Jessie wrung her manicured hands nervously. "She just loved being in love."

I turned the sentence around in my head. *She just loved being in love.*

Now I walk up Amanda Alessi's short driveway, approach the front door, and ring the bell. I stand back to see if any lights come on, ring again.

Nothing. Darkness. Streetlamps seem dim. Across the street, a single upstairs light is burning. Somewhere a dog is barking—yippy and relentless.

I wait another few moments before I put the key in the lock and open the door. I brace myself for the smell, but there's nothing. From the tiny foyer, I can see the whole first level—kitchen, dining, and living areas. The space is tidy, simply decorated with mid-range pale modular furniture and a huge flat-screen television dominating the kitchen, living room area. Everything spotless.

"Ms. Alessi." My voice bounces around and the silence vibrates. "Little Valley Police."

No answer. I move through the house, hand on the gun in its holster.

In Amanda's bedroom, the bed is unmade, covers in a tangle, drawers open, closet door wide. Empty hangers hanging helter-skelter, a row of underthings missing from a carefully organized drawer. A hasty packing job? Or someone wanted it to look that way?

I open the bedside table drawer, hoping for a journal. But all I find is a box of condoms, a bookmark, some hand lotion, a book of positive bedtime affirmations.

Downstairs, I check the small garage.

No car.

Also, no phone or purse anywhere that I can see.

All the first things you look for. Phone especially. If you find it left behind, that's a big red flag that something's really wrong.

Her parents told me that they still tracked her location, and she theirs. A couple of days ago, her location became unavailable. Someone turned it off. Or the phone went dead.

"I feel like someone cut our connection to her," her mother said, voice breaking.

Amanda's place is full of photographs—friends and family. I recognize a much younger Jessie, Amanda's parents. Lots of smiling faces on the walls, on surfaces, in pretty, coordinating frames. Cozy blankets and fuzzy throw pillows, piles of fashion magazines, scented candles. A girl who liked pretty, comfortable things.

On the side of the refrigerator, there's an old-school paper calendar, the little boxes filled with colorful loopy scribbles—*drinks with Jessie, girls' brunch, dinner with M&D, period ugh!* Not on the calendar: Aruba with Paul! In fact, the whole week is filled with appointments, hair and dentist, lunch with Jessie, massage, yoga. If she was planning a trip, I imagine she'd write something like "Yay vacay!" with lots of hearts or something.

It impresses me as a kind of anachronism, this paper calendar when most people Amanda's age keep track of dates on their device. She has a set of markers in a mason jar beside it. The entries are color coded, cute, cluttered. There's joy here, someone connected to her life and its unending activity.

Of course, that doesn't mean that she didn't take off with her boyfriend, or that she didn't kill him in a fit of jealous rage then seek to cover her tracks, or that someone didn't kill Amanda and Paul and dump their bodies in different places.

The good news in this cute, tidy, empty little house? No dead body. So, there's still hope, however slim, for Amanda.

"I'm sorry," I say out loud to no one. Because Amanda Alessi seems like a nice girl, leading a happy life. Hardworking, according to co-workers, attached to her parents, close to her friends. "She's one of those people," said Jessie. "Always there when I need her. Always my ride or die. A true friend."

The distant sound of something clattering to the floor startles me.

Shit. What did I miss?

My eyes fall on a door I haven't opened. I reach slowly and turn the knob, pull it open quickly, gun drawn. But there's only darkness, a stairway down to a basement.

"Little Valley Police," I bark, making my voice deep and loud. "Who's there?"

Silence. Throat dry, pulse pumping, I flip on the dim light, and head down the stairs.

A shuffle, a groan. A rush of cold air.

At the bottom of the stairs, I swing the gun. The whole space is visible from where I stand. Empty. I clock the open window over a craft bench, items fallen to the floor where it looks like someone climbed up. I get up there, look out the window in time to see a slim form in black disappear down the street into the night.

I call dispatch, give them Amanda's address. "I need patrol to circle the neighborhood. I'm looking for a runner, dressed in black."

"Your mysterious woman in black?" asks Judy. "Same one from the park?"

"No idea." I'm frustrated, breathing hard, too big to fit though the little window and give chase.

"Both of my cars are out on calls," says Judy. "I'll send someone soon as I can."

But by then it will be too late. I turn and race up the steps, burst out the front door. I make it to the street in time to see exactly nothing. The figure in black has disappeared, no sign in either direction. I stand, try to catch my breath.

In that lit window of the house across the street, a shadow. Someone watching.

The light goes out, and I head in that direction. The stoop is unkempt, plants dead in terracotta pots. Leaves littered, crunching beneath my feet. Door badly in need of a coat of paint. The windchimes hanging from the eaves are rusted, making a discordant sound. I knock, clocking the camera doorbell, the only thing on the stoop that looks new.

No answer. Again. Harder. "Little Valley Police," I say, not liking the edge to my own voice. Frustration and fatigue are taking their toll.

Finally, the door opens a crack; an old woman in a thin robe peers out at me. I identify myself.

"I already told them, the ones who came earlier. I didn't see anything," she croaks. She has watery brown eyes, face a landscape of deep lines.

"Did you see anyone come out of Amanda Alessi's house just now?"

She shakes her head. "Only you."

"Were you watching from upstairs?"

She doesn't answer, pulls her robe tighter, shuts the door a little. "I heard a noise. It woke me up."

"Ma'am," I say. "Does this camera record?"

"What camera?"

"The one in this doorbell." I tap on it. It looks like it has a direct line of sight to Amanda Alessi's house.

She waves at me. "Oh, my son installed that. I don't even know how it works. Can't even hear it when it rings."

"Can I have your son's name and phone number?"

"I don't have to give you that," she says, frowning.

I take a card from my pocket, slip it through the slowly closing door. "Okay, then can you have your son call me?"

She takes it, nods at me, eyes narrowed with suspicion. I'm guessing the card is going right in the trash.

"Thank you," I say. "Sorry to disturb you so late."

As I'm walking away, "She was a bad girl."

I stop and turn. "Amanda Alessi?"

She wags a finger. "A party girl. Always with someone new. Dressing up, going out. People spending the night. Music! Too late, I told her. Turn it down!"

I imagine this lonely old woman, alone in this run-down old house watching Amanda living her happy life.

"Did you see anything this week that you found unusual?"

She shakes her head. "I already told them. The cops. And the other girl who knocked on my door."

"What other girl?"

"She wanted to know about the camera, too."

"Did she leave a name? A number?"

She nods, then shuffles off, comes back shortly. Through the opening she hands me a piece of paper with a scribbled number and name. Oh my god. Seriously?

"Take it. I'm never going to call her. I could tell. She's a bad girl, too."

"Was this the same woman who was here tonight?" It's a reach. Maybe it wasn't a woman at all.

"I told you. You're the only one I saw snooping around tonight."

"Thank you, ma'am. Please have your son contact me."

She shuts the door. Hard. I stand a moment, stare at the paper in my hand.

I look up and down the street one more time. Peering into the night, I see no one. But I swear I feel like the night is staring back.

Back at Amanda's house, I make one more sweep. Inside, my phone rings.

Beck starts talking as soon as I answer.

"So, I put a rush on the Hayes toxicology screening because certain substances can't be detected in the system after forty-eight hours. The early clinical picture is consistent with death from alkaloids."

"English please."

"The toxins found in conium maculatum, more commonly known as hemlock. It's a common plant in the carrot family, sometimes called Queen Anne's lace," says Beck. "Symptoms start with dizziness, pupil dilation, weak or rapid pulse, eventually impacting the cardiovascular system, leading to death. A very small amount is needed, and it grows wild in this area on public and private land. It's quite commonly mistaken for parsnip or parsley, and there are multiple incidents annually of accidental ingestion in humans and livestock."

"So, it's possible he ingested it accidentally?"

"Sure," says Beck, exhaling sharply, probably vaping. "But he didn't bury himself in the woods."

Truth.

"There's a young woman, Iggy Rose Caine, in a coma at the hospital," I tell him. "Can you call over there and share your findings in case these things are connected and helps them treat her?"

"Will do. Unfortunately, there's no antitoxin for this. You basically have to weather the storm of symptoms and either you survive, or you don't."

"Got it," I say.

But he's already hung up. I take a moment, let the information sink in.

Paul Hayes died slow and ugly. He suffered. As if someone wanted him to pay for something he'd done.

My breath is returning to normal, heart rate regulating.

I open the refrigerator to find it spotless, housing just a few lonely take-out containers and two bottles of Moët.

In the living room, I take another pass at the photos of Amanda's happy, richly populated life. So many pictures of Jessie, in fact mostly of the two of them doing various things—horseback riding, hiking, in bathing suits somewhere tropical. A long relationship, best friends. I wonder how Jessie felt when Amanda got serious about Paul. Jealous? Angry? Left behind.

I keep looking at the photos. And this time, I see something I missed.

In a selfie from what looks like a martini night, Amanda smiles brightly. It's a big group shot. Many of the women are unfamiliar. But there are faces I recognize.

There's Jessie, of course, smiling broadly and cheek-to-cheek with her bestie.

Vera and Ana Blacksmith are also in the frame, as well as Ignatia Rose Caine.

Iggy's grin is shy, self-conscious.

Ana's smile is wide and knowing. Again, an unbidden flash of memory of our bathroom assignation, her breath in my ear tonight.

Vera hangs back in the darkness behind, the corners of her mouth just barely curled upward. They are all holding pink concoctions in frosty martini glasses toward the camera.

Those sisters.

Something tingles down my spine, a single word bounces around my head.

Poison.

PART TWO

EATING CROW

"A person can only swallow so much."
Aunt Agnes's *Book of Cures*

CORALINE

Mr. Hamm drones on at the front of the room, and I pretend to be taking notes, but I'm actually just doodling. Seriously, I could teach a class on *The Scarlet Letter*. Poor Hester Prynne and the big red *A* she was forced to wear for her adultery, and her witchy little child, Pearl, and her revenging old husband, and her secret lover the minister (spoiler alert!) whose guilt and shame was slowly killing him.

I have to ask myself—in a woke world, why do they still teach the Nathaniel Hawthorne cautionary tale? Women beware! Take dominion over your body, your sexual life, and be condemned to a life of shame and suffering! Are we supposed to look back at it and marvel at how unjust, how awful the world was for women *back in the seventeenth century*? Because there are lots of problems now, too. Do women have any more control over their bodies and their lives? Maybe on the surface things look better. But women are being sterilized against their will in prisons—like right now. And *Roe v. Wade* has been repealed. And if I got pregnant because someone raped me, in some places I wouldn't have the right to do anything about it.

Why is that okay?

Autumn is sitting ramrod straight beside me, foot tapping, diligently taking notes. The girl is a wreck. She's neck and neck with Micha for class valedictorian, and anything less than perfection now will have her in the number two spot. Which for most of us would be fine, *awesome* even. But not for Autumn.

And Micha—well, let's be honest, he's a cheater and a shameless suck-up. This is not the common opinion. With his blond floppy hair and pretty face, he's every girl's crush and every teacher's favorite. Micha is homecoming king, and he sings in the school choir; he even volunteers at the local animal shelter.

And, rumor has it that he bought the answers for the last AP chemistry test from a senior at another school who had a special test-taking date because of his alleged ADHD. And so Micha got a 103% with extra credit, and Autumn got a 99%. With just weeks to go before college decisions come in, Autumn is losing it.

I also know that she's cutting herself again. A thing she made me swear to keep secret and *promised* me that she would stop doing. But when we changed for PE last Wednesday, I saw the tiny slices on the inside of her thigh up above the hem of her shorts.

So now I have this secret that my friend is hurting herself. I should tell someone. But I can't because if I do she'll hate me forever. And I know that Micha is cheating, but I'm no snitch. So, as my mother would say: *Coraline, how are you going to solve these problems?*

"Coraline? Thoughts?"

Crap. I look up from my notebook and everyone's staring at me. Someone snickers and Autumn looks down at a piece of paper on her desk. In big letters it reads: Witches!

"There are a couple of characters that might have been witches or who Hawthorne alluded to as witches," I say, looking at Mr. Hamm, who nods. "Mistress Hibbins, who was a reference to a real woman executed as a witch in 1656—she's always trying to tempt people into the forest, which clearly represents sin and paganism. Hawthorne describes The Black Man as a necromancer because of his knowledge of herbal medicines from his time with indigenous people. Even Pearl, who is a child, is often compared to a witch."

"And how do we think that Hawthorne feels about witches?"

"I think he views their persecution as unfair. He was a critic of the Boston Puritan society, even though his ancestors were notorious prosecutors in the Salem witch trials."

Mr. Hamm nods and goes on, talking about the various descriptions of Pearl in the book, Hester's child, the product of her adultery and the proof of her sin. How descriptions of her veer between cherubic and demonic, how she's compared to an imp, a fairy, a rosebush.

I glance over at Autumn, who flashes me a grin.

See what I mean? I might have to drag her through *Red World*, but in flesh school, she's got my back.

Later we meet at my locker, then walk to the lunchroom where Micha is holding court at the table of popular seniors. He sits at the head of the table, everyone turned toward him like flowers reaching for the sun. We grab our usual spot by the window, looking out on the field covered in snow, the barren black trees.

Other notable things about Micha. When we were in first grade he pushed me off the jungle gym and I chipped my tooth. He did it on purpose, but *no one* believed me. Because I was the difficult one, and he was the class angel, beloved by all. The angrier I got about it, the less convincing I became. The only one who believed me was Ana. *The world is populated by men like that*, she told me. *The world thinks they're one thing, but underneath that glimmering facade, there's black rot. Only some of us see it. And when we call it out, no one believes us.*

In eighth grade, he texted naked pictures of his ex-girlfriend to all his friends, and many of them went on to send them to their friends. One of the little fuckers sent the images to *Pornhub* and they went up online for all the world to see. Brittany Lamb was suspended from school for *allowing* pictures of herself *to be taken*. Eventually, she and her family left town.

Did anything happen to Micha or his evil friends?

Take a guess.

No.

Ethan slides in beside me and proceeds to open the bento box that his mother, Charlie, packs for him every day, each little square filled with berries or nuts, baby carrots or hummus.

"Are we eating in silence?" asks Ethan after a few minutes of chewing. "What's going on?"

He follows my gaze. "Oh." Eye roll. "You know, Coraline. This obsession has to end. Like, let it go. We were in first grade."

"You don't get it," I say. "Because you're a man."

"This again."

"Seriously," says Autumn. "There's a kind of man that other men, good men, don't recognize. He's a cheater, a user. A predator."

"I mean look at the world," I say. "It's run by men who *literally* get away with rape, assault, and murder."

Ethan crunches a baby carrot. "Fair. Still—Micha? He's not *that* bad."

"How can you say that?" I ask, incredulous. "After what he did to you?"

Ethan's shoulders hike. "I don't know. Maybe it *was* an accident. I mean, he works at an animal shelter."

"That's his *cover*," I say, voice coming up an octave. "See. It's working."

He glances over at Micha, then gives me a nudge with his shoulder and we both start to laugh.

Autumn still looks miserable. "If I'm not valedictorian my parents are going to disown me. I wouldn't mind so much if I just got my ass kicked fair and square, but how much cheating has he done?"

"It's a *rumor*," says Ethan. "You don't know that he cheated. Maybe he really is just smarter than you are, Autumn."

She gives him the finger. Why do men always seem to do

that, stand up for each other, even the best ones for the worst ones? It's like some biological bro code.

Just then, Micha breaks into song—really hamming it up, standing up on his stool, belting out the lyrics of a show tune—"Tomorrow" from *Annie*. He is, of course, pitch-perfect. Oh, right, did I also mention that he's the lead in the school play?

"Okay," says Ethan, frowning. "You're right. He's a tool."

I reach into my bag and take out two little pouches, slide them over to Autumn.

"Oh," she says, glancing shyly at Ethan. "Thanks."

"The tea bags in the pouch with the pink ribbon are for your cramps. Evening primrose, chamomile, red raspberry, and ginger. That's Great-Aunt Agnes's recipe. The tea bags in the pouch with the blue ribbon are for focus—black cohosh, matcha, peppermint, and blackberry. That's my Aunt Ana's recipe. She says it got her through college."

"And this." I hand her a little metal tub of salve. "This is *my* recipe. Yarrow, echinacea, calendula, comfrey, beeswax, olive oil, and some other stuff," I tell her. "It's for cuts and scarring."

This is my way of telling her that I know she's cutting again. From the way she lowers her eyes I'm guessing the message was received.

Ethan picks up the pouches, inspects them. "Where did you learn to do this?"

"Family recipes," I say with a shrug. He holds up the label I created. On the front is a *C* comprised of vines and flowers, on the back a list of ingredients. Everything is organic from Agnes's garden. "This is nice," he says, nudging me.

I'm proud of the label that I designed on my iPad and printed on sticker paper.

"Got anything for me in there?" he asks, peering into my bag. I reach over to close the zipper and our hands meet. There's like a little shock at the softness of his skin. We've known each other all our lives, but since something weird happened at homecoming, things are different. I'm ignoring it and I think he is, too. Our eyes meet and I feel myself blush like an idiot. I also feel Autumn watching us, which brings up even more heat.

"There's no tea to stop someone from being a dork," I say to cover my embarrassment.

"Ouch," he says, putting a hand to his heart with mock dismay.

I ruffle his hair, and then I see he's blushing, too.

"Huh," says Autumn, eyes back on Micha.

When Ethan gets up to toss his trash, I lean into her.

"Hey," I say. "Would it be the worst thing in the world to come in second? It's still amazing."

She gives me a look, then starts packing up her things, holding up the salve to me, which I take to mean she's going to stop again. She puts it and the tea in her bag.

"If you're not first, you're last. That's what my dad always says."

In what twisted world view I wonder does that make sense? And what does that make me? I think my class rank is like number ten or something. But honestly, I don't take Autumn's psychosis personally.

"That's the stupidest thing I've ever heard. Meanwhile, isn't your dad just like a middle manager at some third-tier investment firm? Life's not just about who's first, is it?"

"Isn't it?" she says, looking up at Micha, who seems to intuit that she's watching and looks our way, gives her an easy wave and a smile that's almost a sneer.

I think about my chipped tooth, which luckily was a baby tooth and fell out a few weeks later. That feeling of anger at not being believed when you were telling the truth; I still remember it. I think about those images of Brittany and how she had to leave school because people were so cruel to *her*, calling her a slut and saying she shouldn't have taken her clothes off for him. But no one said a thing about what *he* did, taking advantage of her innocence and trust. And no one did a thing about a place like *Pornhub* where she gets exploited over and over—forever because of a mistake she made when she was thirteen years old.

"He's not going to win," I tell Autumn.

"How do you know?" she asks.

"Trust me."

Autumn shoots me a worried frown.

"Hey," says Ethan. "What's this one? Why does it have a skull and crossbones on it?"

He holds up a little black pouch that he lifted from my bag. It's inside a plastic baggie.

Shit.

"Coraline," he says in that way he says my name, knowledge, patience, worry. "What are you up to?"

I snatch it back from him. "Mind your beeswax," I say. "And go wash your hands."

He issues a laugh.

"I mean it," I say, nodding toward the bathroom. He obeys. I've taught him a thing or two, so he knows to listen.

"What is it?" asks Autumn, as I bury it deep in my bag.

"It's an old family cure."

"Cure for what?"

We both look at Micha, who's started singing again, drawing all eyes to him. There's something about him. That unearned arrogance, the willingness to hurt others to get ahead. It reminds me of Ana's ex Paul, who obviously needed correction and got it.

"For assholes."

ANA

I haven't slept so I brew myself another pot of the concoction I taught to Coraline—black cohosh, matcha, peppermint, and blackberry. In school we called it Night Owl. It worked its magic for me last night. And I'm still tingling with its effects hours later, but I need another hit.

Since leaving Lisander and a quick visit to Agnes's place again, I've done nothing but try to find someone else who had motive to kill Paul, another narrative for my detective friend.

Paul's picture stares back at me from the screen. The last time I saw him, it was ugly. Raised voices, name-calling. Violence. But there was heat, too, something intense. Something thrilling. *That's not really love*, the kid-shrink told me.

What is love, then? I asked her.

It's up to each of us to decide what brand of love we give and receive. But when it's healthy, it's not violence. It doesn't hurt.

I wish someone had told that to my parents.

Now, the sun rising and washing my small kitchen in pink light, I also toss back an energy drink for good measure. Sometimes nature needs a little assist. My phone pings continuously.

Vera. With all her orders and thoughts, since just before the sun broke the horizon.

Victor and I are getting you at 8. We'll talk in the car.

Be ready.

Let me do the talking when we're with the detective.

Don't answer any questions you don't have to.

Ana.

Answer me.

Have you figured out who that woman was with the grudge?

Wear something conservative. No heels. Nothing too low-cut.

On and on. For fuck's sake. No wonder her relationship with her daughter is a cage match. Has there even been a bossier, more controlling pain in the ass?

The other phone in front of me has been silent. Not a single text or call since I lifted it from Iggy's house.

I scroll again through the texts there from an unknown caller on the day of the brunch. I've tried calling the number, but no one answers, no voicemail picks up. A burner probably. But who?

I can't sleep. I can't stop thinking about it.

I'm all alone out here.

I'm scared.

Only one from Iggy: Don't text me again.

Looking back, Iggy *did* seem tense and jumpy at the brunch. I thought it was just being away from her baby overlord. But maybe there was something else going on. There was a time when we didn't have any secrets. But since I started seeing Paul, and she married Brock, things have changed.

I've tried responding to the texts with an Iggy-like tone: **So sorry I was sharp. This is a lot. Are you okay?**

But no answer has come. Who is texting Iggy? Why was she so cold in response? That's really not like her at all. Was she having an affair? One she regretted and was trying to end?

Never. Not Iggy, the ultimate good girl.

The only other saved text chain on her phone is between her and Brock, a total lovefest, nothing but sweetness and baby pictures, heart emojis and kissy faces. Gawd. Boring.

Not boring: Detective Bandeau. A lover. An enemy. It's a combination I find wildly exciting. I swear I still feel his lips on my throat. That's what *I* can't stop thinking about.

Focus, Ana, Vera would surely chide.

Across my kitchen table, I have my research spread out. A printout of the blog and the text chain I screen shot and sent to myself from Paul's phone the last time I was snooping. Paul's professional portrait stares at me from the printout of his ConnectIn page. I reread the comment left by someone calling herself Jezebel.

One day, you're going to pay for things you've done.

I've gone down the rabbit hole of Amanda Alessi's social media feeds, the things she's done, where's she's traveled, the people connected to her. I have found some things that surprised me. I even swung by her house, talked to her nosy neighbor. Maybe I should become a private investigator. I think I'm good at this.

A theory is starting to take shape, but it's still unformed, out of focus.

The only things I know for sure:
I didn't kill Paul.
And everyone, including my sister, at least suspects that I did. Once that detective starts really digging into my past, he's going to be less interested in me as a fuckbuddy and more as the main suspect in his murder investigation. Our sexual chemistry is not going to save me. Or is it?

The thought that I could go to prison like my mother, that I could die there, fills me with a sick dread. How many innocent women have died for crimes they didn't commit?

Ana. Are you ready?

I look out the kitchen window and see a Range Rover pull into the lot. My sister with our lawyer, Payton's ex, my one-night stand, Victor. We're off to see the detective.
This should be fun.
If I wasn't so terrified, I'd be excited.

TIMOTHY

As usual, the station house is too cold. The furnace is old and the windows are poorly insulated. So, the interview room is just warm enough that our breath is not coming out in clouds.

Give me salty, hot, humid days where even the breeze is warm. Must be the Florida kid in me. This cold, it shrinks you up, makes your shoulders tense and your muscles ache.

Paul Hayes's sister, Regina, hasn't taken off her long black coat, and she leans into the bulky Ross Avidon for warmth. He keeps a possessive arm around her. Plaid wool jacket, black beanie cap pulled down to just about his eyebrows. They seem very coupled. Like their energies meld together.

"Ana Blacksmith is a witch," says Regina. "Like, literally."

Ross looks at her and releases a sigh, like maybe he's heard this before. He rubs at his beanie cap.

"What does that mean?" I ask.

"It means what it means," she says unhelpfully, with a tight shrug and a shift of her eyes. In the hard light of the interview room, her eyes are rimmed red and shadowed by fatigue.

"Can I smoke in here?" she asks.

"No," I say. "Sorry."

I wish I could let her. I'm itching for one, too, and I wouldn't mind the secondhand smoke.

She runs those black-painted fingers over her bright orange buzz-cut crown. I've seen bodies in the morgue with more blush to their skin. Beside her, Avidon sits silently attentive. I note his girth again, his obvious strength. I try to envision them carrying Paul Hayes's stiff body through the woods. Would they argue? They bring to mind nothing so much as Bluto and Olive Oyl, his muscular bearing, her slimness. She seems to fit easily in the crook of his arm. He hasn't said much except to grunt the occasional assent.

"When you say witch . . ." I press.

"She's Wiccan."

"I still don't know what that means."

"It *means*," she says, leaning in, narrowing her eyes, "she's a practicing witch. Like spells and rituals, a worship of nature, trees and plants. Paganism."

"Okay," I say, drawing out the syllable.

"Google that shit," she says, leaning back then coming forward again, agitated. "You *must* know. There's a whole bunch of them here in Little Valley and The Hollows. You know that shop in town with all the crystals and dream catchers, tarot cards, all the books on mysticism? That's where they meet. And out in the woods. In fact, there's a meeting coming up for the first full moon of the year. The Wolf Moon."

Her eyes are a little wide; she's gripping at the edge of the table. And I'm trying to decide if she's unstable, sick with grief, or both. I know the place she's talking about, the occult bookshop on the outskirts of town. I also know about our so-called Wiccan contingent in Little Valley. And our neighboring town, The Hollows, has a wild reputation of dark occurrences, unexplained happenings, is home to a number of alleged psychics and certainly has an unusually high crime rate. I try to keep an open mind about things. But I'm not exactly a believer.

"The Wolf Moon—?" I let the words dangle, giving her the opportunity to say more.

"That's when they do whatever business they do out there." She flings a dramatic arm. "Cast spells, throw curses, worship nature, whatever. They have a big bonfire. People come from all over for it."

I feel like I would know if there was a yearly gathering of area witches. Large gatherings and bonfires tend to attract a lot of attention.

And then there's the "voodoo doll." Which, one has to admit, looks extremely witchy.

"So, you're telling me that Ana Blacksmith is a witch."

"And she killed Paul." She says this with a satisfied nod. "*When* are you going to arrest her?"

Ross puts an arm around her and offers a gentle squeeze. "Babe, we don't know what happened to Paul."

"Then who?" She looks up at him, eyes narrowed.

"I don't know, but—"

"But *what*?" She turns back to me. "You said he was poisoned. Is that right?"

"Toxicology is consistent with that."

She lifts her palms. "Her mother poisoned her father. Did you know that? She and her sister came here to live with her aunt. Who was also—wait for it—*a witch*."

"She was a florist, wasn't she?" says Ross.

Regina snapped back. "*Which* was a *cover* for her *other* business."

"Okay," admits Ross, looking at me as if for help. "In addition to being a florist, Agnes Blacksmith was an herbalist. Like a doctor, but she offered holistic cures for various ailments. Teas, tinctures, salves."

"Spells, curses."

"Regina."

"*Poison.*"

"Stop," he says finally, pulling away from her.

She rolls her eyes at me. "He's just protective because his mother was a Wiccan."

Ross withdraws his arm. "Stop it, Regina."

"You're such a mama's boy."

Ross's face clouds with anger; he folds his arms, slouches. I'm clocking him at over six feet, two-fifty. She's five two if she's an inch. But she cows him. Power is not just about size.

"Okay, look," I say before their argument can devolve any further. Once a couple starts bickering, you're not going to get anywhere with them. "You say you saw your brother last week. He'd just broken up with Ms. Blacksmith."

"And she was in a rage," Regina says, seeming to calm a little. "She was calling all the time, texting, stalking Paul and his new girlfriend, Amanda, in social media."

"Did she threaten him?"

"I think the threat was implied. She was following him. Turned up at work."

"But did she *actually* threaten to harm him?" I press. "Is it documented somewhere, a post in social media, a voicemail that you know of?"

People do get angry, act irrationally at the end of a relationship. But an actual threat gives me a reason to start digging deeper, gives me a reason to ask for a warrant to search her house, or seize her cell phone records.

Regina sags a little, shakes her head. "I don't know," she admits. Big tears start to fall, and Ross puts his arm around her again. She leans into him.

"That was Tuesday, the last time you saw him."

"He came for dinner."

"Did he tell you he was leaving town?"

"No, but he wouldn't. Paul—just did whatever he wanted."

"I understand that there was some dispute between you, over an inheritance."

Her eyes widen in surprise, but then she nods. "Our mother died. Once her estate clears probate, we stand to inherit quite a bit. I wanted him to pay me what he owed me from that sum.

But he was refusing, saying he still needed the money. We were *discussing* it. I wouldn't say it was an argument."

"How much did he owe you?"

She looks off to the side of the room. I can see it in her tight grimace, anger. "A hundred thousand."

I glance at my phone, at the text chain Ana forwarded between Paul and "The Witch." Did he mean his sister? Did he owe someone else a hundred grand?

I don't want this to get ugly, The Witch in Paul's contacts had written.

Things had certainly gotten ugly for Paul.

"Whoa," I say. "That's a lot."

She nods, offers a slight lift of her shoulders. "I loaned it to him when he got fired and started his own business."

I make a show of looking at my notes. "He was fired for sexual harassment."

Regina wraps her slender but muscled arms around her middle. There's a kind of wiry strength to her. I picture again her and Ross carrying Paul's dead body through the woods. I can see them, struggling with the weight, arguing about how to carry him. Maybe it's dark. Maybe they drop him. Old Bob is out there now, taking a closer look, casting a wider net.

She scowls and squares her shoulders. "That—the sexual harassment charge—was like a he-said-she-said thing. I don't know what really happened. He claimed he was innocent and I believed him."

Willful ignorance. I've spent less than twenty-four hours getting to know Paul Hayes and I already know he was a bad guy with lots of enemies, most of them women. The fact that he gave money all over town, including funds that were supposed to save the gym where I volunteer, seems to have bought him a lot of goodwill and some powerful allies.

"Did Paul have any connection to a woman named Iggy Rose?"

Regina purses her lips, shakes her head slowly. "I don't think so. But I didn't know all the women in his life."

"She's in a coma," I say. "Her symptoms are consistent with poisoning."

Regina blows out a breath, looks up at Ross, then back at me. "Did she know Ana Blacksmith?"

I don't answer, slip the photograph I took from Amanda Alessi's house across the table. She stares at it a moment, goes quiet.

Regina Hayes is in the photograph, too, standing in the back, apart, partially shadowed but holding her glass up to the camera. I didn't see her when I first looked at the photograph, only when I was staring at it later. Regina knows Iggy, Vera, Ana, and Amanda, at least well enough to join them for drinks.

She freezes a moment, then shrugs.

"So, we were all at the same bar one night. Small town."

I stay silent, let it sit a moment. I think that she's about to go on when Ross stands up suddenly, scraping the chair back.

"That's enough, Regina," he says. "Nothing further without an attorney present."

I lift my palms. "It's not like that."

"It's *always* like that," he says, voice gravelly.

Ross has had a couple drunk and disorderly arrests over the years. He stole a car when he was a kid, spent a few months in juvie. Been on the straight and narrow for a while, has a YouTube art class that seems popular, an Instagram feed that features all of his tattoos, artfully photographed by Regina.

He offers her his hand; she takes it and rises.

"Ms. Hayes, you told me that you didn't know Amanda or Iggy. Did you lie?"

"No," she says. "I don't know them. Just because we were in the same place at the same time doesn't mean we know each other." She looks at the image. "That was more than a year ago."

"So you remember the night?"

"Enough," says Ross, scuttling her toward the door.

"Is this a text exchange between you and your brother?"

I show her the printout. She stares at it, flushing. She blows out an angry breath.

"Were you in his contacts as The Witch?"

"I don't know."

But the tension in her face tells me she does. I already know that the number is hers. Birch confirmed it earlier. I let them go because I don't have a choice, and I'm not one of those to bluster and issue threats, to strong-arm or bully. I know where to find them. We'll talk again.

"Regina," says Ross. "Don't say another thing."

"Just one more thing," I press. "Do you recognize this or know what it is?"

I slide the picture of the stick doll across the table. Regina takes a step back, a hand coming to her heart.

"No idea," says Ross, ushering her away. "Looks like a bunch of sticks to me."

"It's a voodoo doll," I say. "An effigy."

"Dolls aren't always used to harm. Sometimes they're for protection," she says.

"Hush," says Ross, casting an angry look back at me.

"So, you've seen one before?" I press. "Mind telling me where?"

But they're done, moving down the hallway toward the door, whispering urgently to each other.

I follow them out slowly, arriving in the foyer in time to see the Blacksmith sisters enter from outside with a tall nattily dressed man with a shaved head. Another power lawyer. Great.

I couldn't have timed this better. I stand back to see what type of fireworks will go off as Ross and Regina exit and Vera and Ana enter, bringing the cold in with them.

Outside the day is gray, threatening snow. Inside the station bustles with ringing phones, people coming and going. The Christmas decorations are still waiting to be taken down.

I expect Regina to start shouting, maybe Ana to answer with her own accusations. But nothing like that happens. Ross steers Regina toward the door, and I observe Ana and Regina lock eyes, a kind of stare down, quiet, electric. And then Regina and Ross are gone into the winter morning.

When I look back at the sisters, the elder Vera is staring at me, gaze unrelenting. I feel like she's looking right through me, seeing everything, all my secrets.

Involuntarily, I shudder.

Ana's staring at me, too. I find myself imagining backing her into a corner somewhere and pressing my mouth to hers. She yields to my touch, opens like a flower. Something passes between us, and I can tell she's remembering our encounters, too.

Then she turns and whispers something to the man who is obviously her lawyer. He, too, gives me a look that someone else might find intimidating.

This should be fun. I feel like I do right before I'm about to climb into the boxing ring. Wired, adrenaline pulsing.

I've learned a few things since the last time I saw Ana. And I'm looking forward to landing those punches.

I gesture for them to follow me and we all head to the interview room. Fine for the Blacksmith sisters to be interviewed together. I have questions for them both, and for now it's a good idea to keep things friendly.

IGGY

You know how you can fall in love with a friend? Especially if you don't have any siblings and maybe your family isn't picture-perfect. Especially if you spent your whole life wishing for that feeling that other people seem to consider their birthright, that feeling of being known and belonging, wanted.

Ana and I both had difficult lives before we met in the dorm room of Sacred Heart College that fall. We both knew what it was like to be left out, left behind, to lose. But looking back now, I see that the things that hurt me, that weakened me in some ways, only made Ana stronger. I was ground down by the hard stone of my early life, but Ana was a blade who was sharpened upon her ugly circumstances. Maybe that's because she had Vera and Agnes, and I had no one. Just a dad who left before I was born, and a mother who never wanted me in the first place, who preferred to drink than to mother.

Until I met Ana, I felt utterly alone in the world.

The hospital room is quiet, and Brock is sleeping uncomfortably in his chair. And I look down at my poor body run through with tubes, a machine breathing for me. And the only thing I can think about is Noah. Brock's mother took him away. She's not the warmest woman in the world, but she's a good caretaker. I never worry about Noah when he's with her; she'll make sure all his needs are met, is careful and watchful. And I know he'll never love Marge the way he loves me. That's what they should tell you when you're growing up in a bad place, that when you're an adult, if you do your work, you can make your own family. You can create the thing you weren't given. And I feel like I've done that with Brock and Noah. I want more babies. At least two more. So that no one will ever be alone like I was.

But I can't get back in my body right now. The toxins racing through my veins are wreaking havoc on my organs. I've learned enough to know what they will do, and it will take all of my strength to fight my way back.

I remember the first time Ana brought me to Agnes's and shared with me what they were and what they did. It was Christmas and Ana invited me home because my mother was off somewhere with her new boyfriend, and I was just planning to stay at school with a group of the other kids who had no place to spend the Christmas break.

Agnes's house smelled of cinnamon and pine needles, was decorated so beautifully with organic greenery and real holly leaves, homemade candles, and strands of gingham ribbon. When I walked through the front door, it felt like a dream. Agnes and Vera welcomed me warmly, and I was given my own room. And I knew from Ana that nothing about the situation was perfect, and that she'd often been unhappy and lost her parents. But to me there was something magical about it all. The home, the garden, the kitchen where there was always something wonderful bubbling on the stove. It inspired me.

Theirs was a world without men. And that suited me just fine. Because my mother had a parade of them through her life, each one worse than the last. And they brought with them their wants and desires, their needs. They trampled through our lives and took and broke. I still bore the scars—a cut just under my ear from Ben who threw a glass at my mother in a rage and hurt me instead. The jangle of alarm I feel when I'm inside a room and someone outside turns the knob, from when Alex lived with us and twice after my mother went to sleep he'd tried to come into my room.

I'll always take care of you. You're safe now, Brock whispered the night I told him all my ugly secrets. And he meant it; he is pure of heart. I watch him now, neck cricked so uncomfortably, legs splayed.

"Iggy," he says in his sleep. "Please."

I put a shimmering hand on his forehead, and he seems to quiet, stirs, neck cracking, like he senses me. He should go home and get some rest, but I'm selfish. I need him here. I'm scared. What if whoever did this to me comes back to finish the job? He sighs. If I had a body or tears, I'd cry. And if he could see or feel me, he'd wake up and take me into his arms.

Ana used to say that, too, that I belonged with her now, and that she'd keep me safe. And she also meant it in her way. But Ana is a very different animal from Brock. Brock is a protector. Ana is a warrior. She's happy to harm if it means protecting what she loves—or getting what she wants.

I used to dream of being an actress. I had some middling talent and a decent voice, earned lead roles in my high school theater club. My teacher said that I had a gift for "inhabiting character." I never forgot that. So, as soon as I got to college, I tried out for the theater club. Ana came with me on the afternoon auditions were to begin. I was so touched by that, but also nervous that she'd be in the audience watching. What if I wasn't any good?

But I *was* good. I chose the Angelina Jolie monologue in *Maleficent* where she curses baby Aurora to become Sleeping Beauty. I infused it with all the same notes of barely contained rage, and sadness, and jealous vindictiveness. I think I even captured the irony of her mention of true love's kiss as the only way to waken the sleeping princess. Which of course she and everyone knows doesn't exist. That's what I thought then, too. That there was no such thing as true love. I know better now. There *is* one true love in this world, when it's pure, a mother's love for her child.

When I was done, everyone cheered. Then I sang "Tomorrow" from *Annie*. And again, more thunderous applause.

When I sank into the seat beside Ana, flushed, exuberant, she turned to look at me and grabbed my hand. "Wow," she whispered, smiling. "Just *wow*."

I was good. But I wasn't great. That much was clear when Clara took the stage. A hundred times prettier, more confident. Her voice was stunning.

"She's not better than you," Ana whispered, reading my mind.

"She is," I said. "It's okay."

"No," said Ana, still clutching my hand. "It's you. You're the lead."

I smiled at her, appreciating the vote of confidence. And as the auditions wound on it came down to three of us, all vying for the lead in the Sacred Heart production of *Beauty and the Beast*. The final audition was at the end of the week. And I poured my heart into preparing.

But truthfully, I saw in Clara all the things I knew I didn't have. An effortless beauty, the patina of privilege, style, extraordinary talent. She was an "it girl." I was a chorus girl. She was a star. And I was used to not getting the things I wanted, which I think is better. Because so often we don't and it's okay. Really.

But on the day of the final auditions, Clara didn't show. We waited. Someone went looking for her as I took the stage. We all waited, looking toward the doors that didn't open. Clara never showed. And the part—of Belle? It went to *me*!

Poor Clara had been on the toilet in her dorm room, violently ill from food poisoning, too sick to come to the door or answer the phone. Her roommate took her to the ER, and Clara was hospitalized, returning to school a couple of days later. A couple of other kids who'd eaten in the cafeteria reported symptoms, too. Clara eventually was fine, but bitter in her secondary role, showing up late, flubbing her lines, and finally dropping out.

"Sometimes it takes hardship for people to show their true colors," said Ana when I told her that Clara couldn't handle being second best. "And sometimes," she went on, kissing me on the head, "people like you get what they deserve."

It was months before I put it together. It was a long time before I understood Ana for who she truly was.

Brock stirs awake. "Iggy?"

He looks over at my still, pale body, slides the chair up close, and takes my hand. He kisses it, then bows his head over it and starts to cry. Ana hated that about him, that he cried. But it's what I love most. It takes so much strength to feel, to show your feelings, especially as a man in this sick culture.

The beep and whir of the machines is steady and rhythmic; I feel a surge of hope. I'm still alive. I can still return to them.

"I'm here. I'm here," I want to say. I want to tell him about milk thistle and how it can aid in the recovery of the liver. But I have no voice. And I just hope it wasn't Ana who did this, because I know for a fact that she has no mercy. And that if it *was* her, and she doesn't want me to, I won't wake up.

VERA

The only places I hate more than hospitals are police stations. They share the same cold arrogance, the same black-and-white, right and wrong, life and death. They are places of unyielding consequences and limited solutions, rules to be followed even when the rules are broken and wrong.

I don't love bringing Ana here. But Payton insisted that we appear to be playing ball. And Payton's top-tier criminal defense attorney ex-boyfriend, sometimes lover, Victor, is the kind of man you want on your side. A crackling, no-bullshit intelligence, tempered by a cool, in-on-the-joke-of-it-all confidence, a kind of easy charm that disarms before he muscles you to the ground. Ana knows him, but he and I have only just met. Already, I see why Payton likes him (read: keeps fucking him) but won't marry him. There's an edge to him, something dangerous.

Victor opens the door to the station for us, and we step inside. There's a smell—ink and desperation. I see Regina Hayes before she sees us—looking drawn with distress, wrapped in some kind of dramatic shawl, her hair as orange as copper wire. As we pass each other, she and Ana lock eyes and their dislike for each other is electric. I squeeze my sister's hand. *Keep your mouth shut*, I think but don't say, hoping to communicate it through touch. Ana issues a grunt of disdain but controls herself. Her hand is icy cold in mine. She pulls it away.

Detective Bandeau is waiting for us. Then we're walking back, trailing Victor like baby ducks. A uniformed officer opens a door for us. We enter the interrogation room and sit, Ana between Victor and me. Bandeau stands in the corner, arms folded. I don't like the way he looks at Ana, like he already knows something about her.

"Thank you for coming," he says, as if we had a choice. "Please have a seat."

Victor introduces himself and they shake hands. There's some chitchat about a friend they have in common, someone who volunteers at the youth center with Bandeau, a word or two about some boxing match. It's all very male, very congenial. Then it begins.

"So, Ms. Blacksmith, you were in a relationship with Paul Hayes for the better part of nine months, is that right?"

"Yes."

Instructions from Victor, which echo all the things Agnes told us over the years, include short, truthful (if possible) answers without any unnecessary elaboration.

"How would you characterize your relationship?"

Ana looks at me, shrugs. "Fun, I suppose. Light. Not serious."

Obsessive, oversexed, shallow, performative. But I give her a light nod of agreement.

"Nine months is a long time—at your age." He wears a shadow of a smirk. Ana's nostrils flare slightly at the dig. "Isn't it? I mean, long enough to be serious."

"My client has answered your question," says Victor, voice chilly, all the male bonhomie gone. He holds a black leather notebook, scribbles with a Montblanc held in long lean fingers. A southpaw.

The detective moves on. "When was the last time you saw him?"

"The night we broke up."

"Why *did* you break up?"

Ana glances at Victor, who nods. "He was seeing someone else. Wanted to pursue that."

The detective is also a scribbler, writing in his notebook.

He looks up at Ana. "You must have been angry."

"It's never fun to learn your boyfriend is seeing someone else and likes her better," she says easily. The only tell of her tension is a slightly bouncing heel. "But like I said. It wasn't serious."

"Do you remember the exact date?"

"It was right before the holidays."

He offers a dramatic wince. "That's cold. So not angry about it all?"

"Again. Question answered," says Victor, looking at the detective.

So far I haven't said a word and I'm quite happy to keep it that way, even though I planned to do all the talking.

"Would you say that's a fair characterization of the breakup?" Ugh. He's looking at me, waiting for me to answer.

Ana went completely ballistic, was a total fucking rage case, tearing up her apartment and bombarding me with furious phone calls. I had to leave a PTA meeting and help her pull her shit together. The afternoon ended with her weeping in my lap like a toddler who'd finally burned out on her tantrum while I stroked her hair.

"I think so," I say, looking at her as I imagine a loving older sister would. "As she said, it never seemed serious. I mean of course Ana was hurt that Paul cheated. No one feels good about that. But it's not like she planned to marry him."

I give my sister a sympathetic glance, touch her arm. She smiles sadly, nods. We're good at this, putting on a little show of our sisterly bond.

The detective flips through his notebook, clears his throat.

"Paul's sister, Regina, characterizes the breakup differently." He makes a show of looking down at his notes again. "*She* claims you were enraged, that you stalked him, showing up at his place of work, and at the workplace of Amanda Alessi, who is currently missing. She says that you harassed them both on social media and made threats."

Ana sits coolly. "Ha, that's rich. She should talk. Regina and Paul were at each other's throats about the money he owed her."

More scribbling. I notice that the detective's knuckles are raw and remember the boxing gym at the youth center where he volunteers. I also notice the dark circles of fatigue under his eyes, the shadow of stubble on his jaw. This one has layers. There's more to him than meets the eye.

For some reason, I think about Chief Royer, Agnes's longtime friend and maybe more. I never understood their relationship, but I had the sense that he protected her when he could, and that she helped him in ways she never revealed to us or anyone.

"The inheritance will all go to Regina now," Ana goes on into the silence, leans forward. "Isn't that like detecting one-oh-one? Follow the money?"

The detective holds her gaze; there's the tick of a smile, something between them. Like they know each other. But they don't, right? She'd have told me.

"Regina Hayes is a wealthy woman in her own right," he says. "The amount he owed her wasn't significant."

Ana releases a snort, leans back in her chair, and crosses her arms. "Except that money is never about money, is it? Especially between siblings."

The clock over the door ticks. Victor rustles some papers. "Do you have more questions for my client?"

He glances down at his notes. I wonder if we're done. He doesn't have anything on Ana and he's just fishing.

Then, "How would you characterize your relationship with Kevin Harding? Light? Not serious?"

Shit.

Ana swallows hard, looks down at her nails.

The detective reads over his notes; the silence expands. When did he find out about Kevin Harding? How? I'm certainly not going to ask.

"Kevin Harding, another ex-boyfriend, claims that you tried to poison him," Detective Bandeau says when she stays silent.

"There was never enough evidence to bring charges against my client," says Victor. I've briefed him on Ana's history, and he's ready for this line of questioning. "Meanwhile, there was plenty of evidence that Harding was an abuser and a career criminal."

"Hmm, yes," says the detective. "Assault, domestic violence, fraud. Sounds like a nice guy."

"Love is blind," says Ana darkly.

"So . . . you *loved* him?"

Victor lifts a palm. "You don't have to answer that."

"I ended my relationship with Kevin Harding after he hit me. He stalked me, threatened me, and harassed me for months."

Something like anger flashes across the detective's face. But then it's gone.

"Until," he says, voice softer.

Ana sniffs, wipes at her eye with a tissue she digs from her bag. Nice. "Until he fell ill."

"He was in a coma for three months."

"That's right."

"What happened to him?"

"How should I know? I *ended* our relationship because he was abusive. I didn't follow up on his health."

"And when he recovered did he return to stalking you?"

"No, he moved on to his next victim, I guess."

Outside the interrogation room a phone rings and rings. The buzzing fluorescent lights, among other things, are giving me a terrible headache.

"Kevin Harding claims that you tried to kill him. That he now lives in fear that you might come back to finish the job."

"According to whom?" Victor asks.

"Mr. Harding called our tip line when Paul's death hit the news. Like Regina, Kevin Harding suspects that Ana killed Paul."

A tide of blood rushes in my ears. But I know that my bearing is cool, relaxed. I have practiced control over my face and body language. I force myself to breathe.

"That's ridiculous," says Ana, easily. "Men are such children when they don't get what they want."

"Agree. It's preposterous," says Victor. "My client is an upstanding citizen with no criminal record. There's no real evidence to tie her to the illness of Mr. Harding *or* the death of Mr. Hayes. Just rumors started by a woman who should obviously be your primary suspect, and allegations from a violent criminal."

I glance over at Victor, whose face is still as stone, gaze on the detective unyielding.

Detective Bandeau looks at his notes again. "Going back further isn't it true that your mother was convicted for poisoning your father?"

Okay. Wow. The detective does his homework.

Victor clears his throat. "Nothing whatsoever to do with my client."

"And that you went to live with your aunt, Agnes Blacksmith, who was a known—*herbalist*."

He leans on the word unpleasantly.

"She was a florist," I put in.

Victor yawns elaborately. "Again, little to nothing to do with my client and the matter at hand."

"But it's fair to say that you come from a line of women who are knowledgeable about plants, herbs, and flowers and their effects on the human body."

"My aunt was a florist, master gardener, and the occasional

maker of herbal teas," says Ana. "My father ingested the death cap mushroom by accident. Common, really. Thousands of people die each year from accidental ingestion. My mother had a garden and was known to forage for herbs and mushrooms. It was a simple mistake that resulted in the tragic death of my father."

"But your mother was convicted of the crime."

"Which doesn't mean she was guilty."

"She then died in prison after a visit from your aunt."

Unbidden, the familiar rush of emotion I feel when conversation turns to Agnes and my parents washes over me. Anger, guilt, and a terrible crushing sadness that I'd do just about anything not to feel. When I was younger, I used to try to drink it away. Now, I breathe, let it flow through me.

"I think our mother died of a broken heart," says Ana, dabbing at her eyes.

"It could have been poison," says the detective.

"Well, that was never considered. My mother was a heavy smoker. She was under tremendous stress and grief-stricken at the death of my father, the loss of her children, and facing life in prison."

The emotions pass and I feel a distance from them, from the current situation. There are few topics of conversation I hate more than those about this chapter in our young lives.

"Once again," says Victor, tone sterner now. "What does this have to do with Paul Hayes's murder? Are you just dredging up unhappy memories to rattle my client?"

Bandeau is undeterred.

"Now Iggy Rose is in a coma. Another person connected to you. Do you see where I'm going with this?"

"Ignatia Rose Caine is a dear, longtime friend of my client's. Ms. Blacksmith has no motive whatsoever to harm Ms. Rose."

"Isn't she married to *another* ex-boyfriend of yours? Brock Caine?"

Victor issues a sigh. "Again. Absolutely nothing to do with

the matter at hand. As far as we know, Ms. Rose has a bad case of food poisoning."

"After brunching with the sisters Blacksmith, descended from a long line of—what are we calling them—*herbalists*?"

We choose silence. That's always best. The less you say the better. A dim panic is rattling deep inside me, reminding me that I am more than willing to kill to defend the people I love. And this detective represents an imminent threat to my family.

Breathe, I tell the beast in its cage. Calm down.

The detective opens a file. I catch a glimpse of Paul's dead body and my stomach turns a little. Ana looks away, wipes again at her eye. I wonder if anyone else notices that she isn't really crying. Her eyes are dry as stones.

"We have determined time of death as approximately forty-eight to seventy-two hours before the discovery of the body. We have also determined that Paul Hayes was killed in a remote location, transported to Black River Park, and buried there. This would likely have required the work of more than one person."

Ana is about to speak, but Victor puts a gentle hand on her arm.

"It is my understanding that Paul Hayes had a number of enemies both personal and professional," Victor says. "That he was unethical, a womanizer, and some say was almost sociopathically competitive. He had numerous charges of sexual harassment lodged against him, as well as a domestic assault charge on his criminal record. This was a bad guy."

"So, my question is," says the detective, undeterred. "Where were you on Wednesday night?"

"On Wednesday, I was at my niece's school event—a student art show. We then had a family dinner, not returning home until after 10:00 p.m. My neighbor Tina saw me come in."

"Do you confirm this?" he asks, looking at me.

"I do."

It's a lie. I have no idea where Ana was on Wednesday.

"And Thursday?"

"Girls' night out with my good friends Payton and Esme. Martini night. It was a late one. I met someone at the bar, took him home. I was with him all night."

She smiles at the detective. Is she flirting with him? I tap her with my foot under the table. She ignores me.

"Did you happen to get his name?" he asks, unimpressed.

"I'm afraid not. Chad? Chuck?"

"Is that a common thing for you? That you pick up a man, sleep with him, then forget his name?"

"*Zero* relevance," says Victor with a roll of his eyes.

I love this man so much.

"Are you slut shaming me?" she asks, mock offended with a hand to her heart.

Detective Bandeau has the good grace to blush, clears his throat again. A nervous tick? Do we make him uncomfortable?

"My point is," says Ana, "I had moved on from Paul Hayes."

"Do you have any way to get in contact with your new friend?" Scribble, scribble.

My back is aching in this hard metal chair. And I'm struck again by how much more I feel like Ana's mother than her sister. Did she really have a one-night stand with a stranger?

Ana taps a French-manicured finger on her toned thigh.

"He left before I woke up. It was just a one-night thing. We both knew that. I mean, I suppose I could cast around and see if he turns up."

"Do that."

The detective is quiet a second, clicking his pen.

"When was the last time you saw Amanda Alessi?"

"Who?" she asks stubbornly.

"Paul Hayes's new girlfriend. The *missing* woman."

"Never."

The expression on the detective's face makes my shoulders tighten.

He slips a photograph from another manila folder, slides it

across the table. There we all are. Me, Ana, Iggy. Regina is there, too, toward the back. Some other women; faces I know but their names elude me. Friends of Iggy's I think. I barely remember this night. If I was there it would have had something to do with Ana, or she begged me to go for some reason. I am not the girls'-night-out type.

Ana shakes her head, confused. She squints at the image. "Is one of these women his new girlfriend?"

He puts his finger on the image of a pretty, busty blonde with thick eyelashes and berry-pink lips at the center of the selfie. I recognize her then from the news coverage.

"That's Amanda Alessi," the detective says.

Ana shrugs, looks down at her fingernails, then up at the image again. "This is an old picture. Maybe she was a friend of Iggy's? She might have been there . . . but girls' night is a more-the-merrier proposition, bring friends, co-workers. She could have been at the bar, and I wouldn't necessarily have met her."

"Amanda Alessi had this photo framed in her house. It meant something to her."

Ana doesn't speak again, holds the detective's gaze.

"My client," says Victor, "has answered your question. Is there anything else?"

The detective slides a wrinkled piece of paper across the table. I recognize Ana's handwriting, and her phone number.

"Amanda Alessi's neighbor said that you dropped by, asking questions."

Oh, Ana. For fuck's sake.

"You don't have to answer that," says Victor quickly.

"I was looking for *evidence*." She leans forward. "To prove that *I* didn't kill Paul."

"How did you know where she lived if you didn't know her?"

Ana rolls her eyes like an annoyed teen, leans back with folded arms. "There's this really cool thing? It's called *the internet*. If you know where to look, you can find almost anything."

"Did you kill Paul Hayes?"

Huh, I guess he's decided on the direct route. My shoulders hike; my head is pounding now.

"No," says Ana, with an emphatic shake of her head.

The detective is annoyingly clicking his pen; the room is so cold my hands feel stiff. "Do you know where Amanda Alessi is?"

"I thought she was in Aruba, fucking my ex. Otherwise, no. I got an earful from her nosy neighbor, though. How she was a party girl. Slept around. Maybe she killed Paul, took off. Ever think about that?"

"Are you responsible for Iggy Rose's sudden illness?"

"No." Her voice quivers a little here. "She's . . . my best friend."

He pushes out a breath. "With friends like you, who needs enemies?"

Seems like a stupid move, but maybe he's losing his patience.

Ana pushes her chair back angrily. "Fuck off," she says quietly. She rises. Victor does, too.

The detective, unflappable, keeps on.

"What's this?" He pushes a photo across the table. A doll. An effigy made from sticks. My heart nearly stops in my chest. It's exactly like the one I found on my porch. Except mine was a protection effigy. This one has barbed wire wrapped around its neck. It's a doll meant to bring harm to an enemy.

Victor, Ana, and I lean in to stare at it.

"We found this in the woods near Paul's body," says the detective. "Any idea what it is?"

"No," Ana says simply. Victor nods, looks back to his notes.

Dolls and effigies have been used in rituals since the beginning of humanity. In popular culture, they are seen as evil, a harbinger of black magic. But most often they are used for healing, for protection, fertility, attracting love, and empowerment. White magic.

Of course, there are some who have used them for cursing or

binding enemies. But black magic comes at a high price for the practitioner. I have seen dolls like this one. I have made them myself. Many times. I assume the sticks are bound with hair, crystals, charms, perhaps small personal effects. I could give the detective a lesson on this particular item, but naturally I stay quiet, lean away with a shrug.

"Do you have anything to add, Vera?"

There's something odd about the way he leans on my name, like we know each other. Which we don't. I hold his eyes a moment, then lower them to the worn and scratched tabletop.

"Mrs. Blacksmith-Kline, please."

He gives me a deferential nod that is just north of condescending.

Then, from my bag, I withdraw an ecru correspondence envelope; inside is a folded piece of letter stationery.

"As per your request, the brunch menu, ingredients, who brought what, where we purchased some of the items that were served. Everyone who was there and contact information."

He takes it from me, and there's a sizzle of bad electricity in the millisecond that we're both holding the paper. Victor agreed that this was the right thing to do. Provide all the information that was requested, hold back nothing.

"There's a killer out there, detective," I say. "I suggest you find him before he hurts anyone else."

"Him?"

"Let's be honest. Isn't it usually a man?" I say. "Paul had a lot of enemies. He owed some shady people money from what I understand, had questionable business dealings. There's a pool of suspects a mile deep. Best get to work."

He regards me a minute, then looks back and forth between Ana and me. His eyes rest on Ana; he tips his stubbled chin toward her. "Regina Hayes says that you're a witch."

"She should talk," snaps Ana. "That bitch never liked me. And the feeling is entirely mutual."

"A Wiccan, a practicing witch," he clarifies. "She claims that there are a number of them in the area. It's a collective of sorts, isn't it? A group called The Cove?"

My blood goes a little cold, but Victor lets out a derisive laugh.

Ana's moving toward the detective. I grab her arm; we don't need a violent temper tantrum in here. He doesn't need to see her at her worst, which I promise you is very, very bad.

"Are you seriously asking me if I'm *a witch*?" she asks, voice raised in indignation. "What is this—the fucking *sixteen-hundreds*? Are you getting the stake ready?"

"Detective, that's quite enough," Victor says, still chuckling as he rises, gathering his things. "We came here in good faith to cooperate with your investigation. This interview has concluded. My client won't be speaking to your ridiculous suggestion."

Victor shuttles us toward the door and I can't get out of there fast enough.

"A man is dead. A woman is missing. Another woman is in a coma," says the detective, still seated, voice raised. "They have one thing in common, Ms. Blacksmith. You."

"What about the threats on his ConnectIn page? Or that blog I sent you? Did you even investigate? Who is Jezebel?" says Ana, her tone sizzling with anger.

He looks at his notes. "The post came from an IP address masked by a VPN. Untraceable. It could have easily been you. The blog was published anonymously, no one at the *Jezebel* site knows who wrote it. Again, it could have been you. But essentially, the leads you sent are dead ends."

She has locked him in a dark stare, and he's staring back with an equal amount of intensity.

"What about the texts with The Witch?" she asks.

"We're still investigating," he says vaguely.

"You know it wasn't me," she says. He lowers his eyes, closes his folder.

What is going on with these two?

"Time to go, Ms. Blacksmith," says Victor. "The detective clearly has nothing to hold you. Call us when you have some actual evidence."

We exit the room, hustle through the station, and step out into the cold. Above us, the sky is gray. I'm finding it hard to catch my breath, but I think I'm doing a good job of hiding it. There's an unpleasant spin to the world, the ground and sky tilting.

"They don't have anything," Victor says as we approach the car. He's seemingly unperturbed. "They don't even have theories at this point. No leads. No suspects. They're just fishing, making up silly stories to get a reaction."

"I didn't do any of this," Ana says. "I swear."

"Of course not," he says easily, as if this is a foregone conclusion. "But I would avoid the urge to play amateur sleuth, Ana. Or to communicate independently with the detective. It's not going to serve you."

Ana frowns but stays quiet.

He opens the door to his Range Rover, first for me in the front, then for Ana in the back. In the driver's seat, he's still laughing. "Witches. *Now* I've heard everything."

I lock eyes with my sister in the rearview mirror.

We are so very fucked.

My sister's phone pings. She looks at it then shoves it in her bag. Is that the hint of a smile? What is she hiding?

AGNES

I wait for them to come home, sitting in the dim of the kitchen, sipping peppermint tea, searching for calm. Which one of them did it? The truth is, I'm not sure. They're tricky. Both of them have The Knowledge now. I'm in a state of self-recrimination. Maybe I taught them too much, too soon. It's just that lately I feel an urgency to pass along what I know, so that it lives on in our family. It's a sacred practice that I don't want to see lost.

Sadie didn't want it. I don't have any children of my own. Lisander, my best pupil and dear friend who I love deeply, doesn't have the strength she needs to take my place. She's weak, swayed by emotion. She gossips, listens to rumor, is too concerned with the opinions of others. I've seen her be small, vindictive. Also, she's not family.

The girls, both gifted, are also powerful. Too powerful for their age. I'm thinking about this when in the distance, the school bus rumbles and whines in the hot afternoon. The sky outside darkens with an approaching storm, the trees bending in the sudden wind that's kicked up. My sinuses ache in the barometric pressure, and the windchimes on the porch start to sing. Storm song, I like to call it.

Ana's the sensitive one, Sadie wrote in her final letter to me.

It's doesn't seem like it because she's a tough talker, has that hard stare. But words, actions, hurt her deeply. She cares. Has a terrible temper that passes quickly as a summer storm.

Vera's colder, though on the surface she's the good girl, the rule follower. You think she's the one to get her feelings hurt, to act from fear. But her depths are icy. And she'll do anything for her sister, though they're at each other's throats most of the time. Like we were, remember? But I always knew you'd be there for me. I hope you knew the same was true for me.

No, Sadie. I didn't know that. I lost you to Mac. And before the night you called me to come get the girls, we hadn't spoken in years.

Vera and Ana come in the front door. They're talking in whispers and it's a sound that's grown familiar in this house. I often hear them at night, up late talking. Sometimes when their voices are low like this, it almost seems like they're speaking another language, something only the two of them understand.

They're laughing as they come into the kitchen and find me sitting there. When their eyes fall on me, they stop short, almost comically, exchange a look.

"What?" says Vera, flatly. "What's wrong?"

"Mr. Danvers," I say.

They both freeze, cast their gazes away, looking anywhere but at me. It's Ana who finally steps forward.

"Okay, look," she says, making her blue eyes wide and beseeching. "I'm sorry. I didn't do the reading and got a D on the pop quiz. I'll make it up. Don't worry. I can still end the semester with a B."

Vera stands stock-still, gaze now locked with mine.

"Mr. Danvers has been rushed to the hospital," I say.

If I didn't know them as well as I've come to, I might have missed it. The twitch at the corners of Ana's mouth. A smile fought back.

"Oh, no," says Vera, hand to her heart. Is she smiling just slightly? "What happened?"

"No one's sure," I say. "He collapsed after lunch, was rushed to the hospital."

"Will he—be alright?" asks Vera.

"Maybe not." I shake my head, put my cup down on the table. "Poor man."

"That's awful," she says. A beat passes. Then, "But didn't he have a bad heart?"

"Apparently, yes."

"So, heart attack then?" Vera opens the refrigerator and peers inside; the light washing out paints her pale.

"Girls, take a seat."

Vera lets the door close. They approach reluctantly and sit across from me. I let silence do the work.

"He was a lech," says Ana finally, leaning forward. "He touched me when I stayed after class to talk about my quiz."

"Touched you."

"He touched my hair, moved too close to me. So close I smelled his breath. And I'm not the only one. He's been doing this for years, touching, saying inappropriate things, giving good grades to girls he thinks are 'sweet.' Punishing those with opinions or those who don't let him get close."

"What are you telling me?"

"He's a bad man," says Ana. "If I'd been one of the sweet ones, he wouldn't have given me a D on the quiz. He didn't like my opinions on The Scarlet Letter, that it's misogynistic and facile. That it portrays women of power as witches."

"Ana," I say softly. "What did you do?"

She shrugs. "Nothing. Well, I reported him to the principal. Who said she'd look into it but didn't. I saw them laughing in her office. Old friends, I guess."

I draw in a deep breath. It's hard to tell if she's being purposely obtuse. "That's not what I mean."

She frowns, then seems to get it. "Oh. No. I didn't do anything to him. Seriously? No."

Vera is looking at her sister, her face unreadable.

"Someone has been in The Kitchen," I say. "I'm missing hemlock, mandrake, and henbane."

"Deadly Trance," says Vera, sounding almost like she's in a trance herself. "Soaked in hot water to create a steam, it was the first anesthetic."

"That's right," I say, glad she remembers her lessons. "But unreliable. Often causing the heart to stop altogether."

There are other ingredients missing, as well. Any one of them might have done the job, creating a cardiovascular event that looks like a heart attack. If I'd had to choose, it would have been foxglove.

"It wasn't me," says Ana.

"Then who?"

"Any one of the members of The Cove have access to The Kitchen," says Vera coolly. "Lisander was here all weekend."

Truthfully, I've heard whispers about Charles Danvers, but just that—rumors, a vague uneasy feeling women have around him, that yes he stands too close, says inappropriate things, touches in ways that are uninvited and unwanted. There have always been men like this, those that hover close to the line but don't step over it. But that's not reason enough to make a cure. Just reason enough to make sure that girls aren't left alone with him.

"Anyway, he's not dead, is he?" says Vera, leaning back.

"He touched me. He gave me a D," says Ana. "I don't care if he dies or not. But I didn't do anything. I swear."

"There are rules, girls. We follow them for a reason. Too many incidents in too short a time span in the same area can call attention."

"Old men have heart attacks all the time," says Ana easily, twirling a strand of her raven hair, blue eyes cool. "What's for dinner?"

Outside the sky is purple as a bruise, a storm threatening on the horizon.

The truth is that I'm just not sure what she's capable of doing. Either one of them.

ANA

I avoid eye contact with Vera in the rearview mirror.

She's talking to Victor, but her stare is like a cattle prod. I have to get out of this car and away from them both. I feel suffocated. Oppressed.

I'm still shaking inside from our visit to the police station. When that detective looks at me, it's like he sees right through me, knows all my secrets. I can't hide myself from him, the real me. I don't even want to.

The truth is that I have hurt people.

Sometimes I just get angry. Well, maybe it's a bit more than anger. There's like a little switch that flips. One minute I'm fine, normal, the right version of me. The next I'm not. You know what it is? There's a certain kind of injustice that I just can't tolerate. Someone who uses his position of power—whether it's his place in the system, or his physical strength, or his wealth—to hurt and abuse others. My shrink calls it a trigger. That's about right. The trigger on a gun.

My phone pings. It's Brock. *She's getting worse. You have to do something.*

"Victor," I say. "Can you drop me at the hospital? Iggy and Brock need me."

"Is that a good idea?" Vera asks Victor instead of me. A little lash of anger. She always treats me like one of her children.

Victor bobs his bald head from side to side considering. I remember how the crown of his head is stubbly and left a slight friction burn on the inside of my thighs.

I've got to hand it to him. He's been strictly professional, not so much as a sideways glance in my direction.

"I think it's fine," he says finally. "Probably looks good, that she's attending to her friend and her friend's family. If anyone is watching. Just don't be overly affectionate with the husband or spend any time alone with him outside the hospital."

"As if," I say. "I broke up with him years ago. We try to get along for Iggy's sake."

"Ana, listen to Victor." Vera's voice is stern, bossy. "Do what he says."

A lash of annoyance. "I'm not a child."

"Then stop acting like one."

Victor pulls off the highway and within minutes we're arriving at the hospital. As soon as he stops I get out of the car. Vera exits with me.

"We need to talk," she says in a fierce whisper. "If you're not honest with me I can't help you." She's always been like this, so desperate to control everything. Isn't she exhausted?

"I *am* being honest with you. I've told you everything." I don't love how whiny I sound.

"How much does Regina Hayes know about The Cove?"

"I have no idea."

"Did you tell Paul?"

"No! Of course not. But they've both lived in this town all their lives. There have always been rumors about The Cove. It's like an urban legend."

"Except it's true."

"Look—there are no secrets in the age of social media, right? For fuck's sake, there are online herbalists now, TikTok witches,

Instagram voodoo doll practitioners. There's a Facebook page for modern day *veneficas*." A sorceress who uses potions and drugs for various reasons. "People are practicing The Knowledge out in the light these days. The good news is that there's no such thing as truth anymore, right? Truth these days is whatever your curated social media feed tells you is the truth."

There's a look that Vera saves only for me—some combination of fear, anger, pity, and love. I can't really blame her. I've fucked up quite a bit.

"Where did that doll come from?" she asks.

I have some ideas, but I just shrug. "You tell me."

"It's not one of mine," she says. Coraline told me about Vera's room in the basement. I'm surprised she still makes them, those little effigies for protection. She seems to have left everything about The Knowledge behind her, buried it beneath her supermom, trophy wife persona.

There's something dancing behind my sister's eyes. I get a brief glimpse of that inner beast, the one she keeps locked up in the dark, the one she starves and neglects. I have a fleeting thought.

No. No way.

"I'm going to fix this," I tell her.

"You keep saying that. But what is your *plan, Ana*?"

I hate it when she leans on my name like that, as if I'm one of the kids.

"I am going to figure out what happened to Paul and Iggy, figure out who did this."

It sounds weak because it is. I don't have a plan. I never do. That's one of my biggest problems as a person.

"How?"

"I'll handle it," I say even though I have no idea what to do.

But I do have a way to maybe help Iggy, and that's where my focus is now.

"You'd better," she hisses. "Because I don't like that detective. He's got his sights on you."

If she only knew.

"He knows too much about us," she continues. "This could be very bad. And we're already on warning with The Cove. I didn't like Lisander's attitude. She's not going to help us again."

She grabs my hand, and I see it. Vera hides fear with anger. I remember the look she has now from the night Agnes came to get us from the police station, Mac taken away in the ambulance, Sadie dragged into a police car in cuffs. The ground had fallen away beneath our feet and all we had then was each other. She looks tired now, tiny lines etching around her eyes.

I squeeze her hand, then back away from her, our eyes locked, finally turning to head inside the hospital. Sirens wail as an ambulance approaches, Vera keeping worried eyes on me. I wish there had been someone to protect Vera the way she has always protected me. Maybe then she wouldn't be such a panic case.

Inside the building, I'm assailed by a powerful wave of negative energy. *How can anyone get well in a place so full of sickness, fear, death?* I wonder as I march through the crowded foyer. The energy is not conducive to healing. Healing comes from the earth, from within. Not in a sterile, harshly lit place like this.

In the elevator, I stand next to an ancient woman in a wheelchair attended to by a young male nurse. She looks up at me. The Crone—knowledge and wisdom, a warning that the world is cruel and random, unless you do something about it and even then. She holds a rosary in her hand, worrying fine polished dark beads and a tarnished crucifix between her crooked thumb and forefinger.

I smile at her, and she returns it with a toothless grin.

"Be careful," she says with a little laugh. Maybe she's talking to me. Maybe she isn't. Her eyes are cloudy and unfocused.

"Always," I tell her, putting a gentle hand on her shoulder. The male nurse gives a wave as I step off the elevator.

In Iggy's room, Brock sits head bent by her bed. He's whispering something near her ear.

I wait outside the door a minute, watching them, feeling like an intruder, filled with regret for how I've treated my friend. I remember the promise I made to my sister. That I'd find out who did this. That I'd handle it. I use the moments before I walk into Iggy's room to think.

Okay, what did Paul and Iggy have in common, aside from me? She used to work at his company, said he was an asshole, handsy. There was some other incident at their office. A he-said-she-said thing that Paul said was all lies. No charges filed. That's when he started his own business—with Regina's money. Iggy wasn't too pleased when I started seeing him, told me I should stay away. She told me the stories that I believed were just rumors. I wasn't deterred. We had very different tastes when it came to men. And when she warned me off him, I got mad. Since the argument, since the baby, Iggy and I were spending less time together. But we were still close, still talked all the time. Just there was a tension there that hadn't been there before.

She'd grown closer to Esme. Maybe there's something there? Esme has hated Paul with a passion since the *Business Journal* article. But Esme's a nerd, a gamer. A successful businesswoman. She's no killer, right? And I can't see why she would want to hurt Iggy.

So, who was at the girls' brunch, my exorcism?

Vera, Esme, Payton, Iggy, and me.

And April was there, serving. Vera's little mouse had access to all the food. But what does April have to do with Paul? What reason would she have to hurt Iggy?

We've all known each other for ages. And April's been working for Vera for as long as the kids have been alive. She's a member of The Cove, is Lisander's student. The truth is that April has never even been remotely interesting to me.

Until now.

I enter the room and Brock looks up, red eyed.

"How is she?" I say and he just shakes his head. I give him

a hug. Beneath the negativity, there is a little bit of affection. I did give them my blessing, and I meant it. They're right for each other. Anyone can see that.

I take a little vial from my bag, hold it out to him.

"What is that?"

"It's a milk thistle blend, something Agnes developed to combat the effects of amatoxin—which Iggy's symptoms seem to indicate. It might help to protect her. That's the best we can hope for, to strengthen the organs while the toxins work their way through her system."

"Are you sure it will work?"

I shake my head. I'm not. There are too many unknowns. What she ingested. How much. How healthy and strong she was to begin with. I know she's a fighter, that she loves Brock and the little stinko. So that's something in her arsenal, the will to live. Iggy looks like a doll, Cupid's bow mouth, too red against gray skin, deep purple under her eyes, wrists tree-branch thin. She's fading. I take her hand and I can barely feel her life force.

"Iggy. Don't you dare leave us," I tell her sternly. "Don't leave Noah. He needs you. I've been a shitty friend. And you were right about Paul. *I* need you."

Do her blue eyelids flutter?

I walk over to the IV line and give Brock a questioning glance. He shrugs. I take some satisfaction that Brock clearly knows I would never hurt Iggy. Otherwise, he'd never let me near her. But there's not much hope for modern medicine now. Of course, all modern medicine derives from the shaman of indigenous cultures; all medication comes initially from plants. There is nothing invented, only discovered, synthesized, and refined, measured, balanced.

I attach the vial to the IV line, the way I learned from Agnes, who made frequent hospital visits. Often after her visits, which were ostensibly to offer support, prayer, comfort, patients would grow miraculously better—if even just for a short time.

Sometimes not. Sometimes they would peacefully pass after a long languishing. But sometimes they would become well and walk away defying all odds.

I sit beside her and whisper my aunt's prayer: *May your body use the gifts of the earth to heal. May you find the strength to stay with us or the peace to let go. It is not your will or ours, but the will of the Great Mother whose wisdom encompasses all things, even that which is unknown to us.*

I do as Agnes taught me, fill my lungs with air, draw the energy of the earth in through the soles of my feet, and let it travel from my palms to hers. Then I add my own addendum. "Don't go, Iggy. It's not time."

Brock stands in the corner, watching.

We both startle at the sudden sound of a baby crying. Not crying. *Wailing*, growing closer. Oh, god. Seriously?

Brock's mother walks in looking harried, Noah wriggling in her arms. Her face darkens when she sees me.

"You," she says.

"Hello, Marge," I say flatly. "You really seem to have a magical way with children."

Her nostrils flare in distaste.

I reach for Noah, and she reluctantly hands him over. In my arms, he quiets immediately. I am annoyingly happy to see him. What is it with this kid? He's just so warm and fat in my arms, like a little hot water bottle.

I touch his nose. "Hey, buddy. I know, your grandma is a real . . ."

"Ana," says Brock.

"Sorry."

"I just can't get him to settle," Marge says, looking uncharacteristically distraught. Babies do have a way of unstitching our composure, don't they? I remember when Coraline had colic and Vera, Brad, April, and I took turns walking with her while she wailed. God, I resented the fuck out of her then, swore I would never have children of my own. But she grew on me. More or less.

I bounce Noah a little, give him a couple of hard pats on the back, and finally he releases a big, gross baby burp.

"He's gassy," I say, remembering what Iggy told me. *If you don't burp him right after he eats and then again a little while later, he's a bear.* "You need to burp him after you feed him. More than once."

"I know that, Ana. Thank you," Marge snaps.

"Ana put a milk thistle blend into the IV line," says Brock.

Marge casts a side-eye at me. A friend of Agnes's, Marge knows a thing or two about The Cove. She wasn't a member, but an ally, someone from whom Agnes often sourced herbs she didn't grow in her own garden.

"Where did you prepare it?" she asks.

"In the kitchen, from Agnes's recipe."

She nods. Everyone trusted Agnes. Her work was always flawless. I wonder what it takes to earn respect like that.

"You know what tonight is," Marge says, glancing out the window.

Of course I know what tonight is. The Wolf Moon. I'm a little surprised that she does.

When Agnes was alive it was always a time of celebration, of gathering. I remember the bonfire and the mulled cider, the incantations. The meeting usually lasted for days. People came to learn from each other, to swap recipes, herbs, crystals, books. It was a time of releasing the cold, fallow months of winter, looking forward to the renewal of spring.

Since Agnes's death, it's as if all the energy and joy of it is gone. With Lisander at the helm, it's as dull as a condo board meeting. There's bickering, grudges brought forth, reprimands handed out, and new rules voted upon, which no one follows. I'm sure Agnes is not pleased, if she's looking down on us.

Not as many people come. Agnes was the mother of The

Cove. People came for her love, her energy, her encouragement. They came for her instruction and recipes, for the herbs from her garden, which were known to be special. Now Lisander and a small council are the leaders. The garden produces far less than when Agnes was alive, and not for lack of our trying. It's like it was part of her and now it's slowly fading without her, just like The Cove.

"Lisander wants you and Vera to be there."

"What do you know about what Lisander wants?" I ask, bouncing Noah a little on my hip. How does everyone and their mother all of a sudden know about The Cove?

I don't like the way she and Brock are looking at me, like I'm the kid who got called to the principal's office. Sometimes I wonder if Brock is as sweet as he seems. He is Marge's son after all.

A dark thought occurs: Do either of them have a reason to kill Paul, to hurt Iggy?

I swallow the lump in my throat, back away, and can only manage a nod. I'm still traumatized from the last meeting that was called because of something I was involved in.

Noah takes a chunk of my hair and pulls hard.

"Ouch, buddy," I say, unclenching his little fingers. Seems to be our thing. He laughs, bounces his legs.

"He likes you," says Marge grudgingly. Her hair is dry and frayed as a Brillo pad, her face a landscape of lines and sagging skin. Note to self: moisturize.

"I have to go," I say. "I'll take the baby."

"No," says Marge quickly, reaching for him. Noah looks at her, mouth pressed into a comical pout. Then he starts to squall. Marge lifts her beefy palms in surrender, looks to Brock, who shrugs wearily.

"Where's that baby carrier thing? The one you strap on."

"In the trunk," says Brock, handing me the fob. "Just take the car because it has the seat in it. I'm not leaving Iggy."

I take the baby bag from Marge, who turns to her Brock. "You need to get some rest, son," she says. "I'll stay with her."

He shakes his head, sits back down as Marge looks at him helplessly.

"I'll bring the baby back to the house after a while," I say. "I'll put him down there for the night and stay."

Brock doesn't say anything and Marge waves me out.

I leave them, taking the baby, not even sure why I offered. It just makes me feel better somehow. I have the weird feeling that Iggy would rather he was with me than with Marge, even though I've never evidenced caretaking skills of any kind.

At the car, I strap him into his seat. He happily bats at the toys that hang from the handle. We haven't even been driving for five minutes when I look in the mirror to see that he's sound asleep.

I know where April works when she's not at my sister's beck and call. I have some questions for the little mouse, so I drive that way.

Even though it's just early afternoon, the sky already seems to be darkening the way it does in a northern winter, the stingy sun lost behind the persistent gray ceiling.

As the sun sinks, I have the very powerful sense that the wolf is at my door and my time is running out.

VERA

The first time it happened, Ana was just out of college. The call came late.

"What's wrong?" I answered.

"Something happened," she said. Her voice sounded so strange I remember, flat, cold. I think she was in shock. "Something bad."

"Where are you?"

"At home."

"I'm coming."

Because that's the thing with us. It doesn't matter how mad she makes me, or how much we fight. We're bound—not just by blood. But by the knowledge that there's no one else in the world who would have our backs in the same way. I'd lay my life down for my kids, but I wouldn't want or expect them to do the same for me. Brad? Well, adult love, especially one like ours, is conditional, isn't it? With Ana and me, it's not even a question. She calls, I come. I call, she comes. We do what it takes, no matter what. That's how it was with Sadie and Agnes.

When I got to my sister's place, Ana was sitting at the kitchen table in her little rental house just outside of town. There was a beat-up old Mustang with a torn ragtop in her driveway that I didn't recognize. As I came in through the garage, Ana was holding an ice pack to her face. When she took it away, I saw the black rose of a giant shiner blooming across her cheekbone and temple, her eye swollen shut.

"What the fuck?"

"You should see the other guy," she said, nodding in the direction of the living room.

Indeed.

He was splayed across the floor, having fallen apparently on top of the cheap IKEA coffee table and flattening it beneath himself. The shards of a shattered crystal vase were scattered about like stars on the dark area rug. There was a deep gash on his head. Something about the scene reminded me of our childhood, Sadie and Mac always going at it. These big fights where things got broken, and then they were weeping in each other's arms.

I'm not sure how long I stood there in a terrible storm of shock and bad memories.

"Is he dead?" I asked from the doorway, finally finding words.

"I don't *know*," she said wearily, as if the question annoyed her.

This was before I met Brad, before the kids. Agnes had recently passed. It was really just the two of us then. I imagined her being hauled away like our mother, leaving me alone in this ugly world.

I approached him carefully, my heart thumping, knelt down, reached to a wrist for his pulse and found him alive. At my touch, he issued a groan and I moved away from him quickly. He was too big to move; Ana has always been partial to a big muscle-bound guy, whereas I prefer them lithe, flexible—yogis and runners, not body builders and WWF beefcakes.

"Who is he?"

"Just some guy I met on HookUp."

"HookUp?"

"You know, the app for people who just want to get together for—like a night or whatever."

"You're kidding."

She shrugged. "Don't be a judgy bitch, Vera."

"What happened?"

"He came over. He got rough—like *too* rough. I told him to stop. He lost it, hit me. So, I took care of him."

The man on the floor issued a low groan. A word. *Help*.

"Is that Mom's crystal vase?"

"Was. Yes," she said, sounding momentarily regretful. "I'd like to think she would be happy it served a function beyond holding flowers."

"So, what do we do with him?" I asked.

She looked at me with dismay. "For fuck's sake, Vera, that's why I called *you*."

It was a mistake in retrospect, but I couldn't think of anything to do but call Lisander. To her credit, she was there within an hour. She brought a couple of her young acolytes with her, Bree and Camille—who have both since moved up the ranks of The Cove.

They arrived with purpose at the front door, each of the younger women carrying a duffel bag.

"First, we take care of Ana's injuries," said Lisander.

She was tender with my sister, asking her what happened, listening attentively. She produced an arnica salve, which she rubbed liberally on Ana's bruise and probably fractured ribs—then put her to bed with an ice pack.

"Now we take out the trash," she said, as she closed Ana's door.

"What does that mean?" I asked.

"We just need him to wake up somewhere else, not be sure how he got there, and be humiliated enough that he never speaks of it. Why in the world did she invite some stranger to her house?"

"How should I know?"

Impulsivity. Poor judgment. A lack of foresight. I wish I could say I was surprised. But that was Ana. Act first, think later.

Camille, Bree, Lisander, and I managed together to get the unconscious man in the back hatch of her vehicle, grateful for the isolated property surrounded by trees. We then continued on to a truck stop, Lisander driving the stranger's junky old Mustang, the three of us following in her ancient minivan. The truck stop was a place known locally for illicit hookups and illegal activities. As we arrived several dark, parked cars idled. Windows tinted, vehicles rocking subtly.

Lisander, a registered nurse at the local hospital, had injected Ana's friend with a syringe of Midazolam, a short-acting benzodiazepine utilized in sedation in critical care, a powerful amnesiac.

"Won't it show up in his blood?" I asked.

Camille, who was the approximate build of a twelve-year-old boy but still somehow impossibly strong, shook her head. Her bright green eyes and dark skin a gorgeous contrast.

"No."

She'd done most of the lifting as we hauled the unconscious man from Lisander's hatch to the back seat of his own vehicle.

"Well, only if he goes to the cops, *and* they take his blood," answered Bree, a watchful blonde with short-cropped hair and sleeves of tattoos who had driven the van. "Which he won't."

"And no one who saw us here will ever tell," said Lisander, looking around at the darkened vehicles. "Because everyone here is up to no good."

It was slightly genius.

"He'll wake up, no idea how he got here," said Camille, as if this was something they'd done before. "Hopefully he'll be embarrassed enough to go home, sleep it off, and never speak of it again."

"What if he goes after Ana?" I asked.

"She'll stay with you for a while," said Lisander, easily. "We'll watch her house. If he comes back, we'll manage him more completely."

Lisander reminded me so much of Agnes with her cool certainty that bad people, men especially, were problems to be managed in a variety of different ways from the subtle to the total.

Once a man hits you or harms you and you let him get away with it—Agnes warned us, as I know she warned Sadie, who never listened—*he'll hit you again and again until he kills you. A certain type will come after you when you try to free yourself. That type will need to be put down like a dog who can't stop biting.*

"But we'll give him the chance to walk away and keep his mouth shut," said Lisander.

We got into the van, and Lisander started the drive back to Ana's house.

"Thank you," I said when we arrived.

"Ana," said Lisander, glancing at me. "She's a loose cannon. This isn't the first time we've had to clean up one of her messes."

"I know," I said. "But this was clearly self-defense."

Lisander nodded, tugging on the long gray braid of her hair with heavily ringed fingers. On the back of her hand the tattoo of a monarch butterfly, her wrists covered with inked vines and flowers, line drawings of herb gardens, bees, birds. "I agree—and that's why we're here at all. But you know when we invite danger into our lives, we often pay a high price."

"So, you're saying she asked for it?"

She put a comforting hand on my leg.

"Of course not. I'm only saying that there are good men in this world, and there are dangerous ones. When we find ourselves drawn to darkness over and over, we have to question that impulse. We have to learn and grow from our mistakes, act to protect ourselves—and The Cove. Impulsive actions threaten us all."

She sounded just like Agnes, which was as comforting as it was annoying.

I understood what she was saying, and truthfully it was nothing I hadn't said to Ana a thousand times. *Don't pick Mac over and over*. But maybe when we're young, we learn what love looks like from our parents. And in our case our parents' brand of love was violence.

Victor has left, and I'm alone in the house, mind reeling from the things I've learned at the police station.

As I wrestle the vacuum from the closet to clean floors that don't need cleaning, I think about the crime scene photo of Paul, the detective's questions of Ana. The mention of Kevin Harding, another man who ran afoul of Ana. I feel my grip on things slipping.

Then it's on to surfaces that don't offer even the finest layer of dust, as I wonder how I'm going to get my sister out of this recent mess.

Finally, in the master closet, I go through all the pockets of Brad's suit jackets. Not looking for anything in particular. I like to check receipts against what he's said he's been doing. Once I found a matinee ticket stub for a noon movie. He never mentioned it to me; I never asked. It's not really my business. I just like knowing what he's up to. His pockets are empty except for a receipt from the weekend at the golf club, consistent with his known activities.

My phone pings with a text from Brad, as if he knows I'm rifling around his things.

> We lost another client today. Vision, the data center just outside of town.

Shoot. That's a big fish. A flush of anger comes up. Anything that threatens our livelihood, threatens our family.

Okay, I type back. We'll get through this. There have been challenging times before.

> We might have to let people go.

Brad tends to get very worst-case scenario.

Let's not jump the gun.

Anxiety reaches a crescendo as I fluff the bed pillows. Another ping. This one from Ana.

It's the Wolf Moon tonight. Did you forget?

I look outside to the dim afternoon already hinting at dusk. I didn't forget as much I chose to ignore. It's in these moments when I feel out of my depth that I most miss Agnes.

I need advice, but I can't call Lisander. I don't want her to know that things are looking worse than ever for Ana. And I don't want to tell her that Regina Hayes is running off at the mouth. Because who told *her* about The Cove? Did Ana tell Paul? Did Paul tell Regina? Did she already know about us? What was she doing there the night that photo was taken? Martini night, of all things. I don't even remember it, really.

Meanwhile Ana's right that it's hard to keep a secret these days—the information age and all of that.

Still, women like us have been operating in secrecy for centuries.

There's a long lineage of female herbalists and botanists, tracing our history back to Locusta, who was the poison maker for high-profile ancient Romans like Emperor Claudius, Empress Agrippina the Younger, and Nero. Ladies Catherine and Marie de Medici were implicated in more than a few deaths. These were woman who were respected and feared—they could heal, or they could kill depending on the client, the need. But the 1300s saw a growing hatred and distrust toward female herbalists. We became seen as witches, and over the next three centuries we were burned, drowned, hanged, and crushed. Female power is terrifying.

Because women aren't supposed to kill.

We are the life bringers. We are the ones meant to bear up, to endure, to stand by and do nothing. Men are supposed to take us to their beds with trust and ease. In the kitchen, we're only meant to create things that nourish, not use our rightful place in home and garden to cause harm.

Finally, when things are as neat as they can be, I sit at the kitchen table and open my laptop.

What am I looking for?

Anything that will take Detective Bandeau's attention away from my sister and The Cove.

I enter "Paul Hayes" into the search bar and click on the news tab, scroll through the current spate of articles about his death, the discovery of his body, pictures of the still-missing Amanda Alessi.

Suspect? Victim? Where is Amanda Alessi? reads the headline of one article, including that now-famed picture of the toes, beach, and clinking glasses. The article is just blather, possibly written by AI, published on some obscure crime blog.

But it's a fair point. Where *is* Amanda Alessi? The girl with the framed picture of us in her house? I start clicking around the web.

First, I watch a video of her mother crying, begging for information. I feel a pang, every mother's worst nightmare. Then it's on to social media. On Amanda's Facebook page, there's a post from someone named Jessie Parker. I click on her page and recognize her from the framed picture.

She's posted a picture of herself and Amanda cheek to cheek, along with a plea for information.

Come home to us, girl. We miss you.

The comments are typically inane—lots of crying-face emojis and broken hearts—still I scroll, looking for connections.

Finally, a comment catches my eye because of its flurry of emojis. A closer look reveals that it's from Iggy, time-stamped after the brunch and before she fell ill.

Okay, wow. So, Iggy knew Amanda and Jessie well enough to be engaged with them on social media. Iggy's ill. Amanda is missing.

That's a connection, right?

I do a little more hunting around, find Jessie Parker on ConnectIn. It doesn't take long to discover that she once worked at the same advertising firm that fired Paul.

Another connection.

Iggy's comment on Jessie's post: **Sending all light and love for protection and wellness for Mandy.**

I cast about on Iggy's socials and find that her online business has grown considerably. Ana's mentioned it before, but I didn't pay much attention. Like I said, I ignore The Cove and its members.

Protection.

I think about the effigy the detective found in the woods and honestly, it scares me. Who left it there? Members of The Cove, whatever their practice, are rarely so careless. We have spent centuries hiding in the shadows, fearing men and their persecution. We know how to cover our tracks. The photograph was grainy, so I didn't get a close enough look to see if I recognized the handiwork.

I keep scrolling—articles, Reddit threads, blogs, social media, the typical barfing mouth of the internet. Finally, I am sick with it. Eyes aching, central nervous system buzzing.

There's one image of Paul that comes up again and again in the articles, some executive headshot that manages to make him look smarmy and boyish all at once, his hair weirdly swept to the side, his teeth too white, eyes distant, skin airbrushed and plastic smooth.

The first time I met Paul, Ana brought him to a July 4th

barbecue we hosted at our country club. It was rare, that Ana would bring someone to meet me, to meet *us*, because she considers me to be a "judgy bitch" who "hates everyone she likes." Which I guess is mostly true. I liked Brock, though. He was sensitive and kind and good with Ana, smoothing some of her rough edges. But that obviously was doomed from the start. I figured she'd tire of him and move on, which she did.

Honestly, I disliked Paul Hayes on sight. The way he kept a possessive hand on Ana's back, glanced around at the features of the club, our wealthy friends, the way his eyes fell on my diamond ring, even how solicitous he was with Coraline and Autumn.

But with Brad and Paul it was all backslapping hugs and boisterous man laughter. Apparently, they already knew each other from the local chamber of commerce. It's so easy for them, isn't it? Men know how to lift each other up, giving each other business, recommendations, contacts that can help with this or that.

"I don't like him," I told Brad when we found a moment alone at the bar. I kept my eyes on Paul as he leaned into Ana, whispering something to her. She smiled, sly, eyelashes batting.

"Darling," Brad said, clinking my glass. "You don't like *anyone*. You didn't even like me when we first met."

True.

"Just give him a minute," Brad urged when I didn't bother to respond. "He's an acquired taste."

Later as the event was winding down, and the kids were floating in the pool with their friends, Paul approached me.

I was sitting on a lounge chair, watching the sun go down and feeling a wash of gratitude for the life we had been able to give Grant and Coraline, watching them play and tease each other with ease, their beautiful young bodies, their ready smiles. Autumn was there. And the girl Grant has had a crush on forever but never does anything about, Dahlia. I can't speak for the rest of the kids, but mine have never known fear, or hunger. They've never watched their parents lose control of themselves, their lives.

And that innocence of the world and what could happen if you didn't keep a grip on the reins was a golden halo around them. In the setting sun, I swear I could almost see it.

"May I?" Paul asked, interrupting my thoughts, pointing to the chair beside me.

"Of course," I said.

My husband, Brad, is very pretty with refined features and thickly lashed eyes; his voice is soft, touch gentle, smile ready. He's svelte, stylish, refined. Unlike my father in every way. On the other hand, in Paul I recognized Mac's brand of virility, the squareness of his jaw, the ripple of muscles in his forearm, his gravelly voice. Despite his thick Rolex, manicured nails, that carefully styled hair, I saw him for what he was. A thug.

"I know you and your sister are very close," he said, squinting into the sun. "She means the world to me. I wanted you to know that."

There was a shriek from the pool, and I looked over to see that Grant had dunked Coraline; she emerged from the water laughing, splashing at her brother, who looked very pleased with himself.

"You have a beautiful family," he said. "I hope to be a part of it."

I almost guffawed at that. "Well," I said, turning my attention to him, and making sure to pin him with my gaze. "Let's not get ahead of ourselves."

A slow smile spread across his face. I didn't like the look of it. I felt a wave of toxic energy, and I think right then I knew he was going to be trouble.

"Well," he said, matching my tone. "I think we'll be going. Thank you for an enjoyable afternoon."

I returned his fake smile. "Thank you so much for coming." We?

Ana was part of *my* "we," not his. Still, I watched as he approached my sister, whispered something to her. She threw me a dark look, a wave, and then they were gone. I felt something small and unpleasant squirm in my middle.

Brad sat down beside me where Paul had just been, watched as Ana and Paul disappeared through the doors from the pool deck. "Making friends?"

"I have enough friends."

His smile was loving, indulgent. "He's not that bad. She seems happy."

Even good men don't see what women see. They don't have to. When men hear about crime, their interest tends to be in the perpetrator. When women hear about crime, we more strongly identify with the victim. Women have to stay attuned to cues. Because a misstep leaves us vulnerable.

"He asked for a meeting," said Brad. "He wants to pitch his firm."

I laughed, but it came out more like a bark. "I don't think so."

"I'll hear him out. Just to keep relations."

I gave him a wave to say I couldn't care less what he does. But there was no world in which we were hiring Paul Hayes's advertising firm.

"I hope for his sake he stays on your good side," said Brad.

We exchanged a look, more shrieking from the pool. The poolside waiter in his crisp white shorts and blue polo shirt delivered two flutes of champagne.

Brad took them both, offered thanks to the waiter, then handed me a glass.

"Are we celebrating?" I asked.

"Always," he answered. "Let's drink to Ana's happiness. I know that's what you want."

He was right of course. I wanted Ana to be happy, well coupled, taken care of. I would do anything to protect her from someone who might harm her, because my love for her is so fierce. She's my baby sister.

"And you just want her married so that there will be someone else other than me to take care of her."

"The thought had crossed my mind," he said, clinking glasses again.

"We're a package deal," I reminded him.

He sipped his champagne.

Now, I keep scrolling. Click. Click. Click.

Paul Hayes, *Maverick Entrepreneur*. A phoenix-from-the-ashes puff piece about how he got fired and started his own business in one of those ad-heavy local glossy mags.

Paul Hayes Donates $100,000 to Local Youth Center. Another fluff piece with a picture of Paul holding a big check, surrounded by kids. *"A place like this saved me when I was a kid growing up with nothing. It's truly an honor to give back to the community."*

Paul Hayes Nominated for Businessperson of the Year Award.

This is the most recent news item before the news of his murder, so I click on it, scroll through the article. The award is actually kind of a big deal, not the typical local org offering self-congratulatory faux accolades to the highest bidder. This one was a state award that came with prestige, a glitzy gala that was often attended by high-ranking government officials, and garnered a great deal of press coverage. Brad had been nominated and won a few years back, and it skyrocketed our business.

I scroll through the list of other nominees until I come to a name I know well.

Esme Carlton, founder and owner of *You Play Like a Grrl*, a gaming company devoted to hiring and incubating female programmers, helping them develop games and other tech products in a male-dominated market. Her company has won awards for the most employee-friendly work environment with flex hours for new mothers, on-site day care, generous leave, and health insurance. Most famously YPLG, Inc hired one of the programmers who would go on to create *Red World*, the most popular video game maybe ever. Esme has made a fortune, donates copiously to local causes, and dedicates herself to a grueling speaking schedule where she travels to schools, trying to inspire girls to go into technology fields.

And yet there isn't a fraction of the news coverage that's been devoted to Paul—who was fired for sexual harassment from his last job, then poached all his clients to open his new firm.

Esme railed after that *Business Journal* article last year, "50 under 50." She wasn't mentioned, but Paul was lauded. Ana was angry for her, I remember. But it wasn't more than a couple of months after that that Paul and Ana started dating.

I stare at Esme's picture, that smile, the dimple in her cheek, those glittering dark eyes. If there's one word I would use to describe her it's kind. A corporate killer, for sure, savvy and hardworking. As a woman, you don't build a successful company without being a bit of a badass. But she's a woman who cares deeply about her friends, her wife, her employees. She's generous to a fault. And I can't see her killing a man for a regional award. Still, it stings when someone with far less talent and grace than you possess seems to take all the wins. Not because he's better than you are. But because he's a man.

Sometimes when we're pushed to our limit, there's no telling what we'll do.

I have a couple of hours, since Brad is picking the kids up from school. I decide to pay Esme a visit.

But before I do, I go down to the basement to take a closer look at the doll that I found on my porch, just to see if it offers any clues.

But when I get to my workbench, I draw in a breath.

It's gone.

ANA

After pulling into the quiet lot of the bookstore, I come to a stop in front of the gray wood-framed building. I've been here before—with Agnes as a kid, with Vera, even alone looking for ingredients or information, or other things.

Windchimes hang from the eaves, filling the air with a discordant music I can hear even through the closed windows of the car.

Noah stirs in the back, opens his eyes, makes a noise that sounds cranky. He's going to need a bottle soon, I think, which means I have to get back to Iggy's. See, this is what I mean. When there's a kid around, you can't think about *anything* else. The constant need. How do people stand it?

"Just chill a minute," I tell him in the rearview mirror. He's watching me with that frown he gets right before he's going to start bawling. "Auntie Ana has to figure out who killed Paul and made your mommy sick otherwise I'm probably going to jail, or worse. Okay? It's not just about *you*."

He offers a little chortle, which I take to mean that like all children he couldn't care less about what's going on with me. He turns his gaze away to look out the window, then coos and points at the glittering chimes.

"Let's go see those," I say, getting out into the cold.

It's frigid, the sky an ugly gray, black branches all around like fingers reaching for me. I hate winter. Death. Sleep. I dream of spring when the plants come back to life, when Agnes's garden is in full bloom. Even the deadly residents of her walled garden are beautiful, have their moment preening in the sun.

I find that baby carrier thing in the trunk and strap it on with the kid facing out. God, he weighs a ton. My back is already aching as I climb the stairs to the porch, and push into Make Magic, Little Valley's only occult—a word I hate as it conjures darkness, evil—bookstore.

A little bell rings as I open the door. Inside it smells heavily of sandalwood and sage. Dim light sneaks in from the west-facing windows, casting a milky glow on the books and shelves, a table of tarot cards in colorful boxes, trays of glittering crystals all shapes and sizes, and a painted rose gold wall displaying a variety of handmade dream catchers.

"Can I help you make some magic?" says the woman at the counter, skeletally thin, gray, with those big glasses that hide most of her face, make her eyes look huge. April.

"Oh," she says, recognizing me. "Hello."

It's not that we don't like each other. I mean—we *don't*. But it's not exactly antipathy between us. It's more like distrust, laced with a thread of distaste.

April gazes upon Vera with devotion, something like hero worship, and it annoys me. Vera, I guess, is like a mentor to her, but my sister is far less versed in The Knowledge than I am. She doesn't practice actively, doesn't want to. I don't really either, but I keep up my skills at least. I know how they see me in The Cove. I'm the badly behaved kid sister who's always in trouble. Which is so not fair. Agnes thought I had more talent than Vera. But less control, she was always careful to add. Like a baby rattlesnake. Whatever.

"Can I help you?" April says, pushing her glasses up. She comes around from her perch behind the counter and approaches Noah. "Who's this?"

I'm annoyed when he giggles and closes his little hand around one of her fingers. She smiles and it's like she's a different person—very young, sweet. She's not old; her hair is just prematurely gray.

"Iggy's baby, Noah."

She frowns, looks up at me with her one green, one brown eye. Heterochromia. The Native Americans called it Ghost Eye, believing that one who had it could see into heaven and into the earth, was connected to the divine. But that's all bullshit. It's a simple genetic mutation. Science, people.

"How is she?" April asks, her voice heavy with concern.

"Not good." I quash a rush of fear and sadness. But it's like she sees it, softens a little toward me, puts a hand on my arm.

"I made a doll for her," she says.

I flash on the effigy Detective Bandeau showed us, black sticks bound with twine, most likely laced through with hair, charms, bones, crystal chips. "I've been praying. Let me show you."

April locks the front door and flips the sign to Closed. I follow her into the back, with Noah reaching for every crystal and shiny object as we go, cooing happily.

She takes me to her workbench, which is covered by all manner of weird dolls. April rescues doll parts from dumpsters and Goodwill locations. She weaves, stitches, patches together bodies. Collects buttons, crystals, other charms and objects from flea markets, thrift stores, garbage cans. Then she creates and sells dolls for various purposes. Her "Get Well" doll is the most popular and she makes them to order, sells them online and from the shop.

Among the collection of big-headed, button-eyed, stitched-mouthed dolls of all shapes, sizes, and colors, I see the one she made for Iggy. Small with a wild tangle of yellow yarn hair, big blue crystal eye buttons, a pink stitched mouth, dressed in a gauzy white gown. The Iggy doll lies on a felt bed, surrounded by plant sprigs, herbs, and crystals. I recognize a dried mistletoe sprig for surmounting all difficulties, mint for consolation, lavender, sage for cleansing and healing. In her hands, the doll holds a piece of quartz crystal, the mother of all healing stones.

"Iggy must return to this little one," she says softly, turning to touch Noah on the cheek.

"You were there that day," I say. "In the kitchen, preparing food, serving."

She pauses a second, turns her eyes away from Noah and up to me. Her gaze, when focused, is unsettling.

"She's a mystery," Vera often says of April. "Still waters."

The stare of her green eye is cold. Her brown one seems kinder, more compassionate. Like there are two people on the inside looking out.

"You're not implying . . ." she begins as I lift a palm to interrupt.

"I'm not implying anything. I'm asking."

"There was nothing unusual served at brunch," she says crisply. "In fact, the only ones who brought anything that wasn't store-bought were Iggy and you. Her cookies. Your cassoulet."

"I would never hurt Iggy," I say.

"You two haven't been getting along," says April, turning back to the Iggy doll, tucking the little felt blanket around her tenderly. "You were angry at her, weren't you? For being happy."

Ouch. Okay, bull's-eye. I did resent her happiness a little. After all, she picked Brock up from the curb where I'd discarded him like an unwanted piece of furniture. I wondered about all the time we'd spent together as a threesome. Had she *always* had designs on him? And now they were so annoyingly happy.

Noah starts to fuss a little. I bounce instinctively and he goes quiet, but I can tell he's about to blow. Who doesn't get cranky when he's hungry?

"That's not a reason to hurt my best friend," I say, sounding defensive even to my own ears.

April fusses with her dolls.

"Well, here you are with her baby," she says. "I bet you've been working overtime to comfort Brock, as well. If Iggy doesn't wake up, you could just swoop in and take it all, couldn't you?"

I back a few steps away from her.

April is in tight with Lisander, who owns this store and sits at the head of the small council that's governed The Cove since Agnes passed.

"And Paul broke up with you, found happiness with someone else," April continues. "Funny coincidence . . . I hear his new girlfriend Amanda is also missing. I see a theme: Ana doesn't like it when other people find happiness."

Those weird eyes are flashing with something like glee.

"Paul was a monster," I say. "He had a thousand enemies. Anyway, I was over him."

"So why were you with him?"

Good question.

"Everyone makes mistakes."

"That's why you called an *ex*-orcism? Because you were so over him? The whole point of that brunch was to eradicate him from everyone's life. Mission accomplished, I'd say."

My throat feels thick; I swallow hard.

"You've punished Paul, his new girlfriend, and you're in the process of taking back what you lost to Iggy. That's how I'm seeing it. And I'm not the only one. But you're here to do what, to accuse *me*?"

I square my shoulders to her. "Someone's been at Agnes's. Whoever it is has been reading the book. I think they were in The Kitchen."

"Agnes's is well monitored. Lisander knows who comes and goes."

"Is that so? That house belongs to Vera and me. Why would Lisander be watching it?"

April smiles and shakes her head. "You'll have to ask her."

"I didn't do this. Any of it." I feel like I keep saying this to people, and the more I say it, the less believable it seems.

Noah is getting louder, squirming in his carrier.

"How many times have we heard that, Ana? And how many times has it been true? Kevin Harding was abusing you. So, you poisoned him. That other one from HookUp. He got rough with you, so you smashed him over the head with a vase. Lisander had to clean up this mess. Now Paul and Amanda. Iggy."

I feel a cold finger of fear trail down my spine, start backing toward the door.

"They found a doll near Paul's grave," I say, nodding toward her creepy collection. They all seem to be staring at me with their shiny button eyes and crooked mouths.

April blinks at me. "What kind of doll?"

"A stick effigy."

She draws in a breath. There's a flash of something frightened across her features. "My dolls heal and help only—get well, draw money or love, protection from negative energy, career advancement."

I glance through her collection, and I don't see anything that looks like what they found in the woods. That effigy was crude, radiated a kind of menace. April's dolls *are* different. White magic, not black. Or gray. In Voodoo they call it *gris gris*, a nod to how much in this world and beyond is not good or bad, just gray.

Still, I won't hesitate to throw her under the bus if it comes to that.

"Try explaining that to the police," I tell her. "I'm sure they'll keep an open mind about your voodoo dolls."

Noah makes an unhappy noise. I put my hand on his crown, rub his downy head. I think it comforts us both.

"You keep your mouth shut, Ana," says April. "Those are the rules of The Cove. If you think I've done something wrong, you bring it to Lisander. We don't speak to outsiders."

"Tell that to Regina Hayes. She is running off at the mouth about witches."

"She knows nothing about The Cove," says April.

"Enough to tell the police about it."

"She's not one of us," says April. "She wanted to be, but Lisander denied her. She doesn't have the lineage, hasn't been taught The Knowledge."

I keep flashing on the image from martini night that Detective Bandeau showed us. I barely remember it, truly. Regina and Amanda were there, clearly. But if I met either of them, they faded from my memory. Is it my fault that I don't find most people memorable?

Anyway, those groups get big; many cocktails are consumed. It was true what I said—that people bring friends and co-workers, not necessarily connected to the group.

Iggy had just started the job I helped her get. She had a bunch of normie friends that I never bothered to know. I vaguely remember Jessie, but only because Iggy brought her up when she warned me to stay away from Paul.

In my digging around last night, I made the connection. Jessie was the one who claimed that he drugged her, signed the NDA, went to work for Esme.

Paul said Jessie was unstable, that she threw herself at him and he rejected her. Jessie was angry about it, looking for revenge.

How can you believe that, Ana? Women have to support women, Iggy said, incredulous when I stood up for Paul during the talk we had about him.

I should have listened to her. She was trying to protect me. But I *didn't* listen to her because yeah, I was a little mad about Brock. And I was a little obsessed with Paul. And I'm an idiot.

But now I'm thinking—what about Jessie? If she was still holding a grudge, maybe I need to pay her a visit. From what I remember about her, she was meek and petite. Killing someone takes guts, determination. I just can't see her womaning up to commit murder.

"Ana, are you even listening?" says April, startling me. "I said that Regina fancies herself a practicing Wiccan."

"So maybe it was her," I say, just tossing it out there. "She killed her brother, and is now bitter that she was rejected by The Cove so she's trying to destroy that, too, by telling the police about it."

That makes more sense to me. Now, Regina is a woman I can see doing the deed. She's filled with rage; it comes off her in waves.

April considers, turning back to her dolls, tidying dresses and flattening yarn hair. "She *was* angry with the council. Very angry."

"Okay," I say.

This is really working for me. Regina kills Paul. Since she knew about The Cove, maybe she knew about Agnes's garden, about The Kitchen. Somehow she gained access to the recipes and the materials to end her brother. Then she started blaming me and The Cove, getting revenge on the group that rejected her.

I posit this theory to April.

"But she wasn't at the brunch," says April, petting her Iggy doll. "And what reason would she have to harm Iggy?"

"Maybe the two things are not connected."

She squints at me, like I'm not making any sense. But maybe that's right. Two separate crimes not related.

"I don't know," I admit, wrapping my arms around squirmy Noah. He's fussing with more enthusiasm now.

"The only person I can think of that would have reason to harm Amanda, Paul, *and* Iggy was you. Paul was a toxic narcissist. He cheated on you; you took your revenge on him and maybe his new girlfriend, too. Maybe somewhere along the line you realized that you'd made a mistake leaving Brock. So, you got Iggy out of the picture. And now . . ." She stops, coming closer to pet Noah on the head. "You're moving into her place."

"No," I say, my voice just a rasp.

"And I think a lot of other people see it that way. Including the police. *Including* your own sister."

The space is closing in on me. I'm starting to see how magnificently fucked I really am. I back up, knock over a box of tarot cards, look down to see the Hanged Man. Oh that's just great.

I keep moving, don't bother to pick it up.

I expect April to follow, but she doesn't, just stays rooted where she is in the dim light, becoming darker as I move away, the light from the door casting her shadow large on the wall behind. Not a little mouse after all, it seems.

In the parking lot, I keep looking back at the store as I strap Noah in, expecting her or maybe Bree and Camille, Lisander's enforcers, to come running out after me. The baby is fully squalling now, turning red with angry hunger.

I climb in the car, and drive quickly; Iggy and Brock's place is not far. But with the kid screaming and my heart pounding, the drive seems like an eternity.

My mind is reeling—those images of Paul in his grave, the voodoo doll, Detective Bandeau and our bathroom assignation, my reflection in the cracked mirror over the porcelain sink, April's weird eyes, the last time I saw Paul, how ugly it was. Reflexively, I rub at my arm. It doesn't hurt anymore; the big purple fingerprint bruises have faded to a very faint ugly yellow brown.

I turn onto Iggy's street and am comforted by the normie nature of it. It's peaceful, houses neat and tidy.

The afternoon is growing ever dimmer as I take Noah from the car and bring him inside, looking around me for anyone who might be watching. A neighbor. The police. Someone from The Cove. But there's no one, just some kids playing tag in the yard across the street.

Inside, I mix the formula since the breast milk is all gone now, and warm the bottle with the kid still wailing. Finally, when I take him upstairs, sit, and give him his meal, he quiets and starts sucking immediately.

I sit in the rocker in his nursery, pushing us back and forth. I can't slow the beating of my heart.

"I'm sorry," I say to a smiling image of Iggy in a frame by the rocker. It's a photo of her, Brock, and baby Noah on the day he came into the world. She was so happy that day. I remember not understanding her joy, only that her love was directed at Noah and Brock, and not me. *Ana doesn't like it when other people find happiness.* That's not true. Is it?

"I'm sorry I've been a shitty friend."

I rise and put Noah in his crib. He's already sound asleep. I dim the lights and leave him peaceful, breathing deep.

My phone pings. We seriously need to talk. You can't keep ignoring me.

He's been texting me since the station. But I haven't answered.

I have a loose theory, I thumb back.

I'm listening.

Can I trust him? Probably not. Definitely not. Once again, I leave him hanging.

Down in the kitchen, I get on Iggy's laptop, start casting about for new information on Paul and the investigation.

But the news items are just repeats of what I already know, except now they're calling it murder. Headline: *Local Entrepreneur and Philanthropist Murdered.* Not: *Local Abuser of Women, Cheater, and All-Around Asshole Got What He Deserved.*

Victor said that they didn't have anything, no leads, no real suspects, and it looks like he was right.

My Regina theory makes a lot of sense, doesn't it? I enter

her name in the search bar but there's nothing, just some features on her art, which admittedly is impressive, her gallery, her thriving online business. There is an image of her dressed in gauzy black, eyes thickly lined, some Halloween bonfire rave she threw after a show opening. It takes more than dancing around in the woods all dressed in black to call yourself a witch.

Anyway, I wonder how long it will be before Regina goes to the media with her theories. And what that will mean for me and all of us. There's a vein throbbing in my throat, a roil in my stomach.

My thoughts turn again to the (annoyingly hot) detective, and I enter his name now into the search bar. In spite of our previous hookups, I don't know much about him. I know he stares you right in the eye, that he's physically strong, that he doesn't hesitate to take what he wants, but in a weirdly respectful way.

It's interesting how he presents squeaky clean in his life as a cop. But there's a shadow. There's *always* a shadow.

Decorated officer. John Jay College graduate. Master's in criminal psychology. Youngest detective in Little Valley. Volunteers his time at the local youth center where he teaches boxing to troubled teens.

I click, click, click through articles.

Oh, interesting. He learned to box at the same place, a troubled teen himself. His mother died when he was young. His father was in and out of jail. Raised by his aunt? Okay, wow, we have lots in common. *This place taught me to channel my anger in a constructive way, in a confined space,* he told a *Little Valley Beacon* reporter. *It taught me to control and manage my darkest impulses. I try to teach what I learned here now.*

My darkest impulses. Huh.

I keep scrolling. I'm about to give up when finally, I see something that brings me up short.

A picture of Detective Bandeau with Paul at the youth center. Paul has his arm around Timothy, is holding his signature big check, donating money. Paul loved those pictures of himself handing out money. *It's a huge tax break and I'm a hero for a couple grand.* He was not a person who ever considered an anonymous donation. Had to have the ribbon, the big scissors, the big check, the wide smile, and the press coverage.

And there's our Detective Bandeau, taking the money from Paul.

It's an older article, from before I met Paul, before he got fired for being a disgusting lech and a psychological abuser. I met him after he had "done his work," and was a "better man."

Still, they knew each other.

Another thing the detective failed to mention.

I thumb out a message, attach the article. You knew Paul?

The little dots pulse.

Then, I wouldn't say I knew him, exactly. We were acquainted.

You never mentioned that.

I don't have to tell you things. That's not how it works.

Do you really think I killed him?

I think maybe you could have if you wanted to.

You don't know me.

I'm starting to.

A noise from the hallway sends an electric shock through my system. The detective forgotten, I grab a knife from the block on the kitchen counter. *A woman must always be ready to defend herself, psychologically and physically.*

I move quietly toward the direction of the sound. The afternoon is fading fast, house dim without the lights on.

I listen. Nothing. Stepping into the hallway, I see that the front door is ajar.

"Brock?"

The house is silent. I walk the downstairs rooms, peering into the living room, the powder room. They're empty.

But when I return to the kitchen, I'm not alone.

Lisander is sitting, arms folded, at the table. Her lackeys Bree and Camille stand behind her, dressed almost identically in black—jeans and bomber jackets, heavy boots.

Bree's face is blank, but Camille glances at me worriedly. This cannot be good.

"Ana," says Lisander, cool, easy. It's weird how much she looks like Agnes.

I feel trapped. My heart is an animal in a cage, thumping for release. I'm about to make a run for it, glance at the key fob on the counter, toward the door. But that's when I see that April has come up behind me. She smiles. Those weird eyes are on me.

"Put down the knife and have a seat. We need to talk," says Lisander.

My mind reels. What are my options?

I can't get to the baby and get out of the house. They'll never hurt Noah, right? So, I'm not worried about that.

I'll never get to the key fob and to the car before April, Bree, and Camille get to me. I'm not worried about Lisander. She'll just sit there and let the others do her bidding. These days she can barely walk, needs a cane she refuses to use.

"Ana, honey," says Lisander into the tense silence. "Don't do anything stupid."

Stupid is in the eye of the beholder.

I move toward April, and whatever she sees on my face causes her eyes to widen. She takes a step back, lifts her palms. I've put the kitchen knife down as I've been instructed to do. But now my hand closes on the smaller one in my pocket. I pop out the blade and point it at her in one deft, practiced movement. It's not the first time I've pulled it. Or used it.

"You *wouldn't*," she says, voice wobbling.

"Ana," says Lisander, sounding worried. "We just want to talk. You're overreacting."

That's another thing I'm tired of hearing. When people don't like the way you're responding to *their* behavior, all of a sudden *you're* overreacting?

I'm on April quickly, pulling her so close that I can smell the scent of the bookstore, sage and sandalwood. Holding her bony body tight, looking at my own reflection in those stupidly big glasses, I drive the blade into her side right buttocks, what there is of it.

She issues a roar of angry pain, falls to the ground taking me with her. Camille and Bree are on the move, shouting. I extract the blade from April's flesh, our eyes locking—pure hatred from April, another yowl of pain.

Then I'm up and running. No major arteries in your ass, for your information. I could have easily stabbed her in the heart, or the stomach, throat, or the kidney. But I *didn't*.

And Agnes thought I didn't have any self-control.

The cold air hits me like a wall as I burst through the front door.

I bolt, sprinting up the street and then ducking into the trees past the houses.

Camille and Bree shout behind me.

They're younger, faster. And I can hear them gaining.

VERA

Esme stands aside, swinging the elaborately carved double-height door wide for me, letting me into the grand foyer that makes mine look like a mudroom.

"You look awful," I say.

"Thanks. Just what every girl wants to hear. Come in. But stay back, I've been sick for hours."

She leads me down the marble hallway, padding in fuzzy sock feet, past the dining room where we've eaten at the lavish dinner parties she and Claudia throw, beyond the elegant, but coolly modern living room dominated by white leather furniture, through the gleaming industrial kitchen into a smaller, cozier sitting room overlooking the pool where a fireplace and big flat-screen television dominate.

Esme returns to the pile of fluffy blankets where she's obviously been cocooned, suffering, motions for me to have a seat in one of the big chairs.

I'm concerned. Iggy's in the hospital. Does Esme need to be there, too?

With certain substances, the onset is initially indistinguishable from a stomach bug. And for that reason, most people don't get treatment right away. Only when things have progressed beyond repair—liver dysfunction sets in, kidneys fail, heart struggles—is it clear that you're not dealing with a bout of indigestion. But Esme mainly ate the prepared meal she brought, only picking at the other offerings. I haven't been sick; but of course I didn't eat. What hostess ever does? Neither Payton nor Ana is unwell.

I try to visualize the table, the sideboard. The waxy, fragrant charcuterie board with its artfully arranged offering of meats, cheese and nuts, little pots of jam and golden honey. There was the fresh fruit platter with its bright berries, tart apples, melon balls, and kiwi slices. Fresh bread and crackers from our local bakery. The creamy quiche Lorraine, rich and flaky. A flavorful Waldorf salad. All of these items were catered in from local places.

Of course, there was Ana's cassoulet. April washed all the dishes, took all the leftovers. I am, as ever, grateful for her efficiency.

I approach Esme, tuck in her blanket, take a good look at her. But her skin is pink, eyes clear. There's no gray or yellow tinge to her skin. I put a hand to her forehead. There's no fever.

My mothering instincts turn on. This is not just illness. There's something else. I thought she seemed less than her normally cheerful self at brunch. Now her eyes are rimmed red like she's been crying.

"What's going on?" I ask.

She runs a hand through her short, spiky hair. "Claudia left me."

This comes as a surprise. They seemed so happy, so coupled, had built this home, a big life populated with friends. Their love for each other, their intimacy, seemed obvious, unquestionable.

"I'm so sorry," I say, sitting across the glass coffee table from her. There are books everywhere, lining the built-in shelves, stacked artfully on the end tables, in a stylish pile on the floor. "What happened?"

"I mean—what happens in a long relationship? It's not one thing. Then it's everything. You know?"

Of course I know what she means. A marriage is an ongoing

negotiation—who wants what, who gets what. There are the big fights that almost unstitch you, but then don't. A thousand things you overlook until you can't. Power struggles. Infidelities. Speaking strictly for my marriage.

"You know what's jacked?" she says. "I'd say it was Paul who was really the final straw."

"Paul?" That's interesting.

"You know that whole *Business Journal* thing? I couldn't let it go. He was only chosen because he was frat brothers with the editor. I should have been in that article."

"You're right," I say, because she is.

"And then to be up against him for Businessperson of the Year, knowing that he is—was—probably going to win. I just couldn't stop thinking about it. Like, seriously, it was keeping me up at night imagining the gala where I would have to smile graciously as he took an award I deserved. The humiliation of it."

She draws in and releases a deep breath. I've never seen her so angry.

"What's even worse is that he probably will still win, posthumously. And I'll just have to smile and eat crow. I'm sick with it."

"You don't know that, Esme," I say. "There's every chance you'll win. You deserve it."

But she's not listening.

"Claudia said I was obsessed with him, that I could never just be happy with things as they were. That I always wanted more, and more. She thinks the article is meaningless, that the award is stupid and pointless, and that it doesn't matter who wins. Which hurts, you know? It matters. To me."

When you care about your work the way Esme does, when you've worked as hard as she has, of course it stings not to be recognized, to see accolades go to lesser people for unfair reasons.

"I'm sorry," I tell her. "Of course it matters to you."

She nods, wipes at her eyes. She's normally so positive and upbeat; it's hard to see her so crushed.

"Where is Claudia now?"

"She's in Tokyo for work. Plans to stay on awhile. I'm not sure when she's coming back. Or if she is."

She sinks down under the blankets, looking miserable. "And maybe she's right, that I was obsessed. It's just—things are so unfair all the time."

She bats angrily at her tears, grabs a tissue from a box on the end table beside her. A crystal hedgehog catches the light and casts tiny rainbow flecks on the wall. There's a framed picture of Claudia and Esme walking hand in hand on the beach where they were married.

"Claudia was always like: When is it enough, Esme? And I said, when it's *fair*."

I can see why Claudia might have lost patience with this line of thinking. It's childish to imagine that the world should be fair. It's not, nor has it ever been, or ever will be.

Still, I feel the motherly urge to brew her some tea for that stomach. I know she has my special blend because I gave it to her and Claudia in a ceramic canister for Christmas. I make this suggestion, and she nods weakly. "Thanks."

She follows me to the kitchen as I boil some water, find her fresh ginger, and grate it into a cup. The tea is in her cupboard. I spoon it into a tea ball and let the whole thing steep. Everything in the kitchen is meticulously clean and organized, as if it's never been used.

"So now Paul is dead," I say, finally handing her the cup.

She holds it in both hands, breathes in the strong aroma, blows on the hot liquid before she takes a tentative sip. Tea is a whole experience of comfort, scent and warmth soothing before you ever take a sip. It calms your nervous system, the plants working their healing magic in multiple ways.

I watch her.

"Hmm," she says. "This is so good."

Could she have killed Paul? Did she hate him that much?

Would Ana have helped her, provided the necessary ingredients? Maybe my sister's whole bit of *I loved him* and *I'm going to find out who did this* is just an act.

In all the years I've known Esme, I've never seen her cross, or losing her temper. But that doesn't mean anything. Women are good at hiding their darkest feelings. We learn early that we're not allowed to be angry, get skilled at burying our rage deep. But sometimes it just explodes.

I've been there myself.

"You know if I'm honest, I've wished for it," she says, maybe reading my mind. "Car accident. Heart attack. Fall from a cliff, whatever. But I don't feel any better now that he's gone."

"No?"

"Because as I've been lying here sick what I get now is that I wasn't just mad at Paul. He was just the symbol of all the ways the world is dangerous and unfair for women, all the shit we have to eat. How men help each other, and bend over backward to laud their own mediocrity. Paul's dead but there are a million more just like him."

"Esme," I say, leaning toward her. "They think it was Ana. She's in real trouble. So, if you know something, please tell me."

Her dark eyes grow wide; she puts down her cup. "Vera. No. No way. You think I had something to do with Paul getting killed?"

"I don't think anything," I say, lifting my palms. "I'm just trying to take care of my sister. The police have an easy narrative. The jilted ex. Ana's got a history. I need to figure out who did it before they arrest her."

"It wasn't me," she says. "I wish I had a killer instinct. But I don't."

"Any theories?" I ask.

Esme shrugs. "Probably the list of people who *didn't* hate him is shorter. There's a young woman who works for me now who says she worked late with him one night. After they finished, he poured her a drink. She woke up the next morning in her car in the office parking lot and couldn't remember what had happened. She had bruises, felt—you know—violated."

"Who was that?"

"Jessie Parker. She works in the IT department, a crazy-talented coder."

Jessie Parker, here you are again. I think of the picture she posted, she and Amanda cheek to cheek.

"What about Amanda Alessi? Did you know her?"

"She was Jessie's friend, maybe a little more than that. I got a vibe, like Jessie might be in love with her, but that those feelings stopped at friendship on Amanda's part."

Okay. It might be nothing. But at least it's something to throw at the detective. Someone Paul harmed, holding a grudge. Then he's going out with her best friend. But what kind of friend dates a man who harmed someone she cares about?

She sips at her tea again, some of the color returning to her face.

"This tea. It's like magic."

But she still looks pale, clammy. I put a motherly hand to her forehead, wonder again whether she needs a doctor.

"It's Agnes's recipe. A blend of peppermint and lavender, among other things." Willow bark, which contains salicylates, an organic aspirin, a dash of baking soda to neutralize acid. She called this one Tummy Soother. It never fails. Unless there's something more seriously wrong.

"Let me run you to urgent care?" I suggest. "Or call your concierge doctor?"

She wipes at the slight sheen of sweat on her brow. "I'll power through."

I'm about to protest when she goes on.

"You know what I still don't get? Why would Ana be with Paul at all? We all hassled her about it."

I shake my head and offer a shrug. "Ana has always had dangerous appetites when it comes to men."

Esme runs a hand over the crown of her head, expression puzzled, worried. "The girl is a mystery."

She has no idea.

Before I pull out of the drive, I thumb out a quick text to Claudia, mention that Esme is unwell and should go to the doctor. Maybe it will get them talking. If something happens to Esme, and I didn't do anything when I had the chance, I won't be able to forgive myself.

As I start to drive, I'm still thinking about things she said.

Why would Ana be with Paul?

Why would Amanda? Especially knowing her friend had been harmed by him. What little I know about her, just from social media, Amanda—unlike Ana—doesn't seem like the type to be attracted to an abuser at best, a rapist, a predator at worst.

But we all have our dark appetites, don't we?

TIMOTHY

In the youth center lot, I park by the big oak, sit a minute, stress and fatigue pulling at my eyes, aching in my neck and shoulders.

I draw in a breath, release it. The kids rely on this class. Even though I should be out there working this case—a man dead, a woman missing, another in the hospital—I owe them this hour. Canceling, not showing up, that's what the kids at the gym expect from the adults in their life. I don't want to be another grownup that they can't trust, who doesn't do what he says he will. I remember what it was like when my dad disappeared, that helpless feeling of anger and sadness. So now I come here when I'm sick, when I'm tired, when I've worked a double.

That's why I'm trying so hard to keep the doors open. If the youth center goes away, the kids who come here after school won't have any place else healthy and safe to go.

Right now I'm giving every spare dollar I have to this place, calling in every favor. So is everyone who volunteers here. The GoFundMe page is doing pretty well and hopefully we'll pull some big donors at the fundraising event in a few weeks. But we're month to month at the moment. If something doesn't happen, I'm out of ideas on how to make ends meet here.

I'm also out of leads on my case. And something has to

happen there, too, and soon, or I know how this goes. The Blacksmith sisters have a tough lawyer and won't be easily manipulated. Since the voodoo doll and swatch of cloth, Old Bob has turned up nothing in spite of numerous passes through the woods and at the site.

He agreed to walk with me again in the morning—though the longer it goes, the less evidence we'll be able to find.

I lean back a minute and stare up at the gray sky, think about what I *do* know.

Paul was poisoned. The toxin Beck discovered is consistent with that found in the common plant hemlock—piperidine, alkaloids, coniine, and y-coniceine. According to Beck, who is chock-full of useless factoids, 3,900 a people a year are injured by electrical outlets, but nearly 70,000 are accidentally made ill by plants.

Of course, Paul's death was no accident.

Ignatia Rose, too, appears to have been poisoned, still fighting for her life in the hospital. According to her recent bloodwork after Beck's findings, not with the same substance. They've yet to determine the exact toxin, and are still running tests. The doctor said when last I called that Iggy has a fighting chance. Apparently this afternoon, she mysteriously took a turn for the better, organ function improving. "She's got a lot to live for," the doctor said. "I've seen it make a difference."

If she wakes up, maybe she knows something. That's my dim, faint hope, my only one.

Amanda Alessi seems to have vaporized. No activity on her credit card. The last call on her phone records just a brief call to her parents. Her phone is offline, not even low on charge somewhere because if that were the case it's often still possible for the phone company to grab a signal. No withdrawals from her bank accounts. Even the location signal from her leased car has been disabled. Did someone make Amanda Alessi disappear? Or did she kill Paul and take off for an island somewhere? It's almost impossible to go off the grid these days. Between phones and cameras everywhere, facial recognition software, electronic banking, there's always a digital trail.

Meanwhile, as far as I can tell, The Cove is a bit of an urban legend. A loose collection of mystical healers, herbalists, and psychics spread across the region from Little Valley to The Hollows. The whole idea of witches casting spells is a little silly, isn't it? There's nothing about anything called The Cove online, except a rehab facility out in California. Regina Hayes is just a grieving sister with a wild imagination. I mean, look at her art. There's a lot going on in that head of hers.

Still—that creepy doll, which literally everyone claims never to have seen anything like it before. That was a little witchy to be sure.

So, what's my next move? Above me the branches sway, the afternoon turning to evening.

There's still a half hour before class starts, so I call Chief Royer. He was the chief when I came on the job here, after he'd served for more than thirty years at Little Valley PD, starting in patrol and moving up the ranks. And he's still a very connected person, as well as on the board of the youth center.

He took me under his wing when I came on the job, and he's the person I call first when I'm stuck.

"Son," Royer answers. "Good to hear from you."

"Chief, how's retirement?"

A low chuckle. "Lots of cruises and yard work. But the wife is happy. Has me taking tango lessons if you can believe."

"Sounds nice," I say. Actually, it sounds like my worst nightmare.

He issues a raspy cough. "Heard about your big case."

I give him the rundown, all the details. I end with: "That's why I'm calling, Chief. Know anything about the Blacksmith sisters?"

There's an interestingly long silence. I wonder if the line has gone dead somewhere during my information dump. Then I hear the faint sound of the television in the background.

"Vera and Ana," he says finally, as if pulling the names up from his mental database. "Agnes Blacksmith's nieces. Sure. They went to school with my boy, Chuck. Nice girls as I remember, in spite of their parents and everything that went on there. Though the younger one got in a bit of trouble from time to time. Nothing too serious."

This does not surprise me. Her picture on HookUp was intriguing. Those blue eyes and raven hair, milky skin. A slight smile, like she knew a secret she was dying to tell. When she walked in the door of that roadside bar outside of town, Gina's on RR3—the instant desire I felt for her was febrile. The fever I have for her is only running hotter.

"Come here often?" she vamped, sliding into the booth seat across from me. She wore this tight black skirt that looked like it had been painted on, high heels. Her nails were painted black with silver tips. Her lips, cherry.

"It's my first time."

"That's sweet," she said. "But I'm not sure I believe you."

Honestly, it *was* my first HookUp foray. The dating pool in Little Valley is small, and it had been a while since I had felt *anything* but tired. Some kid I picked up for shoplifting told me about the app. *Brah*, he said from the back seat of the squad car, *it's for real. I get greased on the regular.* He was scrawny, with stringy hair, face faintly acne scarred.

Later that night I downloaded the app, not that I generally take dating advice from troubled teens. That's how desperate I was. The next day, I connected with Ana Blacksmith.

"You *don't* seem like the type," she said, sipping her drink. I couldn't stop staring at her mouth.

"What's the type?" I asked.

"You look like a Boy Scout," she said. Then she narrowed her eyes, smiled. "But with an edge."

We'd barely finished our first drink before she was running her foot up the inside of my leg from across the table. I followed her to the bathroom, locked the door behind us.

"What kind of trouble?" I ask Chief Royer now.

He sighs. "She and her friends stole a car once, took a joyride. The car belonged to one of their parents, who generously decided not to file charges. I shut down a party one night, and she was there, three sheets to the wind. I took her home to Agnes."

"Agnes. Sounds like you two were friends."

"Sure, yeah. Old friends."

"Was she an herbalist?"

He chuckles a little. "Agnes was a florist. But people went to her for various things like teas or salves. Balms. Female stuff, you know? She had kind of a reputation as like a healer type. People went to her when doctors couldn't help kind of a thing. She had a tea for insomnia that even I used sometimes—lavender and chamomile, like that."

Okay. Interesting.

"What about the girls? Were they involved in anything like that?"

"Gosh, I don't think so," he says, blowing out a breath. "Vera's married now to Brad Kline, the fire protection guy. Made a fortune. She's got a couple of kids. Ana has something to do with that social media stuff."

He clears his throat; in the background I hear the sound of the television again. Some game show.

"Ever hear about a group called The Cove?"

There's just a moment of hesitation, but it rings like a bell for me.

"The Cove? Huh, no I don't think so. What's that?"

"The victim's sister said it's like a group of witches that practice in the area. She says Ana and Vera are a part of it."

A belly laugh that also doesn't come off quite right. "Witches. Son, you must *really* be out of leads on your case."

"I am," I admit. "And I can't shake the creepy feeling that the stick doll gave me."

"Yeah, but *witches*?"

He clears his throat. "Well, let me think a minute. We had a poisoning case once. It was like one of those things where the parent makes the child sick so that they can get attention from the doctors."

"Munchausen syndrome by proxy."

"That's it. Long time ago. Kid survived. Mom went to prison. She's out now, I think. Claimed she was innocent, just trying to heal the kid because doctors had failed them. The mom had a bit of a reputation—a recluse, crazy. I don't think anyone ever called her a witch."

"Remember a name?"

"Uh, let me see. The mother's name was Trina. Trina Snell. And the kid. Uh, something that reminds you of spring. That's it. April. Her name was April. Still lives in town I think."

I grab the envelope Vera left with me and open the sheet containing the list of items served at the brunch and everyone in attendance. There's her name at the bottom of the list.

April Snell was working in the kitchen at the Blacksmith brunch.

There's a soft knock at my window and I turn to see Ernie Sanchez with his puppy eyes, and mop of black curls, standing there smiling. I love this kid, I have to say. He came to me a couple of months ago and the changes in him—lost a few pounds, more confident, calmer—are the reason I do this work. I roll down the window.

"Hey, Ernie, get the ring set up for me, will you? Help the other kids with their gloves and I'll be right in."

He gives me a grin, grows like an inch. "Got it, boss."

He jogs off. Sometimes you just have to show kids that they

can do things, that you trust them, and watch them rise to your expectations.

"Was Trina Snell associated with The Cove?"

It's a cheap trick, a cop thing. Repeat the question in a different way. Or pretend that the perp didn't already deny knowledge of this or that. But the old dog doesn't bite.

"Yeah, like I said. Never heard of anything like The Cove. She just came to mind because you mentioned poison."

I hear the television click off in the background. A couple of kids walk up to the gym.

"So, what's your next step?" asks the chief. There's an eagerness in his voice that tells me he misses the work.

"Go back to the location where we found Paul Hayes's body with Old Bob. Keep looking for Amanda Alessi. Hope Iggy Rose wakes up."

It sounds as weak as it is.

"If I were you, I'd be looking close at the victim. What was he involved in? Did he owe money? Did he run afoul of any shady types? Paul Hayes, for all the money he threw around, wasn't a good guy. Sounds to me like someone got sick of his shit."

"Not Ana Blacksmith?"

"You said yourself it would take more than one person to kill him and move the body where you found it. Crimes of passion aren't usually premeditated. Maybe someone just wants it to *look* like it was the ex-girlfriend. Because that's the most predictable story, right. Now she's a witch, to boot? That's an easy narrative to write."

I let the words bounce around a minute. Ana Blacksmith. It's not that she doesn't seem capable of doing bad things. It's just that it doesn't feel to me like she did this. But maybe that's just wishful thinking on my part.

"Anyway, I don't have to tell *you* that Paul Hayes wasn't a good man."

"How's that?"

"It was *his* donation that never came through. The shortfall from his promised-but-never-delivered hundred thousand dollars that was supposed to make the budget for last year is the reason why the center is in trouble now."

This is news to me. I'm not on the board, just a worker bee. And that particular piece of information never reached me—if it's true.

"Are you sure about that?"

"Ask Marge Caine."

Marge Caine, Brock's mother, volunteers at the center, as well as serves on the board. "I'll do that."

That word comes back to me again. *Entangled.*

Ernie's waving from the door. I check my watch; it's time to go in and get started. I tell the chief as much.

"Call me if you need me. And, Tim? Just be careful."

It's an odd thing to say and his tone has gone a bit dark. "Careful of what?"

Another one of those micro-silences. "I don't know. I've got a weird feeling about this one."

"Me, too."

It's almost dark when I head into the gym, air frigid. The boys are waiting. A ragtag group of kids the sight of whom makes me feel like a kid again myself. Not just boys. I have a girl, too, as of last month. Dahlia joined up at the suggestion of her sister, Miranda, from Beck's office and who is raising her since their mother died a couple of years back. Their dad was nowhere to be found. Dahlia, tiny, fierce, has a look of wild sadness, barely checked anger. She's a tiger in the ring; the boys are a little wary of her.

Predictably, as I enter, they're all staring at their phones, not talking to each other. Those devices. I wish they'd never been invented.

I take the big box off the shelf, walk from kid to kid. No one says a word as they put their phones in the box. This is a device-free zone. Even I put mine in, with a twinge of guilt since there's an active murder investigation and that's top of mind.

But sometimes it's these down moments when answers and ideas pop up. I have a lot to bat about after my talk with the chief.

We glove up, put on protective head gear, mouth guards in.

"Ernie and Benji, show me what you got today."

They get in the ring and start to dance around each other. Benji's bigger, but Ernie's fast on his feet with quick reflexes, a smart fighter. Benji gets angry, gets sloppy, but he makes up for it in sheer girth. His fists are like hams. Ernie's creative, adaptable.

We're not here to hurt each other. If things get too hot, I break it up. They go a couple of rounds.

Then it's Dahlia's turn. I put her in and watch her work over Carlos, who is twice her size. I take pity on him, get in with her and let her hit the hand pads for a while. She has a mean upper cut, a killer left jab.

The gym smells of sweat and exuberance as the kids leave tired and happy, wrung out, stress and pain forgotten for a while. There's peace in physical exertion; it's the cure for many ailments physical and mental.

Later, as I lock up, I think about the day Paul Hayes came with the big foam-board check. Everyone keeps telling me what a shit he was, but that's what I remember about him. How he laughed with the kids, even got into the ring. I didn't know it was a false promise. Maybe he wanted to give the money but came up short. Or maybe he just did it for the publicity and never planned to deliver the real check.

Either way, I'm starting to get why he had so many enemies.

TIMOTHY

My old partner, Hitch, used to complain about how so much of detective work has become digital, how once upon a time it was all knocking on doors, stakeouts, and following suspects. Now it's all scanning social media feeds, cell phone signals, scouring email, call, and text records.

Back at the station, sitting at my desk, I continue looking through what I have, hoping for something I missed.

I don't have enough evidence to take Ana Blacksmith into custody, even to get a warrant to search her apartment. After scrolling Paul's voicemail, his texts and email, and scouring his social media pages, as well as Amanda Alessi's, I couldn't find a single angry or threatening message from Ana. No one at Paul Hayes's workplace had seen her lingering, showing up enraged as Regina Hayes had claimed.

I check my own voicemail. There are several messages from Amanda's father asking for an update and what were we actually doing to find his daughter. But even the voicemail, texts, and emails I've been able to access on Amanda's accounts are all innocuous—all twenty percent off at Anthropologie, and confirming your hair appointment, and drinks on Friday?

No tickets to Aruba. No hotel reservations. No Uber to the airport. They never went. They never even planned to go.

Someone clearly had access to their accounts, posted those images. But who? The tech team couldn't find any remote access to any of their social media accounts, meaning that only their authorized devices had been used to log on to each of the accounts.

So, whoever killed Paul had access to his home, his computer, his phone. And Amanda's, too.

My thoughts keep going back to Regina. Access, motive, and opportunity. A big beefy boyfriend to help her move the body. Old Bob said on the initial walkthrough that there might have been a third person moving the body, a third set of footprints at the scene. Could someone else have been helping them? There was a pot of money at the end of that rainbow. Ana Blacksmith was right about that. *Isn't that like detecting one-oh-one? Follow the money?*

I wish I could stop thinking about her.

My eyes fall on the picture I keep on my desk of the day Chief Royer and Commissioner Brown gave me my gold detective shield. It was a proud day, and I remember wishing I had a family to share it with. Instead, it was a night out with the guys—my first patrol partner, the chief, the commissioner, and their cronies.

On a whim, I enter Chief Royer's name into the search bar, and start scrolling through various news articles, some of them quite old. About his being appointed chief, a major drug bust, a standoff with a group of doomsday preppers in The Hollows that ended in a fire where people were killed. All before my time.

But as I read, I notice something odd. I notice how over the years, one or two things seem off. Like when Royer was named chief, another man who was ahead of him for the job suffered a stroke and was forced to retire. Royer got the position. A major witness for the defense in Royer's big drug bust case killed himself in protective custody. Then toward the end of the feed, I find a picture of him at a fundraising dinner for the Little Valley Food Bank.

He's standing with Agnes Blacksmith, tagged as local florist and founder of the food bank. They are arm in arm, smiling. He's wearing a boutonniere of flowers, the article says, from Agnes's extensive garden. Their body language is intimate, heads tilted together, smiles broad.

I'm processing this when my phone rings.

"Detective Bandeau."

"I'm Brent Ellis." The raspy voice of an older man. "My mother gave me your card. Says you need the footage from her doorbell camera?"

"Yes, that's right. Thanks for getting back to me. Does the device record?"

"It does. I like to know who's coming to her door. I installed the camera for her last year. I set it to turn on when there's motion, so it captures all the activity on the street. I usually delete it every month or so. But I haven't gotten around to it."

"Can you email the files?"

"I already did," he says. "I converted the recordings and sent a Dropbox link to the address on your card."

I check and see an email from him in a long list of unopened messages.

"Does it include the last two weeks?"

"The whole last month. Every time the camera detected motion, it recorded. Can I do anything else for you?"

"Not at the moment," I say. "Thanks for your help. And I'll come back to you with any questions."

The files are huge, take forever to download. I brew some coffee in the break room and prepare for a long night.

I sit in my creaky chair, and click through the files, watching people come and go, to work, out on dates, to school activities. Families with kids, couples, singles. It's a diverse group, a mix of races, gender, age, middle income in decent cars. I see the peace of it, the appeal. Safety, routine. Why do I feel like I would suffocate in a life like that?

Finally, I see what I've been watching for. I pause, rewind. Watch it once, twice, three times.

I'm not often surprised. But I am tonight. Some of the pieces click into place.

I'm rising to get into my car when my phone rings again.

It's Beck. Obviously, he's working late, too.

"You know," he says when I answer, "I've been doing a little research. And I think I might have something that I need to share with you."

"Hit me."

I hear his chair creak beneath his weight. "Maybe better if you come here."

"I'm on my way."

VERA

After Agnes confronted us about Mr. Danvers, Ana and I returned to our room. We kept our poker faces until we heard Agnes exit the back door and watched her head to the garden. When she was gone, we both burst out laughing. We laughed until we cried.

"You know what's crazy," said Ana. "Is how easy it was."

It *was* easy. It took a little reconnaissance, a little research, a little patience. But once we knew Mr. Danvers's routine, how he always had a thermos of tea with him, which he drank daily after lunch with some type of cookie or treat; how that thermos sat all day in his unwatched, unlocked cubby in the break room; how he was already taking medication for a bad heart and had suffered a minor heart event last year, it was almost embarrassingly simple.

Just to be clear, we weren't trying to *kill* him. We just wanted him to go away, like medical leave, or better yet medical retirement. He was a lech, and a bad teacher, mean, favoring the boys, and always keeping the "bad girls" after class. There's a kind of man who knows how to walk the edge, push the boundaries. Not outright molesting—but those inappropriate hugs, the lingering touch on the arm, a body brush by your desk. Men and boys don't see it. But women and girls do. There's an inner cringe, the urge to get away, to protect yourself from the unwanted advances of a dirty old man. If you were unlucky enough to be kept after class or called to his office hours, Mr. Danvers might tell the story of how as a young boy he had a terrible crush on his teacher, or say something about how much you'd grown, or how he knows how difficult it can be when girls develop early. He lauded the boys for their mediocre work and took every point possible away from the girls on their tests, or made incomprehensible corrections on their essays. "Too vague!" Or "Awkward!"

We happened to know that there was a younger, better teacher waiting in the wings. Ms. Bane, a Brown graduate studying for her MFA at Sacred Heart College who was his steady substitute teacher. She was passionate, intuitive, in love with teaching.

With Mr. Danvers in a coma, Ms. Bane would be taking his class for the rest of the year. All the girls of Little Valley Academy breathed a collective sigh of relief.

Just—we made a slight miscalculation in the dosage. Coma and possible death were not our intention precisely. Foxglove is a beautiful flowering plant. From stalk to blossom, all parts of this common plant are extremely dangerous, and we knew in Agnes's garden to handle it in our beekeeper suits only. A digitoxin, foxglove can kill, but it can also heal in different doses, is an ingredient in many heart medications.

In the kitchen we grated the stalk of the plant and created a paste, which we kept in a vial. Knowing that Danvers drank his tea with copious amounts of honey, we banked that he wouldn't taste it in small amounts. And he did not.

Of course, because Danvers already had a heart condition, no one questioned his heart event. There was no suggestion or question of foul play. And if there had been, doctors might just have assumed he'd taken too much of the medication he was already taking. Only Agnes suspected.

"I don't feel bad," said Ana, as we lay side by side on our twin beds upstairs later. "*Should* I feel bad?"

I searched my own heart for remorse. A man was in a coma and could possibly die because of what we had done. I found none at all. Maybe it's how we're made, Ana and me. Agnes and Sadie.

Women aren't supposed to kill. We are meant to endure, stand by. There is a kind of strength in that, to be sure. The strength to love, to hope for better, to forgive.

But the women in my family don't have that brand of strength. We're different.

I'm leaving Esme's when the kids start texting about dinner. I call Brad, ask him to order a pizza.

"When are you coming home?" he asks.

"Soon."

"Meanwhile, back at the ranch," he says pointedly. The business, the fire. I've been so wrapped up in Ana's mess that I haven't even checked on ours.

"I'm sorry. What's happening?"

He runs it down, how the publicist put out a press release. How he reached out to some of our clients to offer assurances.

"I learned something today," he said.

"What's that?"

"So, Paul Hayes—you know, after we declined the services of his company?—was spreading rumors. Saying that our systems are subpar, that we get our materials from China though we promise clients that everything we use is made in the US. I answered some of those rumors today in conversations. But I'm starting to get why people hated him so much. He was a snake."

The truth? I already knew about it. The rumors found their way to me through one of the wives. Paul and I had a little chat. Fairly recently. But that's not a thing I plan to bring up at the moment.

"Anyway, he won't be spreading any more rumors about us now."

Almost as soon as we hang up, I get a text from Brock. Hey, have you talked to Ana? She's supposed to be watching the baby at our house and I can't reach her.

A pulse of dread.

I'll find her. How's Iggy?

Actually, she's doing a little better. The doctors are . . . optimistic. Call me when you reach Ana?

I call Ana, no answer. Text her. No answer. I check her location. Her dot is blinking at Iggy and Brock's place. Maybe she's sleeping? Or in the shower?

But the white noise of concern that's been humming since brunch is reaching a roar. Too many bad things happening. The world spinning out of control. I remember that feeling of watching my mother being taken away in the cop car, her looking at us out the window pressing her hands to the glass. *I'm sorry*, she mouthed. Ana was wailing; her cries that night are a sound that stays with me, is sometimes evoked by the calling of gulls.

Outside, evening has fallen. I'm annoyed at Ana for being a problem once again. But I'm also scared, feel my usually iron grip on everything slipping, my world spinning out of control.

Ana, where are you?

TIMOTHY

The medical examiner's building is a few miles from the police station, a typical northeastern concrete block, low and white nestled among a spate of pine. I pull up and gather my internal resources for my meeting with Beck.

I like Beck, I really do. But to be honest, he's a little weird. First of all, he used to be an EMT. And those folks see things that most of us don't, won't, and shouldn't ever see. Broken limbs, bodies in various states of decay, found in ignoble conditions, abuse, self-harm, murder, the ravages of unchecked disease. It changes them; many develop a very dark sense of humor to cope. And what Beck finds funny is often unsettling. The other thing is that as the chief medical examiner, he spends much of his time now with dead people. And I think he likes them better than he does those of us who happen to still be breathing.

I leave the car and approach the building. The smell of chemicals and death hits me as soon as I am buzzed through the doors. The curly-haired heavyset desk clerk waves me through.

"Detective," he says. "How's it hanging?"

Which impresses me as something you're not supposed to say anymore. Probably never should have said in the first place. I just give him a nod, and he smiles, face full of piercings—eyebrows, lips—an unhealthy pallor to his complexion. He's young; I feel like I could give him some advice about getting outside more. But I have found that people generally don't want advice, especially when they haven't asked for it, sometimes even when they do.

Outside the entrance to the autopsy room and to Beck's office is a desk where Miranda Reyes sits. With long black hair and dark skin, deep-set eyes, generally dressed in various shades of black and gray, she's like his undead gatekeeper. Her clear directive is to keep people as far away from Beck as possible.

She's here now, staring at me with that look that says *do you have an appointment?*

"He called me," I say defensively.

"I know," she says, tapping a black-painted fingernail on the desk, pinning me with her thickly lashed gaze.

"Your sister," I say. "She's a tiger in the boxing ring."

She softens a little. "That doesn't surprise me. She's a handful at home."

Miranda, who is raising her little sister, brought Dahlia to me after Dahlia got into a fight at school that almost got her kicked out.

"How's she doing at school?" I ask now.

Miranda nods, twirls a strand of hair. "Better. Calmer. Her grades are improving. She's got some friends. That's you. That's on you."

I shrug. "I'm just wearing her out, giving her a place to vent, teaching her to control her impulses."

"That's a lot," she says. Her lips are painted black, too. It's a look. Black mini, oversized sweater, fishnet stockings, and Doc Martens. She looks like she's headed to goth night at the local club instead of working late.

She nods toward the door. "He's waiting for you."

Tonight, Beck's office is only lit by his desk lamp, and the human skull by his keyboard is staring at me, eyes black pools. I wonder who it was. But I stop short of asking because it's a rabbit hole.

In addition to his role as ME, Beck is also busy, travels to teach, goes to writers' conferences where he talks to mystery authors about how to accurately portray forensic science, toxicology, autopsy results. He even has his own Instagram page: @drdeath.

On his Insta bio: Death is a part of life. To live well *memento mori*.

Something else about Beck, which is a little weird for me but not as weird as you would think. Beck used to be *Becka*, and once after the precinct Christmas party a couple of years ago, we hooked up. And—it was pretty hot. I liked Becka a lot; she was funny and inventive in bed, warm, exciting. But she left in the middle of the night. And then she blew me off, didn't answer my calls. Got a little chilly with me on the job. After her final text: Tim. "No" is a complete sentence, I finally took the not-so-subtle hint and reluctantly shifted back into our professional relationship.

By March, Becka announced that she was transitioning, that she would like to be known as Beck moving forward. That her pronouns had changed to he/him. Anyway, I like Beck, too. He's the same person—whip-smart, wicked sense of humor, cool under pressure. I'd be lying if I didn't say that I still think about Becka, though.

"We don't talk on the phone now?" I ask.

He looks up from his work. "This town—you never know."

"What does that mean?"

He hands me a folder and I sit down in the chair across from his desk. He's growing a beard, looks like he's been working out—broader through the chest and shoulders. His hair, once a shoulder-length bob, is cropped short. Is it odd to note that he's as good-looking a guy as he was a girl? Is that one of those things you're not supposed to notice or say in a professional environment? Is it toxic maleness on my part?

I open the folder and start reading his report.

"Final results confirm my initial findings that Paul Hayes was poisoned. Hemlock. Do you know that Socrates was forced to kill himself by drinking hemlock to answer to his crimes of inciting disrespect against authority, accused of impiety and corrupting Athenian youth?"

"Okay." Maybe I knew that, somewhere in the deep recesses of my knowledge of history.

"Also present was aconite, known as wolfsbane. Greek hunters used it to bait and kill wolves. A blue-flowering plant, it's often mistaken for an edible herb. It paralyzes the nervous system and eventually stops the heart. Even skin contact can be dangerous."

I'm looking through the report, but it's a lot.

"These are common plants found in gardens, meadows, by the roadside," he goes on. "People think plants are harmless, but many of them are not. They have to defend themselves like everyone else."

We're both quiet a moment. I flash on Paul's face, the way his hands were clenched in death to his own throat. Not a pleasant way to go.

Looks like they got their wish. I flash on what I saw on the video footage. My brain is in overdrive, trying to piece it all together.

"Did they run tests on Ignatia Rose?"

He rubs his hands together. "The hospital did not find either substance in her blood. In Ms. Rose's case, based on the menu you provided, they suspect it could have been the death cap mushroom, often mistaken for its harmless relatives. Her renal failure is consistent with the effects of amatoxin. And it would only take a very small amount, less than half a mushroom to harm or kill."

"Did they find evidence of that toxin in her blood?"

"Her symptoms and biomarkers are consistent with known effects of the poison—hypocalcemia, hepatic failure, anemia."

"Is there an antitoxin?"

"No, unfortunately. You just have to hope the body recovers from the ravages of the toxin. Just try to keep the patient alive long enough that they heal. In extreme cases, she might need a liver or kidney transplant."

I sit with it a minute, Beck watching me. He goes on. "Murder by poison is an ancient technique, dating back to the Greek and Roman empires. Circe, Medina, Locusta. Historically, it's a woman's weapon."

I look at him, his gaze as dark and steady as the skull beside him. I try not to think about the night we spent together, but I do. We mostly avoid each other except when we're working now. But there's still something there, a connection.

"So, hemlock, wolfsbane, and the death cap mushroom, these are organic substances," I say. "Growing somewhere nearby presumably."

He nods slowly.

"Have you ever heard of The Cove?" I ask.

Does he startle? He recovers quickly, leans back, releases a sigh. He grew up nearby in The Hollows. He attended Sacred Heart College, got his master's and PhD at John Jay College in Manhattan, then returned to work here. He knows the area, the people, well.

"I shouldn't be talking to you about this," he says softly, as he rises and closes the door.

"It's our job to be talking about this," I say sitting up and turning to look at him.

"Do you think the world is a fair place? That good triumphs over evil and bad people get punished?" he asks, still lingering by the door. He's wearing his white lab coat and scrubs.

"Not necessarily," I say. "No."

I think back to my last domestic violence case, the one that ended in a young woman murdered by her husband in her kitchen, her baby crying in his crib for hours until a neighbor called the police. She was small, maybe five three, a preschool teacher, someone's daughter, mother. I remember thinking, here's a girl who never hurt a single person. She bled to death on the tile floor of her kitchen. We caught up with her husband getting wasted at a nearby bar, his knuckles still bleeding.

Look what she made me do, he kept saying over and over. I could have killed him right there; the rage was an ache at the back of my throat. We were alone, on the deserted road back to the station. I could have pulled over. Just meted out the cosmic justice that he deserved. But I didn't. Last I heard, he was out on parole, trying to get custody of his kid back from the grandparents. It still activates my ulcer when I think about it.

"It's not," he says. "In this work, we know that too well, don't we?"

"What's your point?"

"The Cove isn't just one thing or group. It's like a network. A network of women who help people."

"Help people do what?"

He walks back around his desk and sits again. "Like, who would have believed that ever again we'd need to seek an illegal abortion from the local midwife, herbalist, or shaman? That we're heading back to coat hangers and forced sterilization? And yet, here we are, a woman's right to decide what happens to her body in the hands again of male lawmakers. Women find themselves again at the mercy of a system that wants them to be weak and small, controllable, filled with shame and fear. So, we have to find another way. Back to nature."

My conversations with Vera and Ana ring back. "Are they—*witches*?"

He smiles. "Do you even know what that word means? You think it's potions and cauldrons, bonfires, eye of newt, spells and curses?"

"You tell me."

"*Witch* is just another word for a powerful, fearsome woman in control of herself and connected to the earth. It's a male word, something that justifies the institutional punishment and control of half the species. Because there's nothing more terrifying than a woman who won't submit, who has some secret knowledge that can't be regulated."

"Okay," I say, drawing out the word. "I hear you."

He rocks back in his chair, glances at the door. "The Cove is mainly comprised of people doing good in the world. But as in all organizations, there are always bad actors. People who take things too far."

"What are you trying to tell me, Beck?"

He taps the file. "I'm telling you to find the place where these things grow—the hemlock. the wolfsbane, and the death cap mushroom—and you'll find some answers, or at least more questions that will lead you to the answers."

"And where would that be?"

"Have you ever heard of a poison garden?" he asks.

It's starting to shape, the diffuse edges of the truth solidifying. "Illuminate me."

CORALINE

Let me in.

A text from Ethan.

I walk over to my window and see him standing in the yard, a tall slender shadow among the trees. My parents are out. Mom chasing after Ana again. Dad said he had to go to the office. And Grant disappeared without a word sometime after Mom and Dad left. He's probably somewhere with Dahlia. Whatever.

I use the app on my phone to unlock the front door then listen as Ethan lopes up the stairs. Then he's breathless in my doorway, drops his knapsack inside the door. He flops beside me on my bed, bouncing it wildly, pillows and stuffed animals flying.

"Hey," I say, reaching for Mr. Webby, my big purple stuffed spider, and lifting him back onto the bed hugging him close.

"Aren't you too old to sleep with stuffed animals?" Ethan asks with a snort.

I shift away from him, putting space between us on the bed.

The weird thing that happened between us? We were at the homecoming game, making fun of all the normies—the jocks, the cheerleaders, their perfect plastic selves, their idiotic TikTok and Instagram feeds all arched backs and pursed lips.

Anyway, after the game, Ethan drove me home. His dad gave him the Tesla for the night, and we glided through the quiet streets of our town, just talking. When he pulled in front of my house, we sat awhile, just talking like we always do. The front door light came on, so I knew my parents knew I was home. That's the other thing my mom always says—that there was no LifeWatch or anything like it when she was a kid. That when people left your house, they were just gone. You had no idea where they were, no way to contact them. That just seems *scary*. Like how would that even work?

Just as I was about to get out of Ethan's car, he grabbed my hand.

"Coraline," he said. His voice sounded funny, creaky.

I turned to look at him, and before I knew it, his lips were on mine. Soft. Sweet. I mean, yeah, there's always been *something*. But—Autumn and Ethan, they've always just been there, a part of my life as much as Grant. In my bedroom in sleeping bags, at my family table, in all my most important memories.

We just stared at each other a moment, and suddenly he was different. He wasn't just the skinny kid with a cloud of floppy curls who hates horror movies and amusement parks and is the fastest runner on the track team. Not just one half of Autumn and Ethan, Ethan and Autumn. He was a guy who just kissed me, who was—in a kind of dorky way—actually, almost, *hot*?

I was glad it was dark so he couldn't see me turning red. My cheeks burned.

"What was *that*?" I asked him, heart thudding stupidly.

He smiled, looked away. "I don't know. Just, yeah."

I've never been so glad to see my mother open the front door.

"Good night, Ethan," I said, my voice sounding wobbly even to me.

"Good night, Coraline."

There was no one to tell. I couldn't tell Autumn because it felt like we'd violated some sacred threesome friend group pact.

At no point should two of the friends in the group start *liking* liking each other, because then the delicate balance of the relationship would be irreparably altered. On the other hand, we were all seniors waiting for college acceptances and next year, we'd all be in different places probably. For Autumn it is Brown or die. Ethan wants Tisch School of the Arts at NYU for filmmaking. I want to study botany at Sacred Heart College, which is just an hour from here. My parents want me to go farther, so I cast my applications wide to small private schools around the country. Also, University of California Berkeley and the University of Florida have the top botany programs, but there's little chance even with my good grades that I'll get in either of those places, things are so brutally competitive now.

"My place is here," I told my mother. "With The Cove."

"Over my dead body," she'd said, without heat. "No."

It came up in therapy, minus any mention of The Cove of course, and our shrink asked Mom, "Have you considered that Coraline might need to start making her own decisions? That her life belongs to her."

My mother couldn't keep herself from issuing her signature derisive snort.

"I'm not sure any of us, at seventeen, is qualified to make decisions that impact the rest of our lives," my mother responded stiffly. She really hates our shrink, who seems to be the only person on earth that my mother can't intimidate.

"And yet we all do it," countered the doctor easily.

My mother had the good sense to keep her mouth shut, and since the college applications all went out over Christmas break, there's been no further discussion on the topic.

"Let's just see what happens when the decisions roll in," said my dad, ever the moderator, the wait-and-see-it-will-work-out guy.

Anyway.

I've been thinking about Ethan's kiss ever since, haven't told a soul. It makes me feel all warm and squishy inside and also, like, scared. It's such a rom-com trope. Best friends to lovers. But it doesn't ever work out in real life, does it?

Now we lie side by side, both looking up at the ceiling, his giant sneakers hanging off the bed, legs impossibly long. Unlike most boys, he always smells good, like some mingling of sandalwood and baby shampoo.

"Well?" I say. He's been sent on a recon mission and I'm anxious to hear the results.

"*Well*," he echoes. "According to people who are in the know, Micha has been buying tests from some guy on the dark web—like forever."

Micha and Ethan are on the track team together. And even though they don't move in the same social circles, he and Ethan have friends in common. Micha is a type—teacher's pet, coach's favorite because of his charm and high performance, but someone else with his peers. Sexually aggressive. Someone who won't hesitate to harm, manipulate, or scheme to get what he wants.

"Apparently," Ethan continues, "he's also paying someone to take those online classes he's using to ramp up his GPA."

"Do we have any actual proof?"

"Do we need it?" he asks, rolling toward me. We lock eyes, and I turn away so I don't have to look at his lips.

The first rule of The Cove is: Harm as little as possible for the cure.

The second rule: Let the strength of the cure be equal to the disease.

Third: Question the motives of the client. Investigate claims.

Ana says that this third rule is malleable. "Agnes always relied on her instincts. Sometimes there's no definitive proof, just the word of someone you trust." When I asked if Agnes was ever wrong, Ana just shrugged. "I think she had regrets when she passed. But she never voiced them."

Also, I don't have a "client" per se. Autumn is basically the client; she just doesn't know it.

Number four: Act swiftly. Once the decision is made. Don't vacillate. Don't hesitate to administer the cure.

"No," I answer finally. "I think by now we know who Micha is well enough."

Ethan nods slowly. Micha tripped Ethan once at a cross-country meet, causing him to come in third. Micha claimed it was an accident, apologized profusely in front of the coach. No consequences, except for Ethan who was rattled by it, performed poorly that season and didn't make it to championships, and has a bad ankle now that still hurts at the end of every meet.

"So, what's the plan?" he asks the ceiling.

"I'm still thinking about it."

My LifeWatch app chimes. Dad's on the move. I track my whole family, including Aunt Ana. My dad should be at his office, but I watch his blue dot pulse along the highway, on his way out of town. Grant apparently is at Robbie's place; they're probably playing *Red World*. My mom and Ana are both at places I don't recognize—neighborhoods around town. Everyone's been acting so weird since Ana's ex turned up dead.

I would ask my mom about it, but I try to talk to her as little as possible. Seems like we always wind up arguing, even when I don't mean to. Sometimes, though, she comes into my room at night and lies next to me and strokes my hair, and when neither one of us says anything, we can just stay like that for a long time, and sometimes I fall asleep and wake up and she's gone. I know my mother loves me, and I love her, but we just don't get along most of the time.

"Your mother's love language is control," Ana told me. "She doesn't know another way to be."

Ana's been schooling me in The Knowledge for over a year now. If my mom knew, she would not be happy. But Ana says I have the gift. And it's true that when I'm in Agnes's garden, or the greenhouse, I feel like the plants are whispering to me. I'm comfortable and myself in a way that I'm not anywhere else.

"Can you take me somewhere?" I ask.

"Anywhere," he says, glancing at me quickly.

Hey, a text from Autumn pings us both. **Are you guys hanging out without me? What are you DOING?**

We all track each other on Pop Map, always know each other's location. "You've literally never had an unsupervised moment in your life," Ana said with something like disdain. She taught me how to jigger LifeWatch when we went to Agnes's. Surprisingly easy with the right software. I tap on it now. Anyone looking at it will see my last location and think I'm here at home.

We'll pick you up, I text Autumn back.

K.

I turn off my lights and turn on my nightlight and put on some music, fluff up the pillows in my bed so if someone gives a quick glance in my room, maybe they'll think I'm sleeping.

"Where are we going?" asks Ethan, picking up his backpack at the door.

"To find an appropriate cure for a disease like Micha."

Ethan raises his eyebrows, seems like he has something he wants to say. But he stays quiet and follows me out the door.

VERA

Coraline has stopped sharing her location, the little message bubble on my phone informs me as I pull into Brock and Iggy's driveway.

Funny. My daughter thinks she can jigger the app on her phone to disguise her location. As if. Like I'm some soccer mom who doesn't get technology. She has an app; but I have one, too. It doesn't tell me where she's going, but it does tell me when she's messed with her location on LifeWatch.

I consider texting my very clever daughter, but then *she'll know* that *I know* she can trick the LifeWatch app. Instead, I switch over to Pop Map, where I have a fake account that follows Autumn, Ethan, Coraline, and Grant. Tricky, right? And in spite of all my warnings to never allow someone you don't know to follow you on Pop Map, they all allow "May Linn," cute little emo girl from Hollows High, to follow them, even though she has no posts and doesn't allow people to follow her. Coraline's and Ethan's cartoon avatars are in a little cartoon car, pulling onto Autumn's street. It's a small town. How much trouble could they get into? I decide to let it slide.

Iggy and Brock's place is dark, their electric car sitting in the driveway. I wait a moment, call Ana again. The call goes straight to voicemail.

The houses up and down the street are lit and tidy. Toyotas

and Jeeps in driveways, televisions visible through bay windows, bikes askew on lawns left carelessly by their riders. Normie, Ana would say derisively; but I'm happy for Iggy. Or will be when she's better, home with her family. Sometimes safe and orderly is the best you can ask for in this life. I finally climb out into the cold, look inside Brock and Iggy's car, which is locked and unoccupied, car seat empty in the back. I try the trunk; it's locked, too.

Then I walk up the flagstone path. Somewhere there's a distant strain of piano music.

When I reach the porch, the red front door is ajar. My heart starts to thump. Something's wrong. The energy is bad. I can feel it on my skin.

But calling the police is not an option, so I press inside. I'm unarmed. I still have the knife Agnes gave me on my eighteenth birthday. *A woman must always be ready to defend herself, psychologically and physically.* But the small, easily concealed switchblade is hidden in the back of one of the drawers in my closet.

But tonight, I wish I had it. It's annoying how often Agnes's words and warnings come back to me. How often she was right.

With a gentle tap of my foot, the red door swings open silently on a well-oiled hinge.

"Ana," I say into the quiet dim of the foyer.

No answer. I stand a moment, then step inside, listening to the sounds of the house. Only the hum of the refrigerator in the nearby kitchen fills the heavy silence.

"Ana," I say louder.

When there's still no response I walk inside, then head straight upstairs and to Noah's nursery, the location of which I remember from Iggy's baby shower. At the door, I pause, bracing myself. I try to listen over the sound of blood rushing in my ears.

A dim light shines from inside. The tinkling of one of those wind-up mobiles carries out into the hallway. I force myself to move inside. Over the crib dangles a solar system, nine colorful planets revolving around a smiling sun.

There he is, sleeping soundly in his little onesie and cap. My whole system floods with relief. His breathing is deep, and the urge to touch that soft, plump hand or the pink round of his cheek is strong.

I'm about to reach in and pick him up but decide to let this particular sleeping baby lie—and search the house for some clue as to what in the hell is going on. Did my sister leave the baby here alone? Even she's not that careless, that irresponsible. Then where is she?

Taking the phone from my pocket, I snap a picture of sleeping Noah, send it to Brock, just to put *someone's* mind at ease.

Baby's fine, I type. All is well. Can Marge come to relieve me?

Thank God. Where's Ana???

I debate about how to answer. Finally, I opt for a half-truth. She had to go. Not sure what she has going on tonight.

Or ever.

I back my way out and head downstairs.

In the kitchen I find the baby monitor and shove it in the pocket of my coat so I can keep it with me as I move through the house.

I start rifling through drawers—Post-it notes and pens, receipts fastened with a paperclip, silverware in bamboo dividers, potholders. Everything tidy and organized, clean. The pantry is stocked with staples—neat glass containers of sugar, flour, oatmeal, rows of jars for freshly made baby food. In the refrigerator, I rifle through the produce drawers. Apples and red leaf lettuce about to go off, carrots and radishes. All benign.

What am I looking for?

I'll know it when I see it.

I head down into the basement, flip on the lights as I creak down the stairs. In the cool damp, I look around. A stack of boxes, the washer and dryer, a worktable; again it's all fastidiously organized, nothing out of place. Something's off, though. What is it?

I am about to go back upstairs when I figure it out.

The basement is shorter than the length of the house upstairs, similar to my own. Someone has built a wall. And in it there is a door, locked tight.

I reach up over the door frame for a key, but there isn't one. Noah issues a little squeak on the monitor. But when I pull it from my pocket, the grainy image shows me that he's still sleeping, little legs kicking, fists clenched. What do babies dream about?

In an old coffee can on the tool bench, hidden behind a row of little drawers filled with nails, screws, washers, bolts, I find a key. It slides easily into the lock, and I push open the door.

After I flip on the light, it takes me a moment to register what I'm seeing. A long wooden table, an apothecary cabinet, rows of brown glass bottles, several stone mortar and pestle sets in various sizes and hues. A shelf of beakers, sets of measuring spoons and cups. An elaborate potted herb garden, irrigated, and lit in the orange glow of grow lamps. A leather-bound volume, open on the table. Branches, herbs, sprigs, and stalks of flowers hang upside down, tied with twine drying out.

I walk through the orderly and well-stocked room. It's an apothecary's workshop, much like Agnes's though less involved and elaborate. Lite.

The aromas of sage and lavender, maybe a note of mint, linger on the air.

There's a shipping station, a desk with shelving, storing high-quality mailers, a big roll of opalescent Bubble Wrap, sheets of labels—*Iggy Rose's Cures, Salves, and Potions*. Her logo is a rose comprised of stars, leaves, and flowers. Cute.

More, smaller labels read:

> Love Potion—Attract the love of your life
> Protection—Guard against negative energy
> Money—Bring a flood of wealth into your bank account
> Health—Feel well and be your best self every day
> Tummy Troubles—Soothe your belly
> Headaches
> Colds, coughs, and runny noses
> Girl Problems
> Broken Heart
> Etc. Etc.

When I notice Iggy's Instagram tag, I open the app on my phone and look her up. There she is, most often dressed in white, blond hair flowing, looking ethereal and wise.

"Sometimes it's setting your intention and opening yourself up that invites love in," she says sweetly, staring at the camera with her pretty, heavily lashed dark blue eyes. "But we can all use a little help, so just dab a little love potion on your wrists and neck—this is a proprietary organic blend of herbs, florals, and oils—to lift your spirits and open your heart chakra, making you more able to receive all the love the universe has to offer."

I scroll through similar videos for her other potions, then look through the comments, lots of raves for her products, hearts, and riots of glittery emojis.

I found the man of my dreams on a day I was least expecting it—thanks to your love potion.
  I put your money potion in my aromatherapy oil diffuser. Not only does it smell heavenly, but the very next day I got a raise and a promotion. Thank you, Iggy Rose.

Oh my god. Are people really this gullible?

On her post about headaches and eucalyptus oil, a comment from someone named GirlBoss80 catches my eye.

Do you have anything for revenge? I have a headache that won't go away if you know what I mean. 💀.

Iggy's response: "All my cures and potions are for love and positivity, but DM to talk if you like." I click on GirlBoss80, but the account is private, and the profile picture is a black-and-white sketch of a dark-side Hello Kitty—eyes narrowed, teeth and claws bared.

Interesting.

I dig through Iggy's apothecary drawers—filled with pouches of dried herbs, vials of oils, flower petals, seeds, sprigs, powders. Truthfully, I only find the most innocuous substances—lavender, rose, turmeric, basil, rosemary.

Still, I wonder—what have you been up to, Iggy Rose?

Noah stirs on the baby monitor, just as I hear footsteps creaking on the floor above my head.

I remember Agnes's warning again, and in the tool chest on the worktable in the outer room, I find a claw hammer.

It will do.

I head upstairs. The hallway is dark. Wasn't there a light on when I went down? I pause, listening. Noah chirps over the monitor again. I breathe, take in the night. There's someone here.

"Ana?"

I move quietly toward the kitchen, hammer ready.

A sound behind me has me spinning around too late.

I take a hard blow to the head, the hammer falling, thunking to the wood floor, spinning away. The ground rises up fast to greet me with a hard smack to the side of my face. The world rattles. My first thought is the kids. Coraline. Grant.

The form is just a shadow, masked, dressed in black. The form straddles me, small but strong. A great soft mass presses hard to my nose and mouth. I know the scent—hemlock, mandrake, henbane, poppy. The Deadly Trance.

I watch, pinned and helpless, struggling as a second figure heads up the stairs toward the baby. Another comes to stand over me, looking down. Oh, god.

It's only seconds before I'm overcome, totally paralyzed. Rage and fear are a five-alarm fire inside my immobilized body. Only a single tear can escape from my eye.

Noah crying in his crib is the last thing I hear before everything goes black.

PART THREE

JUST DESSERTS

"A little sugar cuts the bitterness of the cure."
Aunt Agnes's *Book of Cures*

AGNES

Tonight is the first full moon in January. The Wolf Moon, named for the howling of hungry wolves lamenting the scarcity of food in winter. There are other, more significant celestial events in any given year. But this moon is a moment for reflection, the passing of what is old, the coming of what is new. It's a moment of hope. Even in the depths of winter, spring is only weeks away. Soon the garden will start its audacious color show of beauty, healing, and power.

Without fail the earth moves closer to the sun, the seasons turn, what has died is reborn, fresh and green.

I watch as the younger people work diligently, Lisander calling out orders as she and her students prepare the bonfire.

For our meeting, we light the trees, wrapping the bare branches in bright white lights to remind the darkness that a new dawn is coming, to remind the cold that soon there will be warmth. Most winter rituals in indigenous cultures—even the lights on Christmas trees—derive from this practice, a way to bring hope in the paucity of winter when nature can be cruel, light scant, and food hard to come by.

They arrive. On foot, by car, those who have traveled farthest have rented vans or RVs and will be welcome to stay after the meeting has ended. I have left the gate open and one by one they have come throughout the day. The energy is electric, anticipatory. This long night will last until the first rays of dawn.

This will be the first full moon since Ana and Vera have both achieved relative mastery of The Knowledge. I have taught them what I know and now it is their choice whether to accept it or not, to continue their education, to choose a practice. They help Lisander and her young students string the lights. There is laughter; it rings on the air like the tinkling of bells.

The younger members of The Cove bring joy, a fresh new energy that I appreciate. They haven't been raised in darkness, under cover, hiding their power and who they are. Say what you want about the world and all the ways in which it is still cruel, unjust, divorced from nature. But there is a greater acceptance of all the things that make us human. People are freer to be who they are now than they once were.

Once upon a time, women like us, those of us connected to the power of the earth with the knowledge to use its gifts, were hated and feared, persecuted and violently murdered. To be sure, a hateful misogyny still prevails in our culture. But the young women of The Cove have not been raised in secrecy or fear. They embrace their gifts in a way our ancestors could not.

I watch as Ana climbs the ladder, lithe and sure-footed. And Vera stays on the ground calling out her orders. I know Sadie would be proud of them. Ana, though she's wild and in trouble all the time, is intelligent, fierce, gifted in The Knowledge. Vera is wise, disciplined, in charge of herself—and trying to be in charge of everything else. They are beautiful, both of them in different ways, bonded and devoted to each other above all else. Sadie, I was never the mothering type. But I have done my best. I hope you know that.

As for choices, I have made mine.

Tonight is the night that I will name my successor as the leader of The Cove. The day will come when I am no longer able to lead, or won't want to. I understand the world less and less. Technology and its dark magic, its reach, how it is changing everything, even the way we relate to each other, exhausts me. I am not the person to lead the group into the future.

I know Lisander expects to take the mantle when that day comes. In many ways, she, my best student, is the natural choice. And Ana wants the position for herself someday, or so she says without really understanding what it means.

But tonight, I will name Vera, who wants it least of all. And for that reason, I know she is the right choice. Unlike Ana, her gift is underpinned by self-discipline. She is bold but not reckless. She understands The Knowledge but is not made greedy by its power. She is measured, slow to anger, compassionate. She's not ready now, nor am I. But one day, she will lead The Cove. I'm sure of it.

The sun is dipping low, and the sky is painting itself orange and black. The girls are becoming shadows in the setting sun. Someone turns on music. Someone laughs, the sound bouncing off the trees. In the near distance, the graveyard with its low stone wall, where the women in our family are buried. I sense them watching us, looking on in benevolence.

I walk the path back to the house and find Chief Royer walking toward me. He lifts a hand in a wave, and I smile. It's only as I get closer that I see the concerned wrinkle on his brow.

"What is it?" I ask as we come to meet on the path.

I don't see him as he is now—graying with a paunch, a landscape of lines on his tanned face. When I look at him I still see him as he was when we were young and in love. He's still big, powerful through the shoulders, upright and strong. So many years ago. That love is still there, speaking strictly for me—worn and soft, faded.

"Where's Ana?"

"She's down by the graveyard, setting up for tonight. What's she done?"

I hold my breath, hoping it's not the Danvers thing come to haunt. They got away with it, and Mr. Danvers survived, but there were whispers. They've both promised to behave, and truthfully seemed chastened by the whole thing, have been on best behavior.

"Apparently, Ana was with a group last night that stole a car and took it for a joyride. There was an accident, no one hurt luckily, but the parents are considering pressing charges. Ana was supposedly at the wheel."

"She doesn't have her license yet," I protest. "And she was home all night."

"Sure about that?"

He takes out a piece of paper and hands it to me. There's a grainy image of kids in a car. Yes, there's Ana at the wheel, smiling devilishly. There's a date and time stamp, last night after midnight.

"We captured this from a red-light camera."

I draw in and release a heavy breath.

"Meanwhile, I've had some complaints about the amount of people coming through town and heading up here."

"This is private property. We're not hurting anyone."

He gives me a look, which makes me angry.

"I'm sure that I don't need to remind you how you've availed yourself of my gifts."

He lifts his palms in surrender. "I've got your back, Agnes. But I don't know what I can do about these parents. They're on the warpath."

"Tell them I'll pay for the damages. And I'll find an appropriate punishment for Ana. See if that calms them down."

I glance at the image again—Ana smiling, the other kids laughing. I have to press back a smile myself. I guess the chief has forgotten that we were all young and wild once upon a time, sneaking out, getting tipsy at the quarry lake, getting it on in the back of his father's pickup. We're old now. He's married with children, but the fearless, joyful teenagers we were once are still alive and well in my memory.

There's a sound behind me and I turn to see Lisander approaching, with young Camille and Bree close behind. Lisander has her long gray hair braided, the plait snaking over her shoulder. She's dressed in a flowing black caftan, draped in a woven shawl against the chill, Birkenstocks, a heavy quartz crystal on a gold chain around her neck, every bit the earth mother. Her skills are significant. I am proud of who she has become.

"Everything alright here?" she asks easily.

The chief stays quiet, folds his arms, rocks back and forth subtly from toe to heel.

"I'll talk to them," says the chief, giving me a nod. "Try to calm them down and see what we can work out."

A group of other Cove members walk past us, all robed with crystal jewelry, greeting us as they pass on their way to the field. The scent of wood smoke wafts on the air. The bonfire must be lit.

"And I'll leave you to—all of this."

Lisander, Bree, and Camille remain silent behind me. I offer him a nod, feel Lisander rest a hand on my shoulder.

He gives me one last look, then turns to walk down the path. He has come to me a number of times over the years. And I have helped him to the best of my ability, helped his wife when she was ill, made sure his career advanced as it should. He has long been my ally and my protector in this town. Why do I feel like it's the last time I'll see him? Just the Wolf Moon making me anxious, I suppose. Reminding us that we're all in a cycle of continuing change.

The afternoon grows darker as the dipping sun hides behind a thick swath of clouds. Music, the sound of an acoustic guitar, carries through the dusk.

Lisander loops her arm through mine.

"I made you a gift," she says, hands me a little cloth pouch.

I touch her face. "Thank you," I say.

I open it and remove a delicate item. White branches are wrapped with silk thread, crystals woven throughout, glittering in the scant light. It's run through with herbs and flowers, feathers, some small shells. I've made many of these myself with the sprigs and branches from my garden and the found items in the forest that surround the property. This one is for protection.

Even before Lisander knew what they were, when her mother first brought her to me to teach, she was making these little dolls.

I hold it up to the light. In the practice we call them stick effigies, make them for all sorts of purposes—to protect, as this one is, to heal, to keep an enemy from harming us, to guard from negative energies, to make someone fall in love—or out of love. There are darker intentions. But I don't teach those. In The Cove, as long as I hold my seat, we don't practice black magic.

"It's beautiful," I tell her, holding it up to watch it glitter in the waning afternoon light.

ANA

I run, the moon high, the night cold. Branches slap at my face, my feet slip in forest floor detritus. I stumble, come down hard on one knee, get up and keep going.

I can hear Camille and Bree behind me, their voices bouncing off the trees. There's a stitch in my side and I am about to vomit from exertion. Ahead, a big oak towers. I stop, limp. I can't keep running.

Camille and Bree have taken to howling like wolves, and the moon is almost blue in the sky. I walk around the tree and find a hollow, burrow myself into its moist, cold center. My breath is ragged. I shiver, try to center myself.

Agnes used to say that our circumstances are always the exact consequence of our actions. I'm thinking this as Camille and Bree go loping by, yelling my name.

I've made mistakes. I've hurt people. I'm the first one to admit that. But I'll tell you what. I've never hurt anyone who didn't hurt me first. Where does it say in the rule book that you have to let people abuse you? That you have to let people get away with it?

Nowhere. It says that nowhere.

Take Kevin Harding for example, the ex that Detective Bandeau mentioned—who thinks I tried to poison him. Who imagines I'm coming back to finish the job one day. Well, truthfully, I *did* poison him. And, yes, sure, I wish I'd killed him. But Kevin was a sexual deviant and stalker. And after what I thought was a fairly civil breakup (no bloodshed), he *would not* leave me alone. The late-night calls, the vile texts and DMs, showing up at my apartment, my job.

I did the right thing first. I went to the police. I took out a restraining order. Let me tell you. They're useless. Only respectful, law-abiding people give a shit about restraining orders. Kevin Harding was neither of those. Men like him only understand one thing.

When I told him I wanted to get back together, when I offered to come over and cook him a meal, his ego was bloated enough that he believed it. I made him Sadie's famous beef Wellington. He ate more than was reasonable. How is that my fault?

Sometimes, girls, violence is the only answer. Another Agnes-ism, one of my favorites.

Their voices are fading. I hear them in the distance now faint and confused—*Ana! Where did she go?*—I take out my phone, cover the glowing blue light with my hand.

The way I see it, there's only person who can help me now. The last person I want to contact, the last person I *should* call, and the one I can't stop thinking about.

As if I've sent out a psychic distress call, my phone rings. I hit the silence button quickly, pause, listen to the night. Did they hear?

I tap out a text. Then another one.

I can't catch my breath; that stitch in my side feels like I imagine the knife I stuck into April. Ha—still happy about that.

Bree and Camille are coming back, their voices echoing in the night. *Did you hear that? Was that her phone?*

Ana, one of them yells, sounds like Bree with her smoky, young voice. *We just want to talk.*

Ever notice that when people say they just want to talk, it never goes well?

I get up and force myself to keep moving.

TIMOTHY

The road is dark, swimming ahead of me. I need sleep. I'm not going to get it.

I'm thinking about my old partner, Hitch, on the drive from Beck's office. He was a fan of Occam's razor, the rule stating that the most plausible explanation is the most likely. He was constantly saying things like "when you hear hoofbeats, think horses, not zebras."

Of course, Occam's razor is a fallacy. Because the simplest solution is not always the correct one. Life, people, circumstances are impossibly complicated. If Hitch were still here, we'd probably have Ana in custody already. When a man is murdered and his new girlfriend is missing, the ex with a history is the reasonable suspect.

I wonder what he would think of the things Beck shared.

"Agnes Blacksmith had a garden on her property, walled and locked," Beck said. "It's where she grew the flowers for her business, as well as the herbs for her cures. I think you might find what you're looking for there."

"Agnes Blacksmith has been dead for ten years."

He nodded slowly, picked up the skull on his desk, turned it in his hands like a baseball. "But her nieces, Ana and Vera Blacksmith, inherited and maintain the property."

"You're saying that they tend the garden. That they keep a *poison* garden."

"That's what I understand."

"Understand how? Have you seen it?"

"No," said Beck, putting the skull down.

It was clear that he knew more than he was saying. I pressed. "I'll need a warrant to search that property. Tell me why you think I'll find what I'm looking for there."

"I'm telling you that the plants which are indicated in Iggy Rose and Paul Hayes's poisonings grow locally. And one of the places they might be growing is on the Blacksmith property. Other possible places—fields, wooded areas, even places like cemeteries, which are essentially nature sanctuaries."

He slid the file over to me. "Keep it. It's a copy."

What would Hitch think about witches with poison gardens? He'd think that motive is motive. And everything else is just set dressing.

Now I come to a stop at the driveway to Agnes Blacksmith's property. The road leading to the house is gated, a tall wrought iron structure that is locked with a heavy chain. There's no call box, and the stone wall in either direction is high enough that it would be difficult, not impossible, to scale. I climb out of the vehicle to stand in the dark considering it, weighing my options. Above me a rising full moon casts the world in silvery light.

If I enter the property illegally and find anything, it will be inadmissible in court.

I stare through the gate. Is that a glow off in the distance? Is there someone in the house? What's that noise? There's a faint humming.

The place is still owned by the Blacksmith sisters. Pacing, I pull out my phone and call Ana. No answer. I leave a message. Then Vera. My call goes straight to voicemail.

I'm staring at the wall and imagining all the ways I could fuck myself up or over by trying to climb it when my phone pings.

I need help. It's an emergency.

Another ping offers a shared location.
Here is a choice with a lot of layers.
Bad cop: climb the wall and try to find the deadly garden Beck claims is here.
Smart cop: call for a warrant based on the evidence provided by Beck and the video footage I watched. Call for backup, and seek to enter the property to find more evidence to build my case.
Idiot cop: drop everything to answer the text of an obviously unstable woman with whom I'm obviously entangled on all sorts of levels.

Hurry. Please.

The decision is surprisingly easy.
I get in my vehicle, gun the engine, and drive.

IGGY

My baby is crying, his wails distant and angry. I can feel his little spirit. Noah, I knew it from the first moment I laid eyes on him, is a rebel, a powerhouse. But right now, he's just a baby, one who needs his mom. I have to go home to him.

I swim up through layers of consciousness, higher, higher, reaching desperately for the milky light I see above me. I have no body, no voice, no words. His name shimmers in my mind. *Noah. Baby. My baby boy.*

A flutter of light, a flicker. A strange beeping. A harsh white glow. Brock, pacing the room, looking at his phone. He looks so tired, so afraid. Ana thinks he's weak, but he's not. He's a thinker, a feeler, loyal. Most men believe that anger is power. Throw a punch; wield a gun. They think that's what makes them strong. Brock has been taught differently. I am not Marge's biggest fan, nor she mine I'm sure, but she has raised a rare kind of man, one who respects female power.

I try to speak but my throat only aches. A tube. Tubes everywhere, coming from my arms, leading to machines. I try not to panic but my heart starts to race, and the monitor beeps faster. He turns to me.

"Iggy! Iggy! She's awake."

A crowd then, all around me. Nurses, the doctor who's been

here often, young, Indian maybe, with kind eyes and a smooth, earnest face.

"Iggy, relax," the doctor says, keeping eye contact. "You're okay. I promise. Okay, cough big for me. Hard as you can."

I do as he says, and he expertly pulls the tube. It comes out of me and I gag, then I am gasping for air, throat on fire.

"Easy, easy," he says, one hand on my shoulder, one on my arm. The healing touch. He has it. I can feel it travel through my body, soothing me. "I got you. You're good. Breathe. Breathe."

Brock has my hand, his eyes holding mine. "I'm here," he says. "Iggy, I'm here."

As soon as I have my voice back, I rasp, "Noah."

"He's fine," Brock says, but his eyes say something different. "He's with—Ana."

"Ana?" I ask, incredulous, the word just a squeaky croak. *Oh, no.*

He lifts a palm. "She's been helping with him. Actually."

"What's happening? What's going on? Where is he?"

"He's safe at home." Brock holds out his phone, so that I can see an image of Noah asleep in his crib. Seeing him there safe and sound, my breath comes easier, the beeping of the monitor eases.

"I'll give you two a minute," says the doctor. "We'll be back to draw some blood, run some tests. But welcome home, Iggy."

It all comes back to me in a rush. The brunch. Paul found murdered.

"Who did this?" I ask. "It wasn't—Ana?"

"I don't think so, no," says Brock, sitting. "She came with a milk thistle mixture yesterday. We put it in your IV drip. Honestly, I think that's what saved you, Ig. You started to get better right away."

Ana. I should have known she'd never hurt me. That she'd come through for me when I needed her.

I remember the girl she was when we were in college, fiercely loyal, wild, always with me, willing to do anything, go anywhere, veering from one bad relationship to the next. In so many ways, she was my first love, the way you can only love a friend, or a sister. That unconditional bond, which is stronger than anything you will ever have, could ever have, with a man. The reason our relationship is strained now is because of Brock and Noah. Not because she wanted Brock, or a baby, or because she's angry Brock and I are together. It's because my love for him and Noah comes before my love for her. It's the same reason she was angry when Vera got pregnant. She knew Vera would never put her husband before her sister. But Vera's children would be a different story. But Ana has come to love Coraline and Grant in her way. She's a good auntie to them now.

"She's good with him actually," says Brock, as if reading my thoughts.

This makes me smile. I always knew she'd come around and be Noah's loving Auntie Ana as soon as she realized that there was just one more person to love her.

"Where is she?" I ask Brock now.

"I—don't know. I haven't been able to reach her. Vera's with the baby now. We're not sure where Ana went."

Other memories come back, ugly ones, dark ones.

"She's in trouble," I say, trying to get up. It's on the air. I can feel her energy. It's dark and dangerous. She needs me.

But my body doesn't work, my limbs filled with sand, my head pounding. The toxin mingles with my blood, a blackness spreading through my system. I think back to the brunch. What did I eat, drink?

There were pastries, creamy, flaky, filled with jam. Champagne, dry, bubbling in my throat.

Ana's cassoulet.

I ate it like I hadn't eaten in weeks; it was rich and meaty, delicious. I ate it until I couldn't eat another bite.

I think about the table. Payton, chic and powerful. Vera,

elegant and cold. Esme, cheerful and kind. Ana. She seemed fragile to me. In pain, needing attention. Who else was there? There's a fog in my head, obscuring memory.

April.

April Snell was in the kitchen with access to all the food, all the plates, all the glasses, and the serving wear.

She carefully ladled out the portions of cassoulet into bowls, served one to each of us.

Quiet, meek little April. Always in the shadows. Lisander's pet. April's mother, Trina, tried to poison her, made April sick so that Trina could have the attention doctors shower on the mothers of ill children. Trina always maintained her innocence, claimed that she was trying to heal April. But poor April wasn't ill until her mother Trina started to administer her "medicine."

Trina went to prison, but the real punishment came from The Cove. From Agnes, who was its leader until her untimely death. Or so I'm told.

I didn't grow up in The Cove like so many around here have. I joined later, when Ana learned about my gift with potions, and taught me some of the things she knew. She brought me in, and I have loved this sisterhood. Women helping women, using the power of the planet to heal each other. To protect each other when necessary.

But why would anyone want to hurt me?

Unless.

"What happened at the brunch, Iggy?" asks Brock now. I tell him all the things I've been thinking. And he listens, brow furrowed with concern.

The pieces start to fit together.

"Ana's in trouble," I say again. "She needs me."

"Ana has to take care of herself now," says Brock, pulling up the chair beside me. "Noah and I need you to take care of *you*, to get better. If your liver function doesn't improve, they're talking about a transplant, Ig. You have to rest, okay? You need all your energy to fight the poison in your system."

He puts a heavy hand on my shoulder as if he thinks I'll try to get up. As if I could. I'm so weak.

I look at my husband. His expression is loving, gentle but stern. I wonder if he'll understand when I tell him what I've done.

"Honey, I need you to hear me. You have to help me."

In the dim of the room, I whisper to him the truth of what I've done, what I suspect might be happening now, and what I need to do next. He would be within his rights to walk out the door and not come back. He could take Noah away, even call the police.

After I'm done, I hold his eyes. I see his shock, his fear.

"Will you help me?" I manage in the dim quiet, praying he won't get up and walk out on me for good.

"Iggy," he says instead, a gentle hand to my cheek. "There's nothing I wouldn't do for you."

Relief and love wash through me. Outside the window, I see the blue glow of the full moon. The Wolf Moon.

"Then help me get out of here."

CORALINE

"Where are we even going?"

Autumn's getting whiny in the back seat. I knew we should have left her at home.

"To Great-Aunt Agnes's," I tell her.

Ethan weaves the Tesla up the rural road.

"I still have an English essay," says Autumn. "It's due tonight."

"You wanted to come," I remind her. "We're not going to be long."

"Are we sure this is a good idea?" she asks, sounding weepy.

I spin to look at her in the dark.

"Autumn, Micha is *cheating*. Is it fair that he's going to get the valedictorian spot and you're not because of it?"

"No," she says weakly.

"Okay, then." I turn back to the road in front of us, Ethan casting me a look, his hands gripping the wheel.

"It's just that," Autumn says softly in the back, "I don't want to hurt anyone."

"We're not going to hurt him," I say. Which is sort of a lie. "We're just going to level the playing field."

"I mean," says Ethan. "I kind of agree with Autumn. Like if we hurt him, what does that make us?"

"Right," says Autumn. "Why don't we just report him?"

"Okay," I say. "Like anyone will believe us."

Ethan shrugs, keeps his eyes on the road. "But maybe they will. Or at least investigate. Look, I've got your back. But like how much of this is about helping Autumn? And how much of it is about hurting Micha just because you're holding a grudge? Since first grade."

I am about to argue when a pair of ultrabright headlights bear down, coming from the other direction. Ethan veers slightly to the right as a big dark car races past us in a blur, a light flashing on its dash.

"That was a cop car. Unmarked," says Ethan, like he knows something. He's a bit of a buff, fascinated by all things law enforcement. "Where's he going?"

"Where's he coming from?" I ask. "There isn't much up here. Agnes's property sits on like twenty acres."

My heart has started to pump a little.

When we get to Agnes's all is quiet, and the gate is firmly locked. Luckily I have the keys. My mom has kept them hanging on a hook by the garage door. It was easy to take them to a hardware store and get them copied. I've been coming here with Ana and on my own forever. When Ethan pulls to a stop, I get out and unlock the gate, swing it open. After he drives through, I close and lock it again behind us.

"Is there someone here?" asks Ethan, looking off into the distance.

I see what he's talking about. An orange glow comes up through the trees. Glancing at my phone, I see something odd. Both my mom and Ana have disappeared from my LifeWatch, their locations unavailable.

I feel a tingle of unease.

If something feels wrong, it probably is. Ana and my mother have a lot of the same pet phrases. That's one of them. *Follow your instincts.*

My instincts are telling me to leave, to get my friends out of here and not investigate the strange light coming from the house. And maybe, yeah, drop the whole Micha thing because it does violate one of the rules of The Cove: Do not use The Knowledge for your own personal grudges or gains.

But something else, something deeper, is telling me to stay. There's a voice I hear when I'm in the greenhouse or in Agnes's garden or concocting with Ana in the kitchen. No one ever talks about *that* voice. The one that's somehow quieter and louder than any other voice.

"Hey," I say. "Pull the car off the road up there. Let's walk the rest of the way."

Ethan does as he's told. Autumn leans over the seat. "What's going on?"

Above us the moon is rising, big and full. It's so bright. And I remember what tonight is, even though I'm too young to be in on the business of The Cove.

"Something's up," I say. "Someone's here. I'm going to call for backup."

ANA

I've lost Camille and Bree, and I sit shivering in the trees by the side of the road, when I hear the roaring engine approaching.

Bright headlights come fast around the bend. I step from the trees and the dark car comes to a stop in front of me. I'm numb with the frigid cold, with fear. The passenger door swings open. And I hesitate a moment, wondering if this is a frying pan into the fire situation. But I'm out of options. Climbing inside the car, the relative safety and heat are a blessed relief.

I put my hands numb with cold up to the vents, don't greet or even look at the driver.

"Hello, Ana," he says.

That easy, low growl of a voice.

I'm shaking, still hearing April wailing in pain, worried about baby Noah who I left behind. Total babysitting fail. I've really started to like that little chunker; now I bet Brock and Iggy will never let me take care of him again. Assuming I get out of this alive.

"Drive," I tell him, looking through the window into the woods.

A glance into the trees reveals only darkness. It makes me nervous that they gave up the chase so easily. Where did they go? I have a bad feeling. The full moon is a white-blue disk in the sky.

He doesn't ask me where we're going. He puts his foot to the gas, and we peel out.

"I can't stop thinking about you," he says so softly that I can barely hear it over the roar of the engine.

I'm not sure this is the moment for confessing our feelings.

I don't answer him because I don't want to give him the satisfaction of telling him that the same is true for me.

Since our raunchy first meeting, I keep returning to that bathroom, feeling the heat of him, the strength. His mouth. His hands. It's been super annoying, considering that at the moment, he's my enemy. It's also kind of hot.

"And not just because you're the prime murder suspect in my investigation," he goes on into my silence.

I finally turn to look at Detective Bandeau.

"You know I didn't kill Paul," I say.

His profile, strong and angular, looks like it should be etched in marble. He keeps his eyes on the road, expression unreadable.

"Then who?" he asks as he makes a hard right.

I have a theory. More than a theory. But it's a Cove rule to keep quiet; April was right about that much. *The Cove manages its own problems, metes out its own justice to its members. No outsiders. And absolutely no police.*

"How should I know?" I ask. "I'm a *victim* here."

This earns a snort. "I'm thinking you're nobody's victim. And you know more than you're saying. That much is obvious."

He pulls over sharply and kills the engine. We sit in the dark, face-to-face.

"I discovered a few things tonight," he says. He takes the phone from his pocket, and taps it a couple times. When he holds it up, there's a grainy video, time stamped Wednesday night before the brunch, after midnight. What I see there makes me gasp.

"Where did you get that?" I ask.

"Amanda Alessi's neighbor. The doorbell camera footage."

I hand him back his phone, brain in overdrive trying to fit the pieces together. He stows the device, starts driving again.

I had my theories, but *this* I did not imagine.

"That's a mistake," I say, unable to believe my eyes. "Like a deep fake or some shit."

"No. It's not."

"Where are we going?" I ask. Since he hasn't asked me, it seems like he has a destination in mind.

"Is it true that your Aunt Agnes has a poison garden on her property?"

Okay. Now, *who* told him that?

"That if we go there I'll find hemlock and wolfsbane, the toxins of which are consistent with what killed Paul? Or the death cap mushroom, which is likely what made your friend Iggy sick?"

Silence is often the only good answer.

"Is it also true that you and Vera maintain the property and the garden to this day?"

Silence expands, all things I want to say, can't say.

Our bathroom assignation. It was more than just a tawdry hookup. There was—is—an undeniable connection. Still, despite that or maybe because of it, I left and then ghosted him. I feel it again now, a pull to him. A desire to confess all my sins and secrets.

"I—can't," I tell him now. I can't. I won't.

My phone pings, and I look down to see that there's a text from Lisander, and it makes my blood run cold.

> Ana, we have Vera. You both have a great deal to answer for. We would like you to come tonight to observe the Wolf Moon so that justice might be served.

Panic has me shaking. Why do they have Vera?

The answer comes quickly: they think I killed Paul Hayes,

and that she helped me. They won't turn us in to the police. But they will punish us. I've violated the rules of The Cove too many times.

I try to call my sister, but it goes straight to voicemail. I hang up, mind reeling.

"Ana," the detective says, and there's something about his voice that soothes. I look at him and he holds my eyes. He's present, right there, in a way that I have found men are often not.

Who is he? Can he be trusted?

He seems so familiar. I felt that way the first night, like I've known him, that we've met before. I haven't felt that way about a man. Usually it's strangers, *strangeness*, that excites me. Darkness. Violence.

I glance at my phone again, willing my sister to call me back or text me and tell me what to do like she always does.

But Lisander goes on via text about justice and new beginnings, and bringing The Cove to order, eliminating bad actors, blah, blah, blah.

But I'm only focused on one thing: they have Vera.

Why? *What* is happening?

And who am I without my sister? Who are any of us without her hand on the helm?

I look at the LifeWatch app and see that Vera's location is not available.

Equally troubling, Coraline is at Agnes's.

My throat goes dry, heart now a timpani drum in my chest.

What the actual fuck?

I feel suddenly lost, alone. Afraid.

Without Vera to consult about what to do next, I'm ten again, standing in the driveway, watching Mac, then Sadie, get carted away.

I'm standing in front of Agnes's for the first time, realizing that a place I've never been before is now the only home I have.

Every time, no matter how hopeless things seemed, I could

look to my sister. She always knows what to do, what to say, how to get us through. Every single time I call, no matter what I've done, she's been there.

Do they really have her? Is it just a lure to make sure I'll come?

Did Vera have something to do with Paul's murder?

She's tricky, that one. Despite her Stepford Wife, Soccer Mom persona, my sister has a dark side, is capable of nearly anything if someone she loves is threatened.

"Can I trust you?" I say, fear and anger doing a dance in my center. It's a stupid question. He's a cop. But I see something else in him. The shadow.

He doesn't answer me for a moment, then he nods ever so slightly, the lights from the dash washing his face. And in that moment I see in him an ally, not an enemy.

"My sister is in trouble," I tell him.

"What kind of trouble?"

"Take me to Agnes's. And I'll tell you everything."

It's not unprecedented.

Agnes had Chief Royer. He was her ally and her friend, her sometimes lover. He protected her, made sure to direct suspicion from her when he could. She helped him advance his career, protected him from enemies. They founded the food bank together.

Allies in high places are an important asset, she told me when I questioned their relationship since it clearly violated The Cove's rules. But it was more than that. They were high school sweethearts. Even though he was married with children, there was deep connection. *I wasn't the marrying kind. Never wanted kids. He needed that kind of normal life. Our relationship is exactly what it can be.*

"Everything?" Timothy asks now.

"Everything I know."

The detective looks at me a moment, then gives me a quick nod. He guns the engine and I start talking.

VERA

The sky is blue velvet, riven with stars faded by the glowing silver dinner plate of the full Wolf Moon. It's all I can see as I come to, my head tilted unnaturally backward, neck aching, head a siren of pain.

Am I dreaming?

Someone has hung the lights in the trees the way we used to when Agnes was still alive. The air is frigid; my hands and feet, my face numb as if I've been out in the cold for a very long time. I sense rather than really see I am in the field beside the graveyard where the women in my family are buried beneath the big weeping willow. As things come into focus, I see that someone has gone to the trouble of lighting that, as well, with tiny twinkling blue bulbs. Nearby, a bonfire roars and the night is filled with the smell of wood smoke.

I am bound to some big chair fashioned of wood. It's rickety beneath me, the ties at my wrist and ankles tight and painful. With effort, I lift my head. I see them seated at a long table before me, waiting patiently.

Lisander, with Camille and Bree standing sentry behind her. The two of them have grown up before my eyes; they are strong now, Lisander's enforcers. I'm guessing one of them pinned me to the ground and administered The Deadly Trance.

April sits to Lisander's right; she looks pale and clammy like she might be ill.

There are others here, too, all around us, forms that seem to slip from the trees. Some of them I recognize as Lisander's students. Others I have never seen before.

The Cove has grown large and diffuse since Agnes's passing. This gathering used to be boisterous, joyful. Tonight, it's silent.

I try not to panic, though I feel my heart thumping, my throat achingly dry. I won't let them see me flail against my bindings or let them hear me raise my voice in fear.

Instead, I turn my gaze on the quorum gathered before me. I imagine they have come in judgment. But who are they to judge me? I give them my most pitying smile.

Lisander rises, all flowing black robes and crystals dangling from chains around her neck, her long gray hair wild. The candlelight flickers in the breeze.

"You always did have a flair for the dramatic," I say, my voice croaking.

What would Agnes have thought of Lisander's little show?

In the years since Agnes's death, there has only been this loose leadership of The Cove, no one to really steer the ship. That's why it has become so diffuse, practitioners of all disciplines scattered about, posting on social media, selling their services like Iggy. If I had taken my seat, as Agnes wanted, maybe I could have kept things tighter, more organized. But it wasn't my calling, or my wish. When she died, we were still angry with each other—about what she did, what she wanted from me, and what I refused to give her.

"Where's Ana?" I ask.

"Ana's on the run," says Lisander heavily. "We tried to bring her in to answer for herself. But she stabbed April and has disappeared."

Is that true? Did she *stab* April? If she did, it was because she felt cornered. A glance at April reveals that she is seriously unwell.

Would Ana just run away, leave me and the kids behind?

Leave me to face The Cove, and leave Grant and Coraline without their mother or their aunt?

The truth is I'm not sure.

There's a code between sisters, Sadie liked to say. *You don't always have to be happy with each other. Sometimes you might not get along, or even like each other that much. But you always have to be the backup, the ride or die. When the phone rings, you answer.*

No one could say I haven't been there for my sister. As I sit bound beneath the Wolf Moon, I think about all the dark and dangerous things I have done for her, and I wonder where she has gone. If she's okay. I've never really had to call on Ana for help; it's always been the other way around. But I need her now.

"Vera Blacksmith, daughter of Sadie, niece of Agnes."

Lisander makes her voice deep, and it resonates, bouncing off the trees all around us. A stiff wind blows the smoke from the bonfire in our direction. And somewhere I hear the faint call of the screech owl.

I have tolerated but never felt affection for Lisander. She was Agnes's star student, her protégée before Ana and I arrived at the house. So, there was always a bit of tension between us. Then on that night long ago when Agnes named me as her successor to lead The Cove, that subtle tension turned to a deep resentment on Lisander's part. The fact that I declined didn't seem to improve our relationship. I discarded something she wanted so badly, and it only made her dislike me more.

"Tonight, before your peers, you stand accused of violating the laws of The Cove."

See. That's my whole problem with the so-called Cove. It's not a real thing. Like all religions, it's just a doctrine that is only validated by the zeal of its followers. And over the years, what was really just a loose band of Wiccan women who practiced the healing arts, helping and protecting each other in a world where the persecution of female power was the norm, became something else.

"We, the council of The Cove, formally charge you with the murder of your father, of your aunt, our beloved leader Agnes, and of Paul Hayes."

The accusations land like blows, each one of them hurting in a different way. I opt for silence.

On the table before them some of the flickering candles go out in the stiff wind. The scent of sage is heavy on the air.

I am afraid because I know what these women are capable of.

I keep my face still, my breath even. They won't see my fear. I've never let anyone see it, though it dictates so many of my choices and actions.

All eyes are on me, looking at me. All I see is judgment.

"Vera, how do you answer to these charges?" asks Lisander.

Still I say nothing.

"Your father was abusing your mother," Lisander said. "So, I understand that. Why you might decide to end him, put the death cap mushrooms in his beef Wellington. Agnes never believed that Sadie would kill Mac; Sadie loved that man too much. Agnes did, however, believe that Sadie would die to protect you or Ana."

I still feel the rise of acid in my gullet when I think about this. My mother's choices, such as they were. The choices I had to make because she was too weak to protect us properly.

Lisander offers a solemn nod. "I know you have always felt that Agnes was responsible for Sadie's death. That she was pressing you into a life you didn't want. You hated her, didn't you, Vera?"

Hate is a strong word. I wouldn't say I hated my aunt. I wouldn't say I ever really loved her. And, yes, I did hold her responsible for my mother's death. It was a complicated dance—the bouquet she brought to Sadie, my mother's willingness, maybe even her desire, to die. But Agnes could have intervened, or at the very least not made it so damn easy for my mother to end her life.

"So, I can almost understand what motivated you to kill Agnes. You were young, impulsive, and angry."

I bristle at this. These are words usually used to describe Ana. Not me. I am none of those things. And thanks to Sadie, Mac, and Agnes, the inept adults in my life, I have never been young.

"But what about Paul Hayes?" Lisander goes on. "Why take that kind of risk? Killing him like that."

Oh, there were myriad reasons for Paul Hayes to die.

First reason: The women he psychologically abused and manipulated at the workplace, and those he drugged and raped. Jessie Parker, for one. The rumors about Paul made their way to me through the whisper network when Ana started seeing him.

Second: There was the damage Paul did to Esme's reputation and business when they were both in the running for that *Business Journal* article. That she was a drunk; that she was being investigated for tax fraud. Both completely untrue. Brad happened to catch wind of it after the article ran. I didn't share it with her when we spoke because she was already angry enough. But what damage would Paul have done to Esme in order to win the award for which they were both nominated?

Then: It was the fingerprint bruises I saw on my sister's arm at the July 4th barbecue. Don't get me wrong. I know my sister has a taste for violent sex. But in Paul's eyes, I saw the shine of the sadist, the rapist, the hater of women who walks among us doing harm in overt and subtle ways.

Finally: Paul posed a threat to my husband's business, the livelihood that makes it possible for me to provide for our children.

No one, and I mean no one, fucks with my family.

Paul Hayes was a disease that badly needed a cure.

"I don't suppose I get a lawyer?" I say. "A trial, perhaps?"

No answer from the group, remaining candles flickering, then going dark. There are murmurs all around me. I can feel the unease of the crowd, but also the edgy excitement.

"No?" I say, raising my voice a little when Lisander says nothing. "You're right. We should just go back to the 1600s when women were accused of crimes, named as witches, and put to death because people feared them and their power."

"Where is Amanda?" asks Lisander.

"I have no idea. I had nothing to do with Paul Hayes's murder."

"The evidence against you is substantial."

I bark out another derisive laugh at that.

"That's what they all say, isn't it? How many women over the centuries have sat before a row of judges, accused of crimes they didn't commit, fallen under suspicion for reasons of fear, ignorance, or just good old-fashioned jealousy?"

Lisander glares.

"Because isn't that what this is really about? All these years, you've been so jealous that Agnes loved Ana and me best. That she wanted me to take over The Cove. And you're just a poser in a seat you can never quite fill."

In the heavy wooden chair, I'm slowly working my wrists. But the binding is tighter than I thought at first. My head throbs from The Deadly Trance, which I'm lucky didn't kill me already. There's no one in this group skilled enough to handle a substance like that. Fortunately, they must have taken it from Agnes's storeroom. I mixed it and put it there myself. You never know when a good anesthetic will come in handy.

"Is the irony of this lost on you?" I ask Lisander but look at each of the women sitting at her table. "So what's it going to be? Pressing? Drowning? Burning at the stake?"

Lisander clears her throat and keeps at it.

"Witnesses saw you and your husband, Brad, carrying something large wrapped in a tarp from your car and into the woods leading to Black River Park where Paul's body was found."

That's a lie.

"The toxicology report states that the toxins in Paul's blood were consistent with those found in hemlock and wolfsbane, which we all know grow copiously in the garden."

That's true.

"And no one believes that Agnes had a heart attack," Lisander continues. "Everyone saw how much you hated her the night of the Wolf Moon when she named you as her successor. You and Ana used the same substance on your English teacher, Mr. Danvers."

I did lash out at Agnes that night, railed against her in front of everyone for killing my mother. It was ugly. Our relationship never really healed after that. I left for college a few months later and didn't return to the house again for a long time.

Lisander has more to say.

"April overheard you and Brad discussing Paul, how he was talking about Brad behind his back after Brad declined his services. Your company lost clients because of the rumors he was spreading. And then there was a fire. Brad suspected that Paul might have been involved."

I look at April, who can't meet my eyes. I've always trusted her, let her into my home, paid her to take care of my children, cook in my kitchen. Ana never liked her, but I thought my sister was just jealous, being territorial as she can be. I see it now, what Ana saw. *There's always something going on behind those eyes.* She was lurking in my house, listening to our private conversations. I'm angry, but also hurt. And annoyed with myself for trusting her.

Meanwhile, it's news to me that Brad thought Paul might have had something to do with the fire. If he did think that, he never said so. And we most certainly did not dispose of Paul's body together. That's a complete lie.

"None of this means anything," I say easily. "You have no proof. No evidence. Explain to me the doll they found at the burial site, Lisander. Everyone knows that's *your* thing. That you taught April how to make them, as well."

Lisander just smiles wanly. "Are you suggesting that *I* killed Paul?"

"I'm suggesting that you don't know what you're talking about. That perhaps you're being manipulated. You know, that's one of the reasons Agnes didn't name you to lead. She thought you were weak. That you were too easily swayed by opinion and rumor."

I've hit my mark, though antagonizing the person who wants you dead is probably not the best tactic. Lisander flushes and clenches her fist. "Enough," she barks.

"And what about Iggy?" I ask. "Her symptoms are consistent with the effects of amatoxin. And who was working in the kitchen that day? Your little pet, April. She'd know well how to do that. After all, her own mother, Trina, tried to poison her, just a little bit at a time."

There's a gasp. April has gone even grayer, her eyes angry now. She even has the audacity to look hurt. It was a low blow, I know. But did they expect me to just sit here, begging for mercy? They're all a bunch of witches, guilty of a thousand crimes, and they've gathered to judge me. I'm not going down without landing a few blows.

"What reason would she have to do that?" asks Lisander.

"Why don't you ask her?"

But Lisander just keeps her eyes on me. And then I understand.

They are all against us. Both Ana and me. They think we killed Paul Hayes together. The Cove is ending us.

Fear turns to anger. Anger for this injustice, for the betrayal from these women, for the safety of my sister, my children.

"Vera Blacksmith," Lisander says, voice cool as gunmetal. "Your actions have brought danger to The Cove and its members. You have created more harm than necessary and used your practice for your own benefit. For these violations, you have been sentenced to take the cure."

There are anxious murmurs from the crowd.

From behind me a voice cuts through the night. "Well, *that's* not going to happen."

I turn with relief, expecting to see Ana. What took you so long?

But it's not Ana.

It's Coraline.

VERA

Coraline.

With Ethan, Grant, Autumn, and Dahlia in tow.

They don't seem like children, Grant and Ethan towering over the girls who used to tower over them, the girls with shoulders squared and tall, with all the confidence the powerful women in their lives gave them.

Grant and Coraline were babies in my arms. I've wiped their eyes and bandaged their knees, held them after nightmares, cheered them on at the various events of their lives.

Now the kids surround me, Grant undoing my bindings. Coraline walks toward Lisander and the council in ripped jeans and an oversized hoodie, tattered Converse, hair a wild tangle of pink and black.

She is herself, not of me, but *from* me. Making her own choices.

"Mom," says Grant, helping me up. I am embarrassed to say I have to lean against him for support. "Are you okay?"

"I'm okay," I say. "What are you guys doing here?"

"Coraline called," he said. "We came to save you."

"Let my mother go." Even Coraline's voice sounds different. Low and easy, but full of confidence.

The person who comes to stand between me and a group of

women gathered to judge me is not the little girl whose hand I've held. She's a young woman claiming her own power.

"Coraline," says Lisander, annoyed. "This is not the place for you."

Grant tightens his arm around my shoulder. Autumn presses in beside me and I take her hand.

"We got you, Mom," says Grant.

Coraline glances over at me with a smile, and then puts her eyes back on Lisander.

"You're wrong," she says, voice clarion. "*This* is not the place *for you*. This is my house. And it belongs to *my* family."

Lisander leans back, nostrils flaring with anger.

"So, bitch," says Coraline, that wicked smile in her voice. "Step down."

Lisander looks to Camille and Bree, who emerge from the shadows and approach Coraline. Panic sets in and I break away from Grant and move to defend my daughter.

"You stay away from them," I yell, my voice sounding shrill and frightened the way it only can when you're afraid for your children.

"Camille and Bree will escort the children from the property," says Lisander. "They won't be harmed."

"I really don't think so."

Now it's Ana's turn to slip from the darkness. And with her is Detective Bandeau. The crowd erupts in surprise and starts to disperse.

Ana comes to stand with all of us, whispering in my ear.

"This is quite a mess you've gotten yourself into, sister dear. Good thing I'm here to clean it up."

"Took you long enough. They nearly burned me at the stake." I smile, thinking about how much she must be enjoying coming to the rescue.

"Lisander, I didn't kill Paul Hayes," I say.

"That's right. She didn't."

The voice is very faint as a slim figure moves from the trees to stand in the firelight. She's weak, unsteady on her feet, helped by her husband.

"*I* killed Paul Hayes." It's Iggy.

"Oh my god," says Ana, drawing in a sharp breath and grabbing my arm.

"And I killed Paul Hayes." Another form moves from the darkness. It takes me a second to recognize her. Jessie Parker.

"And *I* killed Paul Hayes."

It's Amanda Alessi.

IGGY

I'm weak and shivering, leaning on Brock. I shouldn't be here; Brock's distraught because I should be resting, and we left the hospital against the doctor's orders. Big scene. But I can't just lie there. Not when Ana and Vera, Jessie and Amanda need me to tell the truth.

I think about the selfie that Amanda took so long ago, all of us lifting our glasses, having so much fun, reveling in our friendship. It seems like so very long ago—before Paul, before Brock and I were together, long before our angel, Noah. I remember how I felt that night, young, free, bolstered and surrounded by my girlfriends. It was a happy time.

All eyes are on me and I'm afraid, with the wide full moon above, and the roaring of the bonfire.

"Iggy," says Lisander, looking rattled. Ana and Vera both stare, like they're seeing me for the first time and maybe they are. Amanda and Jessie move in behind me, each taking one of my hands, offering their support. We are in this together. "What are you saying?"

I tell my story to The Cove.

Ana got me the position at the advertising agency, and I was grateful.

I'd been floundering since I ran out of money and had to drop out of college, moving from one dead-end job to the next—bartender, waitress, cleaning lady. My mother had moved in with her rich new boyfriend, and basically didn't want me around.

Still, I managed to scrabble my way to an associate degree in graphic design and social media management, taking classes online and running up a stupid amount of credit card debt.

So, I had a degree and a strong desire for a real job going for me when I interviewed at the advertising firm where Paul Hayes worked, thanks to Ana's connections.

When I got the job offer as an office assistant, Ana and I went out to celebrate. She bought a bottle of champagne.

"You're the best friend I've ever had," I told her.

"Same," she said, and we toasted how we'd always be there for each other. No matter what. I started the next week.

That's where I met Jessie and Amanda, and they became my first real friends after Ana.

Ana was with Brock then, so this was a couple of years ago now.

And even though I had an embarrassing secret crush on my best friend's boyfriend, and the workplace was somewhat toxic—high pressure, low pay, and an obnoxious predator like Paul Hayes lurking in corners, I remember that as a happy time. Lots of girls' martini nights and Pilates classes, and lunches, shopping. I was making halfway decent money, enough to pay off my credit cards and have some fun. Things were good.

Then Jessie had to work late with Paul one night. They had a big client meeting the next day and he suggested that they work through dinner at the office. They ordered in. When they'd finished preparing the presentation, he opened a bottle of vodka, mixed it with some club soda, and they celebrated with a drink.

That's the last thing Jessie remembers.

SERVED HIM RIGHT

She woke up in her car around 3:00 a.m., body sore and sick. *I felt him all over me. I could smell his cologne on my clothes*, she told us. She went to Amanda, and Amanda called me. We got her home and tried to make her call the police. But she was terrified of losing her job. She thought no one would believe her because she'd been flirting with him, drinking with him. So, we did what women do. We stayed quiet.

By the next afternoon, Paul was spreading the rumor that Jessie got "tipsy" when she was supposed to be working with him. He claimed that Jessie was hitting on him, that he'd had to let her down gently, but that she went a little nuts. By the afternoon, the whole office was gossiping about it.

The presentation to the client went well, and even though it was all Jessie—her images, ideas, concepts—Paul took all the credit.

Later that month, Jessie got passed over for a promotion.

Still, we all stayed quiet.

Then Paul did the same thing to me after an office happy hour one night.

Again, it was all so vague and hard to prove. One minute I was at the bar, drinking with co-workers. Paul was there, so funny and charming that I even almost wondered if Jessie was wrong about him. He bought me a drink. I remember feeling sick enough that I excused myself to the bathroom. He followed me. "Everything okay?" he asked, concerned. "You seem a little wobbly."

The next thing I was aware of, I was in my car alone. The party long ended. The parking lot deserted. I felt so ashamed. Was I a black-out drunk? It took a moment for me to realize that I was hurt. My arms aching, my panties down around my ankles.

What happened?

I drove home alone, remembering what happened to Jessie.

That was the thing with Paul; he was handsome and charming. A man's man—always a good time on the golf course, or at cigar night. He always looked good, had a gift for making people laugh, for putting them at ease. It seemed impossible to say that he was drugging women and raping them. At the office no less.

I had nothing if I lost that job, no savings, no safety net from family. It would have just been another failure. So, I'm ashamed to say that I stayed quiet, too.

A few months later, when a young intern came forward, the rest of us who had been harassed or worse decided to do so as well in support. The company offered us money in exchange for our silence. We all took it; though looking back now, we shouldn't have. I used it to start my online business. Jessie started a "fuck you" fund, a savings account that ensured she'd never have to stay somewhere toxic again.

Paul got fired, and despite what we'd suffered, it might have been something to celebrate.

But those of us that had been hurt by him were kind of shunned in these very subtle ways. Promotions passed us by. Invitations to retreats and happy hour gatherings withheld. Jessie stayed on for a while, hoping things would get better, and they did—a little—when a new female boss took the helm. I stayed on, too.

But Amanda left eventually, wanting a fresh start even though she hadn't had any encounters with Paul. Jessie went to work for Esme. She remained bitter, still longing for some kind of revenge. We were both still plagued by nightmares of him.

Ana and Brock broke up. Brock and I got together a little over a year after that. Later, he wanted me to stay home with the baby and focus on my online business. And Paul started his company.

When Ana started dating Paul, I warned her to stay away. Even with the NDA, I told her what he did to me, to others. She didn't believe me. Or she didn't want to believe me. Or she didn't care.

You just don't want me to be happy, she said. She's always been so stubborn. And truthfully with terrible judgment when it comes to men.

Maybe she was just too angry with me then, even though Brock and I had asked her blessing, and she never loved him, for marrying Brock. So, she wouldn't listen to me about Paul. We argued all the time.

Then, when I saw the bruises on her arm, something inside me just snapped.

Ana had been there every step of the way for me, and I wasn't going to stand by while Paul hurt her. I was going to save her whether she wanted me to or not.

Jessie, Amanda, and I got together. We came up with a plan.

Amanda, who had never worked with Paul even though we'd all been at the same firm, decided that she would make a move on him and see how close she could get. She seduced him at the bar of the local club, and soon he was hooking up with her behind Ana's back.

The blend of hemlock and wolfsbane is bitter, hard to swallow. We mixed it with simple syrup and mint and fashioned a specialty cocktail. Paul fancied a nice rum; so Amanda mixed up a batch of mojitos, had him over to her house. Jessie and I waited upstairs.

I don't mind telling you that we were afraid. And his death was shockingly violent; after just a few sips, he was choking violently, clawing at his throat. We watched in horror as he convulsed in Amanda's living room retching. Then he slowly became paralyzed, lay motionless, his eyes darting wildly. It was the longest hour of our lives. Finally, nothing. He was dead. We all sat and wept, so overcome were we by what we'd done.

Then Jessie started to laugh, softly at first, then doubled over with it. Then we were all laughing, cackling like a bunch of witches.

We killed him in cold blood, long after he'd hurt Jessie and me, to prevent him from hurting anyone else, to save Ana, even though it didn't seem like she wanted to be saved.

Ana taught me everything I know about plants, gave me access to Agnes's garden, her stores, taught me about tinctures and salves, teas and potions. Everything we needed was right at our fingertips. It was easy to kill Paul. As easy as it was for him to slip Rohypnol in our drinks and take what he wanted from us and then ruin our reputations afterward.

It was dealing with the body that was hard. It took all three of us to get him into Amanda's car, to carry him up through the trees. It took hours and all of our strength. And none of us had any idea how deep you had to dig a grave. We did a terrible job, obviously. Probably if we'd enlisted the help of The Cove to begin with, things would have gone more smoothly.

And Amanda had to disappear for a while, which has been very painful for her parents. We thought that posting they'd gone on vacation would help with that. And it did at first, though such a thing would have been radically out of character for Amanda.

Then they found Paul's body.

In the winter moonlight, I tell all of this to The Cove. There's a stunned silence when I'm finished, all eyes on me, Jessie, and Amanda. We all stand together. Heads high. We'd do it again.

"And," I say into the awed quiet. "If someone doesn't hand over my child to me there's going to be hell to pay."

That's when my eyes fall on the stick bassinet beside the long table, hear the little sounds he makes. My system floods with relief and oxytocin. Brock and I walk over, and he lifts Noah safe and sound from the bed of leaves and flowers. Noah gives me that goofy, toothless grin that I know is just for me, and I take him into my arms, hold him tight.

I don't know what will happen next.

But I know right now that I feel free in a way I haven't before, even though I just confessed to murder, and that Detective Bandeau was there to hear the whole thing.

There's power in taking revenge. There's a freedom to owning up to what you've done. Ana comes to me and takes me in her arms.

"I'm so sorry," she whispers. "I wish I had listened to you. I wish I'd been there for you."

Noah giggles. He loves his auntie. With Brock and Ana at my back, my baby in my arms, I know I can face whatever comes next.

ANA

I stand, stunned. I can't believe the things that Iggy has said, and yet I know them to be true. My friend, she's stronger than I ever imagined.

I glance around at the people in my life—my sister, her children, my best friend, now Timothy. What must he be thinking? What will he do with what he's learned? He made me some promises. But will he keep them?

Agnes must be turning in her grave.

After that awful Wolf Moon meeting so long ago now, Agnes was bereft. She wept in the kitchen while I brewed her a pot of peppermint tea, generous with the honey since sweetness is needed after a shock.

Vera had raged at Agnes, rejected The Cove, lambasted our aunt for being responsible for Sadie's death, for not stepping in before Sadie had no choice but to kill her husband to save herself. *You let your sister down, then you let her die.*

Vera never, even that night, admitted that she was the one who killed our father. And not just her. Vera and I foraged together for those mushrooms, finding them deep in the woods outside of town, nestled in the fragrant shade of a big live oak. She always took responsibility for it in her heart, claimed I didn't know what we were doing, that I was too young. But I did.

We replaced Sadie's duxelles, the finely chopped mushrooms, shallots, and herbs sauteed in butter included in beef Wellington, with our own. Sadie knew, I'm sure of it. Fatigued as she was by Mac and by our hardscrabble life, ground down to nothing by his violence, by his hateful darkness. She made a show of telling us not to eat it, not eating it herself.

This is special, she said, *just for your father.*

"I took your sister in," Agnes said to me. "I taught her everything."

"She doesn't want it, Aunt Agnes," I told her. "But I do."

Agnes put a gentle hand to my cheek. "You're not ready, Ana. I'm not sure you will be. You lack discipline and self-control."

I was angry that night, at both of them, at everyone, at the world. I think we all cried ourselves to sleep, bitterly disappointed in each other. Family. It's brutal. Am I right?

Now, the bonfire rages. Timothy looks shell-shocked, the firelight licking at half his face, casting the rest of him in darkness. Who is he?

I told him at the gate: "If I bring you here, you have to stop being a cop for a while. You have to forget everything you see and everything you learn here."

"I don't know if I can do that," he said.

It was a desperate move. But I *was* desperate for my sister, my niece. For Iggy. I didn't even know that the other kids had found their way there. I was afraid for Noah, too, who I had abandoned to The Cove. I thought he might be here, as well.

The video Timothy showed me on his phone was of Iggy, Amanda, and Jessie driving Paul's car from Amanda's garage the night of the murder. They all looked stricken, Amanda crying.

"Then leave me to it," I said. "Go where you were going, do what you must, and forget you brought me here."

"I don't know if I can do that either."

I stood waiting, edging away from him.

"Make your choice right now, Timothy. It's *that*—" I nod to the world outside the gate. "Or it's us, it's here. Our world, our rules."

I had no reason to think that this man who was a stranger, a lover, and then an enemy was someone I could trust with all my secrets, our secrets.

But I swear I saw him shift off something he was carrying. And I remember watching him our first night, thinking I'd seen him before, that I knew him. And I had that feeling again as he took my hand, and we walked through the gate.

Now I stand with my sister. I look over at her. Our eyes lock and I see that she's made her decision, so many years later. Better late than never. She nods, steps forward.

Lisander has tears in her eyes, is sagging with defeat. April has the good sense to look afraid when I pin her with my gaze. I know she's the one who poisoned Iggy. No one else could have or would have done it.

But the poison wasn't meant for my friend; it was meant for me.

I gave my serving to Iggy never realizing.

When Vera speaks, her voice is bright and strong. I think Agnes would be proud. "Tonight, under the Wolf Moon, I take the seat that Agnes left for me as the head of The Cove."

Vera looks nothing like Agnes. She's delicate like Sadie, but she has all Agnes's strength, her power. Her voice carries into the night, at one with the nature all around her.

This is her home, our home.

I see Coraline looking at her mother, the way I always have, with grudging awe. Why is Vera so strong? Because she's had to be. Her heart, torn jagged in its broken places, is stitched back together by wrath and love in equal measure. She has all the power of the sister and the mother; she is justice, she is The Cove.

"And I'll take this seat with my sister and my daughter by my side."

"Mom!" says Coraline, running to Vera. Vera takes her in her arms and holds on tight, Grant coming to wrap them both up. Vera kisses her daughter on the crown of her head and reaches for my hand. We stand there together.

Lisander bows her head.

"I'm sorry," she says. "I thought it was you and Ana. That you killed Paul together. I believed that."

"Who poisoned Iggy?" Vera asks.

"It was an accident," says April, rising. "I knew no one but Ana would eat that horrible cassoulet. But she never touched it. And Iggy ate so much of it."

"Why?" asks Vera.

April sticks her chin out, wobbly from her stab wound but self-righteous as fuck.

"Because we knew she'd never let us bring you to justice. She's wild and violent and needed to be contained. And we believed you acted together. Ana has violated the rules of The Cove too many times. She deserved to be punished."

"We were wrong," says Lisander.

I'm calling bullshit. April just hated me. She always has. It was just the excuse she needed to get me out of her life.

"You didn't even know Paul was dead before the brunch," I say.

"Word came to us right away," says Lisander. "A little bird from the medical examiner's office let us know that poison was suspected. And we believed you did it."

"You tried to kill my sister," says Vera, her voice cold. "And you nearly killed Iggy."

April hangs her head in shame, and I'd almost feel sorry for her if she wasn't a murderous bitch who tried to kill me.

"Lisander and April, you have violated the rules of The Cove. And you will have to face punishment. Step down and we will reconvene tomorrow to discuss the future."

April's crying, too, now as they cede their seats. She looks back and forth, between Vera and me, Iggy, Brock, and Noah in their tight little group. And I feel an unwelcome twinge of pity for her. Her mismatched eyes are filled with sadness. We're all just trying to find our place in this world, aren't we? Somewhere we belong, are safe, and known?

Vera's not worried that they will run, that they won't return to hear what punishment she decides to deliver. They don't have any place else to go. The Cove is their whole world.

My sister turns to Timothy. They lock eyes, square off.

"Detective Bandeau," she says. "What did you see here tonight?"

There's a battle on his face. Finally, he shakes his head, eyebrows raised, turns out his palms. "I honestly have no idea."

Vera sighs, tense shoulders relaxing. "That was the right answer."

The bonfire rages. The moon shines down upon us. The members of The Cove disappear into the darkness between the trees. Soon, it's just us in the winter night.

"You came for me," says Vera, as if she's surprised.

"Did you doubt it?" Then, "Don't answer that."

"Did you mean it?" says Coraline. "That I'll run The Cove with you?"

"In time," Vera says. "After college, if it's still what you want."

"I'm really confused," says Autumn. "What is happening? I still have to turn in my essay."

Coraline pulls her into a hug. "Don't worry," she says. "We'll get it done together. There's still time."

Then Iggy is beside me and I take her into my arms.

"You didn't have to save me," I say, wondering if that's true. "I didn't deserve it. I've been such a terrible friend to you."

"You're the best friend I've ever had," she says. "I couldn't watch him hurt you."

We look over to Amanda and Jessie, who embrace by the tree, holding each other. Obviously, a couple in love.

"And it wasn't just for you. We did it for Jessie, too. She's never been right since Paul hurt her."

I pieced it together after I saw the video. Jessie was the blog author. She was Jezebel making threats on Paul's ConnectIn page.

"Sometimes justice is a dish best served cold."

I hand Iggy her phone. "Was it Amanda who's been texting you?"

"Yeah, she really took some big risks for this—for Jessie. For you. She was afraid."

"She was brave." I look over at her and Jessie. I dismissed them as normies; far from it.

Noah coos at me from Iggy's arms. "I hear you're his favorite auntie."

"I'd better be." I boop his nose, and he gives me that gooey smile.

Then Brock is leading Iggy off, back to get some much-needed rest. And the kids are gone, heading back to Agnes's house.

"Can we trust him?" Vera is looking at Timothy, who is watching the fire. "Iggy just confessed to murder. Amanda and Jessie, too."

"I can't explain it," I say. "But I think we can trust him."

Vera keeps her eyes on him.

"I think I might be able to help him with something he needs," says Vera.

"I don't doubt it."

We both look over to the graveyard where Sadie and Agnes rest. I wish I could tell you that I saw them there, shimmering in the moonlight, watching over us, guiding us toward right action. But I don't.

The past is gone. It's just us. Vera. Me. Coraline. The present. The future.

SPRING EQUINOX BRUNCH

"Spring is a time of joy and rebirth. The winter months have passed and that which has survived will grow and bloom again. Life is a cycle, an endless loop of death and rebirth. We are the stewards of what grows from the earth, caring for it, nurturing it, availing itself of her gifts and of her power."

Aunt Agnes's *Book of Cures*

VERA

Our table is laden, rich with flavor, color, aroma. The large sideboard in Agnes's generous dining room is covered from end to end with platters of meats and cheese, fruit and salads. There's Ana's famous cassoulet, and the creamy, rich quiche that Iggy brought. Potatoes au gratin and a sliced ham from Timothy.

This house that has stood empty for so many years is full of life.

Out in the yard, the kids run around, filled with the exuberance that can only be felt outdoors, in nature, after doing work that seems like a chore and suddenly becomes the only thing you can imagine yourself doing with your day. Coraline has Noah in a harness on her front, having taken him from Iggy as soon as they arrived. The baby smiles, overjoyed to be in the company of the big kids—Ethan and Autumn, Dahlia and Grant. The sun shines on them; they all take the fresh spring air into their lungs and their souls.

Ana and Iggy are in the kitchen. Timothy and Brad are carrying chairs into the dining room so that everyone has a seat at this table, set with Agnes's best stoneware and old silver, decorated with fresh greenery and votive candles.

We've spent the day tending the garden, readying for the fecund summer, when the earth bears all her gifts. Those that

SERVED HIM RIGHT

heal. Those that might harm. Many could do either, depending on the dose.

Iggy is still fragile, still struggling with her recovery. But when I look at her, I only see joy. When we discussed punishment for April, Ana wanted her to pay the ultimate price; considering what they had planned for us, it was not unreasonable.

But it was Iggy who called for calm, for mercy. She reminded us that April was a broken person, harmed by her own mother. That Lisander believed I was guilty of murder—Paul, Agnes, and my father. She thought she was doing the right thing by asking me to take the cure.

I remember how Agnes loved her. So there has been mercy for Lisander, as well.

Outside, I see them both—Lisander and April—making their way to the garden in their beekeeper suits, like I used to watch Agnes so long ago. Camille and Bree accompany them, carrying tools. They all work for me now.

"How can you stand the sight of them?" asks Ana.

"I feel sorry for them. I think they really believed that I was guilty of crimes that deserved the cure."

Ana shakes her head. "Lisander has always been jealous of us. She wasn't just dishing out justice. She wanted revenge because she never forgave us for taking her place in Agnes's heart."

"Maybe."

"How can you trust them?" Ana asks, still glaring at them as they disappear inside the garden.

"I don't trust anyone," I say, shooting her a grin.

Ana frowns. "They didn't deserve your mercy."

"Everyone deserves mercy," I say. Well, maybe not everyone.

She pushes out a laugh. "Tell me that when they come for you in the night. Or poison your tea."

Lisander and April have both have asked for my forgiveness and sworn to serve me and The Cove in whatever way I deem necessary for the rest of our days. I have found work for them.

And, so, it is. I know how complicated motives can be. How something we do to protect ourselves might look like murder, or how sometimes violence is the only answer.

"Did you kill Agnes?" asks Ana, making her voice soft.

This is a question that has sat unspoken between us since the Wolf Moon.

The first strong feeling I remember experiencing is anger. Ana and I were small, I'm not sure how old. But I found myself huddled in my closet with my little sister, while Mac and Sadie rowed outside our door. What were they fighting about? Who hit who first? I don't remember. What I do remember was realizing that what we were forced to witness and endure was wrong. The light came in through the slats and Ana shivered under my arm.

"It's okay," I told her. "It will be over soon."

And I knew on some deep level that I shouldn't be the one protecting Ana, that Mac and Sadie were charged with protecting us both. And they couldn't, they *didn't*, were always more consumed with the sick dance of their relationship than they ever were with concern for us.

My anger was a seed that took root in the pit of my stomach, expanded, filled me, informing my choices and my actions. Finally, I only saw one way out—for all of us.

Ana was young and didn't truly understand what we were doing when we replaced Sadie's duxelles with mine. But when Mac fell ill, Sadie knew for certain what we had done.

"You take care of her," Sadie told me. "I can't. I've never even been able to take care of myself. Don't say a word. Don't ever say a word because then Ana will be all alone."

I let them take my mother away. I let her take the blame for me. I kept my promise to her.

On the night that Agnes died, many years after I had turned down my seat, I went back to her to tell her the truth. That *I* had killed Mac, not Sadie.

I still remember the stricken look on her face. Not surprise. Just grief.

Why did I go to her then? Why that night? Who can say why a seed that has lain dormant finally finds the right conditions to break through the earth?

But maybe it was because I was a mother myself then, and I knew finally how badly Sadie, Mac, and Agnes had failed us. I knew because I had worked so hard to provide for and protect my kids, to do better.

No, I didn't kill Agnes, not with any toxin.

But maybe I killed her with my words.

Or maybe it was her regret for not taking us away from Mac before their sick love destroyed us all. Or for delivering the bouquet that my mother used to kill herself. Maybe Agnes would have died that night no matter what, her heart failing. And there was something in the air that compelled me to share the truth with her before she left this earth, the garden, us.

But when I left Aunt Agnes, she was alive. I left her weeping at the kitchen table, that anger a wildfire inside me. By the next morning, she was gone. Do I have regrets?

What difference does it make if I do?

I tell Ana all of this, and she stays silent, still looking toward Agnes's garden. I wonder if she'll judge me. I doubt it.

Finally, she loops her arm through mine.

In my pocket I find the rough texture of the protection effigy my daughter Coraline made for me, just like the one she left on her porch to safeguard her family.

I think of the image of the doll found in the woods by Paul's body. It was Iggy's; she'd been carrying it around and it dropped from her pocket when they were disposing of Paul's body. Careless. I've asked her to be more careful in the future. She assures me her days of revenge seeking are over.

But you never know.

"We'll do better than they did," Ana says.

The kids are all filing in to eat, laughing and free, protected and loved. Coraline, still toting Noah, gives a wave and in her I see the best of all of us.

"That's the plan," I tell my sister.

And we step inside to join them.

ANA

I look around the room. Sun streams in and everyone is talking at once, plates full, laughter filling a space that has been too quiet for too long. Even Vera looks relaxed and happy, as if she put down a terrible burden she's been carrying. Coraline and Grant sit to her right, Brad to her left. And once upon a time I would feel jealous that they get the most of her, but today I just smile.

Iggy is cozy beside Brock, Noah on her lap. Brock feeds Noah soft food with a blue spoon, his face alight with love. Noah and I lock eyes and he coos, spitting his peas. He's all mischief, that one. We're going to get along fine. Iggy has bought Lisander's bookstore Make Magic, and her online business is also thriving. I'm happy for her. Truly.

Love is not small. It's not limited. I think I always believed that it was, that there wasn't enough for me, that what little I had would always be taken away. It's something we talk about in family therapy.

Across the table, Timothy watches me. After the way we met, and the nature of our early days, I didn't exactly expect him to be sitting at the table, eating brunch with our family and friends. But here he is. His smile is slight, those eyes still wolfish. My heart does a little rhumba.

Payton arrives with Victor, beaming. Vera gets up to greet her and accepts Payton's signature bottle of Veuve. I *did* tell Payton that I slept with her ex—as part of my new program of honesty, thanks to the family shrink—and she was pissed at me for a while. Actually, she slut shamed me—which, okay. But now she's over it. And she and Victor are very clearly in love, a power couple, svelte and well-dressed, glowing. I am forgiven. Mostly. Let's see if I get an invitation to the wedding.

Esme and Claudia look a little less happy, still working through issues, tentative and overly polite with each other. And Esme's in therapy, too, working on what she admits is a really deep-seated mistrust and hatred for men. She comes by it honestly, her past one of pain and trauma—like so many of us. Paul and the things he did were a trigger for her and forced her to confront a secret pain she'd been carrying. I believe in them—Claudia and Esme.

There's real love there. And I have come to believe, in spite of everything, that this above all things is the ultimate cure for all that ails us.

Last week we all attended the gala where Esme won Businessperson of the Year. An honor she richly deserved.

"Just a word," says Tim, lifting a glass. "Thank you for sharing your family and this meal with me. And thank you, Vera and Brad, for the generous donation to the youth center. The endowment from your company means that we'll be able to keep the doors open for years to come. I can't tell you how many kids will be helped by this."

"We're happy to do it," says Brad, always magnanimous. "We suffered some bad press this year, lost some clients, but ultimately the Little Valley Police investigation came out in our favor and we're on solid ground. The least we can do is support the community."

More cheers and big smiles all around.

Everyone tucks into their food; conversation, laughter, the clinking of silverware on plates rise up, the music of harmony and togetherness. The sharing of a meal with family and friends, one of life's great gifts.

"So, Detective."

Brad is buff and pretty beside my sister. As ever, they make a striking pair, her cool features, auburn hair, his sandy boyishness, wide smile. He drapes an arm around Vera, and together they're a kind of stylish yin and yang. She always seems softer when she's with him. I didn't understand their relationship at first. He seemed like a boy that needed a spanking. But I see it now for what it is. A partnership. They run a successful business, a home, are raising a family. There's love there, too. But it's foundational, not running the show. Which, honestly, I think is what Vera wants. Not passion. Stability.

"How's the Paul Hayes case coming?"

Tim shakes his head, offers a frown. "The leads have all gone cold. Unless we get a break or someone comes forward with new evidence, I'm not sure we're going to solve this one."

"I feel like that Amanda Alessi knows more than she's saying," says Claudia, leaning into Esme, who looks down at her plate.

"Her alibi is rock solid," says Timothy, with a shrug. "She says she had a bit of a nervous breakdown. She had a lot of pressure at work, was drinking way too much. She broke up with Paul, then checked herself in to Sheltering Oaks, the rehab facility up by The Hollows. Claimed she needed some time to get herself together. She was in rehab when Paul was murdered."

"Without telling her family or her friends?" says Claudia skeptically.

Tim shrugs. "It's not a crime to run away from your life for a while. If Hayes hadn't turned up dead, maybe it wouldn't have been such a big deal that she was missing for a couple of days. It was his murder that made her disappearance news."

"But what about the social media posts?" presses Claudia.

This case is still the talk of the town. Everyone is a detective these days. Too many true crime podcasts.

"Someone with access to both accounts posted those images," Timothy goes on easily. "The photo was just stock, found on any number of sites. But we don't know who did it."

It was Jessie, of course, with her technical knowledge. Also Jessie: the jogger at the scene where Paul's body was found. She knew she shouldn't go, but she couldn't help herself. It was also Jessie at Amanda's house when Timothy came to search; she was checking for any evidence they might have missed, wound up having to escape through the basement window. Messy. But of course, they're amateurs.

"I still think it was Regina Hayes," I say. "Follow the money, right? She finally got her payout, I hear. Didn't have to split her inheritance with her brother. She and her beefy boyfriend just left for Positano."

The table goes a little quiet. I eat a bit of quiche.

"I heard Harley Granger is doing a *Stranger than Fiction* podcast about it," says Dahlia. Grant is looking at her like she gets up and puts the stars in the sky at night. "That he's planning to come to Little Valley to investigate."

"Let's see how that works out for him," says Coraline.

And I'm struck by how much she looks like Vera, how cool she is under pressure. She's the best of both of us in so many ways—my edge, my daring, Vera's discipline and control.

Ethan chuckles. "Yeah, good luck with that."

Coraline nudges him with her shoulder. Autumn smiles at them. The kids. They're all growing up. Coraline will study botany at Sacred Heart College in the fall, Vera finally ceding to her wishes. Autumn will be valedictorian after her competitor was caught cheating, and she's been accepted at Brown. Ethan didn't get in to NYU and is taking a gap year, will work at his father's garage until he decides what he wants from life. I wonder if he's done this to be close to Coraline, but Vera told me not to pry. Imagine that.

"Not every crime gets solved," says Vera, her tone final. She and Coraline exchange a look. "Sometimes justice is served. More often, it's not. In any case, *brunch is* served. Bon appétit."

Later while the kids are laughing at something Brad said, I push my chair back, get up to leave the table. I feel Vera's eyes as I leave the room.

I walk down the hallway, the voices fading behind me. I wait. A few moments later Timothy follows, his big strides carrying him quickly toward me as I jog ahead.

He comes up quickly behind me and presses me into the powder room behind the kitchen, shuts and locks the door.

He offers me the devilish smile I've come to love.

Yes. There, I've said it. Love.

Love, not pain. Love, not violence. He is a man who made me a promise and kept it. One who excites me but doesn't hurt me. He is a man I trust.

"We shouldn't," I protest weakly, not meaning it at all as I wrap my arms around his neck, and he lifts me against the sink.

Though of course, we still love our forbidden, tawdry romps in inappropriate places, can't keep our hands off each other, have this tendency to sneak off and behave badly.

After all, I can't change completely. Nor do I want to.

I'm on the straight and narrow, adulting on the regular.

But there's still a part of me that will always be the bad girl.

★ ★ ★ ★ ★

ACKNOWLEDGMENTS

Fair warning! Spoilers! Don't read these acknowledgments unless you've finished the book!

A shocking news story was the inspiration for this novel. A murder a world away. A family gathered for brunch in supposed love and harmony. But many of the people who sat down at that table fell horribly ill. Some died. The culprit? The savory and oh-so-deadly death cap mushroom. Early on the question was this: Accidental ingestion or murder? Eventually, the truth became clear.

What struck me about this terrible event was how a meal that tasted wonderful, that was offered by a trusted family member at a peaceful brunch, was in fact deadly. And that only after people died did the secrets and lies and past bad deeds come to light.

This news story collided with my ongoing obsession with plants and nature, the twisted and complicated relationship we humans have with the planet. How plants that harm can also heal, how they nourish, shelter, but can also be deadly. Several books were very important to the writing of this novel, though of course all mistakes and liberties taken for the sake of fiction (never let the truth get in the way of a good story!) are mine. If you're a nature nerd like I am, you will find so much to amaze and fascinate in the following books.

The Light Eaters: How the Unseen World of Plant Intelligence Offers a New Understanding of Life on Earth by Zoë Schlanger; *Most Delicious Poison: The Story of Nature's Toxins—From Spices to Vices* by Noah Whiteman; *Poison: The History of Potions, Powders, and Murderous Practitioners* by Ben Hubbard; *Wicked Plants: The Weed That Killed Lincoln's Mother and Other Botanical Atrocities* by Amy Stewart; and many more! For the complete list, visit lisaunger.com.

As ever, deep gratitude to my sterling editor Erika Imranyi for all her vision, patience, enthusiasm, love, and support. And most of all for her sense of humor. Our editorial conversations are in turn deep, hilarious, and inspiring. And they're looooong! We talk *a lot* about pacing, character, and story. And the result is always something much, *much* better than the first draft I humbly turned in to her. I am grateful for her partnership in this process.

Huge thanks to the brilliant and amazing folks at HarperCollins/Park Row Books. They are the dream team and I hope every author finds a home as wonderful as this one. Special thanks to: executive vice president and publisher Loriana Sacilotto and vice president of editorial Margaret Marbury for their wise and fearless navigation of the big waters of publishing; publicist extraordinaire Emer Flounders for his creativity, tireless effort, and—here's that word again—patience! Also: Amy Jones, Sophie James, SarahElizabeth Lee, marketing genius Lindsey Reeder, and indie bookstore and library whisperer Randy Chan, as well as the countless people in sales, production, and art at HarperCollins who contributed to the publication. I have so many wonderful friends! They are cheerleaders, supporters, readers, bookstore stalkers (looking at you, Colleen!), front-row book-signing attendees, social media boosters, and more. Jennifer Manfrey is my ride or die—my walk therapy complain in the park, dig endlessly into some obscure topic, fellow word nerd. Her wisdom and friendship are foundational in my life. And I know there is no one else on the planet who buys as many of my books! To my lifelong (read long-suffering) friends Marion Chartoff, Tara Popick, and Heather Mikesell—just thank you for being you and for putting up with me since middle school, college, and my publishing years respectively! Team Waterside (and Waterside alumni)! My wild neighbor pals, early-readers club, beach buddies, party-bus riders, cheering squad: Colleen Chappell, Kathy Bernhardt, Marie Chinicci-Everitt, Tim Flight, Celeste Van Auken, Rhea Nichols, Karin Poinelli, Cathy Kimber, Heidi Akers, the whole Tang family, Jennifer Outzs, and Barbie Graham to name just a few!

I am a writer because of my parents—even though my dad told me it wasn't a real job! And I should find something else—*anything* else—to do for a living. My mom, Virginia Miscione, former librarian and avid reader, gave me the gift of loving story in all forms—books, film, television, and theater. She remains one of my earliest and most important readers. My dad, Joseph Miscione, passed away this year. Of course, he's still with me in so many ways. I plan to continue to give him a hard time onstage when I tell the story of my writing journey, casting him as the villain. Because I know he loved that! Big thanks to my brother, Joey, for his support and friendship, shameless bragging, facing out books in stores, and always spreading the word.

My wonderful husband, Jeffrey, and our beautiful, sweet daughter, Ocean, are the foundation of my life. Every word I write is for them. They are the sun and the moon and all my stars, filling my life with joy and laughter. Our labradoodle, Jak Jak, is my faithful writing buddy and a constant reminder to stop working so that we can play more.

And, of course, a writer is nothing without her readers, booksellers, and librarians. Some of you have been with me from the very beginning. And I see you out there (looking at you,

Kim Beamer)! Thank you for spreading the word, turning up to events, engaging in social media, and generally making this writing life a joy. It means so much to know that my stories, characters, and words have found a way into your hearts and minds. I simply couldn't do this without you.

Happy reading!